PENGUIN BOOKS

EXILES/PASSAGE TO ARARAT

Michael J. Arlen is the author of *Living-Room War* (1969), *An American Verdict* (1973), *The View from Highway 1* (1976), *Thirty Seconds* (1980), and *The Camera Age* (1981). *Exiles* was nominated for a National Book Award, and *Passage to Ararat* won the National Book Award in Contemporary Affairs. Penguin Books also publishes Mr. Arlen's *Living-Room War, Thirty Seconds,* and *The Camera Age*.

EXILES

PASSAGE TO ARARAT

TWO WORKS BY

Michael J. Arlen

PENGUIN BOOKS

Penguin Books Ltd, Harmondsworth,
Middlesex, England
Penguin Books, 625 Madison Avenue,
New York, New York 10022, U.S.A.
Penguin Books Australia Ltd, Ringwood,
Victoria, Australia
Penguin Books Canada Limited, 2801 John Street,
Markham, Ontario, Canada L3R 1B4
Penguin Books (N.Z.) Ltd, 182–190 Wairau Road,
Auckland 10, New Zealand

Exiles first published in the United States of America by
Farrar, Straus & Giroux 1970
First published in Canada by
Doubleday Canada Limited 1970
Passage to Ararat first published in the United States of America by
Farrar, Straus & Giroux 1975
First published in Canada by
McGraw-Hill Ryerson Limited 1975
Exiles and *Passage to Ararat* first published in one volume by
Farrar, Straus & Giroux 1978
Published in Penguin Books 1982

Exiles copyright © Michael J. Arlen, 1970
Passage to Ararat copyright © Michael J. Arlen, 1975
All rights reserved

LIBRARY OF CONGRESS CATALOGING IN PUBLICATION DATA
Arlen, Michael J.
Exiles; Passage to Ararat: two works.
1. Armenians.   2. Arlen, Michael J.
3. Armenian massacres, 1915–1923.   4. Arlen,
Michael, 1895–1956—Biography.   5. Arlen,
Atalanta.   6. Authors, English—20th century—
Biography.   I. Arlen, Michael J.   Passage to
Ararat.   1982.   II. Title.
DS165.A657 1982   823′.912 [B]   82-9868
ISBN 0 14 00.6311 0   AACR2

Printed in the United States of America by
R. R. Donnelley & Sons Company, Harrisonburg, Virginia

Parts of *Exiles* originally appeared in *The New Yorker*.
The text of *Passage to Ararat* first appeared in
The New Yorker.

Exiles

HE USED TO JOKE ABOUT BEING
frail and weak, about having had TB as a boy, and then
something wrong with his back, and then a car accident
(he had been walking across a street) in Los Angeles—
but he so clearly didn't really think himself frail or
weak, and when things started going wrong for him,
going wrong in him I guess was more like it, he couldn't
countenance it at all. The pain, yes, or things like that.
Discomfort is what they call it. He could manage that
all very damned well. But not the fact of things truly
starting to go wrong.

It happened in the spring, I think. I remember the
time vaguely, April. It must have been spring, but I was
in the Army then and not paying much attention to sea-
sons. Fort Dix. White board barracks. All that dust,

and boots beside the bed, and those baggy dusty fatigues. A weird soft life, soft amid the weapons, the rifles, the machinery, the sounds of tank battalions and howitzers on the distant ranges. It was a telegram—one of those long telegrams with some of the key words hashed up by the local teletypist. They called me out of formation one morning, into the orderly room—the soft-faced, big-bellied, indoors sergeants sitting around at their desks having coffee. Some corporal handed me this thing, and I opened it and read it standing there. It seemed to read so easily, I read it right through. YOUR FATHER GOING INTO HOSPITAL TODAY . . . SUSPECTED CANCER . . . EXCELLENT DOCTOR . . . CHANCES ARE GOOD . . . WILL KEEP YOU ADVISED. And in a strange way I believed it, believed anyway the calm codelike positivism of the message. *Suspected . . . Excellent . . . Chances are good . . . Will keep you advised.* My mother had a way with telegrams. It was one of the sergeants who snapped me out of it. "What is it, kid? Your girl got pregnant?" No, I said, my father's going into the hospital for an operation; and then I told him some more, and then they all started wheeling into line, stirring things up, papers, forms, one of the roundest and most dough-faced of the sergeants tap-tap-tapping out an emergency pass on a tiny typewriter in the corner. It was very nice, one of those acts of complicity. I couldn't quite understand it at the time and felt apart from them—these strangers who were evidently expressing their own fears and worries. I was too cool for that sort of thing. I could take an emergency three-day-pass or leave it alone. But then I got into New York, and we were suddenly there, inside, in one of those blank, beige, tiled, airless hospital corridors, my mother and I, and I could understand quite a bit.

We walked up and down, walked up and down, and sat. My mother smoked. I told her about Fort Dix. Nurses passed, and all the doctors in the world. Finally, Doctor Gregson appeared—that was his name, Gregson. An excellent surgeon. One of the great surgeons. One of the really great, the very best. He was carrying a trim blue canvas case that unmistakably contained a tennis racket, and was buttoning up his jacket. He had just come from changing and was obviously in a hurry. "I think we got it all," he said to my mother. "It had spread quite far into the lymph. We had to take out a lung . . ." A few more sentences like that, and off he went. My father was never the same after Gregson, which is unfair to Gregson, since he doubtless would have died sooner, and probably worse, without him. Maybe if I hadn't met Gregson just then, and just that way, that busy on-my-way-to-the-River-Club look, that bloody tennis racket, like a figure out of some second-rate country-house comedy, I wouldn't still have such a particular sense of that moment in time, of an act ending that afternoon in the hospital. But it's true, he wasn't the same afterwards. There was something crucial gone from him, and not just the lung either, although that certainly didn't help; and neither did the information we received later that the removal of the lung had been more in the nature of a "hunch" than a step that had been absolutely necessary.

It was so terrible really. He knew the lung was gone, and hated that, one more infirmity, and tried to make jokes about it although the jokes wouldn't take. But he didn't really believe about the rest. He would just lie in bed, at first in bed at the hospital, and then in bed at home, and then sitting up at home, and wait for something to happen to him, something to come back to him. In appearance, it wasn't quite all that passive, and much of the time he seemed "fine." He had the wit and the irony and the strength or whatever it is that enables some people not only to survive bad things but somehow to move with grace above them—he could do that part of it very well, and down to the moment he died, about one year later, he managed to "be himself," to be elegant, to be amusing, to be even gay. But there was something gone, and he was then only sixty, "only sixty," whatever that means, and sometimes a look would cross his face, and linger there for a second, and surprise even him, I think, with its weight and bitterness.

In Paris, I remember, about six months later, we met, the three of us, a ghastly meeting really, the weather gray and sour and full of wet, which sometimes doesn't matter too much but then it seemed as if the whole earth, all the grass and trees and leaves and everything bright and sunlit had disappeared, was disappearing, and for good and all. I'd gone over to Germany in the Army, and my mother and father had recently gone back to Europe on one of those trips that are supposed to give sick people a health-instilling change of air or scene—I don't know why hanging around hotels is supposed to be good for people who are feeling lousy, but it seems to be something that people who feel lousy find hard to resist. Anyway there they were, two weeks at the bright and tacky Dorchester in London, and then to the Lotti in Paris. I can't imagine why the Lotti, with its hush, and tiny shipboard corridors, and half-dead old ladies in the lobby—I think they probably felt that the gap between the way they were really feeling and the way the Ritz would expect, or would remind, them to feel would be too great. I came to see them there one weekend. They were in one of those small-windowed, thick-carpeted old rooms with lots of gilt and low-watt lightbulbs. The breakfast tray on the bed. A pile of books on a chair. Detective stories. *The Devils of Loudun*. The picture my mother always traveled with (a small blue watercolor of a Mediterranean scene, an island) on the bedside table. The curtains drawn. They both were very quiet.

My mother's sister was then in Paris, and so was one of my mother's few old close friends, Louise Ferande—

Madame Ferande, who did something at one of the couture houses, a tiny bony woman with one of those sharp, animated, uninterested faces. That first evening we all had drinks together, the five of us perched around a table in the tiny Lotti bar, my aunt talking at length about her hardships, which was okay, since she led, more or less by intent, a life so full of human drama and collision that, like a racing-car driver, she seemed to exist most naturally midpoint between some past near-miss and some awaited one. Right then she was having trouble with her lawyer, who was trying to cheat her, so she said. We talked about that for a while. My father didn't talk much at all. These women could be such bitches really, and then when he had left the bar for a moment they all crowded over the table and cooed and trilled about how marvelous he was, in such good shape, so elegant, not thin at all, well maybe a few pounds, but not *thin*, such good *color*. He was nearly dead by then, I think my mother knew that. I think he was beginning to know that. And then the next day it almost happened. In the morning, at dawn, he had some sort of seizure, something to do with the heart, the heart maybe working too hard because of there being only one lung. I don't know, it doesn't matter. But off he was taken suddenly, a now-strange city, a strange hotel, a strange doctor, a strange hospital, some small place out near Neuilly. He was okay, they said out there. The doctor was okay too. Nice. Sympathetic. But christ how crummy it all was—wet, gray, faraway; and he lying there in bed, he seemed so small, and getting smaller. I would go out there with my mother, or sometimes alone, and sit beside the bed, the French nurses running in and out, and try to tell him things about my life, what-I-was-doing, because that seemed to please him. What I was doing. Nothing. I was in the Army. He had this funny idea, I remember, about the Army, about me and the Army, and he hated for me to tell him that I thought it all a lot of nonsense, or especially that I was messing around with it at all. Sometimes, in order to liven things up, I would tell him of some small adventure, an over-stayed pass, a wangled assignment—and he really wouldn't have any of it. He wanted me to be a good boy in the Army. The sheet that covered him up to the neck, I remember, rose and fell with the slow rhythm of his breathing. The sound of his breathing filled the room. I talked informatively of the military life.

He got better for a while. The heart was okay, they said, but naturally one must take it easy. He left the little hospital in Neuilly. He was so pleased his heart was okay. He would take brief walks outside the Lotti in the pale sidewalk sun, and have a gin with Joe Baldwin at the Travellers, and get absurdly, miserably, tired. But he was somehow pleased, maybe at just being alive. And then, around the middle of May, they went on down to the South of France. It was a good time for them, I think. They stayed at the Carlton, the big white dumpy Carlton, with the two domed towers, and the dingy little beach, and the bar, the great Carlton bar, where everyone had once sat around, where everyone had once waited for everyone else. Now everyone gone, or nearly, or just not around, or no longer interested. A p.r. man from M.G.M. where Willie Maugham once sat. Two dozen outboards rocketing and churning up the Mediterranean. But still the Mediterranean. In late May my sister went down there for a while. He seems much better, my sister wrote me, hoping it was true. My sister was then attempting to recover from a disastrous romance with an Egyptian (to whom she had been introduced by my aunt), and had taken briefly to writing me letters. My mother also wrote me letters. They were having a nice time. They took walks. They had seen such-and-such. My sister was still being very silly about Ari, who clearly had no visible means of support, and was a bounder, and so forth. Once, on a mostly spurious assignment for the Army newspaper, I ended up one May afternoon in North Africa, covering a golf match at a Moroccan air base, and phoned my parents, full of my new role as foreign correspondent (a military-golfing foreign correspondent), to announce that I might just "drop by" through Nice, where I knew the Air Force ran another flight. But they were having none of that. "That certainly doesn't sound sensible to me," my mother said, which in her language was the equivalent of cursing solidly for twenty minutes. My father naturally didn't want to hear about any of it. If the Army says you should be in Germany, he said, you should be in Germany. But they were well, or sounded well, and that really was good to hear. In a number of ways it must have been horrid then in Cannes, but they had managed a nice time, and that says something about something. I think it was probably the last nice time like that either of them had.

They came on home to New York later that summer, and my father thought he was actually on-the-mend, getting better, feeling better all the time, longer lunches, longer walks, improvement, health, perfection, life, everything better. But then it wasn't so at all. It wasn't better. It was worse. It was awful, that—he couldn't understand it. He was suddenly so tired, couldn't do anything. He felt very bad one day on his way out to lunch, very very bad, and went to bed. He postponed the lunch, which was with a man from *Time* who was researching a piece on Aldous Huxley, postponed it until the next week, but he never went out again. It was clear then that the doctors hadn't chopped it all out after all; that the excellent bright-eyed tennis-playing surgeon hadn't quite "caught it all," whatever "it" means in these instances. Cancer. The black dank specter. The fifth horseman. He so clearly had it, and even then would not quite believe it. Certainly no one told him that he must believe it, why should anyone tell a man that? He was indoors all the time then. Upstairs in bed for

most of the day, and then sometimes, later in the afternoon, downstairs in the library. I had since come back
from Europe, back from the Army to my job at Time-
Life, and in a fit of filial affection (I think it was that)
had set aside my plans for getting-my-own-place—girls,
wild parties, at least the pleasures of leaving one's dirty
laundry in the middle of the floor—and had moved back
into my old room in their apartment. There was such
death in that place. In a way, it had always had something of that feeling—an indoors, inward-facing apartment to begin with, short on sunlight, and heavy with
my mother's tastes in embroidery, tapestry, thick fab-
rics, dark wood, dark things, closed curtains, little frou-
frous here and there for "gaiety" which only made it all
worse. And now there was real death. Sometimes you
could almost see it moving into him, the thin edge of a
tide moving across the open water. He was so bright, he
was still so bright. Mostly he read all the time now, or
slept (or slept while reading), and sometimes talked a
little with a faint, troubled, hard-of-breathing voice. But
sometimes he would connect with something, a memory, an object moving far off across the horizon, and for
a few moments would come awake, really awake, the
eyes alive, that marvelous quickness, lightness, that so
un-Anglo-Saxon passion pushing its way back into his
voice, taking him with it, taking him now in some pain,
in some considerable pain because of it, even laughing,
his breath very short, his eyes seeming to see *out* for the

first time in days or weeks; and then suddenly over, the sentence finished, the eyes dull, the breath coming in great gulps, while we sat around him feeling love and fear, fear for all of us. Death is a hard person to have in the house with one, and I don't know that I was too much help. I couldn't bear the smell of death, couldn't in fact bear to be there, was always finding reasons to get out, and later feeling terrible for having done so. Swearing I would act better. Would not duck out after dinner like that again. For whole days, maybe two days, would sit there dutiful, attentive, providing little bits of talk and whatever affection seemed transmittible—until one evening there I would be again. I'm sorry. I forgot. Have to meet. Won't be long. Won't be late. Didn't think you'd mind, yes, have a good night. See-you-in-the-morning.

He died in June, the last week in June. It was one of those steamy New York summers, everything unnaturally hot, the air heavy, dusty. I'd just come back from an assignment up around Boston and was downtown at the office typing up notes. My sister called me there in the afternoon. He'd gotten very bad, she said, the doctor was there. I went on home. The doctor was leaving when I arrived. He said he was okay, which seemed an odd thing to say about a man with obviously terminal cancer, but he meant he was okay for then. Okay, considering. I went up to see him, but there was a new nurse. He's resting, she said. I went back down the stairs. My mother came down presently. He had this pressure on the lung, she said, almost instructively, and went on to tell me the details of where the pressure came from, what had happened, what the lung could take and so forth. She lived in the details, they supported her. How is he now? I asked. He seems back to normal, she said. It all seemed crazy, and I knew that he would die tomorrow, or that night, or the next day. The next morning he was awake and I went in to see him. He was pretty tired, but smiled, and we exchanged a few words. I told him a little about the Boston trip. "It's important you go to the office," my mother said. "It's important things go on as normal." I went down to the office, towards the office, getting as far as Sixtieth Street, and then came on back. My mother was angry but it didn't matter too much. I stayed in my room reading, or doing nothing, and then around lunchtime I went in again to see him. It was around twelve o'clock, about the only time of day that room ever got any sunlight. He was sitting up in the big bed, with a tray, but not very mindful of the tray. Such a small fierce man. He seemed extraordinarily alive just then, his eyes a deep deep brown and full of life and warmth. We talked, or rather, for the first time it seemed in weeks, in months, he talked. Not very much. About books, as I remember. Some book of Arnold Bennett's that he'd been re-reading, or trying to: *Riceyman Steps*. "I know you don't read Bennett now," he said, "but you ought to look at him. He wrote some good books." And: "It's funny, isn't it, when I was your age, Bennett was one of my Field Marshalls. I was a corporal, and Wells and Bennett were my Field Marshalls." And: "Bennett and I had lunch together once. I can't remember why. At the Savoy. Bennett talked the whole time about money." He smiled. He seemed very happy. Charles Hughson, a friend of his from England, was in town, and I mentioned that to him, and he talked a little about when they'd first met—Hughson a young reader or some such at Victor Gollancz, and he then new to London, new to writing, new to everything, a young man in a small room off Shepherds Market. His breath seemed almost steady then. He held my hand for a moment. His eyes were half closed as he talked, the man in the bed in New York talking across the years to the man in the small room in Shepherds Market. And then he said he was tired. I think I'll just sleep for a while is what he said. And I took his tray up, which had a thing of custard on it that he hadn't touched, and carried it down. And twenty minutes later, the nurse, who had looked in on him, came down the stairs to tell us he was dead.

AN OLD BROWN-TINTED PHOTO-
graph mounted on thick cardboard. A round-faced,
plain, American-looking girl, but with fine eyes; fine,
wide, brave, open eyes. At least, that is the way she
seems in the photograph. A long time back. New York.
The date, 1881, which was the year, I just remember,
that Henry James (who signed himself then Henry
James, Jr.) first published *The Portrait of a Lady*—
not that they ever met, had tea (which later wouldn't
have been all that unlikely), or had any kind of actual
connection with each other, but I suppose I make some
kind of connection between them in my own mind. Two
émigrés.

Her name was Abby Wright. Abigail Pankhurst
Wright of Cleveland. The youngest of several children

of a Cleveland businessman. A small businessman. I don't know anything about the rest of her family, about her parents. She had red hair, and was short in height, even for then, about five feet or so, not more, and was said to have a magnificent temper; and she was my great-grandmother, my mother's grandmother. Only by the time I knew her she was no longer Abby Wright of Cleveland, looking as proud and scared as a serving girl in the unfamiliar studio of an unfamiliar New York photographer; she was somebody, or something, called Madame la Princesse Daria Kara-Georgevitch, and she lived in a huge house down the hill from us in Cannes, the Villa Fiorentina, with its endless terraces of Italianate gardens (box hedges garishly trimmed into shapes of animals, birds, whatnot), footmen, camellias, a lovely chapel right beside the house that members of the family used every five years or so for weddings, and that I used in between times to hide in and make great resonant, wheezing sounds upon the foot-pedal organ in the upstairs loft.

When I look at that early photograph, the one from 1881 of the young girl with the round plain face, it's so hard to try to even imagine what it all must have been like then. She'd married early, at seventeen or eighteen —a man called Edward Wright, also young, a young man of ambition who had started a steamship company on the Great Lakes, the Garland Steamship Company of Chicago, and had done that for a few years; and then shortly after their first child was born he had decided apparently to get away from Chicago, which was where they were living, to get out of the Midwest, and steamships, to do something more adventurous. And so he had gone out to Montana—there was talk of mining and mineral rights and great finds in the earth. It must have been an adventurous time then, and so he went out that year, and he was killed. Nobody ever seemed to know why or how, but he was killed. I think I was once told "by Indians," which certainly might have been true, but my guess is that I made that part of it up. In those days it could have been by any number of ways, and the more I think of the very little I know about him, the more I think it is probably truer to just leave it the way they all had left it at the time—he died somewhere in Montana, somehow, in 1880. And a year later, his young wife, very young, with a small baby, faced, one guesses, with the prospect of living out her days in Cleveland or Chicago, under the umbrella of various parents and relatives—well, she clearly had her own ambitions and she got the hell out.

And went to Europe. The two of them. London first; then "the Continent." It must have been very strange, although she had some money then, which doubtless helped. The Garland Steamship Company had made some money, and in due course she sold her shares in that and let the bank in Cleveland handle the rest. She had, I guess, plenty to live on in a modest sort of way, modest hotels, modest "resorts," and so that is what they did, my great-grandmother and the small girl who was my grandmother, they toured, they traveled around Europe. Steamer trunks on railway platforms. Porters. Luggage. Aix-les-Bains. "The mountains." Paris. London. "The seashore." And periodically they would come back to Cleveland—endless three-week voyages on cumbersome, rolling, sailing-steamers, deck chairs, winds, spilled food; I remember my grandmother once telling me how terrified she used to be of "the crossing," although I'm afraid that part of her inheritance from those hotel years turned out to be that she became terrified of nearly everything. She married young, too—my grandmother. She always seemed to me a sad, strange, lonely woman—pretty in that depressing fragile way, which was maybe more the fashion then, although I doubt that it was ever the fashion. All those years *en route*. Governesses teaching one French verbs in small hotel rooms. She married at eighteen—my mother's father. Alexandre Mercati. Count Alexandre Mercati, a young Greek on the rise in "court circles" in Athens. They met one winter in Saint-Moritz—there is a lovely picture of him then. Tall, dark, a bristling mustache, stiff collar, hair plastered down. A real Count right out of a Phillips Oppenheim novel, which he really wasn't like at all. (Privately, anyway; he liked to farm.) But looking at the photograph, and remembering my grandmother, who seemed so frail and fragile and falling-down at forty-five (one could imagine her in a per-

petual swoon of vapors all her girlhood), it's not hard
to conceive of the attraction between her and this stern,
dark, impassive man. They were married at any rate,
and lived in Athens, lived for a half dozen years in
Athens, where my uncle, mother, and then my aunt
were born (three children with neo-classical names:
Leonardo, Atalanta, Daria); and he, Alexandre, attended well to his duties—attended to the King of
Greece, did God knows what, was sort of an arranger,
an aide, a staff man, became something called Chamberlain, Lord Chamberlain. I remember one summer
we were in Athens, long ago—he came by our hotel
room with his court uniform on (it was the first time
I had seen it), a splendiferous thing with braid and
silk, and knee breeches, and lots of medals. There was
a small revolutionary scuffle going on in the streets that
day. Anarchists. Socialists. Some rifle fire across the
square. He took the medals off in our hotel room, I
remember, and put them very carefully in a case, a
blue velvet case, and hurried out again. He was quite
beautiful. He visited us a few times in the South of
France. A tall, grave man. Gray-haired. A great gray
mustache. On sunny days he'd get up very early in the
morning, long before anyone else, and sit outside on
the veranda steps polishing his boots, and sometimes
take revolver practice across the empty lawns. He was
a very nice man, I always thought, although I don't
know that we exchanged two words.

A few months after the birth of their youngest child

(my aunt), his wife left him to run off with "another man," another strong, stony young man on the rise in diplomatic circles, an Austrian called Emerich von Pflugl (Baron Emerich von Pflugl in point of fact), not exactly a mellifluous sort of a name, and not exactly a very mellifluous sort of a person. Imre we called him. Uncle Imre—none of this step-grandfather business, which is what he became. I don't know how it all came about, how does anyone else know these things? The usual reasons probably, abetted by the fact that my grandmother felt herself congenitally hard-done-by and full of unattended-to sensibilities (and disliked Athens), that my grandfather was doubtless more than usually aloof and impassive even for those days, and that Imre (I don't think I'm really being unfair here) knew a good deal when he saw one. There are some letters remaining from that period, in a way terrifyingly inhuman letters despite the heat of rhetoric, full mostly of the sounds of social embarrassment and a kind of detached outrage. How could she & so forth. How could you. Think of my position. Think of *my* position . . . It must have been awful, though, awful all the way around, and especially for Mercati because he really was a warm familial man, although he mightn't have been too adept at being so for her. Imre, Lord knows, didn't seem any better. He was okay in a way, but so damned Teutonic. Prussian. He even looked a bit like Erich von Stroheim, at least when I knew him.

Round, bald, bullet-head, and, yes, one of those eye patches—he'd been wounded in the First World War, in the Austro-Hungarian cavalry—and long after my grandmother died he lived out his days, which is just exactly the way it was, in the Hotel Continental in Cambridge, Mass., in a tiny room (I was in college nearby and would have stiff lunches with him once or twice a year; which seemed enough for both of us), compiling some sort of Philosophy of Militarism.

But my grandfather, Mercati—well, he was left the children, including this young baby, while his wife was scooting off and away on the high seas back to America. And then, soon afterwards, his own life started to really fall apart, in the sense that he was simply and definitely on the wrong side of the great social upheavals that were beginning to take place all over Europe. In Greece, there was a revolution led by the socialist Sophocles Venizelos (evidently a remarkable man; great shock of hair, blazing eyes) and the King was tossed out. Everyone connected to the King was tossed out, and those especially connected to the King were shot. My grandfather was taken to be shot, but wasn't, because—I later found out (found out from various sources, one of which, in those nearly predictable ironies of history, turned out to be Venizelos's chic granddaughter, whom I found myself taking to fox-trotty little New York dances some thirty-five years later)—because apparently even Venizelos thought he was a nice man (I guess the translation for that is "harmless") and because he had all these damned children on his hands. He, and they, were sent into exile instead, on the island of Zante, which is one of the islands up there on the northwest coast of Greece, some hundred miles due south of Corfu. And stayed there for about ten years. My uncle and mother and aunt more or less grew up on Zante, a small house on a barren lovely island, not entirely barren—donkeys, goats, shepherds, small villages, farms, olive trees. Mercati's sister, Cecile, took care of the household. French ladies would arrive every so often to teach the children arithmetic, and verbs. My uncle and my mother tried to keep scorpions as pets. Mercati wrote in his journal. And then eventually a counterrevolution took place, and brought them all back again—to schools, and proper clothes, and big houses, and "mountains" and "seashores" and Saint-Moritz in the winter, and a curtsy to the King at birthday parties, and yes, Balliol for my uncle, and finishing schools in Paris, and God knows what else, what all, except that when my mother peered back through her life, back through her marriage, before her marriage, one sensed that all she ever seemed to see that made any sense to her was the dust of Zante, the donkeys and scorpions, a passing remembrance, for instance, of her father one afternoon standing solitary by the sea; and that, in the strange ways of the world, everything thereafter had been a kind of exile.

Marriage, even. Or especially. It's indeed hard to know these things. When my mother and father married—in many ways they were very old-fashioned; and in many ways they were some of the first "modern" people, not so much in that my mother smoked cigarettes in public, or that my father would rather fly the Channel than take the boat across, but in that the possibilities they, and people like them, were beginning to live with were already then, dimly, unknowingly, beginning to outrun their resources. Possibilities everywhere. The ability to move. To seize new ground. New people. New money. One still had the old, of course. The old everything. (Franz-Josef himself was not so many years dead.) Then, one still had the old, the carpet underfoot, the furniture nailed in place, although one was moving away from that with every breath, every year. My father and mother met, as it happens, in Saint-Moritz, and fell in love. My father would have been then twenty-nine, and already "successful," a celebrity of some sort, but definitely not the right sort—a novelist, a foreigner, really the most unbecoming kind of foreigner. They fell very much in love that winter, and then spent an anguished year alternately together, apart, together, apart —her father disapproved. An adventurer is what he said he was. "No better than an adventurer." I have one of the letters. It is hard to realize that people once actually spoke like that outside of novels, but then they often don't speak all that differently now. They decided to get married anyway, she running off towards the South of France, to Cannes, to where my great-grandmother lived. Her father, the Count, sent quiversful of letters in pursuit. Telegrams, those portentous, expensive telegrams of the early days of "wireless." He disinherited her by telegram—it sounds so funny now. Disinherit? We are above all that. But it must have been bloody awful at the time (the man on the beach at Zante); rejection in any form is bloody awful.

In the end, though, it was okay, as these things often seem to be if you have the nerve for them. A big wedding. (They used the chapel once again.) Marriage. Even Mercati relented a few years later, and re-inherited her, or whatever, with some real estate outside of Athens, which the next government promptly impounded. It was a very good kind of match, and also very bad, although I grant that it is difficult to tell about these things by looking in from outside the window. They were both of them beautiful. They were also, both of them, in a kind of exile, and sought to find a home, a country, in one another, and very nearly did, came as close as maybe it is possible to do, but they were each so deep in exile when they met—and how would they have known that? My father, so successful, full of energy, in command of things. My mother, so seemingly established—a title even, money somewhere in the background, big houses, gardens, furniture, wax for the furniture, polish for the silver, manners, style, and more than style or manners, a seeming feel for independence, for being a "new woman." But the house my mother grew up in was a dead house, and when my father, running out of success, and nerve, and stamina, and command, came finally to seek shelter in that house—it turned out to have no room, it was already sinking, sunk. And my mother, seeking to escape from her (still unknown) exile, from all those mannered, fragile, assured, protected, self-protective people into this unusual man's vitality, life, imagination, energy—well, as maybe with many men, it turned out to be a fragile, an especially fragile kind of energy. So delicate, really. Too delicate. But that was all for later, for much later. It was later that they found those things out, or didn't find them out, just lived them, lived under them. In the beginning, though, it must have been lovely, as it often is. There is a picture of the two of them on a rock near Cannes, a picture of two bodies really, pleased with each other. I mean, there are clothes, and they are looking in different directions, and there is even someone else in the picture, a friend, but the picture is of what I said it was, and life must surely have been like that for a while. The South of France. The early 1930's. A white house on the side of a hill above Cannes, wisteria, magnolia, lemon trees, fig trees, green lawns, bamboo—about a half mile or so above my great-grandmother's house. Madame la Princesse—about ten years previously she had finally remarried, at fifty-five, to somebody called

Alexis Kara-Georgevitch (M. le Prince), a nice man I gather, one of the thousands of Kara-Georgevitches unleashed upon an unprepared world after the disappearance of Serbia, who then died a few years later in a seaplane crash. One of the *first* seaplanes, she used to say with genuine pride. She considered herself a true modernist, or tried hard to be. I remember this machine she had downstairs in her salon, a room full of marble and porcelain and velvet, immense Chinese screens, a harp over by the window—and there off to one side, built into the wall, one of the first automatic record-changers, a marvelous untamed contraption consisting of a gramophone turntable and a sort of obscene metallic hand, a *hand*, that whirred and clanked and extended slowly out of the wall, and grabbed the record, and then usually dashed it to bits against the floor. I used to go there sometimes for lunch. The two of us (only one footman). Lamb chops. Mint sauce, the smell of mint everywhere. Sunlight. She had very white hair then, and a kind, no-nonsense smile. I don't remember what we talked about. And afterwards we'd sit for a while outside, and she would read, and fall asleep, and I'd throw gravel at the peacocks.

I HAVE AN IDEA, NOW, FINALLY, OF what my father was like when I last saw him. Of what he looked like. Of what he sounded like. Even (I count myself lucky for this) a small idea of the kind of man he was. I have a picture anyway of him and me in the last couple of years before he died, a picture in which we are both fairly clear, are clear to each other, seem to touch. But all those years before. There are few pictures, and the ones that still remain seem now so very blurred. I've wondered how clear they were to him.

THERE WAS THAT TIME in California. Right after D-day, I remember. I was at school in New Hampshire. St. Paul's, that fine, sleek, red-bricked, well-mowed, well-scrubbed Episcopal school that my mother had finagled me into just before the start of the school year. At least that was her story and I had no reason to doubt it. "Freddy Boissevain has been such a help," she said to me later. "You are lucky to have him on your side." Freddy Boissevain was apparently the man who had done the finagling. Freddy Boissevain was a trustee of the school, a tiny pink man with a soft face who would now and then drop by my mother's small apartment in New York and talk to her about electric utilities. He was a "fixer," my mother would say of him admiringly—he fixed people into weddings, and into clubs, and through customs, and into hotels, and maybe in and out of electric utilities on the side, and now he had fixed me into this fine sleek Episcopal school. I was terrified by it. I loved it. All those hymns. They were the same hymns I had been mumbling through at English schools and Canadian schools since the age of eight, and now I knew them nearly all by heart, I could yell them almost, and sometimes did when the music was loud enough, standing blazered and half asleep in chapel every morning beside the sturdy blond Protestant figures of the sons of stockbrokers and lawyers in the pews beside me. My mother kept telling me I should feel lucky to be there. I did feel lucky to be there. Showers that ran in never-ending streams of hot water. Food of such extraordinary delicacy that it could frequently be eaten without catchup. Teachers, even, who seemed to have taken up

their calling with at least a semblance of vocation—at
any rate unlike my previous masters, who had generally
given such evidence of despising both the school and
their profession that one assumed they had been sent to
it, like us, for some sort of as-yet-unrevealed misde-
meanor. It was a nice place, that school in New Hampshire. Lots of trees, and grass, and woods, and ponds. I
had two friends there that first fall, Dick Hobart and
George Brock (I don't remember why they were good
friends, but they were), and we used to skip football
practice some afternoons and go roaming through the
woods in the back of the playing fields, nothing very poetic about it, we were looking for a supposed secret way
into a nearby village, and eventually found it; but it was
nice crashing about in the woods, even when it got cold,
towards November. Even when the sun went down very
early, and the trees were bare, and the ground hard, and
everything in the world seemed brittle, except us, I
think. And then my mother phoned me one evening. It
was a big deal then, being phoned by one's mother. Messages were taken, transmitted, passed up channels,
down channels. One was summoned to the housemas-
ter's office. One was given slips of paper. Fear. Excitement. One called New York . . . New York City. The
Butterfield number. "It's me," I said. "Well of course,"
she said. And then: "He's coming over. He left a week
ago. I just got the cable." My father was finally coming
over from England, in some Brazilian freighter or

something, bound for Halifax, Boston, New York, the long way around. She was quite wild at first, I couldn't make her out. I didn't feel much of anything myself, except her wildness, her excitement. I hadn't seen my father for nearly four years, and when she'd say "your father" this, "your father" that, I really had no face at all to connect the name to, just a sort of shape, a feeling. An overcoat, in truth, was what I most had to connect with in my mind—there was this overcoat, this arm stretching from a dark overcoat that pulled me, tugged me, laughing, running, down a street off Berkeley Square. But anyway I was to come on down for his arrival. It had been arranged with the school. A certain weekend. Travel arrangements were being made; were made. One week later I went on down. Concord to Boston. Boston to New York. The junior master who put me on the train at the Concord station kept tying tags to my lapel, and I kept tearing them off—there ought, I felt, to have been some benefit accrued by then from all those past train journeys, at least to the extent of not having to wear some damned tag on one's lapel. "Don't forget you change stations in Boston," he said. He was a nice young man called Mr. Stevens, who taught French, and had been on the crew at Yale. "I know," I said. "South Station," he said. "You change from North Station to South Station," he said. "I know," I said. The train chugged in, I stepped aboard. "Have a great time with your dad," said Mr. Stevens. "Here," he said, "take this—" and handed me the newspaper he had under his arm. I went down to New York but my father was not due in for still another week. My mother had just found out that morning, a cable from the ship—there had been some sort of trouble in a storm, they were bypassing Halifax, their speed had been reduced . . . My mother was too distracted by it all to give much thought to whether or not I was disappointed, which I wasn't. Something was supposed to have happened which apparently wasn't going to happen, at least not on schedule. But it was all too remote for disappointment. She wasn't disappointed in that sense either—just in limbo, not there. Not here. Not there. We went out to lunch that Saturday, I remember, and she asked me vaguely about school, and offered to go to a movie afterwards, but neither of us could think of one, neither of us much wanted to sit inside a movie house, she clearly couldn't sit still anywhere. I went on back to school, and then, indeed, about a week later my father phoned from New York, from that apartment. I spoke to him on the telephone. I had never heard his voice before, had quite forgotten it —and he then had all this feeling in it; he kept reaching out, and I knew it, felt all sorts of strange and powerful things myself. But I had never heard his voice before. "How are you?" he kept saying helplessly, and I, equally helpless, would answer "Fine," or something like that. It must have been very hard for him. So many things must have been hard for him then, only the least of them being a three-and-a-half-week North Atlantic crossing on a glued-together Brazilian freighter. He was forty-eight years old. He had wanted to be so good, so shining, so flashing, such a proud exotic animal—he had had all these things, nearly had them, had his hands around them, had fondled them. The books. Money. The sun shining on silver. Flame. All those bright bright whites and blues beside the Mediterranean. The big silent cars. The speedboats. The drive along the Corniche and over the hills to Monte Carlo. Byzantium. At Maxine Elliott's, he and Willie Maugham would lunch (serene amid all those monkeys and the half-mad wild deer she kept about her); and Vincent Sheean; and Freddy Lewisohn; and sometimes Churchill would come by, Winston, who was writing all those pieces for *Collier's*, and talked, and drank, and sometimes went off to paint in the afternoons. And then it had all begun to go. The sun on the white houses. The sun on the Mediterranean. The sun on everything. Even as a kid I can remember it changing—a whole new sequence of snapshots. My father listening each evening to the B.B.C.'s Empire Service. Fouchard, the old gardener, absently oiling his 1918 rifle. The evil-looking, brown-tinted drawings about gas masks and tanks and barrage balloons that started appearing in *The Illustrated London News*. It is easy enough, I guess, to look back with hindsight and talk smoothly about "Europe dancing" while the "storm clouds gathered," and I suppose there was some of that going on, I suppose there always is. But the people I peer back towards—I don't know that in the end they will turn out to have acted much differently towards their time than you or me; which is to say that when the dark shapes finally rose above the horizon, finally appeared, inescapably visible, above the horizon line, they worried, felt bad, were scared, were not scared, tried to do certain things knowing that the things they tried were only things, no more than things, and that by then, irreversibly, they were in the grip of "forces." My father, as I think of it, and people like him, lived his life in terms of a never-ending adjustment of his dream of it to what he saw was there to be adjusted to, lived with; and although I think it sad in many ways that this should be so, I'm not sure that many of us in any generation get much beyond that. It so happened (I believe) that his dream was shinier than most, full of wilder colors, plumage, smoke, honeysuckle, scents, the feel sometimes (it must have been) of perfect ivory; but then his view of what lay before his eyes at any given moment could also be colder, harder than most; full of less self-pity. And so the world he had tried so hard to blow his shiny dream upon turned cold and sour, and he knew it, I think, as well as anyone; knew why; felt powerless to stop it, which is neither particularly to his credit nor his discredit. It is just the way things were for him. And then the war did come, arrived. We were in England. I had just gone off to school, my first school, a posh little cold-showers-and-Latin boarding school in Surrey. And we disbanded, our family, for "safety's" sake—I first, in a boatload of sniffly, properly capped-and-jacketed English boarding-school boys bound for another school in Canada. My mother and sister to New York. And he stayed there. In England. It was his adopted country, he used to say, conscious that people did not expect that sort of sentimentality from him, and conscious that he felt it, helplessly and absolutely. He was in London first, and then in Coventry, where he was what he could be, an air-raid warden—in actual title an "information officer" for Civil Defense, but mostly an air-raid warden—and felt proud of it. There was a lot of bombing there, in that war, in that place (as is remembered by some), and he did what he could, which was usually nothing, and felt scared and angry. I used to read some of the letters he wrote my mother then—he'd make as if he just moved through everything, moved through the streets, the night, fires, rubble, people. He and a gigantic Scotsman called MacAndrew who worked with him were walking home late after a raid, he'd write, and MacAndrew, "who then smelled beautifully of whisky," had fallen out of sight into a hole in the street. "The hole was a very large one, containing interesting rocks, and which led in turn to a tunnel, which led into the deposit vaults of Barclays Bank. MacAndrew, being Scots, refused to leave, and I, being Armenian, felt unable to persuade him. I enclose clip-

pings of the arrest." He was often very tired, he used to
write, and sometimes afraid, and "on dark nights have
other dark thoughts I cannot name," and that was the
most he used to give away in those days of his own feelings about it all. And then when the bombing had
quieted down a bit, had quieted down considerably,
seemed to have stopped—well, it's hard to understand
how these things can happen, but of course one knows
how they happen, they happen every day, in every country—on one such day, in early 1944, a "question" was
raised in the House . . . as to why a person of "foreign
ancestry" was in "these crucial times" allowed to occupy
such a "key position" in an industrial city; and shortly
afterwards he left. There was no other course. He left,
and went back to London, where he tried to get something to do in one of the Information Offices, but things
apparently were rather sticky for him, his "situation"
had suddenly become rather sticky—it must have been
a small nightmare. I mean, he really cared. He had cared
a lot. And so he packed, and got himself a bunk aboard
this freighter, this Brazilian freighter, and went finally
off to join his family. Forty-eight years old. No money
(the little he had left being "blocked" in England). The
memory of a flashing career. His wife and children
living out of a small apartment-hotel off Madison Avenue. He was quite marvelous even so. Tired, marvelous. But then he worried about the money. My mother
had since come into a little, a small trust from her

mother, which in fact was what we lived on. A few days after he landed in New York he had taken my mother out to dinner, to the Colony, I think—the first time both of them had been together that way in a long time. It had been nice, I gather. Big fusses made (he'd known old Gene Cavallero from before the war). Champagne. The works. The next morning he woke up in high spirits, and announced plans to take a half dozen people to "21" for dinner that evening, and my mother then told him that they just couldn't do that sort of thing any more. He went out that noon, went down to "21" in fact, feeling terribly serious and solemn, and full of all sorts of resolves about economy—a last drink at "21" or some such, where he ran into Louis Mayer, whom he had known when *The Green Hat*, his big novel, had been made into a movie in the late 1920's. They had lunch together. There was a whole crowd of people, I gather, and lots of booze, and talk, and at some point Mayer leaned over and asked my father what he was planning to do. "I was just talking to Sam Goldwyn . . ." my father began, which was true—he'd met Goldwyn outside in the lobby and Goldwyn had advised him to buy race horses. "How much did he offer you?" Mayer asked quickly. My father thought for a moment. "Not enough," he said. "Would you take fifteen hundred for thirty weeks?" Mayer asked. My father said yes, and went home that afternoon, and called up lots of people to go out to dinner, and told my mother that he was now a screenwriter for M.G.M. He left for Los Angeles a few weeks later.

IT WAS MY FATHER who decided I should come out to California and join him just before Christmas. He was already working on a movie. Within a few days after his arrival there, to his surprise, to everyone's surprise, they had put him onto a movie—it was a William Powell, Hedy Lamarr movie, in fact, that was already in production and that some other writer had been messing around with. He sent letters and phone calls back to New York that made it all sound very busy and glamorous. He said he missed everybody. He said he didn't know if he'd be able to get home much before Christmas, and then hit on the idea that I should come directly out there from school. We would have a reunion, he said. Good times.

The train took me out to California that December, a bright cold East Coast December. Bleak Chicago. Servicemen everywhere. I had heard stories of the resplendent private cars of movie tycoons, and looked for them on the sidings, but they were nowhere to be seen. I sat up for nights and days looking out the grimy windows at the clean spare Western states. I was fourteen years old, and rode beside a young Air Corps captain returning home to Idaho, who answered my questions about airplanes and showed me pictures of his parents and girlfriend. There was a woman too, a girl, she must have been twenty-three or so, Ann Sheridan hair—the dining-car captain had seated me across from her the first night out of Chicago, and I found her very beautiful and fell in love with her the instant she laughed at one of my stories, or whatever it was that I was telling her. She took my hand at one point, or so I thought, or so I remember. I spent the rest of the trip searching for her about the train, but when I found her she was usually seated in one of the club cars with other men, or groups of men, not laughing usually, just sitting. Once I remember going by her, some sort of colonel was holding one of her hands, and a man in a business suit had an arm across her shoulders.

My father met me at the station in Los Angeles. I didn't recognize him at first, which was okay, he was still far away, with one of those wide-brimmed dark hats he used to wear. Everything was smaller, less than I'd expected. California was smaller, less, and he too. My *father*, I wondered, knowing full well that this man advancing down the platform was inalterably my father. Arms outstretched. A sudden wave. We hugged. He had tears along his face. This stranger. I hugged him hard, harder. This stranger. I kept looking at him, trying to do so in a way that wouldn't be evident. We walked, the two of us, back down the platform. How big you are, he kept saying. How well you look. How is everything at school? I answered dutifully, trying not to be dutiful. He seemed so small to me, I hadn't realized he was so small, no taller than I was really. We went outside and took a taxi to the hotel, the Beverly Wilshire. I have a room for you, he said, just down the hall from me. I let him propel me about. Hotel clerks. Bellboys. The Beverly Wilshire seemed dark and garish, and I felt myself withdrawing, withdrawing all the time, not wanting to—wanting to be there. Breakfast, he kept saying. You must be hungry. I said I wasn't. Of course you are, he said. We'll have breakfast together. Shall we have it up here? he asked. Or shall we go downstairs? The dining room isn't much, he said. You should have seen the food we had in England, he said, when the waiter and table arrived. Everything is amazing here, he said. The Americans are amazing. I looked at him across the hotel table in that hotel room. I didn't mind hotels. There had been that hotel in London. Each winter, for a few weeks after Christmas. Cold winds outside. Inside, the smell of porridge. One called it porridge. Wheeled in on a large table. Gaiety. Warmth. My father had been there too, in the next room in fact. And now here he was. This man. His mustache was thicker than I'd remembered. I spoke to him about my school, and said "thank you" a lot. He seemed not to notice any of it, although once he suddenly reached out his hand across the table and clasped me, and I tried to clasp him back, and there was something in his eyes just then, but I don't know what it was.

We went out that afternoon to "the Studio." M.G.M. Culver City. He had a limousine for us. They sent a limousine for him every day, he said. It was part of his arrangement with Mr. Mayer. He made it all sound very posh and debonair, and I felt better as we drove. The studios were big. Impressive. Great white and gray buildings. Sheds. Lots of people. We drove on through the gate, and over to a large nondescript building, where the offices were, he said. I got out and thought that we would go up together to his office. I was curious about what his office might be like, having read somewhere about Selznick, or was it Zanuck, having an office full of tiger skins and elephant tusks, but he said for me to wait downstairs, he would be back in a moment. It was a ramshackle sort of building on the inside, narrow corridors, pasteboard walls. Men and a few women, none of them beautiful, passed in the halls, greeted each other. My father seemed uncertain of his way. I hoped people would greet him too, but they didn't. I waited by the guard's desk while he disappeared upstairs. He came down again in about ten minutes. "We'll go and watch some of the shooting," he said. "Nothing's open today," said the guard. We went out anyway. My father was talking about the techniques of "special effects," but as far as I could see only for my benefit. He was telling me about a scene in an Errol Flynn movie that was then being filmed, about how they used a great tank of water, and wave machines, and had all these ship models—he was walking beside me across the M.G.M. lot, smiling, discoursing about this tank of water, and Errol Flynn. Errol is an old friend, he would say at several points. We walked between sheds, around sheds. People all around. We looked into buildings. A few sets were open, but nothing was happening. There were lots of actors in Navy uniforms on an empty stage. Lots of cameras. I had this feeling that neither of us could stop walking, that neither of us knew how to stop walking. He asked a guard where the tank of water was that they were using for Errol Flynn's movie, but the guard appeared not to know anything about it. "For Mr. Flynn's picture," my father repeated, as if the "Mister" would somehow set it straight, but the guard was having none of it.

We walked some more, in a kind of desperation, so it seemed, and then we went on back to Beverly Hills. I felt he must surely want to get rid of me, for a while anyway, but he kept thinking up things to do, things that neither of us much wanted to do. Have tea. Go to some sort of movie museum. I suddenly realized that it was I who wanted to be off, and hated myself for feeling that. I said something about being tired, and went to my room anyway, and lay stiffly down on the bed for a few minutes, hoping indeed that I might be tired. But then got up and went downstairs and out of the hotel. The sunlight seemed very yellow, glaring, just then. Palm trees in the sidewalk. Careful lawns. Small genteel shops. Beverly Hills in those days wasn't so different from what it is today. It was all of it, anyway, a new world. America. The school in New Hampshire was America, with all its fine-looking, athletic, confident, East Coast boys, their settled houses, their settled families, their settled talk of summer places. Going-on-to-college. Parties in winter. And here clearly was America too. The tanned open-shirted men. The palm trees. Motion. Big cars and slangy waiters. The assumed assurance everywhere. I thought of my father upstairs in his room. I couldn't fit him in anywhere, which troubled me —for thinking about it in the first place. I went back into the hotel later, not wanting to go back in, and we went out to dinner. I kept hoping that things would somehow get better—I don't know what I wanted from him. I had told myself that I hardly knew him, had only memories. I knew that he was kind and loved me. I knew that from memory and instinct, I suppose, and what I wanted was to love him. And so we went out to some place like Chasen's. No, Romanoff's that night. Mike Romanoff. Another "old friend," who actually did seem to be a friend. There were some other people with us, Bill Hartwood, a screenwriter, and his wife, and then some others, two men and a woman. The woman's name was Mrs. Danvers. My father kept referring to her as Mrs. Danvers. She had that Lana Turner blond hair, and body, and a nice distracted smile. She asked me about school. Everybody asked me about school—

they would periodically interrupt their own conversations, which were mostly stories, anecdotes, to pause, and lean over, and ask me about school. My father was being very funny, I could tell. Bill Hartwood and Mrs. Danvers laughed a good deal. It pleased me, that. I felt taken aboard, at ease, and then it suddenly all seemed to go wrong—somebody else had been telling a story, one of those Hollywood stories that I think I still dislike even now as much as I did then (some last remnant of primness, I guess), what used to be called a dirty story, but which seemed somehow different there, more than that. Nasty. I can't explain it much beyond that. There was a burst of laughter anyway, and then my father started to add to it, to extend the story, but nobody was paying him any attention. It wasn't as if they were pointedly ignoring him, it wasn't as if anything very definite was happening, had happened. There he was, telling this story or whatever it was (a starlet story, I remember, although I've never been able to remember anything more), trying—it seemed suddenly and awfully—to be like *them*, and being in the end so different. Not enhancingly different. Just different. Invisible. I hated him for tagging onto that story, and I think I hated him even worse for seeming just then so different from all the others. And I began to look for this, this difference between him and all the rest—it seemed so like a threat to all of us, my family. And I felt awful about it—I know it sounds self-serving to say that, to be self-protectively demanding of someone else and then say one feels badly about being so, but that is how things were. I had felt so often (and unwillingly) like a spy in the world, in the several worlds I had entered, halfway entered, been nudged into; and now I felt like a spy with my father. I don't know what he felt with me, but I knew it was not working out well, my visit, his idea. Our reunion. And it was to go on for seven more days—I truly dreaded each of them. And something began to build up inside him too. Maybe impatience at me, which he couldn't accept, and which anyway took the form of worrying that he wasn't showing me a sufficiently "good time"; and so he started taking me around even more, more dinners at Romanoff's, Chasen's, more producers, parties, stories, that kind of hard-baked, crackly, ungiving laughter that I still associate with Southern California, although I haven't heard it there for over twenty years.

We were to go out to Santa Barbara that weekend— Clark Gable had a place out there. Clark was an "old friend." We went on out. The limousine. An hour's or so drive up by the Pacific. My father very silent. We got there around Saturday noon. Gable was not there, in fact was not going to be there, but there were a number of other people. Tanned, tall Americans. A big Jewish producer. Women. Everybody seemed to be drinking. My father, I'd come to be aware, drank a good deal, but not usually the way they were drinking then, bottles of bourbon and Scotch set on the table, people pouring it into glasses. My father began drinking too. We were all sitting around inside. People talking, trade talk. He would start in to say something, take hold of something, try to take hold, some line of wit, or style, a curl of sentence, but nobody was interested. I could tell it. I didn't know if he could tell it. Nobody seemed interested in what he said, in him. Everyone nonetheless friendly, or whatever it is that passes for friendliness. They talked—it is hard now to remember what anyone talked about, but I have still a feel of that Saturday afternoon, a long afternoon it was too; the big pink house, the phony ranch, great lawns, and colored flowers; the sea somewhere around; a huge green pool; and everyone indoors, stuffed silky chairs, a glass-top table mounted on a piece of driftwood. Blond girls with beautiful lipsticked mouths seated low around the driftwood table, smoking, giggling. The men sitting, sprawled, talking about movies, about real estate, about the Japs, about nothing really, everybody very languid, savvy. The war in the Pacific was still going on, although it was hard to tell. Someone said something about that—I forget again what it was. Something about bombing, the bombing of Germany, and my father suddenly, I remember, became very loud, unnatural. Angry, but the anger not seeming to have anything to do with anyone or anything in that room. And everyone was silent, the girls in their big lipsticked mouths blowing out cigarette smoke, and looked at him. Cigarette smoke. And then somebody said, in that grunting offhand open-necked leathery way—he should have another drink and not take things too damn seriously; and then he was silent. He did take another drink, but he didn't say much of anything again, didn't even seem to be listening to the others, and then he left, walked out of the room. "A very well educated man," the Jewish producer said to me, in a confidential tone, after he had gone out. "A class writer, and clearly a very well educated man." I stayed on there around the table for a little while longer, trying at the same time to be part of the group and to be invisible, a difficult combination. One of the blond girls had moved up on the couch between two of the men and was kissing them alternately, neither of them paying much attention to her. One of the men, in a sort of absent-minded, slow-motion fashion, reached over and put a hand on her breast. "That's nice," the girl said. The man took his hand away and the girl looked at him and got back down off the couch. I found my father outside by the pool. He was sitting by the pool—it was one of those new fancy-shaped things, green tiles, a rubber raft was floating on the water. I sat down on the grass, beside his chair. "I was out here a long time ago," he said. "We used to play tennis. Thalberg—he always wanted to talk about literature." He put a hand on my shoulder. "I worry about you," he said. "I can't give you happiness but I want you to really know about things." He stood up.

"I've missed you," he said. Then: "Let's go back in."
He stood for a moment looking out across the cypresses
at the sea. "You know, that's a very very boring ocean,"
he said, and we went back into the house, and said goodbye, and drove into town, and had dinner later that
evening with Charles Brackett, a funny man, and Mrs.
Danvers.

THERE ARE THESE PICTURES OF HER as a girl. Fifteen or sixteen. Dark hair down to the shoulders, a girl's hair, young. Dark eyes. A nearly beautiful, becoming beautiful, face, although a little plump just then. "I used to be so shy as a girl," she once said. "You would not believe how shy." The girl in the photograph wears a long print dress, and stands between two small trees, real trees, some country place, the farm outside Athens perhaps. Everything is young in the photograph, motionless as in a studio—the trees, the lawn in front of the trees, everything is charming, civilized, fixed firmly in place, save for the look on the face of the girl, which is not a shy look.

There are other photographs. Later. The girl is beautiful now, seems very far from girlhood. The hair sleeked back. The eyes very proud. The face, especially from the side, quite perfect. The dress is now a bride's dress. White. The look on the face dark, dark as a Spanish princess. And later the pictures with the children. Children on lawns. Children in English clothes. Children on the beach. The woman's face is still proud, darker even. The eyes look out, dark eyes, the face of a dark madonna. The eyes are not a madonna's eyes.

MY MOTHER DIED when I was thirty-three. Her husband, my father, had died eight years before that. She had never, it would now seem, really made it in life, connected with the world; had connected only with him, through him (his connection itself so haunted and peripheral), and when he died, she was left, a little like an astronaut cast adrift from his spaceship and spinning slowly, slowly off into the void; she herself spun wildly, angrily, with fits of rage and bitterness, and drink, and pills, and complaints, and sickness—she who had never been sick, now sickly, now suddenly prey to headaches, backaches, complaints, *complaints*, her body itself turning on her, the skin sagging not so much with age as with malaise, the body swelling not from flesh or fat but from something no longer tenable; she, too, slowly slowly drifted off into her own universe—somebody's universe.

It was such a lousy time for her—for me too, really.

But mostly for her. So much going wrong, so much hidden in mist and vapor. All the sunlight gone. There was this apartment, their "home" in New York. They had bought it, she had bought it about five years before my father died. A commitment to the New World. A commitment to something. It was on Park Avenue, Seventy-fifth Street, one of the inner apartments, quite large, quite elegant in a way. The crystal chandelier was brought over from Fiorentina and installed above the winding staircase. Furniture was brought over. Aubussons. Some Chinese stuff. Their home. And, of course, while they were getting it, arranging it, my sister and I were readying to leave. We had our rooms, were given our rooms, and my sister indeed kept and used hers for quite a while, it was *her* room. But mine was never mine, my rooms anyway had always been at schools, at college. And the apartment itself had this dark, heavy, morbid look. Even then, when I didn't think about morbidity, at least not in the same way I do now, it had this look about it. Things turned inward. Things waxed over, covered. There was a photograph she kept on her desk, a photograph of the two of them seated beside a pool near Cannes, near Antibes probably, both of them so young, glistening, nearly naked in the sun, as naked anyway as the 1930's would allow, glistening bodies, you could feel the heat and see the sun everywhere—the sun was nowhere around now, was not even looked for. The curtains always drawn. The beautiful curtains. The curtains were of some Veronese silk, and previously had belonged to Mama, and to Grandmama before her. The curtains were drawn every evening at five o'clock, and opened again when the maid made her rounds in the morning. Curtains. Carpets. And after he had died (had died upstairs at "home," made it a point to do so, was proud of that), she continued there, seated most every night in that sofa in the library, the right side of the sofa, *her* side, eyeglasses beside her on the cushion (she wore glasses now to read), a book open on the table but barely read at, often the television on but not looked at, sometimes with the sound off, a drink nearby. I would come by to visit, to talk and be dutiful, and she would rage at me— doubtless (among other things) for just that, for talking, or listening, and being dutiful. She would sit there on the far side of the sofa, her body which had once been so beautiful, slender, proud, now swollen, not immense, but swollen, stout; doctors kept finding various names for her swelling, for this expression of her body, "colitis" it was sometimes called, or "pancreatitis," as if naming it would somehow wrest some sense out of it. She would sit there and I would sit in the big chair opposite, and we would drink after dinner, and talk about this or that, some movie, something ordinary that had happened, once I remember it was about as harmless a subject as a recent speech of Conant's about education that she'd fastened on in the *Journal-*

American, and then she'd erupt—a wild dark storm, a
mad queen, the elegances gone, the water suddenly rising, the waves coming seemingly out of nowhere, the
trees bending, straining, everything threatening to come
apart. I had been selfish toward her. I had turned her
aside, betrayed her. I never understood much of that
then, don't understand much of it now—some things,
psychiatry to the contrary, are not much, or usefully,
amenable to understanding. But it was difficult then,
difficult for both of us, and especially for her because at
first the only way I knew to manage it was by making
myself invisible. An act of self-protection, like all those
other wretched acts of self-protection, of hiding oneself
under the coverlet, the tarpaulin, as if the force that
seemed to menace me was *in fact* a storm, a raincloud, a
torrent, something out of nature, implacable—instead
of what it was: another human, reaching out. Reaching
out madly at times. But reaching out. Yes indeed, I would
say, cool in my chair. Maybe, I would say. You have a
point, I would say. *Vous avez raison. Vous avez tort.* A
soft voice turneth aside harsh words. It seemed to me a
civilized, grownup way to act, and probably was. And
then one spring they found she had breast cancer, suddenly, the way they do. And so they operated, and then
said she was fine. She had some X-ray treatments for a
while that made her feel rotten. Burned. But then all
that stopped, she seemed okay. Things quieted down between us in a way. We even did things like have lunch

together, although rather guardedly, each of us careful
to keep the conversation out of reach of the dark mon-
sters. And she loved my children, as grandmothers do,
and you could see in the raw passion with which she
sometimes embraced them a glimpse of the forces that
had often swirled up and out of her in her own life; what
one saw of her with her grandchildren seemed more an
intimation of what she was keeping back, keeping un-
said—of the wildness that, as an act of will, she kept *out
of* most relationships, rather than of what was still
there, which was considerable. And then one year later,
feeling better, she decided to spend the summer in
Greece. She had been there often in the recent past, she
liked it, although in many ways she now found it as
alien as New York, as alien as everywhere. The friends
she had in Athens, it seemed, were really no more
friends than the friends she had in New York, an exchange of handshakes between cripples. But the earth
there must have meant something. The place. The presence. Something more than mere memory anyway, more
than names in an address book, and chatty lunches at
Kefissia. I saw her off one evening at the airport, late
one evening, very late, the plane delayed—we sat in one
of those lounges and had a kind of dinner, and talked,
nothing very much. It was fine. I suppose it wasn't
"real"—a relationship sustained mostly out of memory.
But cozy. Quiet affection. Friendly chitchatter. Minor
fussings about my sister. Serious discussions about my

four-year-old daughter and the proper age to be taught swimming or not. That kind of thing. Just nice, and then she left to get on the plane. I'd never got used to her looking thick, and neither had she, but anyway I watched her walking away down the corridor or tunnel or whatever out to the plane, she had on a rather sweet dashing hat, a feather in it I remember, and carried a huge bag stuffed with all sorts of stuff, a half pint of Scotch included—and turned to wave, the way one waves. But it was nice. I think that was really the last time I saw her. I say "I think" because I did see her later, two months later in fact, but by then she was nearly dead.

By then she was no longer thick. No longer with that strange stoutness. Everything now drawn in, brought in, reduced. Ah God I hate that diminishment of cancer. My sister, now in Athens, had wired me first, saying she thought something was going wrong. And then when I phoned my uncle (who lived there), he had said he thought something was wrong, but that the worst thing would be to "worry her," to do anything rash. Etc. One was never supposed to do anything rash. I took something like the next plane over there, and even then it turned out that she was nearly out of it. She had been staying at the Hilton in Athens, one of those crazy Hiltons, and the afternoon I arrived, my sister in tears meeting me at the airport, she was already being readied to be taken to the hospital, to a small clinic in fact, about a mile up the road from the hotel. It was August, the middle of the tourist season, which was big and blooming that year. The Hilton full of drip-dry suits and cameras and restless kids from Minneapolis, a lunatic sort of carnival. We went in, then all of us went back out again through the hotel lobby, the hotel management anxious to have us out of there (a death in the hotel! an imminent death in the hotel!), that part of it so grisly I don't remember even noticing it, just remember one's feet clicking across the marble lobby, the attendants struggling with the stretcher. The hot hot air outside in the street. Hot and full of dust, and something else in the air that felt like chalk.

She could barely talk by then, my mother. She lay in bed in this clinic, which was a pleasant one really. The nurses were nice. Little Greek country girls. And she would sleep most of the time. They called it sleep, but it didn't have much to do with sleep. She lay there and disappeared, was disappearing, and now and then would emerge, eyes opening, looking out, even smiling, as if she had just been trying something out, practicing something for awhile, and now was briefly back. She lay in bed there I don't know how many days, three or four I think, the days seemed to merge into one another. She was so frail and thin by then, her face so thin, as if something inside her had been sucking everything in—something inside her which one could now almost visibly see, the belly swelling, the belly hurting. They gave her drugs now. She seemed in a state of constant dreaming, but then periodically would wake up, as if to surprise us with the unsurprising fact of her vitality. One afternoon old Nico came by, Nico Baltazzi. A large, cheery, stolid-faced Athenian. An old friend of my mother's, an old beau. I told her that Nico was outside —she was asleep, half asleep, but I wanted to tell her anyway. She woke up instantly. He can't come in right now, she said. Tell him to wait a few minutes, she said. And bring my bag. And so I did, both things, told Nico to wait, and brought the bag, and then she made herself up. She had barely the strength to hold the compact. It sounds perhaps a bit grisly, it wasn't grisly. It was quite marvelous. They were old friends, she and Nico, going back, way back. First parties. First dances. Nice Nico (he had recently married a fine English girl, after his first wife's death). He came in then, on "command," and they talked, or rather, he talked and held her hand, and then a while later he left, tears streaming down his big face. Good tears, though. And hugged me. I remember Nico's visit, but not much else about that time. Hours passed. Relatives were around. Her sister, my aunt, flew in from Geneva, full of distress, and anticipated grief, someone who had already seen the burglars prowling outside the house and whose mind had then gone rushing on to counting up the expected losses. My sister was there too, being nice, trying hard even now to please my mother, fetching and carrying little things that my mother was too far gone by then to care about. I spent a lot of time then opposite the clinic at a small outdoor bar-café, drinking that watery Fix beer, trying vaguely to read Greek newspapers. And walking back and forth between the clinic and the Hilton—the Hilton which seemed to have no connection to anything beyond itself: an interplanetary object. And mostly at the hospital, watching my mother who was dying, was nearly dead, who lay there on the bed, propped up on pillows; pillows on all sides of her so that she would not move too much (because, when she moved, her belly caused her pain), her face seeming now so small, the hair which had been worn for much of her life in that brave sweep atop her head, now tousled, all askew, the hair of someone who has been sleeping on it for too long. The room was whitewashed white, a nice white. A nice room. The air was hot everywhere, even inside the clinic, which was air-conditioned, but imperfectly. A Greek summer. The clinic doctors had round calm faces. The nurses had thick legs and deep curling girlish smiles. Life amid death—and one could sense the impatience on everyone's part for death, could begin to feel it in oneself. We were waiting for her to die. There was no way left but that she would die (we were all sufficiently secular in our faith to thus accept the word of science), and bit by bit one could sense this invisible unspoken expectation begin to close in, to hover above us all. It was quite terrible to realize that. This woman

lay upon the bed, my mother, my sister's mother, my
uncle's sister, our kin, our flesh; and now and then she
would struggle back from that far land she for the most
part lived in now, and look at us, whoever of us was
by her bed, my sister, myself, my uncle, a niece sometimes, the doctor (he was a kindly man, an Egyptian
émigré, who told us stories about Farouk), her eyes
half open, and smile, smile up, almost a girlish smile,
not exactly of hope, of something else, beyond hope, and
less insistent. And whoever of us was there would stroke
her hand, or place cold cloths upon her forehead, and
speak words to her, smile, and she would go back to
sleep—and later we would gather outside the door. How
is she? She seems comfortable. She is resting nicely.
She had some broth today. She is less fevered. The
phrases of concern, the technicalities of care and treatment would clatter back and forth between us, and all
the while the expectation of death hovered in the air,
and we breathed impatiently.

The day before she died, she virtually went to sleep,
as if she had already gone so far away, had all these past
days, while we sat about, and milled in the corridor, and
brought water, and held her hand, had all these past
days been quietly taking all her baggage, suitcases,
mysterious possessions over to this far place, and now
that she had everything safely over there, she had no
longer need to be back here, with us. She went away,
she was away, although still leaving behind something:

the woman in the bed. The woman in the bed, propped between pillows, small head on the pillows, the skin on the face now parchment-thin, the breath coming in great, strangely rhythmic gulps of the warm air. And then she woke up once, as I was sitting beside her, my hand on her arm, an effort of will to make my hand a living presence, not one of those damned gestures. She looked at me with open eyes, and smiled, and stroked my hand, such a feathery bony hand hers was; and then she closed her eyes, and said: "Let's take the road down by the sea this time. It will be longer, but nothing really starts until ten anyway . . ." and smiled, and fell asleep; and I realized that she had just then gone way way back, her body misshapen now by aging and disease, the glistening dark skin now yellowing and hurting, all the hurts of the last years, all the miseries, the not-comprehending, she had gone back to some evening when my father and she were young, and in love, and happy, and spun with the world, their feet in place, their bodies light; and on that particular night were driving out to Monte Carlo, because that was the road she most liked to take, the road by the sea. There have been so many times when I have railed and wriggled out of being taken for my father's son, my father's second; but then, just then I felt how cruel of life that he should not have been there himself, and also quite extraordinarily glad that it was me. And then she died, about fifteen minutes later. Without a sound. The nurse and I were talking about something by the doorway, and then she went over to the bed, looked at the still figure in the bed, and looked at me. All silence.

THERE ARE FOURTEEN BOOKS BY HIM, all in a row on one of the shelves in what real-estate agents would call my "library," but which in fact is just a fairly large wide wall of bookshelves. White shelves. From floor to ceiling. I used to like to keep books, to own books, a whole lot more than I do now. I can remember certain periods of time, school holidays and so forth, when the sequence between buying a book, reading it, and sticking it into a neat row in the small bookcase I had (a neat row full of captured prey) seemed wonderfully complete and satisfying. I used to buy books and read them just for this strange capture, and then later find myself looking at the books on the shelf, the trophies, with a sort of gloating; and feel terribly embarrassed; and go right out and do the same thing again.

But now I have all these books. They seem like a lot
to me anyway. Some of them picked up when I was at
school. Most of them bought, I think, at a time right
after college when I went in for what must have been
my final fling at the bookman's booklover's métier, running around to Village bookstores hunting up uniform
editions of Conrad, sending away to Blackwell's in Oxford for a complete set of Forster. Once, sending away
to Blackwell's for a five-pound slab of Wordsworth's
Prelude, I can't imagine what in hell for. It sits there
still, one of the very few books I own that I haven't read,
or at least opened. My father's books are there, too—I
put together a complete set of them after my mother
died, my sister and I shuffling copies of *The Green Hat*
and *May Fair* back and forth across the floor of the now-
stripped library. A row of them, just above my uniform
complete wonderful set of Conrad, and below some
Greek and Latin prize books I received at school, and
which I hang on to for mingled reasons of snobbery and
affection and pride.

My father wrote a lot of books, it seems to me, in a
short space of time, although I think it's true that novelists in those days usually did write lots of books. Certainly the novelists of those days whom he looked up to
did, Wells, Bennett, Lawrence, and so forth. The first
book my father wrote was called *The London Venture*,
a collection of sketches, London sketches, written in the
first person, about a young Armenian (the narrator)

called Dikran, who is trying to make it in London, and in
the course of things has several highly talkative affairs,
or encounters, with girls with names like Nadine and
Shelmerdene. My father's name was then Dikran,
Dikran Kouyoumdjian. At least it was when he sub-
mitted the manuscript to William Heinemann, the publisher, who said he'd take the book but advised that my
father change his name—a change I think he was fully
pleased to make, he was never much for Armenian
ethnic pride, at least not when he felt it limiting. The
book came out under the name "Michael Arlen," a name
he'd made up (and had then checked out through all the
available international phone directories in the Post
Office Building to make sure there weren't any other
Arlens anywhere else; there weren't in 1919). A strange-
seeming name at the time, a strange-seeming book,
rather more fin-de-siècle Paris than postwar London; at
least more George Moore than Wells or Bennett. Some
people actually thought it might be George Moore
under a pseudonym, and in fact Alec Waugh, Evelyn's
elder brother, a kind warm man who became a lifelong
friend, reviewed it as such. "Is This George Moore?"
(After my father's death, my mother gave Alec his big
astrakhan coat, the fur collar still intact, and it is both a
bit odd and very nice to still sometimes walk beside this
coat, Alec inside it, down from the Algonquin after a
lunch.)

The London Venture did all right in a modest way,

its popular success probably not helped very much by the fact that my father's brother-in-law, Marco, in a typical fit of Armenian help-thy-kin-if-it-kills-thee-both gesture, decided one fine day, as a really nice nice thing to do for Dikran, poor literary Dikran, to buy up all the available copies of his book; and did so; and suddenly there were no more. My father never found out what happened to that speedily (and mysteriously) disappearing first edition until twenty years or so later when he received a letter from some warehouse in Buenos Aires, where Marco had "business interests," saying that they were still keeping all these crates of books for him, and what please would he like to have done with them.

It was a nice book, I always thought, that first one. A small book. Nothing very grand. Straightforwardly written, almost gentle. And I guess maybe what I mostly like about it still is that it's the only thing he published (that I know of) where he ever set down anything interior of himself—for all to see, for himself to see. To be sure, it wasn't the fashion then for novelists, or aspiring novelists, to write confessions or autobiographies. Novelists wrote *stories*. Works of fiction. I can even remember my father telling me, in a manner I always felt he must have picked up from Wells or somebody, that no novelist worth his salt, no novelist who could tell a story, ever put *himself* too much into his own books. For me anyway, there were nice things in that first book. Small things. About living alone in London. About wanting success. About what it felt like to be a foreigner, to feel like a foreigner, in England—some almost very passionate things about that; I say "almost" because although there is anger and passion in a few places where he talks of being an Armenian in Anglo-Saxon England, the anger and passion remain mostly as hints, as coloring, are in the end kept tame in a context of amusingness. "An Armenian in London finds quickly that his nationality is something of a *faux-pas* . . ." and so forth.

The London Venture came out in 1920, when my father was twenty-four years old. He had no money then (and didn't make any to speak of from *The London Venture*), and lived alone in a small room above a shop in Shepherds Market, and worked like hell. I used to talk, or rather listen, to some of the friends who'd known him then, the few surviving, who'd tell me how carefree and debonair my father was in those days, how although everyone knew he had no money he was always showing up at "the best places" in "the company of beautiful women," and so forth. I really don't doubt either of those things, certainly not the beautiful women. I don't doubt any of it. But, my God, he was so ambitious. He was this young, slight, short, foreign-looking man, dark hair, long nose, dark face—and intelligent, talkative, nervy, and desirous to please in that endearing and awful way of certain foreigners in a strange court. His family were these small businessmen. Armenians, merchants, who now lived around Manchester and Liverpool. His father and mother, old people in rimless glasses and black clothes, who could still barely speak English; his three brothers and sister —the brothers already small businessmen since infancy: textiles, import-export, jobs in banks, little brick houses, not poor mind you, not rich, certainly not rich, above all cozy, semi-ethnic, little back-gardens dotted about Lancashire. His father, whom I've only seen in photographs (stolid, white-haired, a marvelous Levantine face), had taken the family out of Armenia at the time of the first Turkish massacres, had stopped en route in Bulgaria, where my father was born and the family ran a sort of general store, and then three years later headed for England. My father was the youngest brother. The other brothers had all gone into the family business, or anyway into business. My father was supposed to do the same; went to a second-run boarding school called Malvern; and then, in a final fling at career responsibility, or trying to please his parents, went off to the University of Edinburgh to study to be a doctor, got fed up after three months, quit, and headed down to London. He wrote book reviews. Journalism. Some pieces for a new magazine called "The New Age." *The London Venture.* He knew he had something. He didn't know what at first— it was Lawrence, he said, who nudged him into the kind of fanciful writing, the kind of fanciful vision that even-

tually formed books like *The Green Hat* and *May Fair*
and *Young Men in Love*. He used to go down to the
country to visit Lawrence, he would tell me. When he
was very young, and deferred to Lawrence greatly.
(Lawrence, in fact, later wrote him into *Lady Chatter-
ley* as Michaelis.) He would bring him stories that he
was working on, and read them aloud to Lawrence, who
would offer his advice. For quite a while, before *The
London Venture*, he had been trying to write "realistic"
Bennett-type stories, and hadn't been having much success. One weekend, he showed Lawrence a new thing he
had been working on, a romantic, highly stylized fable
about a girl (which later became one of the sketches in
The London Venture). Lawrence, with all his didactic
authority, said that Dikran should obviously stop trying
to imitate Arnold Bennett, and should write fantasies.
Or something like that. My father, at any rate, was always pleased to say that it was Lawrence who turned
him towards his particular style, probably because it
was partly true (Lawrence, I think, did take a genuine
interest in him), but more probably because he liked to
have been to some degree friends with these titans he so
much admired, the serious literary men, the Lawrences
and Wellses and so on. I remember once my mother describing to me how he had taken her round to meet
H. G. Wells shortly after their marriage. They were to
have tea or something. And my father so nervous. Fuss-
ing a lot beforehand. Changing his clothes several

times—not dressy enough, too dressy? And then, once he got there, all nerve and suaveness. My mother said that Mr. Wells was very "dear" to her, and that my father did most of the talking.

Anyway, after *The London Venture*, he began to write like hell. The personal, alienated, young Armenian of the sketches disappeared, and was supplanted by the sisters and brothers and friends of the young Armenian's fantasy girls, Shelmerdene and Nadine and such. Lots of short stories—about silly young Lords, who drink champagne in the morning, and marvelous new 1920's women, who swear (ever so slightly) in public, and are bored with silly young Lords. The writing very mannered, in places wonderfully mannered, full of wit and elaboration (very exotic, people would say; very "Arabian Nights"), in places too full of curlicues and overwritten. But something new. With lots of style. Books of short stories called *May Fair* and *These Charming People*. Romantic novels with titles such as *Piracy*, *Lily Christine*, *Babes in the Wood*, most of which are right on the edge of romantic melodrama (and some, it's always seemed to me, which are right over the edge). And then there was *The Green Hat*. He wrote *The Green Hat* when he was twenty-seven years old. He'd gone back up to Lancashire one summer to visit with his parents—stayed there two months, in the little house in Manchester, and in the course of that time wrote a novel. It began as follows: *It has oc-*

*curred to the writer to call this unimportant history
"The Green Hat" because a green hat was the first
thing about her that he saw: as also it was, in a way, the
last thing about her that he saw. It was bright green, of
a sort of felt, and bravely worn: being, no doubt, one of
those that women who have many hats affect "pour le
sport."* It was enormously romantic. And lushly written.
And very "modern" (in a way that few popular novels
had been up to then), in that it at least admitted the
possibility that men and women sometimes had affairs
outside of marriage, and dealt more or less openly with
such non-drawing-room matters as syphilis—handsome, dashing Boy Fenwick ("the most gifted of God's
creatures"), who marries the heroine, beautiful Iris
March of the green hat, commits suicide on his wedding
night because of having had syphilis. In the end, much
later, having all along been in love with somebody else,
Iris kills herself by driving a Hispano-Suiza into a tree.
The moment he'd finished writing it (he said later anyway), he knew that it was going to be a popular success.
Success—all the years I knew him, he had this ambivalence towards success, intensely wanting it, then seeming
not to care about it at all. He used to speak of the mixed,
unsettling feelings that he'd had when he realized, first
from his publisher's enthusiasm, later when the book
came out and had started to take hold, that somehow,
more or less by chance (although not entirely by
chance), he had happened to strike one of those chords

that a very few writers strike each generation, or semi-generation—and that people out in the audience fasten on to with a kind of hunger because the new sound seems suddenly to tell them who, and where, they are. He loved the success part. He loved having money, and being asked to dinner with Otto Kahn, and buying speedboats, and all that stuff. He was probably better equipped to run gracefully with a lot of money than most young writers have been. But there was this something else, too, and I know it is terribly corny to remark of so-and-so who has just struck oil, oh yes, well of course he doesn't object to the fame and money, but deep down he believes there is something more important in life than mere riches, etc. The thing is, my father wasn't like that either. I think he loved the glitter, popular recognition (such of it anyway as he had), embraced it, and at the same time was coldly detached from it, as if knowing all along that there was something within him he ought to be taking care of, but not really knowing what it was, saying in fact, well if I don't know what it is, it can't be that important. But my guess is it probably was, although that is only a guess, and a son's guess at that.

I think I would have liked to have known him in *The Green Hat* period. When he was young, and full of dash, and neither quite a gentleman, and neither not; and he really did make quite a splash. It's hard, I think, for people nowadays to realize about things like that then.

Nowadays, there are seemingly hundreds of people so well known or publicized for one reason or another that their names are household words. But then the celebrity business hadn't been around very long. The 1920's more or less invented it. Channel swimmers. Movie stars. Even writers. It hadn't been all that long ago that writers, in England at any rate, weren't really allowed out of the kitchen. Writers were as bad as journalists, usually worse, since some journalists at least had power. Today, of course, writers are not only out of the kitchen, they're all over the house and in most of the bedrooms. But then—I don't know much firsthand about it, but later on, when I was at college, and my mother had brought a lot of our old things over from the South of France, I used to come in late sometimes and look over the scrapbooks that he or his publisher had kept of those years, the late twenties. Reviews. Photographs. Newspaper stories. Mr. Michael Arlen has taken up golf. Mr. Michael Arlen has left for Biarritz. Mr. Michael Arlen is in Saint-Moritz. Mr. Michael Arlen has signed a contract—with *Cosmopolitan*, which made him at that point the highest-paid short-story writer on either side of the Atlantic. The day he arrived in Chicago, the *Daily News* ran a front-page story—saying that he had arrived in Chicago. He was on one of the early covers of *Time*. It must have been a wonderful, strange world he moved in then. He arrived in Chicago that morning, as it happened, for the local opening of the play he had

made out of *The Green Hat*, which had been one of
Katharine Cornell's first big roles on Broadway. He was
thirty years old. Dark, brushed-back hair. A bristly
mustache. A marvelous photograph on the Chicago station platform, in big twenties hat and astrakhan overcoat. "Mr. Arlen, what do you think of yourself as an
artist?" a reporter asked him. He paused for a moment
(the reporter wrote). "Per ardua at astrakhan," he replied. He was very good at that sort of thing. In those
days, they named children after him—at his funeral I
remember standing in the back of the church, and this
family, this group of people I'd never seen before, coming in the door, walking down the aisle, man, woman,
several children, clearly not from New York, not friends
of his. They were the Martins from Detroit. Her name
—she had been born in the late twenties—was Michael
Arlen Martin, and now she had brought her husband,
and her whole family, to the funeral.

The Green Hat made him rich, although not as rich
as most people seemed to think. He used to give out all
these stories about the money. (Never believe what a
writer says about how much he makes, he often told me
later; he's nearly always lying.) People seemed so to
want to believe that he'd made a fortune. One million
pounds sterling. Half a million pounds sterling. In fact,
it was a good deal less than that. There weren't all those
paperback rights then, and although M.G.M. did make
some sort of a droopy movie out of it, with Greta Garbo

and John Gilbert or somebody, they certainly didn't pay anyone $500,000 for the property. He did okay, though, better than just okay. And you didn't have income taxes to worry about then. He could buy a long damn canary-yellow Rolls-Royce. And speedboats. And good clothes. Things like that. And he could afford to marry my mother, in the sense that they could take a fairly large nice house in the South of France. Have nice things. Invest in the stock market in 1928. Scott Fitzgerald came by one evening, hours late for dinner, striped blazer, white flannels, full of booze from one of Gerald Murphy's parties, embarrassed, garrulous, then silent, leaned his head down on the table top (hair halfway in the soup). "This is how I want to live . . . this is how I want to live," he said. And fell asleep.

THERE WAS THIS WHITE ROOM I remember. At the end of a long corridor. The walls in the room were all painted white. Blue curtains, a deep blue. Sunlight. A Persian carpet on the floor, a kind of brown and blue color. The big desk. Some chairs. Papers. Books. The smell of kippers in the early morning—a breakfast tray, silver and china, off to one side of the desk. I would come down the corridor after breakfast, after my breakfast, and knock on the door, and he would say come in, and I would go on in, and fuss with the papers, and fiddle with the paperweights, and do what is known as

"saying good morning," and go on out again. The smell
of kippers, and all that sunlight. It seemed a magic
room. I had no real idea of what he did in there—writing. It seemed as if that must be a fine thing to be doing.
He was writing books—those few books he wrote after
his big successes in the twenties, and while the world
beneath his feet and all around him was changing, and
while he was changing too: *Man's Mortality. The Flying Dutchman. The Crooked Coronet.* Nobody liked
them much. He liked some of them, or thought he did.
Man's Mortality he liked a lot, he had a lot at stake in
Man's Mortality, his first "serious" book, a futurist,
slightly Huxleyan novel about life in 1980, when the
world is being governed by a supra-national "air transport cartel" called "Airways." It was okay, too. It wasn't
brilliant, it wasn't the best thing anyone had ever done.
But it was an interesting book, and written with imagination, and with an intelligence that was only then
finally beginning to take itself seriously. But nobody
else much liked it. The people who had liked him for
being so charming and amusing and elegant disliked
him for trying to be serious. The people who had disliked him for not having been serious enough now disliked him even more for trying to be serious and for not
being better at it. And then, to be sure, there was the
swirl of the thirties all around, the thirties of the Depression and the disappearance of canary-yellow Rolls-
Royces, the thirties which turned against Fitzgerald's

Tender Is the Night as being irrelevant to the period. I
think probably everybody had a point, everybody usually does. But I am thinking now of the man who wrote
in that white room, that lovely white room, surrounded
by all the things he thought he had finally achieved—
fame being only a small part of it. A splendid wife,
whom many admired. A son, a daughter. A family. A
fine house. This room he wrote in, with its big Empire
desk, especially built for him somewhere in Paris. A
secretary, nice old Miss Livesey, who would come in
during the afternoon, while he played golf, and tran-
scribe his longhand into typescript; and then later, after
golf, after a drink or so at the club or at the Carlton, he
would come back in after dinner, and make a few cor-
rections in the margins. Like that. It must have seemed
a lovely life. It must have been a lovely life. I can remember sometimes, after lunch, my lunch, being driven
down into Cannes beside him. He had this small sporty
Ford then, a small black car, he at the wheel, myself
beside him, the two of us gliding and winding down the
roads out of the hills above Cannes, down towards the
beach, the town, wherever. I can remember him singing
—such an ordinary thing to remember. But I think I
can remember him singing only once or twice in my life,
and that would be once; in the car after lunch. Usually I
would drive down with my mother, once a week or so,
and we would go to the little nanny-packed beach in
front of the hotels on the Croisette. A narrow strip of

sand. Umbrellas. Old men selling peanuts. And then afterwards, sometimes, my mother would take me by the Carlton, the Carlton bar, and I would sit there quietly, and be given one-franc pieces with which to play a machine they had in there (you operated a kind of pincers and tried to pick up "valuable objects"), and wait for them until they were ready, he was ready, and we would all drive home together, back up the hills.

It seemed to me a marvelously happy time. Even now, looking back on it, having some sense of how the world was turning then, having some sense of who the people I lived with really were, it still seems a marvelously happy time. Full of light. And space. And spaces between people. And water. He had a speedboat then. The *Swallow II*, one of those huge lovely mahogany Gar Woods, with a pennant on the front, and lots of brightwork, a windshield like a racing car, and Rafael, a wiry, gleaming Portuguese, who took care of the brightwork and the engine, and who sometimes drove it—a speedboat chauffeur. In the spring sometimes, we would go on afternoon excursions to the Ile Sainte-Marguerite, small islands a little way off the coast, not really islands at all, clusters of rock, outcroppings in the water, the *Swallow II* larumphing across the flat waters of the bay, laden with hampers, satchels, my mother and father, I, Rafael. We'd anchor off one of the larger rocks and go swimming, all of us, my mother sleek and purposeful with her bathing cap and sidestroke. And later, just

Rafael and I, the water beautifully clear, green, so clear you could see right to the bottom twenty or so feet below. Rafael would fill his lungs with air and go down beneath the surface, down to God knows where, whole minutes at a time; I tried to follow him, a dark shape way down beneath me, gliding above the sand and coral, but had no lungs for it, and no stomach either. Once, I remember, he caught an octopus, a tiny thing, not much bigger than his hand, all white and quivering. He killed it against the side of the boat, and then on the way back he would grind it against the planking of the deck. "It makes it tender," he said. His hand and arm moving in a circular motion. The red-brown boat jumping across the bay.

And all the while my father wrote these books, wrote at these books in that lovely white room in the morning. And Lord knows what was really going through his mind. My mother told me many years later that one spring afternoon in 1936, I think it was, he came down after lunch, and said that he was leaving, that he couldn't stand things any more, and needed to be by himself, and left, and went away, took the train up towards Paris, then to Cherbourg, got aboard the *Aquitania* bound for New York—but then got off again at Southampton and came back home again. "He never told me what had been on his mind," she said. "I asked him later," she said, "but he kept saying, Oh it was nothing."

AND THEN YEARS LATER there was this other room; a darker room now. The desk was still the same, shipped over from Cannes after the war. The desk stood in front of the windows, which looked out directly onto a gray-brick building across Seventy-fifth Street, and which were always covered by curtains. The desk had on it all the artifacts of writing. Pencils. Paper. Notebooks. Pens. Ink. And around the walls of the room were books. The walls were painted green, a darkish sort of green. My mother had many wrangles with the painters over just the right shade of green. There were some pictures on the walls. Two Boucher little girls. Two prints of birds. A watercolor of a hunting scene done very recently, reds and whites on some kind of greenish paper. The greenish paper went very well, she used to say, with the green walls. The room was called "the library," and was in my mother and father's apartment in New York, and it was where my father worked. Or was supposed to work. Or tried to work. Or something. For years, since the end of the war, he gave out all these airy stories about his not working, about his being retired. I'd come down from college then, sometimes on weekends, on vacations, and meet him for lunch at the St. Regis, where he nearly always lunched with friends, writers, editors, movie people, vague acquaintances who would simply drop by there around one o'clock or so, knowing he would be there. From time to time some one of these would ask him what was he doing. What was he doing? And he had all these marvelous answers; his hard-working (or, at any rate, employed) table-companions loved him for these answers. I do nothing, he would say. I am retired. I read a lot. He had little set speeches he would sometimes make: "I have the affection of my wife, the tolerance of my children, and the friendship of headwaiters. What more do I need?" To reporters and columnists (who still interviewed him despite the fact he hadn't published anything in fifteen years), he stressed the financial aspects of his retirement. "The mistake most writers make," he would say, "is to declare that when they have enough money they will retire. Since they never have enough money, they never retire, and so poor Willie Maugham goes on grinding out book after book. I tried to be more modest. I said, when I have x-amount of money I shall retire. And, as things turned out, I eventually had x-amount of money. And retired. And lived happily ever after." He seemed to be living happily ever after too, although in truth I don't remember his having any friend close enough in those days to have known the difference. Nor any friend he would let that close to him. A great many people seemed glad of his company, always had been glad of his company. He really was a very good talker. Witty. Knew about a lot of things. Had opinions about a lot of things. Had style. Sitting there in the St. Regis. The elegant mustache. The English-tailored blue suit. The gray silk tie. The pearl stickpin. The malacca cane

beside him. *Time* editors would come for lunch, and
then agree—he really had the system beat. Why, he
hadn't written a book in years and clearly was never
happier. Better. Happier. Happier . . . And then later
in the afternoon, I would come back home, back to their
home, this dark elegant apartment, the Chinese screens,
the fine-old-pieces, the chic little hallway, Grandmama's
rugs, the whole place dark, silent—I'd go upstairs to
what was supposed to be my room, get ready usually to
go out again, sit in a chair for a moment reading a magazine, and from downstairs, just below my room, from
the library I'd hear these footsteps. Footsteps pacing.
Back and forth. It was a small room really, the library. I
don't know how many thousands of times he must have
walked around it. The big desk up against the curtains.
The paper laid out for him. The pencils. His favorite
pen. The books all around. He used to tell me sometimes
that he "liked to pace," which in some ways was probably true. But for ten years or so he paced. No longer in
that little room in Shepherds Market. No longer in that
white white room, with the green of French hills around
it, and a semicircle of the Mediterranean down below.
Now there were all these books on the shelves above
him, beside him, many of them his. Spanish editions of
The Green Hat. Old George Doran editions. Leather-
bound volumes of his earlier successes, which Heinemann's had done up for him at various long-past Christmases. He said, he used to say (he had this way of

seeming so offhand about important things), that he was not really a writer, that he just happened to "turn to" writing, and maybe that was so, although I doubt it. I think of him still in those days, all those New York days, for there were a great many of them, pacing back and forth around that dark library. The walls must have seemed unbearably close at times. And then later, after dinner, he would seem so tired after dinner; he would sit in the big green chair in the corner of the room and read.

A Christmas in Southport: the first winter of the war, which was also the first winter I'd been away at school (in Surrey, Abinger Hill), we all went up north to spend Christmas with my father's family, my Uncle Taki's family, who lived in a town called Southport, about a half hour or so from Liverpool, which was where Taki worked. My father's mother then lived with Taki, too (I think that would have been the last year she was alive). I don't remember much about her—a dear, small, old lady, seemingly always in black, and lace, and rimless eyeglasses, and with a smell of old flowers, strange kitchens, of something indoors about her, not speaking English very well, a penny apiece for each grandchild for being such good grandchildren, plump white face, beads, warm warm

eyes. My father would sometimes get impatient with her
(he, the youngest child), chide her for not speaking
English better, for not wanting to, for hiding behind her
foreign-ness. He would get impatient a bit with Taki,
but not really. Taki's actual name was Takvor. He was
the eldest of the brothers, a round genial man who liked
to play bridge in the evenings, and went nine holes of
golf each Saturday, in checkered plus-fours out on the
golf course near his house, a pleasant red-brick sort of
residential row-house on the outskirts of Southport. The
war was just beginning then, was three months old.
Barrage balloons floated above London. Antiaircraft
gun emplacements in Hyde Park. Sandbags. Soldiers in
khaki and tin hats. The air-raid wardens carried gas
masks. Down where I was at school, you could lie
awake at night and in the far far distance watch the
slender beams of searchlights poking around the sky. A
German boy called Schoenfeld, I remember, was given
much trouble in the locker rooms one afternoon. Several
hundred, or thousand, German paratroopers were reported to have landed in nearby Abinger.

In Southport, everything seemed more peaceable.
Schoolboys in caps and shorts and jackets riding bicycles down the street where Taki's family lived. Taki's
two sons (my cousins John and Sarkis) home from
school, and playing Benny Goodman records, that noisy
American jazz, in the cellar. Taki going off to the bank
each morning. Taki carving the roast at Sunday dinner.

In the evening, Taki and my father would listen to the B.B.C. news, the hefty brown radio on the bridge table in the living room, and sometimes I would come in with them, lying on the floor with my cousin Sarkis's new edition of *Jane's Book of Fighting Aircraft*, and studiously subtract the announced losses, German, French, English, Polish, from the totals in the book. I was given a new bicycle. My sister took riding lessons, a small figure with frizzy blond hair, perched atop an enormous horse, going slowly round and round inside the wintry paddock. My father took me to the zoo. One afternoon we went to the movies. Disney's *Snow White*, the awful witch. My sister and I, my mother, and Anais, who was Taki's wife, a nice nice woman, who still lives in that same house today (as John and Sarkis live in nearby Manchester). I thought both Taki and Anais were very nice. The house had a good smell about it. Leaded bay windows in the front. Small garden out back, with flowers and little vegetables. And Taki, this marvelous Armenian, not trying to be English or anything as pushy as that. But English all the same, such a fine solid English voice, such fine solid English concerns. He had a reddish face, and a big-hearted laugh, and liked green, and gardens, and vegetables growing in the garden, and small things in the fields outside in the special way that only Englishmen do. Takvor Kouyoumdjian. He was truly a very lovely Englishman. And he felt my father to be something very rare too, and I liked him for that. It wasn't that he and my father really talked to each other much, talked about things, about life, about careers, about God knows what. But I can remember the way he sometimes looked at my father, the way he'd say things, casual things, the way we'd all go into dinner, his arm over my father's shoulder. My father loved him back, although at times with prickles and impatience. My father loved all his family, really loved them, really cared for family, deeply extravagantly cared for *family*, as maybe only an exile can (or the child of exiles), and also yearned, just yearned to be free of them and glide above them. His two other brothers, Krikor and Roupen. His sister, Ahavni, an extraordinary woman, short, tiny, bright red hair, full of life and sex and gaiety, a really lived-in face. Ahavni's husband Marco, who was considered family. They were all businessmen, not unsuccessful either: small import businesses, and firms, and holding companies all over the world. Buenos Aires. Brisbane. Paris. Manchester. Montevideo. And each with this special Armenian characteristic of being at the same time enormously devious about business matters, and enormously loving and loyal about family. All my father's family, as I think of them now, seem so very warm, and almost childlike— oh, they were tough as hell about business and textiles and import-export or whatever, it was what they did in Manchester and Montevideo; but in the interior of their lives they were so unabashedly familial, tribal; and despite how much they became parents themselves, had children, they remained, more than any other people I've known, themselves children of parents. My father, I used to think, was the exception to this, but I am not so sure. He handled it differently though. He made it look different; he made people think he was the odd one, the one who broke the rules, the one who had escaped, which was all true, but it was not in the end, I think, an escape very far down the road. He used to tell me how, when he was married, at his wedding, in that chapel at Fiorentina in the South of France, an Armenian Orthodox priest had suddenly turned up. Literally showed up at the beginning of the service. Striding down the aisle. Flapping black robes. Black hat. The beard. He gave my father a knowing look, and whispered in his ear that he had been sent all the way from England by his mother, who feared that he would not be married properly amid these pagan Mediterranean rites. He stood immovably a few steps behind my father through the service. The Catholic priest intoned the Latin phrases. The Armenian muttered his own in a just-audible chant. My father said it was a ghastly experience, although he made it funny.

That Christmas his mother, I remember, gave me a book about King Arthur. I was nine years old and would have preferred *Jane's Book of Fighting Aircraft*, but I went upstairs to her room, where she was in bed most of the time, and gave her a kiss (she had hair on her cheek), and later read the book, which was a good one. That Christmas. It was a simple, friendly time. I think mostly of Taki's laugh. And of John and Sarkis standing in the hallway in their long, schoolboy scarves. And of my mother and Taki playing checkers after dinner, which was something I had never seen her do. Our other Christmases had nearly all been in Cannes—one, I think, had been at a hotel in Vienna, but I can barely remember it, except for people dancing, and someone going about the corridors late at night dressed as the devil. We'd have an enormous tree, big enough anyway so that my mother and Monsieur Puigue, the chef, would have to stand on a stepladder to hang the lights. Lots of decorations. Colored balls. My mother knew where each one ought to go, packed them away in order, took them out in order. A big party for children on Christmas Eve. My father dressed up as Santa Claus, distributing presents from a large sack to dozens of mostly strange children, who seemed to have materialized out of nowhere. In Southport that winter, we sat around the living room on Christmas Eve. And listened to the B.B.C. Light Programme. And played round-robin checkers against Taki, who was very good, and won. The next day, Christmas, Taki and Anais gave me a flashlight, one of those long silvery things with lots of batteries, which would last forever. My mother and father, among other things, gave me a model airplane. I remember we put it together in the morning—it didn't take much, it was nearly assembled, an expensive bright-blue job from Selfridges. And my father and I took it out for a test flight in the afternoon. A cold gray afternoon. Gray sky. We went out towards the golf course. There was an aerodrome nearby, they called them aerodromes, a ragged wind-sock fluttering beside the runway. My father and I stood on a rise in the golf course, winding up the rubber band, tossing the little blue plane into the air. It was a nice one and flew quite well. Taki appeared. Those marvelous plus-fours, and wearing a checkered cap that Anais had given him for Christmas. He had a golf club under his arm. He'd been out practicing a few drives, he said. Taki took the plane, and wound it up, and tossed it into the air. It flew a few hundred feet and almost landed on a putting green. We all laughed. On the far side of the fairway, from off the runway, two R.A.F. bombers took off into the twilight —dark, bulbous, insect-like things. Jet black. The roar of engines. We flew the plane a few more times. Then Taki said: It's getting dark. It had already started to drizzle. A sea wind bringing the light rain in off the Atlantic. My father picked the plane up, and handed it to me. We walked on back. Taki between us. I held his hand. He had his arm around my father.

N EW YORK IN JUNE. AT THE BEGIN-
ning of every summer we left New York—not so much
left it as flung ourselves out of it in the direction of some
"resort" or other. At first, just my mother, my sister and
I (and the inevitable tight-mouthed, army-booted, Swiss
governess); then later my father, after his arrival from
England. Apparently it was something one did if one
lived in New York. One got the hell out by the middle of
June. Trunks and suitcases all over the apartment.
Short tempers. Windows open in the New York heat.
Soot. Sweat. Traffic horns. Why don't you children go
out and play in the park. Why don't you children go and
roller-skate on the sidewalk. Can we take our roller
skates to the country? No. Piles of clothes everywhere.
My mother striding about in her slip. "Where are your

short-sleeved shirts?" I'd go rummage through my school trunk and reappear with a couple of wanly-colored cotton things. "How do you expect to get through the summer with these?" It didn't seem the kind of question that required an answer. The governess would bring in a black metallic suitcase, which I knew contained only walking shoes and chocolate, and place it in the middle of the living room. My sister would drag herself slowly down the hallway and stand in the doorway, modeling last year's riding breeches. My mother looks at her with a *Vogue* editor's eye. Detached. "You're pushing your stomach out," she says. "I'm *not!*" my sister says. My mother walks over and tugs at the bottom of the breeches, presumably to see if they will stretch. My sister stands still, St. Joan at the stake, making faces. My mother sighs. Stage-right, the sound of a door opening. My father on his way out. "I'll be back later," he says. My mother dabs at her forehead with a handkerchief. Lights a cigarette. "What about your Palm Beach suit?" she says to me.

These resorts we used to go to were a sort of nightmare. Each year, it seemed, we went to a different one. Northeast. Edgartown. Once to New Hampshire: the White Mountains. For days on end we sat around this New Englandy inn. A swimming pool out back. Some tennis courts—the tennis pro had played (he claimed) number 3 on the Princeton team, which I thought was pretty hot. My father said: "All he ever talks about is drinking beer. He calls them brews." The year after that we went to Hot Springs. Hot Springs, Virginia. The Homestead. That huge white place. Long corridors. All those black slaves gliding up and down the carpeted corridors with trays balanced on their heads, those kinky woolly heads so justly famed in song and story. My father played gin rummy a lot. I took tennis lessons, from a leathery-faced Norwegian called Toby Hansen, who taught a nice straight backhand and what was then called an "Australian twist" serve. My sister was supposed to be taught riding, and was quite good at it, although my sister was not to be taken seriously. My mother went on walks, and also played tennis, and sat at table beneath the colored umbrellas of the Casino and watched while my father went into his fifth hour of gin with some Detroit industrialist. All around us the swirl of American girls and boys. Young men. Memphis. St. Louis. In other places they had been from Philadelphia. Boston. Long Island. Long-legged. Girls with breasts beneath white shirts. That summer I was in love with five different girls from Memphis, and spent much time in the swimming pool because all the girls from Memphis were in love with Allen Clayton, the swimming pro, a fair-haired muscular young man who had been something really terrific on the North Carolina swimming team, and who now walked up and down beside the pool with his beautiful tanned legs and beautiful white bathing suit. I had a dumpy blue bathing suit and wanted hugely to be like Allen Clayton. "Let's kind of take it a little easy there, old buddy," he would say. Later in the afternoon I'd go back to our room. "Let's kind of take it a little easy there, old buddy," I'd say to my sister, but she was usually in tears, or close to tears, because my parents were always threatening to cancel her riding lessons, and was never good for much response.

I could never really understand what we were doing there, or in any place like it. I knew one was supposed to go away from the city in the summer. I knew people went to "resorts." People *fixed* themselves in resorts. There were Edgartown families. Northeast families. Certainly Homestead families. My father and mother seemed rather to move through these places like émigré royalty, the innkeepers (and guests) vaguely conscious that somebody unusual was among them but not quite sure what currency they would be paid in, or when; my mother and father diffident, remote, not so much bored as disconnected, and with small gift for camouflage. I can remember us gliding into that wretched Homestead dining room each evening—it was one of those American resorts where the dining room was only open between some ridiculous hours like 5:30 and 7:30. My father in dark evening suit, well dressed, too well dressed, a boutonniere, a cane. My mother really very handsome. Hair up high. Jewels. My sister and I trailing along, each conscious of the Detroit and

Memphis eyes on all of us. And then would come the dinner scene: my father disdaining the relish tray. Each evening my father would disdain the relish tray, would look at it in fact, held in the hands of some hopeful moon-faced Virginia girl, some girl whom I would have paid money to like me—would look at it as if it were some joke that was being played on him, which in some ways of course it was, a joke to which he had been an accomplice (which must have made it worse). My mother (very regal, but trying to be creative): What are those little things in red? The waitress (not very bright, but trying to please; never run into this kind of rum crowd before): They're candied crab apples, ma'am. They come from right around Covington. A lot of the guests . . . My father (as if waking up): *Candied crab apples?* For dinner? I should certainly hope not! My mother: You've never tried one, Dikran. My father: I don't intend to. (Smiling sweetly, like a cougar, at the poor girl) Can you bring us an Old-Fashioned and a whisky right away? The waitress: Oh, I'm sorry sir. I'm only in charge of the relish tray. My father: Etc., etc. He and my mother would complain their way through dinner. I would squirm my way, conscious of every assault delivered by them against the system, which seemed a perfectly okay system to me (I liked relish trays, relish trays were wonderful, who would want to be so odd and alien as not to embrace a relish tray?); conscious that all their sniping and snipping was heading directly into some huge composite American ear, that would surely in turn spew maledictions back at me. Afterwards we'd usually all troop into the movie. The Homestead showed movies each night in its own plush little theater. And then my sister and I upstairs to bed. My parents to the lounge or some place, where they drank, and my father sometimes played more gin. "He usually had good cards," my mother used to say. She sat beside him while he played, reading a book, or smoking—to "bring him luck." The stakes weren't very high. I think he won a hundred dollars once. I hoped that some of the men he played cards with would become friends. All have dinner together. Get together "in town" after the summer. But it didn't seem to be that kind of a thing. Later at night, my sister and I would sometimes wander back through the hotel, hunting up groups of older boys and girls, but then she once got caught necking in the back lobby (I think it was just a kiss) with Foster Thompson of St. Louis, the riding teacher, and we were both confined to quarters for a while. I won a swimming prize in August, second place in the backstroke, but got no closer to the girls from Memphis. My sister went on a pack trip with her riding class. Towards the end of summer, a large family from Cleveland arrived. The MacAllisters. Nice people really. Big bouncy unsexy girls. Everybody very tall, and tousled, and surprisingly gentle. And it turned out they were "old friends"—in the great long ago, somebody had once "played with" somebody, gone to the park, gone to birthday parties in Cleveland after the First War. Not very *close* friends. Still, it was nice. I hadn't known we were so American. We all went in to dinner together one evening. For a moment everything seemed wonderful, and I looked forward immeasurably to more.

H ER NAME WAS AMY WELLS AND
she said goodbye to me at the station. At Back Bay, just
outside Boston. The train was late. It was one of those
unnaturally hot spring days towards the end of May.
She was wearing a hat that morning, I remember. A big
straw hat. A yellow ribbon. It was really very hot. Her
face was pink under the sun. And tense. We walked up
and down a lot. We kissed. We walked up and down.
Finally the train came in. There were a number of other
people from college on the platform, a group of boys
and girls who must have been freshmen or sophomores.
Corduroy jackets and khaki slacks. The girls wore raincoats and smoked. They all seemed so young and full of
good things to look forward to. I was twenty-one and
felt horrible. "Phone me," Amy was saying. "Phone me

right away." I said yes—it all seemed stifling, especially that "yes"—and got on the train.

New York in May. I should have taken a cab from the station and gone right home, but I walked instead, hot, sweaty, past the same shops I had walked by so many times before. I didn't want to go home at all. I knew that was weak, cowardly, that I was putting things off. Evading. I stopped at the drugstore on Seventy-fourth Street and had a milkshake, couldn't drink it. I went on home, remembering in the elevator that I hadn't told them I was coming. Teresa opened the door, tugging at her uniform. Oh, nobody told me you'd be down, she said. *They're* out, she said. Your mother will be back first. I began to pace around the empty apartment, suddenly crazy with impatience. I had to *do* something. I went into the library and tried sitting down in the big green chair, but that wouldn't work at all, I kept springing out of it. I snatched up magazines, put them down. I went over to the sideboard, fumbled together a drink, a bit because I wanted one, mostly because it seemed a serious and grownup thing to do, to pour a Scotch and soda down one's gullet at three in the afternoon. I heard my mother come on in. A rattling of keys. Sounds of parcels being put down in the hallway. I appeared out of the library, drink in hand. "Oh, it's you," she said. "Whatever are *you* doing here?" Suddenly my impatience vanished, mysteriously drained away. I stood there in the hallway. Tense. Gray flannels. Seersucker jacket. Probably gesturing vaguely with my arm. "I just came down," I said. "Well, I can see that," she said. Then: "Wait a moment." She picked up the two or three packages and started upstairs. "I have to get these out of their boxes." She was halfway up the stairs. "I want to talk to you," I said. "What?" she called. "I said I wanted to talk to you." She stopped and peered over the banister at me, and then went on her way upstairs. I went back to my drink in the library. The telephone rang. I heard my mother answering it in the bedroom. Some woman, Margot Humphreys it sounded like. I picked up one of the magazines. I thought of Amy. I thought of Amy's mother. I thought of the funny smell of Amy's lipstick at the train station. I wondered what she was doing just then. My mother swept on into the library. She had changed into one of those great flowing gowns. She carried her reading glasses and the afternoon paper. "It's so hot in here," she said. She swept on out and into the salon. I went in after her. She was sitting in one of the two rose-covered armchairs beside the window, leaning back a little, she could have been tired, although I didn't think she was. It was a nice room, really, pinks and oranges and glass. She was doing something with her hair, poking in or pulling out a pin. "Well, what is it you consider so—" she began in that special voice of hers. I couldn't stand it any more. "I'm planning to get married," I said.

Her face froze, unfroze, took on that unreal skeptical

look. "Who are you planning to marry?" she said. I sat there opposite her, leaning forward, knees wide, barely sitting at all. She knew perfectly well who. "Amy," I said. "Amy Wells." She said nothing for a moment. "And what does Amy think about this?"

"Well, naturally she wants to get married. I mean, she's very happy. I mean, she wants to marry me." Oh God, that disjointed speech. I could feel those awkward, so inelegant, so uncontrolled, so adolescent stammers beginning to well up in me.

"Have you discussed this plan of yours with Mrs. Wells?" she asked. The voice soft, cool, an edge now on the word "plan." I sat back in my chair. Unclasped my hands. Crossed my legs, trying to look confident and casual and grownup. "Not in so many words," I said. "But I think she knows we want to get married and—" My mother suddenly rose to her feet, her face carved out of some dark stone. "If you've come to me for my approval," she said, "I absolutely will not give it!" I had never seen her eyes so full of temper. "You must be out of your mind!" she said, almost yelling. "You're only a child."

"I'm not a child," I said. "I'm twenty-one."

"Twenty-one," she said. "I'm not going to stand by while you ruin your life."

"I am not going to ruin my life," I said. "I love her. We love each other."

My mother seemed to peer at me as if I had just

changed shape. I stood beside my chair. "Amy Wells!"
she said. Then: "You're both children." She was really
beginning to cry. And: "I thought you were more intelligent than that."

Later. In the library. My father still not back. My
mother at the far end of the sofa trying to read the *Jour-
nal-American*. I stand in the doorway. I sit down in the
big chair. My mother turns a page in the paper. "I don't
care what you say," I say suddenly. "We're going to get
married anyway." My mother glances up from the
paper, looks over at me. "Do you have to get married?"
she asks.

"What?"

"Do you *have* to get married? Is this Amy of yours
pregnant?"

"No!" I yell wildly.

"Well, that's something," my mother says.

Dinner. My father arrived home just in time for dinner that night. He'd been with John McClain at the St.
Regis. He talked about John, about John's new wife.
The three of us around the oval dining table. The usual
chicken broth. Toast. Teresa tottering around with little
slices of veal. The usual rotten gravy. Once I caught
Teresa's eye. She made a strange clandestine grimace at
me. Intended-to-reassure. Teresa and I locked in a conspiracy. My father seemed blithely unaware of what had
been going on, my mother seeming to refuse to recognize that anything indeed had gone on, everything ap-

parently in its place, except that my mother had slightly red eyes, and I probably did too, and felt sick to my stomach. Towards the end of the meal, my father (who had seemed quite unsurprised to find me at home) finally asked me some innocent question about exams or some such. "I don't imagine," I heard my mother say, "he's had too much time for examinations lately." The battleship *Schleswig-Holstein* had evidently moved into place for the shelling of Dresden. My father predictably said "Oh?" and looked at me (I sat at table between the two of them), and while I sat there thinking of what precisely to answer, what best to answer, which of the seemingly eight hundred possible answers to nudge forward onto the tablecloth, the guns of the battleship all swiveled into place, the guncotton was rammed down the barrels, the fuses lit, the sailors all running back for cover . . . "He's planning to get married," my mother said—and, for brief wild seconds, dinner, my father, me, the table, silverware, life, everything exploded up into the air, my father and I seeming to tumble about in midair like Dorothy and Toto in the Oz tornado, his strange mad face peering vaguely at my strange mad face. And then everything settled down again, and he and I had a "serious discussion" in the library. I don't remember much about our talk that night, or rather his talk, except that he seemed so sad. And that he cried. In a way it was all very sweet, gentle (and I was so hugely upset). "You're so young," he kept saying. "But you were young," I'd say, mindful of how many times he'd told me of how at nineteen he'd gone down to London on his own. "But I was thirty-three when I got married," he'd say, but not (as I remember) with any note of triumph. He was very nice that night. I felt we were close, the way I'd hoped we would be, could be. Late at night we walked upstairs. He put his arm around my shoulder. We kissed, I think, and said good night. But the next morning things were not so okay. "It's just too sudden," he said. "Too rushed. You're much too young to get married."

"I'm not too young."

"You're still at college. You don't even have a job."

"I'll get a job."

Then suddenly: "Your mother and I didn't send you to all those schools, St. Paul's, Harvard . . . all those schools, for you to end up driving a truck!" He was red in the face. Angry. "For you to end up as nothing!" I didn't know what he was talking about. Driving a truck? He seemed then very strange. I don't know what I said. I probably said that I was twenty-one years old. My litany. "It's out of the question for now," he said.

I went back to Cambridge in numb despair. I hadn't told Amy much on the telephone. She met me at the station. She was wearing some sort of summer dress. No sleeves. Nice. Bare skin. She looked as if she had been at the beach, Tahiti, the last two days. I felt I had just come from the lions' den. We rode solemnly out of Back Bay in the back seat of a cab. I kept wanting to kiss her. She kept wanting to know what had happened. I was scared to tell her just how badly it had gone. She usually thought of me as very old. Mature. I usually thought of me as very old. Now, the two of us in a taxi. A lot of those well-okay-if-you-want-a-kiss kind of kisses. Nothing very satisfactory. I think I wanted her to make love to me in the taxi. Then I told her what had happened. Something of what had happened. Amy started to cry. I started to cry. "But we can get married anyway," I kept saying. "It won't be any good like that," she said. And then: "*What* will we do?"

We drove in towards Harvard Square. A sunlit afternoon. The red-brick buildings. At Mt. Auburn Street, a traffic light, she jumped out of the cab. Suddenly in tears again. She waved to me not to come after her. I went back to my room. It seemed like a grownup masculine sort of thing to do. I fiddled with things. Opened a beer. Then lunged at the telephone, started calling her. She wasn't in. I went tearing off across the college, across the Square, down all those tranquil side streets, and finally found her sitting calmly on some stone steps out near the building where she lived. We went and got my car, and drove, as we'd often driven before, out towards Ipswich. Ipswich had been where we'd first gone. March. March winds. Still cold. David Kennan's empty house. David Kennan's parents' empty house. Ipswich had been good luck, had been the real spring. We went out there again, drove down Argilla Road. Amy was very silent. There was this restaurant down near the beach. "Do you want to eat?" I asked, nearly gag-

ging over the word "eat." No, she said. We went down
on the beach. There were other people there now. Sum-
mertime approaching. It felt unfamiliar. A family was
having a picnic. We went past them, Amy holding her
shoes. I looked along the line of dunes. I was trying to
avoid the precise places we'd been to before. It was late
afternoon, the sun going down. The sand on the beach
was still warm. Everything seemed quite lifeless and
frightening. We sat down behind a hillock, out of sight.
Amy slightly in front of me. I put my hand on her
shoulder. Bare skin. She was looking out at the water.
"I always thought your mother was so *nice*," she said, in
a kind of bewilderment. "It doesn't matter what my
mother thinks," I said. "I don't believe you," she said.
"Besides I'm not like that. It matters to me." We talked
in low, thin chords. Suddenly I wanted her very much,
wanted something, and pulled her around, pulled her to
me, kissed her, a very dry kiss from her, I held her hair,
her head, and could feel her brain thinking, whirring,
kissed her again, some more, could feel her change, the
sea change—we made love violently, at least I thought
she came to it as violently as I did, but then all of a
sudden she was twisting her head and saying no, no, no,
but I kept on anyway; there was no love on either of our
parts just then, I'd never known that to happen: to have
love at stake and then find nothing.

We sat up afterwards. It must have been like a
movie. We were both hurt. And playing hurt. A lot of
staring at the sea, the mild Ipswich sea, which by then

was so dark and black against the night sky that you couldn't make out anything, except the soft swish of waves. And hands placed on hands. On arms. Elbows. Thighs. My hand on her arm, but the nerve ends in the hand, as well as in the arm, now each seemingly turned inward. She was nineteen at the time. She had blue eyes. Brown hair. Wore neutral lipstick. She had had her coming-out party two years before at the Far Hills Country Club. She was writing her term paper for Mark Schorer on "sexual symbolism" in the Malabar Caves, which I thought very exciting. Everything was terrible. "I want to marry you," she said. And then: "I can't marry you." It went on like that for most of the two weeks before the end of college. We'd scrape at each other, rub each other raw, clasp, unclasp, take hungry nighttime rides off in the country, endure the ritual of movies, of little dinners at little Cambridge French restaurants. One evening she said that her mother was planning to take her on a trip to Canada that summer. But you can't go, I said. She looked confused, defensive. How can I get out of it? Tell her you don't want to go, I said. But how? she asked. *How* can I get out of it? I don't know, I said. I wrote my mother to stop sending me my allowance. I was old enough to be on my own, I said. I was old enough to be married. My allowance arrived a few days later in the mail. Amy wouldn't come back with me any more to my room off Henry Street. It didn't seem right, she said. We'd walk instead. We must have walked a couple of thousand miles in those late evenings, the air warm, sweet, leafy, the trees now full of leaves, the feeling of end-of-term in the air; boys and girls (they seemed like boys and girls) gliding cheerfully by in the streets, bicycles, book bags, books, exams. We were taking exams too, although I don't remember much about that. I did okay in history, but not so well in Greek, and nearly failed Proust-Joyce-and-Mann, which gave me a dull scare. Amy did fine. Schorer gave her an A, and asked her to tea. "He's a really nice man," she said. I nodded yes. We'd sit on a lot of fences. Walls. And stand. And walk and walk. "Maybe your parents are right," she'd say. "They're not right," I said. "Maybe we should wait," she'd say. "There's no point in waiting," I said. "Where will we live?" I used to carry my jacket over my shoulder. "In New York," I said. "Then maybe Europe."

"Oh, where in Europe?"

"Paris," I said. Paris seemed a nice place.

"Oh, I'd love to live in Paris," she said. Suddenly happy. Delirious. Laughter. We'd kiss. Kiss more. "Come home with me."

"No." Then: "Yes." Then: "How will we live?"

"I'll get a job. Come home with me."

"What job?"

"Oh, I'll get a job." Angry. Trees overhead. People walking by us on the sidewalk.

"I don't know," she said. And: "Maybe they're right." And: "Please. Oh *please*. Think of something."

A few mornings later. A lovely morning. I was sitting

beside the Charles on that strip of lawn in front of Eliot House. The grass was warm, had just been cut. There were some scullers on the river. I was sitting out there with Douglas. We were supposedly studying. For the last exam. Some friends came by. Most of them younger, most of them staying on at college. A couple of girls were with them, girly-girls who went to a school out near Dedham. A boy called Harris was going on about the problem of getting out the next issue of the magazine. He had on khaki trousers, a blue button-down shirt, sneakers, and sat beside us on the grass, talking about cartoons and freshman candidates. There was talk of parties. Bashes. Somebody asked about this boat that Henderson had chartered to take everybody down to the Yale-Harvard races. Was I going on this boat that Henderson had chartered to take everybody down to the Yale-Harvard races? The air seemed very warm and liquid. Somebody said he was about to flunk Elder's course. George was going to finish his story by the weekend. George wasn't going to do the editorial. We'd have to find somebody else to do the editorial. I suddenly couldn't stand being at college another moment, all those endless, seemingly endless years of academies, institutions, schools, games, baseball, football, cricket, soccer, masters, teachers, rectors, deans, Yale-Harvard, khaki slacks, parties, bashes, Henderson and his lunatic cherubic face. The lovely red-brick buildings. The lovely scullers upon the lovely river. I tried to reach Amy on the telephone, couldn't. Alone in my room

that afternoon, not really having planned out anything
at all, I picked up the phone and called a man I knew, a
man I'd briefly met, David Palmer, who worked on *Life*.
He was an Editor. An Associate Editor. Thirty years
old. He'd been at Harvard before the war, now edited
the Nature Department. I said simply that I wanted a
job. "I thought you were going to Cambridge," he said,
which had been one of my vague studious plans, the last
time we'd met, that I go and take a year of modern history or something in England. "That's changed," I said.
"I'm going to get married. I need a job." He was very
nice to me on the phone, he wished me well about "the
girl" (in his formality making the whole thing sound
more real to me than it had felt in weeks), and said
when would I like to come down. I said "right away"
and he was nice about that too, he said he'd set something up for me with "Mr. Bermingham." I went on
down the next morning. I didn't tell my parents about it,
went right down to Time-Life, up up in that elevator.
My new brown J. Press suit. The hair well-combed. Mr.
Bermingham sat behind a large desk, a small soft-
spoken man. I sat on the edge of my chair, as usual,
clutching a manila folder full of bits of college magazines and tearsheets. He started to interview me. He
would begin each sentence, most of which had something to do with "picture journalism," floating the first
part out to me across the desk, then swiveling as he
spoke, swiveling slowly in his chair, so that the end of
the sentence, most of it in fact, was wafted out the win-

dow, out into the spaces of Rockefeller Center. It was like a guessing game. I was so serious. I felt everything was at stake. I spoke with what must have seemed to him a quite lunatic enthusiasm for "picture journalism." For "group journalism." I thrust my manila folder across his desk. He accepted it calmly. He said he'd "be in touch." I went back to Cambridge that evening. Amy was studying for her last exam. I told her what I'd done. "Oh, I *know* they'll take you," she said. "I know, I know." I didn't think so myself. But two days later I received a message to call Mr. Bermingham in New York, and called him, and he said when can you start. Right now, I said. I phoned my parents, my mother in fact, and told her I now had a job and so would not be at graduation. "A summer job?" she asked. "A job," I said. "A real job." I felt truly excited, pleased. "I need money to get married," I said. "Oh," she said. "You're still thinking of that, are you?" But I didn't pay her too much heed that evening. Later my father phoned me, pleased at the job, it's a good company, he said stolidly. Harry Luce and I don't always agree on things, but it's a good company. I hear they give you plenty of time to write on your own. He was clearly worried, though, that I would not get my diploma if I failed to attend graduation. They mail it to you, I explained. Which was true. He seemed doubtful. I think he had imagined something with a bit more organ music. Ceremony. Choirs of angels. "It doesn't sound right to me," he said.

I started work at *Life*. Amy came down from college.

I'd spend my days shuffling through wire-service photo-graphs, neat little piles of UP, AP, INS, and then at six in the evening, trying not to show unseemly haste, but obviously showing it, would tear off uptown to Amy's place, or, more precisely, to Amy's mother's place. Amy's mother was drinking champagne that summer. The refrigerator was always full of the stuff. I thought Amy's mother was very sophisticated and intellectual. She read Yeats. She had known Sherwood Anderson "personally." That summer, *Life* was in the process of publishing Hemingway's *The Old Man and the Sea* and I'd bring galleys home with me—an indication, which I hoped everyone would find reassuring, of how far I had proceeded into the professional world. Galleys! We drank champagne. We had literary discussions *à trois*. One evening, Amy announced that indeed she and her mother were going off to Canada. "But how *can* you still?" I was stunned. "Mummy thinks I should have a rest."

"You don't need a rest," I said. "What do *you* think?"

"I don't know," she said.

"Don't go," I said. "We're going to get married." I started to cry. I must have spent that entire summer al-ternately sweating and crying.

"Nobody approves," Amy said. Patient. Explaining to a child.

"But why does everyone have to approve? We can just get married. We can get a room somewhere." I was very big on getting a room somewhere, it seemed like such a nice idea. Amy began to cry. Her mother appeared from downstairs. "Aren't you two going to have any dinner?" she'd ask. "We're not hungry," Amy said. Her mother sat down on the big sofa. Amy on the far end of it. I now on a chair opposite. We would have another literary discussion. Champagne. The time that Sherwood came to the house that summer . . . More champagne. Eventually, she'd stir her feet a little, say, Well I think I'll go to bed and read for a while . . . Then a bit more champagne. The time that Heywood Broun was glimpsed in Madison, Conn., that autumn . . . I'd try to catch Amy's eye, make some sort of conspiratorial sign. Amy, the dutiful daughter. Prim hands. Legs tucked under her. At last, her mother standing upright. Her mother moving forward. Her mother, great admirer of the poets, friend of Sherwood Anderson, glimpser of Broun, trudging off to slumberland with the new Ellery Queen clutched in her hand. The sound of the bedroom door opening. The bedroom door closing. I'd dive for Amy. "No!" she'd say. "Not yet. She can still hear." The Irish serving girl caught between-stairs by the uncouth laird. Oh those inelegances, the big blue sofa, the rumpled clothes, the back-seat-of-the-car fifteen floors above Park Avenue. "Don't leave," she'd say. "Please leave. Don't leave." It sounds good in stories but it was nerve-racking in life. One had those rubber things then, awful things in trim little tinfoily packages. Amy saying yes and no. White legs against the blue sofa. Yes and No. Just a moment, Amy. Wait. Yes and No. The little package in one's hands. One's body suddenly feeling stupid. For a time, I tried putting the damn things on beforehand—standing upright in the bathroom at the cocktail hour, the sound of champagne glasses in the living room, her mother trilling on about something, my fly unzipped, tugging on this wretched rubber, pushing, pulling. Soft rubber. Limp flesh. The whole thing ridiculous, and doomed. Once, coming out of the bathroom after much flushing of toilets, walking debonairly, airily back into the living room, I could feel the damned thing slipping off, slipping, slipping, I could feel it fall down inside my trousers. I stopped. Tried to keep looking straight ahead, felt around with my foot. "Whatever are you staring at?" her mother said. "What a funny expression."

A few hours after such an evening, such a morning, Amy and her mother left for Canada. For two weeks. I thought I would use the time to remain more at home. To be with my parents. I thought this would be nice for them. After dinner, my father and mother would be reading in the library. "What do you hear from Amy?" my mother would ask. I had heard nothing. "Nothing," I said. Besides, I resented the question. "I imagine she's having a nice time," she'd say. "I guess so," I'd reply. My mother would pick up her Daphne du Maurier. "Well, I imagine she probably appreciates a little time to think things over." In seconds I'd be out of my chair.

Smoke. Fire. "She is *not* thinking things over!" I'd say. "I am not a child!"

"You're both children," my mother would say.

I'd glower at my father. He pretended to be reading. "I'm going out," I'd say. I had some friends at *Life* who lived in an old building down on Fifty-third Street. The men were very lean and tall and hard-working and sincere. I admired them hugely. The girls were okay, soft, matter-of-fact. Pleasant. It was all very professional. We drank whisky, and talked about assignments and stories and editors, and how all of us would do things better. It was nice. And nobody cried. I could spend whole evenings with these people and none of them would suddenly break into tears, I wouldn't break into tears. The world seemed rational. I laughed. Made jokes. The feel of hard ground underfoot. Sometimes walking home late at night, I had these mad rushes of desire for Amy. But in the morning, waking up, thinking of her, she had no face. I tried to remember her face. The week was odd that way. Then one day the office boy brought me a letter, the postmark Canada, the address in her handwriting, a script that made a brave but not very successful attempt to escape the Farmington curlicues. I dreaded it suddenly, put it down. Didn't want to open it. Opened it, read. She was miserable, lonely. She was coming back. I felt very strange. And then she did come back. "We have to do something," she said. The edge of her elation, like mine, was fierce, but very thin.

She seemed unhappy. I didn't know what I was. "We'll get married," I said. "But how can we?" she said. "We don't need everybody's approval," I said. "I'm not a child. I'm twenty-one. I have a job."

"I'm nineteen," she said.

"I know. Your mother will approve."

"I'm not so sure she will any more," she said.

I went to lunch with my father. You look miserable, he said. I'm not miserable, I said. Do you really want to get married now, he said. Of course I want to get married now. Suppose you have children, he said. I want children, I said. We talked like that, and then walked uptown staring at shop windows. My mother seemed close to rage all the time. "That wretched little Mrs. Wells!" she finally flung out at me, about nothing really. I'd just mentioned her name. "What do you mean?" I said. I knew what she meant. I couldn't bear that she would think it, say it. I went with Amy to visit friends of hers in Connecticut. A big ample cozy house. The friends were married. Everything there seemed so firm, stable, nailed down. I loved it all, desired it. I sat alone with Amy before dinner in the big living room. Maple furniture. Abercrombie & Fitch ashtrays. I put my hand between her legs. It was very quiet. Peaceful. Later, everyone asleep, she would not make love. We wandered around fields drearily the next day. Back in town on Monday. "I love you," I said. "I love you," she said. We stood outside of Schrafft's at Seventy-ninth

Street. "Let's go away," I said. "Where?" she said. Doubtful. "It doesn't matter where," I said. "It matters," she said. Once again at home my mother asked me if she were pregnant. I screamed back No. Amy said she thought her mother would let her get engaged. She talked of parties. She would have an engagement party. She drew up lists. She said her mother was fond of me. She said her mother considered my father a very sophisticated writer. One day she met me after work. Standing down by the elevators. Her face white. Drawn. She said her mother had told her she should go back to college. I don't know what to do, she said. *Do* something. She wouldn't make love any more. She was afraid about having children, she said. But if we're going to be married . . . I said. I want things to be right, she said. I then determined, decided, that we should be married. I rented an apartment, over on East Eighty-eighth Street. Unfurnished. Two rooms. I ordered a bed from Bloomingdale's and called them nine times a day to assure that it be delivered instantly, at least within the next two weeks. I began to be very scared, I didn't know of what. I began to have great tearing crying fights with my mother—the library late at night, hot tears, indignation. "I don't care what you think," I said. And: "It's my life." And: "You don't understand." My mother on her tenth drink, her voice very deep. My father asleep upstairs, or trying to be asleep. "If she loves you that much," my mother said, "she'll marry you whether I approve or not."

And then I began to hear Amy's voice, as if I hadn't been hearing it for months and months, had been hearing something else, something she'd briefly become. One fall evening, I remember, we'd gone to a party. A dance out in the country somewhere. Long Island. Some friends of my sister's were giving it. On the way there, we talked, Amy and I. Chatter. About how much too old we felt for this sort of thing. Lester Lanin. "Just One of Those Things." Those elbow-wiggling little schoolboy dances. I now had all these new friends at *Life*. Professional people. We drank whisky together and talked about careers. At the party, Amy looked very pretty. I danced with her a lot at first. I really wasn't much interested in most of the people there. And then later, walking into one of the smaller rooms by myself, I saw her over by the piano. Somebody was playing the piano. She was with a group—boys, girls, young men I vaguely recognized, whom she'd known before we met. Yale. Far Hills. She was standing beside the piano, keeping time to the music with her head, her shoulders. She seemed so light. Sexy. Young-sexy. Carefree. I felt this great pang and thought at first it must be jealousy. I must be jealous of Dick Thomas or Ned Somebody. But no, I knew I wasn't jealous of Dick or Ned. And then, still moving her head, her body, a kind of private dance, she turned, saw me, and oh God the sudden gravity—the start, and then the gravity seeping back into those eyes. And then it left, and something more operable replaced it. I wanted to say, no, *please*. But I knew it was true, something had been true then. Something had been true in that surprised look. I really loved her very much just then, more than I had loved her in months and months, since Ipswich in March maybe, and dancing on the windy beach, which was the first time I had been in love with anybody. And I knew what it all meant, too, about the shoulders bobbing to the music, and Dick, and Ned, and the engagement party lists, and the gray-silk dress she wore, which she had worn two summers ago to her own coming-out party—I knew at least enough just then to say you love me but you don't love me that much, nor do I probably love you that much, and neither of us should have to. I knew enough to say that, but I didn't. I wanted her. Or something. I never ever told her any of that, which I think was true.

It was September then. And afterwards October. Early October. I remember very well the time. The air now clear and turning cool. A time of year I'd always loved, a time of birth—and hated then. She was wearing a new coat. Black. A small fur collar. Her face very white. Tense, washed out. She seemed the grownup one just at that moment. My mother says I have to go back to college, she said. I heard her, heard the words, had heard them before. It seemed like such a procedural consideration. I said, But you can go back to college later. If you don't want to go back now, you don't have to. We were standing outside her building. Close by the wall. "I don't know any more," she said. "I love you," I said. I looked at her. There was by now this great thick screen between us. "You should have *made* it right!" she suddenly cried. "You love me," I said. "You should have *made* me marry you!" she screamed. And broke into tears. And ran inside. Her mother called me the next day at the office to say that she was taking Amy "to the South" that afternoon. Amy left, and then she came back briefly. A brief pale ghost. And then she and her mother went to San Francisco for the year, and I was in the Army.

I'VE OFTEN WONDERED HOW MY
mother and father were together in bed. Have wondered lately, I should say, because at first I didn't think
about it at all, except secretly, that sudden wild thought,
the image of two people on the bed, forcing itself almost
physically into the side edge of one's mind, exploding
briefly, and then gone. And later, still not thinking
about it very much, I more or less assumed that they
were very good. Whatever that meant. They loved each
other a lot. They kept telling each other that they loved
each other a lot. They told me that they loved each other
a lot. Oh, I knew they had their arguments, their tem-
peramental differences. They would display their dis-
agreements sometimes, almost as an act, the sort of act a
well-teamed husband and wife might perform publicly

together. Look now, we have these differences. In actuality, they had few fights. Doubtless they had some in private, or I would hope so anyway. But I guess one learns that if husbands and wives fight much in private, sooner or later they fight in public, or at any rate "before the children," and there wasn't ever much of that. My mother seemed affectionate and deferential towards my father. My father seemed adoring and considerate towards her. Friends would often compliment them on their marriage. I see them together of a certain evening. The library. Curtains drawn. A guest is there, talking to my father. The guest is English, togged up in one of those steel-thick suits. He is enjoying, he keeps saying, one of his "last days of civilization" before setting off on a lecture tour of South Dakota. My father sits in the green chair. Gray trousers. Beige Sulka shirt, silky, open at the neck. An ascot around the neck. A brown-checked, loose-hanging jacket. There is a rustling in the hall. My mother comes into the room. Long flowing gown. Dark hair, now very gray, piled high, swept high atop her head. She smiles. Gives her hand. My father and the visitor are standing. My father brings her a drink. She settles down into the couch. "Jocelyn was just telling us about . . ." my father says. Conversation. It is all so lovely. It is a ballet. The little glasses in everyone's hand. The room so quiet, private, enfolding. The visitor makes more jokes about South Dakota. Another drink. The maid comes in to pass around bits of things upon a platter. "How simply marvelous," the visitor says. After a bit he leaves. We all have dinner, and then I go out, and then they have coffee in the library, read. Read. Drink. My mother drinks a lot, I know. At first I don't notice it, try not to. At first, long ago, I'd rather liked it—back in those first years in New York, coming down from school on holidays, I used to make her drinks. Old-Fashioneds they were then. Sugar. Bitters. Slice of orange. I never got it quite right about the bitters. Now it is mostly Scotch. Scotch and soda. Before dinner in a short glass. After dinner in a tall glass. Most evenings now she stays up very late, long after my father has gone to bed. "It's a good thing I always nurse my drinks," she says. One whole evening I watch her. Like a spy. Awful. She drinks a great deal in those days. Sometimes she erupts in sudden black rages. America. The Bloomingdale's credit department. Me. General Eisenhower. My father paces alone all afternoon inside that library. And all the while, this adoration . . . *dearest . . . my beauty . . . beautiful.* My father is so gentle towards her, in his ways of telling her she is beautiful. He tells *me* she is beautiful. Your mother is a very beautiful woman, things like that. (My mother, what the hell. Annabelle French, who lived on the third floor, was beautiful. But still I know . . .) Gentleness. Consideration. Love. I have some of that in me, now grown, this gentleness, and much of it is false—false gentleness—and so I wonder how much of that was in

him. Another speculation, unanswerable. But sometimes I read his books again, look into them, catch mo-
mentary, almost thrown-aside flashes of him from inside
his writing. Real flashes. The flash of how he looked at
times. Alone. With other people. I wonder (one of the
many things I wonder) how all that nerve and passion
got so locked in, allowed itself to go underground.
Fear? One talks so facilely of fear these days. Indeed he
must have been fearful of so much, and how I can imagine him detesting that sentence, and how I can imagine
the people who knew him reading that and becoming
angry. Fear? Why, he had all the nerve in the world. Do
you not remember how he first came on to London? Do
you not remember how he won your mother? Do you
not remember that time when Goebbels was staying at
the Imperial, on the floor below, and stepped onto his
balcony, and your father went to the sideboard, mixed a
Martini, very exquisitely called down to Goebbels, and
poured it on his upturned face? Do you not remember? I
think I do, or partly so anyway. I remember a lot, because the two of them, this man and woman, were vividly drawn, and in the foreground, and I paid (it
seems) attention more to figures than to landscape. Still
I wonder about them in bed, because although "bed"
doesn't tell you everything about anybody, what it does
tell seems true to itself, inescapably true to itself; and
maybe the history on many people's faces has at least a
good deal to do with trying to escape what is told at

night, in those odd moments. I think sometimes of my
father when he was young (and out of sight to me). I
try to imagine how he must have been—the afternoon
he first heard from Heinemann's of their enthusiasm
for *The Green Hat*. (He told me that on his way back
home he stopped in at Cartier and bought himself a jeweled stickpin; my mother gave it to me after his death, a
little duck, blue and white on gold; a jaunty thing.)
And later. All the photographs. They were a very
striking pair. Much love. There are all these photographs remaining, often of the two of them looking at
each other. I really wonder what they saw. The other
night I brought some of them out, laid them on the floor.
I was looking for one for this book. It is quite haunting
to look at photographs of any two people, young, *connected*, beginning one of those mythic, meshed, knowing, unknowing journeys. Austria. Golf at Antibes.
In-front-of-the-Savoy. I thought of him, his family, spinning, whirling, spinning away from them (the old lady
in rimless glasses in the room in Lancashire), the ambition, driving forward, momentum, momentum, success,
reaching out now for all the shiny things he'd dreamed
about, *reaching* (and now the woman beside him,
the marvelous woman, golf at Antibes), catching—
catching what? Warmth? Beauty? Children in English
clothes? Sometimes (one guesses) the air must have
been as stifling as death. And she, the girl in the new
golfing jacket, quiet-looking, beautiful, hanging back a

little in the picture, a slightly "foreign" look, a not quite gentle smile, the girl who worried over what to say to Mr. Maugham, or what to write in a thank-you note to Lady Mendl, who embraced her children (sometimes) like a peasant, who surely needed (those deep eyes) more than being made love to, or wrapped in endearments and adorations, to be fucked—there is no other word now, is there? What of her? Golf at Antibes. Death. Things in between. I picked up the photographs and stashed them away. There is a place I keep them in the basement, an old suitcase.

Ashbury College: the fact that they called it a college when it so obviously wasn't seemed typical of the place, although I shortly learned that a number of the other private schools in Canada called themselves colleges—a wishful note of dignity, I guess. Ashbury consisted of one main red-brick building. Three stories tall. Gabled. Dark red brick, much more ominous and Victorian and English than anything I'd seen in England. The building was T-shaped, with the dormitory rooms in front, then classrooms along a narrow corridor, then out in back a gym of sorts, and outside the playing fields. The whole thing enclosed in a perimeter of Cyclone fence, although whether to keep the heathen out, or the young gentlemen in, was never clear. Also another small building off to the side, white clapboard with a green roof. The headmaster's house. The headmaster then, the "head," was a man called Faircloth, Andrew Faircloth, an athletic Canadian, probably in his mid-forties, with a cheery pale angular face, thinning blond hair, also a large stern wife, and three daughters whom he kept as far away from the school as possible, except on Sundays, when they all sidled into church together. Three blond girls in gray uniforms. One of them was pretty, too. "Onward Christian Soldiers" was Mr. Faircloth's favorite hymn, and we sang it fairly often there in Sunday chapel, standing upright in the wooden pews, bellowing out the warlike phrases, sunlight coming in the stained-glass windows (which had not been fully stained as yet, owing to a deficit in the stained-glass-window fund), thinking the usual thoughts about sports or what to do the rest of the day, or directing imprecise covetous glances at Polly Faircloth.

Ashbury was a school originally intended for about one hundred and fifty of the sons of the more prosperous Ottawa businessmen, and now, by virtue of the bonds of Commonwealth, and maybe of yearning for a little more tuition, contained an additional hundred or so of us evacuees from Abinger in England, most of us younger than the Canadians, smaller, still wandering around, that first autumn, in our English schoolboy uniforms of brown blazers, brown shorts, those little peaked caps. Rooms, linoleum corridors lined with rooms. Five beds to a room, where usually two or three had been before. A metal bed. A chair beside the bed. A washbasin inside the room. One hung one's towel and washcloth over the metal bar at the foot of the bed. Bedroom slippers were to be placed beneath the chair. Cake of soap on top of the chair. My mother sent me clothes up from New York, that faraway place I'd not yet been to. More shorts. "None of the boys wear shorts any more here, except the Abinger boys, who don't have anything else," I wrote. Some long trousers arrived, my first long trousers—corduroys, as thick as buffalo hide. "I have asked Rogers Peet to send you up some trousers," my mother had written, "but naturally, since you refuse to send me your proper measurements, as to outside seam, inside seam, etc., they certainly will not fit. I ordered corduroy since the material is durable and will last longer."

Everything was very strange at first at Ashbury, and dreary. That dour red-brick buliding. The classrooms with their smell of chalk, and ink, and little copybooks. The gray cold streets of suburban Ottawa outside. On Saturday afternoons we were allowed to go outside the fence. Right after lunch, one lined up in the corridor outside Mr. Marsden's office, and waited in turn, and stepped inside, and called one's name, and Mr. Marsden dipped into a petty-cash box and handed one twenty-five cents' allowance. With twenty-five cents one could do one of two things: one could walk with it out the gates, and down the hill a mile towards Rockcliffe, where there was a sort of glop-and-candy store, and buy some glop, usually a huge bottle of soda and some squishy cakes, and take it back to school; or one could sweat out the need for glop and candy that particular Saturday, stay at school, kick soccer balls around the empty fields, and then next weekend, armed with fifty cents, one could take the streetcar into Ottawa for ten cents, see a movie for twenty cents, and then come back out again in time for dinner.

That first fall I shared a room with a boy called George Sargent, who had been at Abinger with me, a nice boy, about my age, ten, tousled blond hair, fair skin (very fast and scrappy on the soccer field); he'd grown up in Yorkshire, where his father had a small livestock farm. His young brother had come over with him, Nicholas, a roly-poly little English boy, no more than eight. He was in with us too, a room at the end of one of the corridors, the three of us, and two Canadian boys. It was all in a way very friendly, and lonely. I remember Nicholas crying a good deal, especially at night, and George telling him crossly to "be a man." George and I practiced soccer maneuvers together after the regular practice was over. Corner kicks. George was going to go back to England and be a great left-wing for Yorkshire. One morning, I remember, they called him out of class and told him, I think it was Mr. Faircloth who told him, that his father, who was in the R.A.F., had been

killed. For days and days he didn't say a word, didn't
speak, cry, anything. He had told Mr. Faircloth that he
would be the one to tell Nicholas, no one else. Each evening, George would sit on his bed—he had a model airplane he was building, and he would lay all the pieces
out, precise little slivers of balsa wood, and glue, and sit
cross-legged on the olive-colored blanket, and arrange
and rearrange the pieces, and now and then take up the
knife and cut a little slit in one of them, and fit two together. Then one evening he began to cry. Nicholas sitting at the foot of the bed, as he usually did. George
holding pieces of his model airplane, tears trickling
down his face. Nicholas didn't know what to do. I remember George then holding Nicholas, all I can really
remember is how Nicholas seemed, the back of Nicholas's head, curly hair, and Nicholas at one point saying,
"But was it really a Spitfire?" (which had been the
plane their father flew), and George just holding Nicholas, eyes so tightly clenched, that English thing of
fighting back the tears, nodding his head. All that time
my mother wrote me letters. I wrote her letters back. I
looked at some of them the other day, my mother saved
everything. "Dear Mummy, I am glad to hear that you
are well. The Latin is going well. Mr. Marsden says it
is the equal of first year at Eton. I am trying out for
right wing at soccer. Jonathan H. plays inside-right but
I think they are going to move him back to half because
he is slow. Well I think I had better run. Love . . ."

And then one day, one weekend, later that year, she came up to visit me. We walked around the school. Mr. Faircloth showed her the hockey rink. Mr. Marsden showed her the infirmary. She was staying in Ottawa, at the Château Laurier, a big hotel opposite the railroad station. I thought the Château Laurier very grand, it was not a side of Ottawa life I'd been much exposed to. I went in there with her the afternoon she was to go back to New York. She had her suitcase open on the bed, a number of books beside it. She'd brought up all these books for me, books about trains, books about animals, books about fish—I remember especially the book about fish, *Wild Game Fish* I think it was. I could still almost remember back in Cannes when she'd sat on my bed, when I had measles or something, and had drawn pictures of animals with me, for me, and now, reaching out, reaching out doubtless of her own limbo for something to have connective between us, had reached out and found a book on fish. I remember thanking her for the books, sitting on the bed beside her, the books on my lap, in truth being very pleased. And then we went down to lunch, it seemed like years since I had had lunch with her. There was one of those big overstuffed hotel dining rooms, and we went in there, and for brief seconds it was as everything had always been, the world in place, my mother ordering her drink, the way she lit a cigarette, the rings on her hand. "They must be starving you," she said. And, "You must eat everything you want," and of course I couldn't eat anything, but that was okay. She couldn't either. And then we went upstairs, and I made sure to get the books together, and took the rattly streetcar back to school.

THE WAY I FINALLY CAME TO GO TO school in the United States was like this: in my fourth year at the Canadian school, springtime, sitting at dinner one evening in the big green dining room, ten long tables, two dozen thirteen-year-olds all in a row tossing down creamed beef on pieces of bread, I was handed a telegram from my mother. My mother usually wasn't much of one for the casual telegram. This one said: "You just accepted St. Paul's School New Hampshire starting September letter follows. Love . . ." A letter duly followed a few days later, four pages of my mother's great slanting thick-nibbed handwriting, and virtually all about clothes. I should remember to bring all my white shirts. I should be sure to bring both parts to my suit. My black shoes. My socks. My head. There was something at the end, about asking Mr. Faircloth to send my "files" (which sounded very sinister) to somebody with a decidedly religious-sounding title at St. Paul's. My mother seemed very sprightly about it all, especially the business about clothes, which was one of those subjects, like packing, which she clearly enjoyed getting hold of, and then swinging around her head like an iron ball on the end of a chain. I wasn't at all sure I wanted to go to St. Paul's. To begin with, I'd never heard of it, and there was some airy reference in my mother's letter to its being a "church school," which conjured up (not entirely unjustified) visions of incense and ecumenical robes and the singing of "Onward Christian Soldiers" twelve times a day. Also, I was beginning to get used to Ashbury. In the past year or so, nearly all the Abinger boys who had come over with me on the boat from England had gone home again, or to other places, and I had begun to settle in at being Canadian in a now all-Canadian school. I cared a lot about the Ottawa Rough Riders, the local football team. I collected bubble-gum cards of famous Canadian hockey players. I was getting to know Ottawa as though I lived there, which I suppose I did. And then there was the cricket.

It seems odd to me looking back on it now, something far away and remote that surely must have happened to somebody else, but there was a time when I cared very much about cricket, and got to be quite good at it. I started in England—I started actually in France, my father lobbing cricket balls at me to catch (it never occurred to me until this moment to think of my father as a sort of expatriate Little League parent). But in England, at my first school, I realized that there was at least one genuine certifiable 100 percent *English* thing I could do reasonably well, which was to catch a cricket ball; and so made the best of it, going out into the fields after those high teas we used to have, late afternoon, evening, until the twilight finally made it impossible to see the ball, taking turns with some amenable friend at batting balls up into the air, standing under them, dizzy, afraid, the red ball against the sky, the red ball very hard, bare hands, very hard.

There was a history master at Abinger called Sykes, who had allegedly "played for Kent," quite an honor if true, and it probably was (he wasn't much at history anyway), a great muscular left-hander, an immense left arm. He was a bowler, I wanted to be a bowler, and he came with the school over to Canada, where he taught Cromwell and the Long Parliament in a fine county accent in the morning, and cricket to us and the Canadians in the afternoon. The Canadians were very keen on cricket then, I suppose it was the colonial thing, but in any case it was the big spring sport at all the schools. The R.C.A.F. had a team. The Canadian Navy had a team. I used to watch every match I could, and would at times sneak out of study hall to watch the Ashbury "first eleven" practice, those great eighteen-year-old giants in their white shirts, white flannels, long white flannels, the little caps—the "nets," where the batter stood at one end, the bowler at the other, Sykes standing by, smoking a pipe, some ancient faded English university blazer around his shoulders. "You don't need all that run!" he'd say, the universal coach's strange mixture of impatience, diffidence, worry, the desire to somehow lay little tongues of fire upon the unanointed. "Use the shoulder more! Get the weight right—" And then sometimes Sykes himself (he couldn't have been much over thirty) would take up the ball, and measure off his paces behind the bowling wicket—I can still see that great left arm dangling, freaklike, wonderful—and start his run, a fairly short run, almost a lope, then suddenly the slight turn sideways, the arm coming way around, the whole body pitched forward—Sykes really threw a very fast ball, with lots of control. I thought it marvelous, bowling marvelous (him marvelous), and practiced for hours, usually by myself on weekends, there not being much else to do, or with such companions as one could find, or sometimes on Sunday afternoons with Sykes himself, who didn't seem to have much to do either.

Then one day Sykes told me I should meet him at such-and-such hour the next Sunday morning in front of the school, and be sure to wear your best flannels, he said, and do you have a clean shirt, he said, and get your shoes in shape, he said. I couldn't tell what was happening, spent the whole night before arranging and rearranging my clothes, putting that white gunk on my shoes, sitting down, lying down, getting up. I met Sykes at the appointed time. He was standing in front of the school, leaning on his bicycle—long white trousers, a very splendid blazer, and a little peaked cap with all sorts of gorgeous colors. "Now get your bicycle," he said. And we rode off, Sykes still not saying much of anything, a mile or so down side roads where I hadn't been before, thick trees, a sort of park, and then we were at the gates of what I knew was the Governor-General's estate, guards, policemen, we cycled blithely through, Sykes puffing on his pipe, me pedaling hard to keep apace with him, great avenues of elm and maple, expanses of lawn, garden, trimmed hedges, and then at last a sort of white pavilion, some few cars, a cricket field, men in white flannels. We left our bikes beside the pavilion, I followed Sykes. Some of the men called to him by name. A large red-faced man, also in white flannels, with a great walrus mustache, came up to us. He shook hands fiercely with Sykes. "So this is the boy?" he said, looking at me. I stood speechless. "Well, shake hands," said Sykes in a kindly way. "This is Colonel Knox." I shook hands with Colonel Knox. "We'll see," he said cryptically, and strode away. Colonel Knox, it turned out, was captain of what was called the Governor-General's Eleven, a very grand (to me) and gentlemanly team of cricketers, who played the R.C.A.F., and Navy, and various university teams (various lesser university teams, I should now imagine); and after that Sunday, in which I played about five minutes, five terror-stricken minutes in an obscure part of the field, one not normally hit to, and made no mistakes (I think I stopped an extremely slow-moving grounder that nobody was running on anyway), I was taken on, obviously as Sykes's protégé, as a sort of utility infielder, a sort of bat boy who now and then got up to bat.

I think those Sundays were up to then the happiest I had been: meeting Sykes in front of the school, cycling down those great shaded avenues on the Governor-General's grounds; and then the whole ritual of the game itself, which must have been so extraordinarily colonial (this was wartime after all)—the Ottawa ladies in their flowing Bournemouth gowns, the men in Old School blazers, the little garden-party lettuce-and-tomato sandwiches passed around on trays between innings. I remember the first thing I thought after getting that telegram from my mother was: would I play cricket at St. Paul's? I imagined probably not, and when I thought about my budding career with the old colonels of the Governor-General's team I felt very sad. I mentioned my forthcoming departure to Sykes, who was going back to England himself that summer. "Don't worry, boy," I remember him saying. "There's always a way and a place to play cricket."

The next Sunday, because of Sykes I think, they let me bowl two innings against a local Army team. I had never been so nervous in my life—can still remember being handed, as is customary, the ball by the umpire, walking off my steps, and then looking down the suddenly unbelievably long pitch towards a gigantic, mustached and bearded Army major, crouched in front of the wickets, making furious little motions with his bat. I didn't get anyone out, but nobody hit me either. "Not bad, not bad," said Sykes later, as we got ready to bicycle home. "I thought you were getting a bit careful with Anderson, but then he was playing it fairly con-serv-ative himself." I rode back to school that afternoon literally exhausted with contentment, Sykes and I pedaling easily down the narrow roads, those two great cricketers, Sykes and Arlen, pedaling back across Ottawa, back across Canada, cheering villages, townspeople, happiness. A few days later, Sykes called me into his study, which as usual was filled with uncorrected exam books, and smelled of the linseed oil he used to oil his cricket bats. "Here," he said, "this may be good news," and handed me an old *Registry of American Schools* opened to an even older engraving of the Worcester Academy cricket eleven, vintage 1896. "I wouldn't be at all surprised," he said, puffing on his pipe, "if some of the solider schools down there still played the game." I must have looked doubtful. Sykes himself suddenly looked doubtful. "Well anyway," he said, "you can always play baseball." He stood up and draped that beautiful overlong left arm over my shoulders. "I hear they play it wearing gloves," he said.

My MOTHER WENT UP WITH ME TO
St. Paul's that autumn. The night sleeper out of New
York to Boston. The ratty steam-heated little train out
of North Station to Concord, New Hampshire—my
mother sitting upright on the faded green horsehide
seat, hair swept high atop her head, a scarf around the
neck, some jewels, one of those stiffish nineteen-forties
suits top-heavy with shoulder padding and lapels, the
Vuitton bottle case open on the seat beside her. Around
us, the coach half full with soldiers, sailors home on
leave. A dozen or so schoolboys up front, giggling,
punching each other on the arms, passing, puffing,
stuffing lighted cigarettes into their mouths like candy.
My mother doing her nails as we chugged past the red-
brick mill towns of New Hampshire. Later, we walked

around the school a bit. Green lawns and clapboard buildings. Gardeners, trees, boys in blazers walking in a kind of gentle shuffle down the pathways, it all seemed quite lovely, not like a school at all. We went in to see the man in charge of admissions, a dour, crinkly-faced Scot called Mr. McAndrew. "He'll be in the Second Form," he said, looking at me, "live in the Lower School. We're a bit crowded now. Has he had French?" "Of course he's had French," my mother said. "Has French," Mr. McAndrew repeated, and wrote in pencil on some kind of chart. We went in to see the headmaster, here called the Rector, a stoutish, pink-faced, relentlessly urbane clergyman called Dr. Peavey, who swept around from behind his desk to meet us, more or less transported us into two chairs placed opposite it, offered my mother a cigarette from a gold cigarette case, settled back into his own chair, beamed, rang a little bell—a woman in a maid's uniform appeared. "Tea?" the Rector said. A great paraphernalia of teacups, teapots, cakes, biscuits, spoons and so forth was brought in. The Rector said that he was sorry my father could not be with us. He was still in England, my mother said. The Rector said that all of us would remember the Battle of Britain. The Rector said that London was his favorite city. He and my mother talked about London for a while, my mother sitting attentively, legs crossed, almost shy, smoking a cigarette, declining cakes; the Rector, hands clasped in front of him, prefac-

ing each sentence with "As you doubtless know," "As
you certainly are familiar with . . ." Then they talked
about me for a while, mostly in the third person. "He's
had quite a varied education, hasn't he?" the Rector
would say. Or, "I'm sure he'll get along very nicely here
. . ." and then beam in my direction as if to show how
nicely I was getting along already. "He's been doing a
lot of Latin and Greek," I heard my mother say at one
point. "Is that so?" the Rector said cheerily. "Well, we
have an excellent classics program here." He peered
over at me. Tortoise-shell glasses. Clerical collar. His
entire shirtfront seemingly crisscrossed with chains and
medals and little gold keys. "There's no training like the
classics, now, is there?" I nodded dumbly. "We were
hoping that he might be able to start in at his own
level," my mother continued, in her best between-us-two-
professionals tone. "You see, he is quite advanced . . ."
The Rector directed another smile at me, this one equal
parts radiance and wariness. "Quite *advanced?*" he
murmured. I tried to become invisible on my chair. "I'm
certain," he said briskly, "that he will find the work here
fairly challenging." We shook hands all around. "A
great, great pleasure," he said to my mother, placing a
fatherly hand over my shoulder. Then a smart clap on
the back. "Well, well, young man! 'Arma virumque
cano'!" He shook hands again with my mother. "I make
it a point to re-read a little of the poets every summer,"
he said, and ushered us out the door. "Really quite a

civilized man," my mother said thoughtfully, as we walked over to the Lower School. The dormitory there already seemed to be filling up with boys, occasional parents in hats and raincoats lugging in suitcases. I was assigned a little cubicle, one of fourteen cubicles along one side of a long room, a bed, a dresser, a chair, a curtain across the front. My mother sat on the bed while I unpacked my suitcase. "It seems very nice," she said. I agreed. It seemed in fact quite elegant compared to Ashbury. A young master came by, stuck his head in. "I only sent him up with six white shirts," my mother said. The master looked bewildered. "Oh yes," he said. "That's fine. White shirts." I wished my mother would leave. I wished she would never leave. "I hope you'll work hard now," she said. And, "I know you'll make friends quickly." And, "Be sure to write soon." She fished into her handbag and produced a ten-dollar bill and gave it to me. "I don't know if they'll let you spend this," she said, "but I'm sure it will come in handy." I helped her on with her coat, and we walked down the corridor, past the other cubicles. Boys' voices. Laughter. A football bouncing down the floor. A deeply tanned young boy came slowly in, followed by a woman in a large hat, and a chauffeur carrying what seemed to be a fishing rod. The chauffeur climbed on top of a radiator and tried to shove the fishing rod over one of the cubicles. The boy and I stood off to one side, trying not to look at each other. My mother and I stood on a brick walk outside the dormitory, beside the line of yellow taxis waiting to take away the parents. She kissed me fondly. "You're a good boy, I know you'll do well here," she said. "Be sure to write," she said, and got into the cab, and waved, and blew a kiss.

Awinter's evening in New York, 1946: We live in the Hotel Volney, an apartment-hotel on Seventy-fourth Street, just off Madison. Gray limestone front. A green awning above the sidewalk. The doorman is Irish: Fred, who sits on a chair just inside the lobby and shuffles to a half-rising position whenever anyone comes in or leaves. Few people seem to do either. The lobby is dark, oak-paneled. The elevator man is also Irish: James, thick chest and one of those wide seminarian necks, pale bloodless face, glasses. He follows the horses in the evening *Sun*, although he says he does not bet. At night, the front desk is empty, save for Miss Rasmussen, a Swede, who sits by the switchboard, and smokes, and reads movie-star magazines. At the far end of the lobby, beyond the switchboard, there is a dining room. Also dark, oak-paneled. Glass doors. A large round table near the entrance covered with a display of fruit and pastries which never seems to be changed, or moved, or eaten, or touched, or to have any acknowledged existence at all, except possibly as a kind of warning to diners. Tonight, as usual, there are few diners. Mr. Binton, the manager of the hotel, a tall, dapper and morose gentleman in his late thirties, sits at his accustomed table against the far wall. Mr. Binton has been manager of the Volney for nearly a year, something of a record—managers of the Volney seeming to come and go like South American dictatorships. Mr. Binton has veal chops every evening, and reads the paper. Close by Mr. Binton there is a table with two elderly ladies. The two ladies are what is called "permanent residents," wear strange long dresses, are very quiet, and sometimes have the startled look of sole survivors from some unimaginably far-off shipwreck, who for unknown reasons have been washed ashore to die in the Hotel Volney, most probably in the Hotel Volney dining room. There is also a small table containing Dr. Hesseltine, who is an oculist, very gaunt (also a "permanent resident"), who wears thick glasses, and reads a magazine. Also a larger table in the middle of the room, the empty middle, which contains two men and two women, evidently husbands and wives, quite dressed up too, little hats on the women, small bursts of laughter—a decided air of the tourist about them. One

imagines them having strayed into this oak-paneled cat-
acomb by mistake, perhaps lured in by the elegant plac-
ard displayed on the sidewalk in front of the hotel: *The
Volney Restaurant. Guests Welcome!* The solitary
waiter, Giovanni, a thickset Italian, shuffles to and fro
between the tables and the kitchen. He has on a white
jacket, slightly frayed, and a clip-on bow tie. "What do
you recommend this evening?" asks Dr. Hesseltine.
"Everythingza very good," Giovanni says. A relationship. Over against the wall opposite Mr. Binton are the
remains of a dinner just eaten by my sister and me. Two
plates probably containing something which the Volney
menu describes as "Salisbury Steak," and some green
stuff, which the Volney menu calls "Broccoli à la
Volney." Also a copy of *Seventeen*, which my sister has
left behind and will pick up tomorrow evening. My sister and I are back upstairs. The seventh floor. A four-
room suite, so-called. A small living room, which contains a couch, some chairs, a table, a small desk, where
my mother pays the bills and writes her letters; a bedroom for my mother and father; a room for my sister;
and a small room off to the side, which has another
desk, a day bed, and is described alternately as my
father's study, or as his dressing room, or as my room,
when I am home from school. My father has been back
from California over a year. He is fifty years old. Has
much gray in his hair. Also a cane, and a slight limp
(the result of a car accident in Hollywood) which soon

goes away, although he retains the cane. My sister, now twelve, is lying on her bed. She wears a flowered bathrobe, feet sticking out in white wool socks, her hair in curlers, those little rubbery things to get the ringlet effect. She reads a book, something about horses; she is keen on horses then, will hear no harsh words spoken about horses. My mother is in the bedroom nearby, once her room, now (since my father's arrival from England) their room: her own pink pillows upon the bed, a watercolor of an island scene upon the bedside table, the dressing table filled with jars and bottles. My mother sits at the dressing table: pink slip, stockings, dabbing at her face with bits of things, hair hanging down below her shoulders. A cigarette burns in the ashtray. An Old-Fashioned, sipped at, somewhere nearby. My father glides in and out of the small rooms. My father in shirt and trousers, white silk shirt, English trousers ending up somewhere in the small of the back, braces. My mother is holding a dress up against her in front of the mirror. My father glides in. Thick hair combed back, drink in hand. You-look-lovely-dear, he says. My mother stares at him. My father glides out. My father discusses horses with my sister. My sister wants to ride in the Grand National. My father describes the cavalry of Genghis Khan. "You should have more light to read by," he says. My sister pulls a face. My father stands in front of the mirror in his-study-dressing-room-my-room, tying his tie. I am in the small slip-covered chair beside the desk, reading a book. The desk is empty, save for a yellow pad, and three pages of a story begun by him six months ago and never finished, a romance between some R.A.F. officer and a nurse, now hidden in one of the small drawers. The tie is silk, gray silk. He ties it with great care. The wide end down and over, like this. Then through the loop. He stops to show me. I watch, half skeptical, half loving. It suddenly all seems very gay somehow, despite the dinginess, the darkened dining room, the tatty gentility. My father puts a small pearl tiepin in his tie. "Come here," he says. "There is a way to do this that doesn't spoil the tie." I come up close. His voice is deep, matter-of-fact, instructive. He moves the tiepin through the silk. I watch his hands, the silk, the tiepin. We are in a canoe together. A fishing trip. My father and I whirl great fly-lines through the air. We cook food together on metal skillets beside the river-bank. He threads the tiepin through, smooths the tie back into place. I feel unbearably happy. My mother appears, fastening an earring onto an ear. She corrects a strand of hair. My father puts on his coat. Good night, good night. My mother tells my sister to read by a better light. The cane, her heels sound in the hallway outside. They wait for James to haul the elevator up.

EACH SCHOOL VACATION IN NEW York there was the ritual of having lunch with Uncle Hugh. Uncle Hugh was not my uncle, or anywhere near it. He was a man called Hugh Payson Courtland (in point of fact, for most of his life Hugh Payson Courtland II, his father having finally, at age ninety-two, removed both himself and his roman numeral), and he was my father's new friend. My father's new American friend. Hugh was a little over six feet. Close to sixty. Silvery-haired. Bright blue eyes. One of those marvelous ruddy Episcopal faces that always looked as if it had just been scoured with a steel brush. Uncle Hugh had himself been to St. Paul's, and Harvard. He had been an aviator in the First World War. He had been some kind of a lawyer. Now he was some kind of a businessman.

He was a director. He was on "boards." Uncle Hugh
had lots of brothers and cousins, who lived on ancestral
acres in exotic Englishy-sounding places like Beverly
Farms and Bedford Village. Hugh's father apparently
had been a long-ago famous New York senator, and
there were countless photographs of the old gentleman
all over Hugh's house, mostly on horseback. Uncle
Hugh was clearly Very Old Family, the near-end-of-the-
line in fact of one of those proud, rich New England
families—Hugh himself, one gathered (from Hugh),
represented the more or less Bohemian, or renegade, aspect of the family; mostly, it would seem, by having
married a French wife, a pale, decent woman of considerable forbearance. I remember dinners at Hugh's
house, a rather shambly but nicely lived-in brownstone
in the East Seventies, with Marie, his wife, downstairs
on the ground floor, in the kitchen, and Hugh three
stories above in his elegant little library: drinks, cigars,
old books on the shelves, Hugh in his evening clothes
("I think it is good for the morale to dress for dinner"),
Hugh prattling on with his stories—Hugh was the only
man I've ever met whose conversation consisted entirely
of stories. Marie downstairs in her long dress, it always
seemed to be the same dress too (a long purply thing
with a couple of hopeful strands of silver), Marie down
in the engine room way below, hauling up the ancient
Courtland china and the ancient Courtland silver on the
dumb-waiter, creak-creak-creak-clank, Hugh and his

amusing stories, sounds of creaking rope, Marie hauling
up the roast, Marie hauling up the veg, clank-clank,
sounds of pulleys, sounds of glasses being rattled, Hugh
telling us about the amusing thing that had happened to
his Cousin Sandy at a Turkish bagnio in 1922, Marie
finally appearing in the doorway to announce dinner,
poking pins back into her hair, brushing off her dress,
Marie managing a smile, Marie looking as if she had
been down at the docks all afternoon unloading sacks of
flour and would like just now to go to bed.

I usually felt ill-at-ease alone with Uncle Hugh,
mostly because he was always trying to tell me dirty stories, and because I couldn't make much sense of him,
although the last I didn't much require. I very much
wanted to be friends, though, or whatever it was I was
supposed to be with Uncle Hugh, because he was my
father's friend; because then he was the only actual
friend I was aware of my father having. Our lives, my
father's life, had always been peopled for me by these
dim far-off shapes of his "old friends," the barely visible
outlines of such as Maugham, Noel Coward, Clark
Gable, and the like. It didn't bother me that I had almost
never seen these men, although naturally it would have
pleased me like anything to impress my Wall Street and
Oyster Bay schoolmates, sons of Merrill Lynch and
Winthrop Stimson, with my acquaintance in the wider
world. Mostly it bothered me that my father didn't seem
to see them either, or that when he did (one might run

into Gary Cooper at the theater, exchange a few words), it seemed like dinghies bumping. Noel Coward would be in town for the opening of a new play. Noel would come by for a drink. Noel admittedly was more of a genuine old friend than the others (my father, I knew, had been one of the key backers for Coward's first play, *The Vortex*), but even so, it seemed that no matter how much gossip and wit and anecdote they nudged across a coffee table at each other every few years, they remained two people clearly in private untouching worlds. I don't know what I expected—Coward and my father on a walking tour of Belgium together, or sharing a Thanksgiving turkey, or drinking a lot and cuffing each other on the shoulder. Uncle Hugh at any rate seemed to have the makings of some kind of visible ordinary friend. For one thing, he came around a lot. He professed to take an interest in our family. He may have been a grade or two off as to what year my sister was in at school, but at least he knew she was at school, and more or less where. And he seemed genuinely to like my father. He and my father "did things together." Other people's fathers, I knew, "did things together" with their friends—playing golf, or cards, or going in a large boat to fish for marlin. My father and Uncle Hugh, I think, mostly walked back from lunch together. It seemed enough. I remember seeing them together walking down Fifth Avenue. An October afternoon. Hugh in a dark suit, gray vest, a bowler on his head. My father with his cane, no hat. My father gesticulating with his hand, talking. Hugh laughing. Comrades. And then, once each school vacation, once each school vacation for at least five years, Hugh would take me to lunch at the Racquet Club. I both looked forward to these times, because having lunch with Hugh Payson Courtland at the Racquet seemed like such a nice snobby thing to do, and dreaded them, because I felt that although Hugh wanted to like me and take-an-interest in me as part of his role as my father's new friend, in fact he disapproved of me because I didn't laugh at his jokes, or worse, laughed in that awful obvious way of trying not to disappoint the teller. The routine never varied much. I'd put on my "good suit," try to find a tie without egg on it, shine the shoes, hop a bus down to Fifty-third Street, present myself at the big door always in the hope that the Swiss Guards who manned the entrance would instinctively assume me to be a member. Mr. Hugh Payson Courtland would be waiting in the bar. Much handshaking and clasping of shoulders. Drinks, a brandy and soda for Hugh, a beer for me, a brief torrent of jokes and stories about Hugh's days at St. Paul's. We would then go to the oyster bar, which I also dreaded, because I could barely look at oysters or clams in those days without wanting to throw up, but at my first lunch with Hugh I had somehow got myself into the fix of saying, Oh yes, by all means the oyster bar, I love oysters, etc. If I couldn't give him much return on the

jokes, at least I wanted to cooperate on the shellfish.
And then lunch. A small table by the window. Hugh
sitting opposite me. Another avalanche of anecdotes,
and then the jokes: I really shouldn't tell you this,
Hugh would say with a giggle. And then some damn
thing about American aviators and farmers' daughters.
Or about President Roosevelt and his secretary. Hugh
elaborating on the detail. Me sitting there, gravely,
primly (desperately not wanting to be grave or prim),
waiting, waiting for the punch line, I must be able
to spot the punch line coming, rearrange my face so
that my burst-of-helpless-laughter (in reality a sickly
grin) will be vaguely plausible. The punch line. The
sickly grin. Hugh giggling, giggling, I really used to
hate those giggles, that pink face, soft, the eyes all
squinched up, the hand reaching across to my arm. "I
really shouldn't have told you that." A kind of wink. I
once tried to say something of my discomfiture to my
father, but it just didn't make any sense to him. Uncle
Hugh after all didn't tell dirty jokes to *him*. "Hugh is
very naughty," my mother would say sometimes, but I
think what she mostly had in mind was Marie and the
dumb-waiter. I don't know what it was my father really
felt for Hugh. He liked him, I know, because he used to
speak of him in a certain way, that simple offhand way
that people use when they like someone. I think Hugh
must have entertained him, to some degree anyway.
Mostly, I'd guess that he found in Hugh, and in Hugh's

place in America (Hugh's alleged place in America), some kind of solid object to hold on to, not that he ever seemed to be holding on to it very tightly. I think he probably liked to have it around. And they had good times together.

I remember sitting in class one morning up at St. Paul's, and someone coming in to say that classes were being let out for the next hour for the purpose of listening to two visiting dignitaries who had just come up to address the school. We all filed down into the big study hall, partly pleased at being let out of class, partly wary as to just what in hell was coming next—and there, seated on either side of the great glowing Rector, were Uncle Hugh and my father, grave, serious, terribly serious, in their best Supreme Court manner. And then they spoke, my father first, something about Literature and Life, at least it was supposed to be about that. I remember Aldous Huxley being mentioned, and several stories about Sam Goldwyn—I was too generally dizzy and embarrassed to listen properly, but the faces around me seemed suitably attentive. Some laughs. Applause. Then Uncle Hugh spoke, something about Paris and Business and Rebuilding Europe, which he seemed to be making up as he went along. Also a success. I went up to see them after it was over, that seeming to be the logical thing to do. They were full of good spirits—had been up in Boston the day before attending some Harvard thing Hugh had been involved in, a big party, a lot of drinking, and somewhere along the line had decided to come up to the school and lecture at it. We had lunch at the small inn nearby, my father and Hugh congratulating each other on the fine reception accorded their talks, the attentive quality of the students, the general splendidness of young-people-today, and so forth, both of them extremely pleased with themselves. It was very nice. We all had brandy after lunch, which gave me a warm buzz between the ears, and then they went back to New York. It was the first time, now that I think of it, that my father had ever been to the school.

My father had one other friend around that time, whom I've almost forgotten because after my father died he moved right out of our lives. His name was Nadal, André Nadal. He was Iranian, I think. Some generations back anyway. A dark tall man, with a bushy mustache. Thick brown curling hair. A kind face. He was an immigration inspector and he lived somewhere in Queens. I think my father had met him when he'd first arrived from England—I don't know much about the connection beyond that, except that for a long while in New York the only two people, *friends*, I could have imagined "dropping by" for Thanksgiving dinner (if one had been having Thanksgiving dinner) would have been André and Uncle Hugh. André I think of as a truly gentle man, with one of those lovely, warm, seemingly untroubled laughs. He would sometimes come by for lunch when my father kept that table at the St. Regis, taking his place quietly along with the others, the flashy talkers, the great English-suited figures, the Rockefeller Center boulevardiers—André seated there listening, saying a few words, the rumpled brown suit, the long hair, André laughing. And then when the others would leave, André would stay on with my father, and sort of gently chide him for his frivolities. Not chide him very much. I think of André as being an intelligent, sensitive man, and the only man I can myself recall who used to talk seriously to my father about "life," and things like that. André was very proud of his job; of "government"; of being in the civil service. I remember once our families all had dinner on a summer evening. André took us out to the Tavern-on-the-Green—André; his wife, a nice large lady who seemed even friendlier than André; their daughter, a girl of about ten; and the four of us. I think we may have had one or two other dinners together, but I just happen to remember that one. I don't really remember very much about it. My father talked about his brother Taki, and his family in England. André talked about Government, and the "role of Congress." Everyone seemed very happy. Some seven or eight years later, at the funeral service for my father, I remember seeing André coming into the chapel, standing alone at the back. I went over towards him—it had been a long while since I had seen him, since any of us had gotten together. He was just standing in the back, a bit the way he used to sit there in the St. Regis, the only man there as far as I could see who seemed to be shedding the kind of tears that actually make you wet.

BLUE WATER. THE MEDITERRANEAN. The faint blue you could glimpse down through the trees at Cannes. The blue-green water off the rocks at Antibes. My father's dark hair below me off the rocks at Eden Roc. Black rocks. Umbrellas open beneath the sun. The water is very clear. My father moves slowly, ten feet below, a far distance, treading water, a sort of breast stroke. A blue bathing suit. He, like most of the men, has recently given up the top to his bathing suit. My mother is nearby somewhere, beneath one of the umbrellas. There is nobody else in the water. "Come on in, jump," my father says. Also the beach at Cannes: in front of the hotels. A narrow strip of sand. I think of the sand as being gray. The great garish faces of the hotels lined up behind it. The Carlton. Majestic. The Miramar. The beach strewn with children and with nannies. White starched uniforms. Standing upright on the sand. There were lifeguards and swimming instructors. One of them, I remember, a German, blond and tanned. He had a long bamboo pole, like a fishing pole, with a tire of sorts, maybe an inner tube, attached to the end of it. He stood at the end of the dock. One was told to climb inside the inner tube, hold on. And then flung off the dock. He was very hearty and believed in physical fitness, and I never asked what else. There were sailboats in the harbor. Sometimes a submarine. The English battle cruiser *Hood* appeared one day, peacetime maneuvers, moored five miles off. My father was invited out to tea one afternoon, took me along. I had an interest in ships. There was a mess table laid out on one of the forward decks. White tablecloth. Tea. Cakes. The great gray guns overhead. The little sailboats back against the harbor. There were shellfish along the beach. Sponge and coral in the sea. We took a sailboat down the coast to Italy one summer. My mother's cousin was along. He wore a bright blue blazer. A small harbor somewhere. Lemon houses. We stayed mostly on the boat. The captain fished. He chopped up little bits of squid for bait, put them on hooks. My father water-skied. Blue water. Outside the harbor, the waves chopped against the sides of the boat. We sailed all night one night.

And then there was one summer we went to the

mountains. It was a place in Austria, in the Tyrol, called Semmering. I don't know why we went there now, I suppose my parents wanted a change. We took the train out of Cannes one evening. I remember all of us on the platform: my parents, my small sister, the nanny (Nanny Nye)—and then suddenly Monsieur Puigue, the chef, our chef, and the whole staff, came hurtling onto the platform in an old pickup truck, all of them (not that there were that many) looking a bit dazed, as if they had just been tumbled out of bed, Monsieur Puigue in charge of the show, Monsieur Puigue still in his white apron, little thin mustache, presenting something to my mother in a box, a cake, much waving of arms, expressions of gratitude, affection, and then we were off. We stopped for hours at the Italian border. Some nuns got on at Genoa. My sister threw up a lot. In Venice, my father took us all to lunch at the Grand Hotel, which must have been a treat for him. Nanny Nye bought postcards. They put the electric engine on somewhere inside the Austrian border, an immense fat brutish thing, and for what seemed like several days we wound up into the mountains, steep faces of red rock, pine trees, tunnels. Semmering was a kind of spa. We stayed in the big hotel, which was full of Austrians, Germans, and English businessmen. There didn't seem much to do. My sister and I went for walks in the hillside meadows, and into the forests that grew down the mountains. Once, I remember, we walked quite far, through very dark glades, wildflowers, mushrooms, occasional bright patches of sunlight that seemed even more disturbing than the darkness. There were some big buildings. We went inside one of them. A great dark room. Huge. A gymnasium. All sorts of strange equipment. Machines made up to look like animals. Large leather contraptions that seemed to run on electricity. And suddenly through one of the far doors a double line of boys and girls marching in step. Fourteen, fifteen years old. All tanned, beautiful. White shirts, trousers, white tunics. They formed a square. An older boy stood in front of them. They did calisthenics and then sang. I don't remember what they sang.

In the course of that summer, my sister and I became quite close. For one thing, Nanny Nye was old, and fell asleep much of the afternoons. We were also bored with Semmering and made plans to run away. One day after lunch, I swiped some rolls from the dining room, a bar of chocolate from my parents' room—my sister and I went down the hillside, down the meadows, rocks, small pine trees, slithering, all those dark glades. I remember pulling her after me, she was very small and blond, held on to my hand. She was excited by all the chocolate. We left the road, the path, went down through the trees. The hill became very steep; it was a mountain really. We fell a lot. Brambles. I had never been so far away before. And then there was a larger road. I think I had some idea it would lead to Vienna, which was about a hundred miles away. A big touring car came by, stopped. Wide running boards, windshield. A man got out. A tall German chauffeur. He opened the back door of the car, motioned to us to get in. We got in. Going back in that car, it didn't seem as if we had been far away at all. Soon the driveway. The hotel. We weren't allowed to go on walks alone for the rest of the week, which meant we had to play in the dreadful hotel playground on the swings and seesaws. Sometimes in the late afternoon then, my sister and I would sit on the balcony outside the Gramophone Room and watch the train from Vienna coming around the side of the mountain opposite us. There was a certain time and place that it always appeared, a glint of sunlight on the great engine. The mountains really were beautiful, although too grand. I tried collecting rocks, then lizards. Towards the end of summer there was a tennis tournament at the hotel, which was won by a businessman from Wales. His name was Llewellyn, which I remember because he had a son called David. David Llewellyn. We were never close friends, but after dinner we would sometimes sit outside on the lawn and talk. About battleships mostly, and airplanes. He said he had seen tanks in Germany. I said I had seen tanks in France. There was a big dance in the hotel one night. The women all in evening dresses. Japanese lanterns. An orchestra from Vienna played fox-trots and waltzes.

MY SISTER AT SEVENTEEN. MY SISter at seventeen is actually a nice-looking girl: blond hair (which after all those years in curlers she now wears straight and in a pageboy); blue eyes; what is described as a "good figure," which means nice breasts, which I feel I am not supposed to notice but dart astonished and unsettling looks at anyway; about my mother's height, which in fact is on the short side if you discount the pile of hair atop the head, but without my mother's coiffure or Lady Windermere bearing, and without confidence, which blows everything. "I don't feel very attractive," she confesses to me at times, although I am not much of a person to confess this sort of thing to then, my own self-confidence being such that were I able to change my own un-American face into Gary Cooper's left elbow

I would gladly do so. I mumble something off into her direction, continue to take batting swings in front of my mirror, have vivid dreams of Ava Gardner, impotence, fertility, sterility, think steadfastly about myself. "Oh, definitely attractive," my mother tells her helpfully, "although not beautiful." My sister sits in her room a lot (which she has been allowed to paint the color of her choice, pale blue), plays Ella Fitzgerald records on the record player, takes baths throughout the day. *My Funnee Val-en-tine* . . . Bathwater running. My sister lies on her bed in a white quilted robe, her feet in furry slippers, says she would rather know the straight truth about her looks than be led on by vain dreams and delusions. My sister also worries about her eyes, which are on the weak side, and cause her to wear reading glasses. She also worries about her nose, which she suddenly considers too large. My father agrees, in what one imagines he regards as a friendly fashion. Father taking an interest. My sister's nose is in fact a fine nose, a fine Armenian nose, which in the women runs admittedly a bit to width, and most closely resembles that of my father's sister, Ahavni, that of his sister-in-law, Anais, and indeed to some degree his own. "You should have it bobbed," he says to her one evening. My sister smiles bravely. Father taking an interest. There is talk of the silent-film star Carmel Meyers, and of her nose-changing operation—of some *mot* my father had delivered at the time (about cutting off one's nose to

spite one's race), which had caused him to be banished
from several homes in Hollywood. Laughter. There is
talk of Ahavni. Of Ahavni's nose. "It's only a small operation . . ." my mother is saying. "They have
excellent doctors," my father says. "All they do is remove a small bone. Somewhere in here." He pats his
nose. My sister sits there opposite me, between them,
tears streaming down her face. She runs from the room.
"I'll never do it, I'll never do it," she sobs later, face
down on the bed. On the table beside the bed is a clock-
radio I had given her for Christmas, a glass of beer, a
copy of *Gone with the Wind*, which she is re-reading for
the eighth or ninth time. She gets to her feet, goes over
to the mirror, peers at her face, which is now puffy from
crying. "I'll never do it," she says. "It's not so bad." The
subject is dropped. "You'd think we were trying to force
her into an operation," my father said some time afterwards, when noses were again fleetingly mentioned.

By THE END OF MY LAST YEAR AT ST.
Paul's, all the things I most wanted to be I wasn't. I
wanted to be a great school athlete and win the revered
Gordon medal (presented the day before graduation at
a special ceremony around the flagpole by old Mr. Gordon himself). I would have settled for being what was
known as "extremely popular" (a quality much admired
in those days, as I guess "personality" was in girls), a
leader of the school, an important figure on the student council—one of the four Sixth Form toffs who sat
in special ornamented seats in chapel, just in front of the
special ornamented seats of the Rector and Vice-Rector.
None of these signal honors seemed in the cards, or anywhere near it, although life there on the whole didn't
seem too bad, mostly because the school was then (and

I imagine now) so full of the kind of young men I admired very much: young men who could play hockey very well, or squash, or who could kick 25-yard field goals at crucial moments, and who owned cars on the side, and sometimes sailboats, and had summer houses as well as ordinary houses. There was a time, quite a long time in fact, when I think I envied nearly anyone who had a house—well, not really any house. If pressed closely on the subject, I think it would turn out that what I chiefly envied were people who had houses in places like Greenwich and Old Westbury. Marvelous desirable Greenwich! O great wondrous mowed lawns! And little boats at Indian Harbor! Club memberships! Yacht Club parties! The heady presence of older girls ("women") who went to Smith, and older men ("men") who went to Yale and Princeton. And all those beautiful red-faced, flush-nosed Wall Street Dads (no damn Daddy nonsense there), with their billowy sports coats, and fuchsia slacks, and brand-new Chryslers, and elaborate bars with electric ice-smashers, and hearty laughs, and jokes, and deep grave interest in the Yale football team—and all those blond, well blondish, Mums, or Moms, or Mothers, with their sleek county look, their cashmeres, stationwagons, teensie-weensie drinkies in the evening, *their* equally deep grave interest in the Yale football team! I stayed close to all these people, or tried to stay close. Roomed with the more lustrous athletes. On vacations, tried to be adopted by their parents in Connecticut or Long Island. About all I really thought I had going for me then was that I was a "good student," but even that I secretly believed to be a sham. Not so much the factual, the achievement part. I knew I was a good student because I had the grades to prove it. St. Paul's, in those days at any rate, was a great believer in the authority and importance of grades. Once a month the "ranking list" of each form was tacked on to the main bulletin board, the name of every boy in the school listed on immense sheets of graph paper and, beside his name, the grade he had received in each subject figured out to the nearest decimal point, such as 88.7 (being naturally a better grade than 88.6). On the whole I was very good at this sort of thing—getting good grades. In truth I had no idea, or very little idea, of whether I was intelligent or not. For the most part, I believed I wasn't—but I knew how to study very hard. I knew, for example, that if I painstakingly underlined and then wrote out the correct meaning of every word in my Latin homework I didn't know, and then looked at them over and over again, and over again, I would get them right. And then the results of all this pleased my father very much. He liked for me to do well at school, to get good grades. In fact, he counted on me to do well. Each vacation time the reports would be mailed home. "History: 84.5. He continues to show an interest in the subject and has a strong grasp of the information. But his essays lately have shown a tendency to be unsure and general . . ." I see the history is down a bit, my father would say. Yes, I guess so, I'd say. Then: It's all that stuff after Napoleon. It doesn't seem very interesting. Not interesting! he'd say. That's a curious explanation. After Napoleon? The Second Empire? I·thought history was one of your best subjects, etc. And so forth. He took an interest. And I did too most of the time. But then in the spring of my last term there I began to slack off. Or rather, I just stopped taking all those pains. No special reason; maybe just being the last term, spring, sunshine, end-of-school. And then, scant weeks before examinations, I realized that my beautiful grades had dropped considerably in the past month's rankings, and that from the way things were going I wasn't going to emerge with honors at graduation even as a student, which admittedly seemed a poor third to the Gordon medal, or being on the council, but which I knew would be a good deal better than nothing.

There were a number of prizes to be awarded each graduation, and while most of them were for the high hurdles or hockey or something of the sort, a few were for "scholarship," and of these one of the better was called the Baxter Prize for History, which in some corner of my mind I had always reserved for myself. And so I decided to really study for it, because in actual fact I had had a pretty good chance of winning it, only now my monthly grades were down so that I would have to do extraordinarily well on the exam (and my rivals would have to do very much less well) for me to pull it off.

All the exams were scheduled for the final week of school, with history on the last day; and so, while paying some small attention to the other subjects, I allotted myself, each day, every day, a certain amount of time for reading over the history book. It was the standard Morison &. Commager American history text: a big blue thing. Two volumes. The exam would be on the second volume. Most everyone studied in their rooms or in the library, but I would go over to the schoolhouse right after dinner, the big red-brick building with most of the classrooms, which was supposed to be unoccupied at night, and hole up in a back room—hard wooden chairs, one of those circular tables, blackboards, maps, charts of chemical elements, travel posters of the Loire. I re-read every word in Morison & Commager. And then I re-read it again. I tried to imagine what the questions might be, and then I'd seek out the relevant chapters, and just gaze at each page, page after page, late at night, sometimes no longer knowing what I was reading, what I was doing, until two or three in the morning when my eyes were so blurred, and I was so tired, that I'd pack up and go back to my room half a mile away, where my hockey-playing roommates were fast asleep. I remember taking the exam that final day, the day before the two-day graduation ceremonies began, and when my parents were due up. It didn't seem too difficult an exam, and I thought I'd done well; at least I'd written it very rapidly, which was usually a good sign, and with a sense of what I was doing. Anyway it was over. I suddenly wanted terribly much to get the prize, and I figured I had a fair chance. My mother and father were due in around noon. There was to be a track meet and crew races in the afternoon. Sometime while all that was going on, Mr. Harding was going to post the history results. I was pleased about but rather wary of my parents' arrival. Originally I hadn't wanted them to come up. Not so much because of the usual filial embarrassment, although I certainly felt some of that. Mostly because their actual physical presence reminded me that I couldn't realistically hope to be adopted into one of those beautiful county families in Greenwich or Long Island—I already had parents of my own; and in fact there they were, walking down the brick walk beside the schoolhouse, two figures clearly different from all the others who had just now come into view—no billowy sports coat on him, no B. H. Wragge on her, no Old St. Paul's blazer, no straw hats, no jolly laugh, no jolly group: a short dark man with a mustache, an excessively tailored suit, a cane (he'd brought a cane, for God's sake!), and a woman with an exotic hairdo, also a tailored suit, and a kind of presence that seemed both to advertise and disregard her total ignorance of football at Yale, or anywhere else. We went through the usual peculiar ceremonies of greeting-in-public. "What do you want to do?" I'd say. Shifting from one foot to the other. Hands thrust into pockets, thrust out of pockets. "But it's *your* school," they'd say. "You show us." Benign. Cooperative. The elders of the tribe remind the young brave that it's *his* Initiation Rite, after all. "Surely you don't want to see the crew race!" I'd say wildly. My mother would beam as if I had just proposed a moonlight visit to the Taj Mahal. "Crew race? But of course we want to see the crew race. We certainly don't want to miss that. Your uncle was once on the crew at Balliol . . ." and so forth. And off we would go, me staring at the ground, nodding distractedly at friends ("That nice boy seemed to be trying to speak to you . . ."), some yellow rented schoolbus to take us all out to the pond, hearty alumni in old crew blazers, my friends, their parents, younger brothers—and there we all were on the banks of Long Pond, my mother and father standing on a little hillock of grass, my father leaning casually on his cane. "Is there any particular boat we should cheer for?" *Cheer* for? My sense of lunacy and gloom would deepen. It seemed quite bad enough that they should suddenly be there. Visible. But audible too! Cheering! The boat races proceeded. Two little eight-oared shells nudging down the middle of the dark-blue pond. A handful of motorboats trailing behind. It was too far away to see much of anything. Loud cheering from the bank. "Come on, Shattuck! Come on, Halcyon!" (The names of the two rowing clubs.) My father was talking with Mr. Enfield, the Latin master. The importance of a Classical Education, and so forth. My mother seemed to be staring into the middle distance with a sort of contented bafflement. I looked out at the boats, privately thought they were both marvelous, and worried desperately about the history exam. Finally, the races were over, we went back to the school. I ducked my parents— they were going to some tea at the Rector's house, I didn't even bother to worry whether or not they would embarrass me there—and ran over to the schoolhouse, where the grades would be posted.

On the bulletin board there was a brand-new list. My form. History. I looked at it, found my name, felt a wild feeling of apprehension and excitement, read across the graph-paper line towards the grades. Zero. O. I couldn't believe it. Zero. Nobody got zero. I read quickly down the column of numbers. Everyone else had done pretty much as expected. Holmes, my chief rival, had an 89. I had zero. I felt quite sick, saw some people coming, ran out the door. I wandered around the back of the schoolhouse for a bit, not knowing what to do, hoping dimly that if I wandered around enough the zero would somehow change itself, which it didn't. Then I went over to see Mr. Harding. He had a small suite of rooms in one of the Fifth Form houses. I wasn't sure whether I wanted him to be in or not. I knocked at the heavy brown door. Silence. I was about to go away, then knocked again. The door opened. Harding appeared.

Gray baggy trousers. Dark vest. Gold watch chain in the vest. He must have been around fifty then, although he seemed older. Thin gray hair. Straight nose. Eyes that were very clear, and sometimes kind. "I don't understand about the exam . . ." I began. I must have been very close to tears. "What don't you understand?" said Harding. I was sitting in a small chair beside his desk. He seemed very cold, remote. "The zero," I said. "The grade." Harding reached over for a stack of blue books, riffled through them, produced what seemed to be mine. A large, unmistakable zero in red crayon had been inscribed on the cover. "I think the grade should be perfectly clear," Harding said. Then: "I am not a fool, you know." I looked at him dumbly. Then: "The answer to the essay question that you have written here is an exact word-for-word transcription of pages 94 through 97 in *The History of the American Republic*." He more or less flung the exam book at me. I opened it, looked through it with thick fingers, not really seeing anything, even my own handwriting seemed strange to me—felt sick, felt very scared, began to cry, then eventually tried to explain. All I could say really was that I hadn't cheated. Sir, sir, I hadn't cheated. I had just studied very hard. I had (it seemed) studied so hard, or relentlessly, or stupidly, that I'd in fact memorized the bloody textbook. We went on like that for a while. Then Harding stood up and went over to a shelf. He produced a fresh exam book and put it in front of me. "All right,"

he said. "You will sit here and write me the same answer to the essay question that you so kindly gave me
yesterday. I will now repeat the question." He leaned
against the side of the small leaded window, closed his
eyes, unrolled the question, which I remember had to do
with Woodrow Wilson, the League of Nations, and the
period just after the First War. "You have thirty minutes," he said, and left the room. For whole moments,
minutes, endless minutes, I just stared dumbly at the
exam book in front of me. I opened it. Stared at the
blank page. The inside of my head seemed absolutely
inert. Woodrow Wilson. The League of Nations. I was
supposed to remember and write out a 700-word or so
stretch of text that I hadn't even known I'd memorized
some days ago. Eventually I began to write. I began
somewhere, and just wrote. Some of the phrases seemed
familiar, plausible. Some of it was blind. I wrote on and
on, and finished. I called out to Mr. Harding that I was
done. He was in the other room. "All right," I heard him
say, but he seemed not to be coming nearer, and so I
left.

I went back to try to find my parents at the Rectory.
Everybody I passed or met, I felt sure, was looking at
me. Everybody *knew*. My parents must surely know. I
saw them talking with Mr. Francis, who was the Vice-
Rector. They all looked very grave. I felt absolutely
sick. "Mr. Francis has been explaining to us about the
summer teaching program," my father said, in his new-

found parent-teacher voice. I stayed with them, silent, fearful. Later, at dinner, the three of us in the little tea-roomy inn, a din of parents, old graduates, boys around us, I longed to tell them of my misfortune, my disgrace, but couldn't bear to. "Is something wrong?" my father asked at some point. "No," I said. "He's probably tired," my mother said. Before going back to my house, my father and I took a short walk down beside the Lower School pond. It was one of the places I'd liked most at St. Paul's. Not a big pond at all, quite gardened and tended-to on the near side, where we were walking; but on the far side, full of coves and inlets, tall wild clumps of rushes, reeds, small swampy places, hidden places. In my Fifth Form year, George Brock and I had kept a small beat-up rowboat hidden there, an old thing that barely floated but that we'd patched up somehow, and spent what had seemed like most of the spring aboard it, fishing late at night, smoking, discussing the true meanings of life, hockey, sex. My father seemed intent on talking to me about a summer job. "I think it's time you began to get into something," he said. And: "Now that you're older . . ." he said. I paced beside him, trying to be manly, glancing out mournfully at the darkened pond. Ah, the simple past! George and I had bought a fishing rod in Concord one afternoon, quite an elaborate, expensive fly-fishing thing, and used to try to instruct each other in the evening, standing knee-deep in mud and swamp, the pond eventually lit only by stars and half a moon, the fly-line whistling, singing above one's head, landing inevitably in trees and bushes, landing in bulrushes, now and then, invisibly, unnoticed, upon the water. "Fantastic, fantastic," George would say. "Don't make a sound for Christ's sakes!" (I never figured out what role silence was supposed to play at those moments.) Now I walked beside this pond, beside my father, feeling him not at all, listening in a way quite placidly to his admonitions about summer work, but with only this one thought in my mind, of Harding's zero. I knew I didn't want to tell my father about it. It wasn't that I was uncertain whether he would understand or not; I didn't even take it that far. I just didn't want to tell him. We walked along. I said I agreed, a summer job would be a good thing. I said I'd thought of trying to get a job as crew aboard Dave Whitney's sloop. "That's not the kind of summer job I had in mind," he said. We talked a bit about the new apartment in New York, about my sister, about my cousin Sarkis who had been visiting, and then said good night in front of the inn. Good night, good night, a light male-to-male brush of the cheek. I went back to my room. My roommates were all up, all very cheery. I went into the bedroom, undressed, got into bed, turned towards the wall, tried all night to sleep.

The next day, graduation in the afternoon—well, the story has a happy ending, this one anyway, although when I look back on it, it all seems foolish, no one comes forth. The Baxter Prize for History. Me. The Rector resplendent as the Pope of Rome upon the platform, two books thrust into my hand. My parents were very pleased. "Interesting books, too," my mother said. Afterwards, Harry Thompson, especially wondrous in his blazer, hair wetted down, huge long arms, inarticulate, introduced me to his parents, then in a wild fit of politesse introduced all his parents and semi-parents to mine. "And this is my mother, and this is Fred White . . . and this is my dad . . . and this is Jane . . ." Jane, the stepmother, an elegant suburban Theda Bara whom I greatly admired for her charm and sophistication, discussed packing and the size of suitcases with my mother. Harry Thompson II clasped my father around the shoulders and looked happy. It was all very gay. The next morning, the cars began to drive up to the dormitories. Some with chauffeurs, mostly not. Harry's father had a big green convertible. A trunk and hockey sticks and records and baseball gloves were loaded in. My mother and father and I went back by train, a nice trip really, we stopped at Boston, had lunch at the Ritz. My father talked about the importance of having a "really good education," and about the Rector, who was always trying to tell him of his deep admiration for the English people. We laughed a lot, the three of us. I remember the thick blue goblets they used as water glasses, and still think of them with pleasure.

It was several more years, well into college, before I

out of it in any strong light, except possibly for old Harding. He'd decided to believe me at any rate—the second exam I'd written had turned out to be more or less exactly like the first. This still left him, and me, with the problem of my having answered a history exam more or less by rote. He gave me a 90, which is what I'd usually had (except for the past two months), and this got me the Baxter Prize. I remember that evening sitting between my mother and father in the study hall, the cavernous Middle School study hall where the prizes were awarded. Row upon row of wooden chairs. Everybody's beautiful parents on either side of me. Masters in their black robes. Some girls. The whole world seemed to have returned to life. My great good friend, Harry Thompson, the wondrous hockey player, sat two rows behind me, between his mother and stepfather, and stepmother and father. His father, Harry Thompson II, had also been a wondrous hockey player, although I gathered that he had been "too light for the Varsity" at Yale. We waved, exchanged cheery greetings between the awards. Charlie Prescott had already received the Gordon medal, which was no surprise to anyone. Dick Vandiver, head of the student council (reportedly so mature that he had to shave twice a day) received the Merrick Prize. Some other prizes. The Charles Henderson Hubbard Prize "for that boy who, in his qualities of sportsmanship, leadership, and school spirit, most resembles the late Charles Henderson Hubbard," and so stopped trying to memorize things, and then it wasn't by any decision, I just stopped. I guess I dimly began to be aware that my mind had a life, an existence of its own. A couple of years ago, though, one of my daughters, who was studying something in school about the War of 1812, asked me a question about the shipping trade between England and the Caribbean colonies, and I found myself answering with a column of statistics, average annual tonnage, molasses, rum, Jamaica, London, Boston, that I remember having memorized in the Fourth Form at St. Paul's, when we studied those things too. But maybe the statistics were wrong, at least I rather hope so; I stopped in mid-sentence anyway, told her I didn't know, that she should look it up. One more small thing: I wrote a story about that incident once, the incident with Harding, the prize, graduation. It was the first story I ever sold, right after college. I had it pretty much the way it all had happened, only in my story (it wasn't much of a story) the boy did manage to tell his father. They walked down along beside the pond, and then he told his father, who was angry at first, for a "brief instant." And then clasped the boy to him. The mother had blond hair, green eyes, and was called Nancy.

MY MOTHER WAS NEVER MUCH
for reminiscing about herself. By which I mean that
Thanksgiving, for example, was never one of those opportunities for everyone to sit around the table singing
and drinking and crying and eating, with the old folk
periodically lurching off into remembrances of bygone
festivities and familial happenings. Now that I think of
it, Thanksgiving in our house wasn't much of an opportunity even for eating, my mother having no use for
turkey, and my father professing not to understand
whether pumpkin pie was a dessert or a vegetable, and
neither of them really caring very much for the holiday
in the first place, which I suspect they observed more in
the spirit of naturalized citizens paying their first taxes
than out of any great desire to connect themselves more

deeply into American mythology. In any case, I hardly ever remember my mother sitting down with us and launching into one of those when-I-was-a-girl or when-I-was-a-boy things that most people, I find, myself very much included, will do at the drop of a child's question. It wasn't that my mother seemed anxious to erase her past, her childhood, to pretend it hadn't existed. To the contrary, in fact. At times, and especially as my sister and I grew older, she seemed quite desperate to convey to us something, if not of her own identity (whatever that may have been), at any rate of the texture of her past life, her own life; as if suspecting that my sister and I, in our all-too-evident attempts to Americanize ourselves, our all-too-evident acquiring of baseball mitts and bobby-sox, were also at the same time trying to erase *her*. She almost never spoke discursively about herself, and usually refused to answer personal questions if pressed—at times with a kind of genuine embarrassment (who would really want to know about *that?*), at times with an equally genuine pride and sense of privacy, let's keep the children out of that room anyway. But every so often she'd throw out clues. One evening I remember my sister muttering random complaints about the amount of homework she had to do, and my mother, more or less in the act of passing through the room, saying "You oughtn't to complain so much about school, I never went to school"—which wasn't exactly fair to the subject of homework, since my mother had certainly had a succession of governesses for most of her life, and had indeed gone to school briefly a couple of times (there had been some sort of "finishing school" in Switzerland when she was seventeen); but it was nonetheless true to her own feelings about it, and in any case was the first time that either my sister or I had been let in to that considerable segment of her life. And then both of us later trying to pursue the subject. Gosh, tell us about all those times you never went to school—and my mother resolutely dismissing the whole business. "Oh, *that!*" she'd say. In this diffident, prideful, hit-and-run way, my mother served up to us selected portions of her past existence, bits and pieces that she doubtless cared about, and which it must have pained her that we couldn't have somehow guessed at. Couldn't have either ignored or known about intuitively. I can't imagine, for example, *her* mother ever having sat down with her and having a serious talk about who *she* was, and where she'd been to, and the fact that my mother now could do it, even to this small degree, with her own children, has come to seem to me rather gallant and adventurous. I knew, for instance, that my mother had once been good at sports, at a time when very few women were, when it was only then being discovered that "sportswoman" was an enhancing adjective, could be a sexy concept—not entirely limited to photographs of Babe Didrikson throwing the javelin at the Olympics. She and I played tennis

a lot in the summers, until I was about sixteen anyway.
She was quite okay too, a lot of very solid low flat base-
line stuff, a lot of running too, a fair backhand, not a
bad serve. (Cautions and bad temper at the net.) Now
and then, apropos of nothing much, she'd toss out clues
about this part of her life—"the summer your uncle and
I played in the doubles tournament at Nice." Or: swim-
ming-between-the-islands. Or: "the winter Lillia got
sick and we had to ski out twenty miles to the
doctor . . ." Then, having placed the object, as it were,
upon the table—not as an ability at something, but as
an indication of a certain point of view, a feel for life—
the object, the clue, would be taken off, brushed to the
floor. I remember one summer afternoon at the Homestead, in Hot Springs—we'd just been playing tennis,
she and I, three sets of singles on a hot afternoon, and
were sitting under one of the elegant umbrellas. The
tennis pro had come by, one of those leathery, wiseguy
club-athletes. Forty-eight-year-old virility. Misplaced
charm. Later she murmured something about Suzanne
Lenglen, the great French player in the twenties, *her* father who used to be the pro at the Carlton, and, as if
forgetting herself, slipped into an account of some
doubles game they'd all played one afternoon in Cannes
—and then stopped. It wasn't a name-dropping story, a
self-advertising story. Anyway she stopped, and then
afterwards when I asked her, quite diplomatically I
thought (I was really interested), about Mlle Lenglen

and tennis and about the tournament in Nice and so forth, she looked at me as if I'd made the whole thing up, and then said, "I don't know, I don't remember."

The one area in my mother's life that I couldn't figure out at all, and used to think about a certain amount as I got older, sixteen, seventeen, was men. I couldn't for the life of me imagine what sort of life with men my mother had had before she was married, what sort of sexual life, what sort of any life. I know she would have been outraged to think that I was thinking about such matters, as indeed she would be outraged now, but the fact is I was, and that was that. I can't say I thought about it very much—considering the amount of time I devoted to thinking about my own sexual life, or lack of it, I didn't have very much time left over for thinking about anyone else's. But one of the things that mystified me was this apparent contrast between my mother's evident sexuality, which seemed so strong and earthy, and the quite girlish ways with which she seemed to clothe *her* sense of her presence in the world of men. To begin with, there hadn't really been men—there had been "beaux." The names of certain men would crop up in conversations. Somebody marrying somebody. Somebody dying, arriving. Somebody glimpsed somewhere. Oh yes, Freddie. He was an old beau. Hugo was once a beau. Henri was a beau. Each time my mother said the word, each time she connected it to one of these invisible men, I had this picture of some Oxford undergraduate, pink blazer, straw boater, strawberry smile, my mother in a kind of 1919 garden-party frock, the two of them strolling-beside-the-Isis, sound of mandolins, pretty, pretty . . . It didn't make any sense to me. It seemed to me that my mother probably wasn't *pretty* in those ways. I didn't know, of course. I didn't know what any of it had been like. My father sometimes referred to women whom he had been "in love with" before he and my mother were married—Nancy Cunard, Marilyn Miller, Louise Carnarvon—and it never occurred to me that any relationship he had had with, say, Marilyn Miller, and which he was agreeable to describing as "love," could have consisted in its entirety of strolling along riverbanks together, or sending her boxes of candy. Besides, there were always the books. You could find out a lot from books. As a kid I can remember reading in some book of literary prattle by Beverly Nichols or somebody about a Christmas party given by my parents in Cannes, and thus finding out that my father was indeed Santa Claus. Or vice versa. A few years later, at school, I can remember reading in a biography of D. H. Lawrence about an "affair" my father had had with Lady So-and-so. Hey, what's an affair? I asked brightly. "It's when two self-indulgent people have an infatuation with one another," said Mr. Waddington, the English master, "and it usually ends badly." So much for affairs. My parents, at any rate, seemed always very much of the flesh, which was less troubling for what I could imagine than for what I couldn't, or could only imagine with difficulty. My mother and her "beaux." Freddie Chatham. In *bed* with Freddie Chatham! The beast with two backs with Freddie Chatham? Old Freddie Chatham. It wasn't just a question of age. "Freddie's in town for a few days," my mother would say. "Such a sweet little man. He's coming for drinks." Could it be possible that my mother and sweet little Freddie Chatham had once made love, had touched, had flown to the moon together in some flat off Chester Square, in a hayfield, in Hampstead Heath, on the back seat of a bicycle, anywhere—instead of just strolling forever arm-in-arm along the banks of the Isis? "Atalanta, so nice to see you," Freddie would say on arrival. "What marvelous *parquet*." Freddie at sixty-three. That drawl. The beautiful smooth cheeks. The beautiful lemon-colored cuffs, which seemed to support the wrist, which barely seemed to support the drink. None of it seemed possible. And so, if not Freddie, who?

ONE SPRING VACATION, down from Harvard, I remember two things happening. To begin with, my sister, in perhaps her strongest bid yet at Americanizing herself, had lately expressed a wish to marry a boy called Leroy Taylor. He really was a boy, about nineteen, and his name really was Leroy, which made it doubly, no triply, difficult. Each time my father would speak his name, which he did with a mixture of consummate politeness and disbelief, my sister would break into tears. He was a nice guy, too, studying "business administration" at Babson, rather tall, and skinny, and hopelessly free from guile (also from some of the harder intelligences). Leroy would come down from Boston on vacations and take my sister to basketball games. The N.C.A.A. championships. After the game, they would come home and play Tony Bennett records, and sometimes sit around the library and engage in conversation with my parents. "Mr. Arlen, did you play basketball in high school?" I remember Leroy asking one evening, and my father replying, in really (for him) a reasonably natural and friendly manner, No, he never had, and Leroy saying something about how he guessed height was an important factor, and standing up to show his comparatively extreme height, and my father looking at him in a strange way and saying, "That's very interesting, Leroy," and my sister saying, "Stop it, both of you," and beginning to cry. Then one weekend she went up to visit Leroy's parents in Providence. Then another weekend. The third weekend she announced she wanted to get married—I was home on vacation and I can remember listening in my room one evening (it was all so loud you didn't have to go down and sit on the stairs) to my mother and sister doing what is known as "thrashing it out," which meant in actual fact that my eighteen-year-old sister was issued a paper sword and a clockwork horse, and my mother sat twelve miles offshore and lobbed heavy shells at her for a couple of hours. At one point, though, in the proceedings, I remember my mother saying, "Have you gone to bed with him?" and my sister saying, all sobs and defenses, no, no, she hadn't. "You *haven't* gone to bed with him?" My mother suddenly surprised, angry. My sister still saying no. You little fool, my mother saying, and then much more—about all the "little girls" and "little boys" who rush into marriage just so they can sleep with each other. It sounds pretty sensible as I write it down here; in fact the logic of it is indeed sensible, as little girls and little boys are maybe finally beginning to find out. But then, that evening, it was really very rough, and, as with many of my mother's rages, it didn't stop anywhere definite, it didn't have any specific destination in mind, the train just kept on going, knocking down women and children and innocent bystanders and sometimes whole villages and railroad stations, until at last it ran out of steam, and drew up quietly some place in the green countryside. In a way, this was the first time that either my sister or I (and I was eavesdropping) had heard my mother express herself about sex. It wasn't really a matter of prudery that had prevented it, at least not the usual sort of prudery. Neither of my parents, for example, had ever made much of a thing about wearing clothes around the house, or not wearing them. But there were just some things you didn't talk to kids

about. Like money, for instance. You didn't pretend that
money didn't exist. You made it damn clear that you
knew that money existed, and was important. But you
didn't talk to kids about it. Kids, the idea was, would
find out about money their own way, and when they
needed to. Sometimes, to be sure, you helped kids a little
to figure things out. Hey, that's no way to use a fish
knife! But most of the time you acted on the premise
that kids would discover and sort things out on their
own, or with their own kind at school, or at any rate
with the help of masters. It wasn't a bad system, as
these things went; at least it was true to the people involved, which is to say that if my mother could barely
bring herself to talk about her tennis playing in public,
or in front of the children, it hardly seemed expectable
that she would conduct earnest informative discussions
about the birds and the bees and the 137 favored Oriental positions. Nor did my father ever discuss sex with
me, my sex life that is, or his, once that I can recall;
there was never any doubt that these areas existed, one
assumed they existed, one just didn't go on about them
at the dinner table, or anywhere else. The trouble with
all this reticence, though, was that when the wall was
finally broken, when the subject finally was broached
—the broaching itself took on a quite excessive significance. For instance, by the time I overheard my
mother telling my sister that she ought to sleep around,
which was my on-the-spot interpretation of what she

had been storming about, I was already spending much of my time swimming in the sort of excessively mental sexual seas that I guess many or most adolescents find themselves roiling around in—and the net effect on me of this overheard outburst was for a time to absolutely rivet my attention, not on Leroy, or my sister, or on what boys and girls ought to be doing, but on what it seemed to reveal about my mother's own life. For days afterwards, all these "beaux" hung suspended before me in a kind of wild erotic focus, even old Freddie Chatham. I found myself looking at my mother across the dinner table with a mixture of admiration and suspicion, and God knows what else. One evening I remember actually trying to steer the conversation around to some weekend long long ago in England, in the early twenties, when (she'd once fleetingly mentioned) she'd gone to a ball at Oxford with some other nameless Freddie. What was it like? I'd ask. Where did you stay? And *then* what did you do?—my mother looking back at me with that vaguely amused, slightly baffled expression, and starting to answer, and then stopping almost in mid-sentence, the vegetables being passed or something like that, stopping, shutting up, nothing more.

INTO THE MIDDLE OF ALL THIS one day appeared Henri Bonnard. Monsieur Henri Bonnard. Dear Henri. One of the most frequently mentioned, and until then most invisible, of the old beaux. My mother and Henri, I understood, had "gone to dances" together in the long ago. My mother and Henri had been on a "ski excursion" in Switzerland. My mother and my uncle and Henri had once spent a weekend shooting in Scotland. I had never seen Henri in my life, had never thought much about him, but suddenly all these remembered sentences, references, these casual one-liner reminiscences that my mother had thrown out at us over the years, started clicking together in my mind. Henri was in town. Henri was due to come for drinks one evening. "For drinks *only?*" I found myself asking my mother. "Unfortunately, yes," she said. "He's very busy. He's only here for a few days." Unfortunately . . . very busy, too busy— I looked at her for stronger signs of disappointment, but found none. As the big evening approached, I looked for deeper indications of tension, excitement, nerves, but still found very little. I observed my father closely. Surely *he* knew—I had inalterably decided by then that Henri Bonnard had been my mother's lover, and felt at the same time very grown up about the knowledge, and protective towards my father (after all, he was the one who had married her), and also vaguely angry at him for risking having this Bonnard person around her again—for not just standing up and saying, Goddamnit, madame, you had your chance with him once, for God's sakes now let him be out of our lives! Something of the sort anyway. During the first part of that week, my mother would come bustling in the door in the late afternoon, back from Bloomingdale's or the hairdresser, at least that was where she said she had been, and I would find myself regarding her as if she were some sort of exotic object, a stranger certainly. She'd be standing four feet away from me, back half turned, putting away her coat in the hall closet. I'd suddenly see her twenty years ago meeting secretly with Henri Bonnard. I would imagine them lying in bed together. An enormous villa just outside Paris. (The set from *Marienbad*, I think.) Rumpled bedclothes. Tearful farewells. Balconies. Alas-I-am-going-to-marry-another. "I thought you were making me a drink," my mother would say. And then on Thursday evening, 6:30 prompt, Monsieur Bonnard, the invisible lover, finally stepped through the doorway in the flesh. "Henri!" my mother greeted him. He kissed her hand. He acted friendly to my father, who acted friendly to him. I watched them all like a hawk. "And so this is young Michael," said Dear-Henri-Monsieur-Bonnard, advancing towards me. I shook his hand gravely. I wasn't going to blow the whole thing by acting like a kid over something that had happened twenty or thirty years ago, especially seeing how suave and cool everyone else seemed to be behaving about it. On the other hand, she *was* my mother, these were my parents—I wasn't going to let any Parisian gunslinger come sidling through the front door and start stirring up trouble in the old homestead. We all sat around in the library and sipped at drinks. I watched Henri closely. In truth, he was a very good-looking man, taller than I'd expected. Over six feet. A nice, quite strong face. Thinning gray hair. Evidently in his early sixties, but with the bearing and physique of a man who once was very good at sports, and still keeps up. I looked at my father. Well under six feet. Decidedly frail. No longer kept up. I glanced over at my mother. She was sitting on the far side of the sofa, listening to Henri. She smoked a cigarette. Henri was telling a story about her friend, Louise Ferande. He had seen her recently in Paris. My mother laughed. My father seemed very calm. I marveled at everyone's restraint, and vowed that when I was older and had marvelous affairs, I too would bring everyone together around drinks or tea or soup and be extraordinarily calm. Now and then, it seemed to me, Henri would look over at me, appearing to catch my eye (not too difficult a feat since most of the time I was staring straight at him), and would give me what in hindsight I would describe as a strange smile. I continued to stare fixedly back. I could be as goddamned sophisticated as all the rest of them, I decided, but I wasn't going to let anyone get away with anything. "How are you getting along at college?" Henri suddenly asked me. "Are you doing as well at your studies as I hear you did at school?" "It's okay," I said stiffly, and took an immense swallow of my drink, which I hadn't especially wanted to have at all just then. Henri went back to talking with my parents. He was in New York briefly "on business." He owned some perfume company, I knew, outside Paris. A fair-sized perfume company. He looked sleek and successful sitting there in his dove-gray suit. I wondered if my mother was secretly regretting not having married him, because of his perfume company. Henri said that after his business meetings he was going up into Canada "to shoot." I wanted to ask, "Shoot what?" —I was actually interested. Henri was leaning back against the sofa, laughing, the three of them now talking about some hunting expedition that he and my mother's brother had been on some while ago. In my mind I was doggedly reviewing the various Canadian animals that Henri could be likely to shoot at this time of year. "Elk," I said suddenly. They all looked at me. Henri's smile remained unchanged. "Do you like to hunt?" he asked. "The boy's never hunted a thing in his life," my mother said. I could have killed her right then. "No, no, I was wondering . . . thinking about what you were going to shoot," I muttered. "Not elk," said Henri, "although sometimes I have shot elk . . ." I wished he would stop smiling at me. I could suddenly see him, in that sleek gray suit, Tyrolean hat, boots, kneeling beside some crag in the Canadian Rockies, rifle braced, telescopic sight in focus, pumping lead into some poor damned antlered elk. Smiling. I looked over at my father. He was sitting in the big green chair he usually sat in, leaning a little forward. He seemed to be staring at the carpet. All this big talk about hunting, I knew, was finally beginning to get him down. After all, it was bad enough having to sit around being restrained and sophisticated while your wife's former lover barges into your house—your wife's six-foot-two, athletic, perfume-company-owning former lover—without having to listen to a lot of aggressive masculine stuff about hunting and shooting into the bargain. Henri turned to me, that smile again. "Sometime, if you like, I'll take you with me on one of these expeditions," he said. "Why, *that's* a nice idea, Henri," my mother said. To me: "I'm sure you'd find it a very broadening experience." I looked back at my father. Smoking a cigarette. Silent. My mother smiling. Henri smiling. Broadening experience, indeed. "Unfortunately, I can't take you this time," Henri was saying. "But next year, maybe . . ." I glared at Henri. "I don't *like* to hunt!" I said suddenly, with lunatic passion. (In fact, I had always wanted to hunt but had never had the opportunity.) "I don't *believe* in hunting! I don't think hunting makes you a better man than—than anyone else!" Silence. "Oh," said Henri finally. "Well, maybe we could do something else . . ." My father got to his feet and offered to make more drinks. Unhappily, said Henri, he had to leave. I felt very proud. My sister came in the front door. Flurry of greetings. Then goodbyes. I hovered solemnly in the background, which seemed all right with everyone else. At the last moment I walked up to Henri, shook hands with my firmest grip. "Goodbye," I said, looking him what I hoped was square in the eye. "Goodbye, Michael," he said. Then he patted me lightly on the shoulder, and smiled. And left. Afterwards, at dinner, my mother and father seemed unusually silent. My sister talked for a while about somebody called Gunther, who I gathered was to be Leroy's replacement. Gunther was currently in his last year at Trinity College, and hoped to make verse drama his career. As we all went out of the dining room, my mother paused, turned to me. "I hope you never act like that again," she said. I looked her, too, square in the eye. I felt very calm, and sure. Paul Henreid singing the Marseillaise in the Casablanca nightclub. Jackboots all around. The inner peace. A-man-must-do-what-he-has-to-do. "Okay," I said diplomatically. I could afford to lose a couple of rounds. I followed them into the library and passed the coffee cups around in a wild transport of familial solidarity.

In the very early 1950's, in 1951 I think, when he was around fifty-five (and I was in my last year at college), something good seemed about to happen to my father. At the time, he really wasn't doing a damned thing except having lunch with people. That table at the King Cole Bar in the St. Regis. Mr. Arler's table. He would arrive there around one o'clock, he said, although actually it was closer to 12:30, and he would leave around 2:30, he said, although actually it was usually after three. Not that it matters. He wasn't doing anything else. And it's probably unfair of me to say that he was only lunching with people; in fact he was talking with people, or to people, and he did that very well. Sometime the people were eminences, distinguished, men who indeed were something in the world, or who had been something in the world. When he was in town in a show, Rex Harrison would come by. Or John O'Hara. Thornton Wilder. Noel Coward. The occasional presence of such people gave "the table" a certain cachet. "The table" would be mentioned in the columns, Leonard Lyons, that sort of thing. But in truth most of the men who joined my father at his lunches were of a different sort, the sleek, rather too affable, rather too easily smiling men-about-New York, men with carefully trimmed fingernails and small public-relations firms, men in charge of advertising at Condé Nast, recently arrived editors at *Time* or *Life*, pleasant men on the whole, of tepid body temperatures, who liked to stand close to something warmer. I used to drop by the table often, at first on vacations from college, then when I was working in New York, and what I mostly remember is this semicircle of perpetually tanned, relentlessly sophisticated, New York-and-I-hope-Southampton-in-the-summer faces, and my father talking, talking, being often amusing, entertaining, being often truly sharp and intelligent, and these faces ringing him around—George and Richard and John and Harry. "*Great* to see you, Michael," George would say, sliding into an empty chair. George in his beautiful gabardine suit, George who commuted to Bermuda, where his wife's family was "active" in real estate, who found the weekly plane trip useful because it allowed him to "keep up with his reading." Also, around the time I'm talking of, 1950, 1951, my father—almost in direct proportion to his own withdrawal from writing—began somehow to fasten on my own slow, amateurish, and really not very promising progress towards it. I knew even then that this was all very understandable and plausible, that no parent is capable of absolute detachment towards the accomplishments of his children. But all the same it used to trouble me that my father should seem so *very* pleased by what I was then doing, by the tiny triumphs I was then managing in the small arenas at Harvard— "the college magazine," "the college musical show." It's not that I myself was especially modest about these things. I felt an enormous glow of pride, pleasure, what-have-you, whenever I got a story into the college maga-zine, which wasn't in the least diminished for me by my knowledge that, on many occasions, I was the only per-son writing for it, and was the editor as well. I realized, too, that fathers were supposed to be pleased by their sons' achievements, or semi-achievements, and I was certainly glad that mine liked what I'd been doing, didn't disapprove, didn't ignore. But it was more than liking, father-taking-an-interest, and it began to seem out of balance and disturbing—something more, or at least different, than a son's usual embarrassment at his father's coming on too strong about his Little League fastball. I didn't even particularly admire my father's work in those days—secretly disapproved of a lot of it in fact, cloaked in my new-found serious Harvard high-

literary standards to the point of being quite agreeable
to sharing with Edmund Wilson, Lionel Trilling, Cyril
Connolly, et al., *their* already published embarrass-
ments at the "excesses" and "modishness" of *The Green
Hat.* But at the same time, I think this is true to say, I
knew damned well he was a real writer. I knew when I
read some of his stories, especially some of the things in
May Fair and *These Charming People*, that there on the
page was a real presence, an energy. Somebody. There
sure as hell was *something* there, something that not
many other men had—I didn't know what it was, and I
didn't even like most of it then, but I knew it was special. *He* was special, in a way that none of the Georges
and Richards and Johns and Harrys seemed able to
comprehend, or at any rate meet, with their thin laughs,
and anecdotes, and endless savviness. And now he
seemed no longer to comprehend it. He seemed to have
let it all go by, as if it had been somebody else all along.
We'd sit around that circular table at the St. Regis—he
talking, conversing, conversing with himself, reminiscing. Set-pieces. The time he and Conrad and Shaw were
on the *Aquitania* together. D. H. Lawrence at the Café
Royale. D. H. Lawrence, Michael? Which Lawrence was
that? Lawrence sketched in five sentences for the benefit
of a cosmetics account executive, who kept inquiring if
Noel Coward was "in town," and looking hopefully
around the room. And then one year, for a couple of
months in that one year, something good seemed about

to happen. It was a television show, the possibility of being a sort of narrator-host on a new "dramatic" series. My mother wrote me about this while I was at college. "Your father is very excited," she said. "He and Mr. Tobin have begun work on an idea for television . . ." I remembered Mr. Tobin slightly, I remembered him in fact as being one of the Georges and Johns and Richards at the St. Regis, a tall, dark-haired, handsome, soft-faced man in his late thirties, vaguely aristocratic good looks, the sort of man who always seemed to be wearing an open-necked silk shirt and an ascot whether he was or not. He'd met my father at a party somewhere, and had started to drop by off and on at the St. Regis. He was a writer. He had written a number of unperformed plays, one gathered, "in the Freddie Lonsdale manner." He was now working on the outskirts of the new television drama programs—and he had this idea for a series. It was to be called *Knaves and Aces*, which still makes me wince as I write it (what would my old companions, Wilson, Trilling, and Connolly, think of *Knaves and Aces?*), and was to be a series of thirty-minute plays; of thirty-minute, elegant-and-sophisticated plays, which my father would introduce from a sort of mock-up of his St. Regis table. Peter Tobin would write the plays. My father would be the front man, the "host." Hosts were very big on television then—Ronald Reagan on G.E. Theatre, Alistair Cooke on Omnibus, etc. One could probably say that *Knaves and Aces* was doomed from the start (although God knows how one could ever be too damned sure about anything on TV being doomed, or not doomed, from the start). Among other reasons, Peter Tobin, a nice man, just wasn't much of a writer—in the sense that it's uphill enough being Freddie Lonsdale himself, let alone writing "in the Freddie Lonsdale manner." But they did one show, and it ran on NBC one evening. My father was pleased as hell about the whole thing, and that's really what I remember. He knew that Peter Tobin wasn't much of a writer, that the whole project was unlikely, an outside chance. But it was as if, for a brief period, he'd woken up, come alive. Again had a connection out into the world. Most of the preparations for that first show took place that December of 1951. "I'm afraid I won't be at the St. Regis today," he'd say. "I have to be at the studio." There were conferences with "wardrobe." Conferences with Tobin. Phone calls with John Gregory, the producer. Tobin was trying to get ready a couple of other plays for the series. One of them, I remember, was about a jewel thief, and had a lot of references to polo and to an elderly female character whose name was Mrs. Bottomley. I remember my father shaking his head over the manuscript and trying to rewrite it. The first episode was shown in January. Everything "live," the way they did it then. My father sitting at this table, very suave, the cigarette holder, the cane, a few well-chosen words, the old storyteller himself—in fact, very pro and not bad at all. The story itself, some damn thing also about jewel thieves, a girl, and a "rich playboy." Grace Kelly, I remember, was the girl—I think this was her first part. She wore a raincoat and looked pretty. I forget who the playboy was, maybe Freddie Lonsdale. And that was it, not too bad, not good enough; and I mention it all here not because the event had some large melodramatic significance in my father's life—you know, the big comeback at the Palace, the old Writer setting his hopes on a great TV success, working his heart out, then having it all fall through. In fact, he was fairly cool about the whole business: interested, hopeful (a bit), but cool, very much the way he was about a lot of things, and I write about it here less for the events involved, whether or not the show was deserving or not, whether or not *Knaves and Aces* would have led to something, than for the recollection of a very brief time, in his mature years and in my semi-adulthood, when I saw him, so to speak, in a kind of *motion;* when I saw him connected, and connecting. "I'm afraid I won't be at the St. Regis today. I have to be at the studio."

THE NEXT TIME I came down from college, March of my senior year, we met once again at the St. Regis. It was fine. He looked very well. John McClain and Hugh Courtland were there. The inevitable George came by, not in a gabardine suit, but wearing dark glasses.

"*Great* to see you, Michael," he said. McClain had just been down to see a Jed Harris play opening in Philadelphia. There was some talk about that. Hugh Courtland was going to Paris. My father asked me to stay on with him after lunch; he had some errands to do, he said. We walked out of the St. Regis down Fifth Avenue. A nice brisk day, sunshine. Not cold. My father now quite short beside me. A dark-blue overcoat. The cane. He had an envelope under his arm. At a street crossing, I spotted the lettering on the envelope. *Esquire*. Had he written something? I asked. In a way, not believing it was possible, believing anything possible. "Oh, it's nothing," he said briskly. "Just a thing." I let the matter drop. We walked on down the sidewalk, went into Cartier's. He had a watch to pick up. On the way out again he said, "*Esquire* is publishing a story of mine." Great, I said, or something like that. I was really very pleased, and felt quite strange. I knew that one of these days he would start again to write, and I felt both gladness and lots of other quite nameless things as well. He handed me the envelope as we walked. I took out the contents, a manuscript. At the top of the page: *The Golden Bridegroom*, by Michael Arlen. I started to read, then stopped. "But this is one you've already done," I said. "Yes," he said. Then: "It was published in England." Then: "I've made a few changes. I think it's jolly good, if you ask me." I didn't read it then because we were walking, put it back in the envelope, returned the enve-

lope to him. I'd already read it, I think in *The Strand*, or
in some similar magazine, one of the scattering of odd-
pieces he'd done before the war. We did some other errands that afternoon, I forget which, something about
shirts at Sulka, a foray into Scribner's. I didn't usually
go shopping with my father, in fact I didn't usually
think of him going shopping. It was very nice. And then
it began to get late. We were on Fifty-second Street and
Fifth. "Let's drop in at '21,'" he said. We went on in,
sat down at one of the small tables downstairs. Mac
Kriendler, one of the owners, came by. "How come you
don't drop in any more?" he asked. "Are you still on the
Coast?" It was about 5:30 then, a nearly spring evening,
nobody much there. My father had a Martini. I would
have liked to have had a beer, but I had a Scotch-and-
soda, feeling that to be more the kind of drink expected
of one in such fancy surroundings. We talked about this-
and-that for a while. College. Some Spaniard that my
sister was threatening to marry. "I don't even believe
he's a real Spaniard," my father said. The manila envelope was lying on the table in front of us. My father
picked up a corner of it, fingered it for a moment. "I was
surprised at how little *dated* this is," he said. "I mean,
some of the references aren't right for today, but the
story itself holds up very well. The character of Pull-
man, for example. I think he comes off very well . . ."
He looked at me. I don't know how I must have seemed
to him. He put his hand on my arm, the way he some-

times did. Sometimes he had the goddamnedest deep brown eyes I've ever seen. "It would be nice to be in print again," he said. And then very quickly: "I heard the most astonishing thing from Hugh . . ." The eyes quite different. Hugh. Some story. A swirl of words. Funny. We stayed a while more, he finished a second drink, and paid. We walked out slowly through the room, which by now was nearly full. Men, women. Talk. Suddenly a voice boomed out: "Michael!" My father stopped. The room seemed quite dark. Over in a far corner sat Hemingway. Unmistakable. The beard. The face. I walked on over, following my father. "Good to see you, Michael," he said with evident feeling. He was apparently being interviewed. "Sit down, sit down," Hemingway kept saying. My father demurred a bit, the interview and all that. Hemingway appeared no longer aware of the newspaperman. We all sat around the small table, and Hemingway and my father talked to each other. I guess I should remember what they said, what who said to whom, but it wasn't like that at all. Mostly I remember a kindness that seemed to exist between the two men, in the resonance of the voices, in the eyes, in the echoes that moved back and forth across the tablecloth. Hemingway himself had recently been having a very rough time. *Across the River and into the Trees.* Bad reviews, a bad press. He'd just been getting over a skin disease. He kept rubbing the side of his face with the flat of his hand. "Those damned doctors," he said. "All that money to fix up one's hide." Then: "I wrote the bloody book for $25,000." Then: "I don't think it's too bloody bad. I could have written five hundred pages just about Cantwell."

"Cantwell is a marvelous character," my father said. "You really did him very well, Ernest."

"They've been tearing it all to pieces," Hemingway said.

"You don't have to worry, Ernest," my father said.

Hemingway asked me briefly about what I was doing. He spoke of his son, Patrick, who was in Africa. John O'Hara. Do you see much of John? They spoke of John O'Hara. Of old friends in Paris and London. Hemingway was hoping to get out to Idaho soon. He had a cabin out near Sun Valley. There was a very real warmth across that table, and I remember Hemingway pleased, my father easeful, a kind of ease I'd rarely seen in him, none of that wit, that dapperness, that St. Regis amusingness. I don't want to make too much of what it was or wasn't. Briefly, I think, for a few moments in the dark of that room, he must have felt himself on hard ground again, known. We finally got up to leave. Lots of handclasping, shoulder clasping. Hemingway so big. My father small, very handsome, not leaning on his cane. "Give my love to Atalanta," Hemingway said. "I will," my father said. "She'd like to see you." Some other men came up. More newspaper people. They were calling him "Papa." "Goodbye, goodbye," Hemingway said. Then: "I still owe you a favor, Michael." A big laugh. "Goodbye, Ernest," my father said. We walked out the door, back down the street. Fifty-second Street. My father was very quiet. The cane tapping on the sidewalk. "What did Mr. Hemingway mean about the favor?" I asked. "Oh that," he said. He laughed. A nice laugh. An old private joke, he said. "One autumn in Paris I introduced Ernest to a girl I was with," he said. "Duff Twysden. Ernest later made that book around her. You know: Lady Brett." We turned on Fifth and headed north, uptown. "At some time or other everybody was in love with Duff Twysden," he said. We walked along beside each other for a while, this short dark man, the cane, the manila envelope under his arm, and then found a taxi close by the Plaza and went home.

Passage to

ARARAT

———

At a particular time in my life, I set out on a voyage to discover for myself what it is to be Armenian. For although I myself am Armenian, or part Armenian, until then I knew nothing about either Armenians or Armenia. That is, almost nothing. My father had been Armenian—a child born of Armenian parents—but he had been brought up in England and educated in English schools. His citizenship had been English and, later, American. More to the point, he seemed to have virtually no connection with Armenia. At home, he never spoke the language. He rarely talked about Armenia. Professionally, he was a writer of romantic novels that were set for the most part in English society, and with hardly more than one or two exceptions he never wrote about Armenia—or Armenians. The exceptions were mainly deprecatory or amusing. One of his lines went "Now who would claim he was an Armenian if he was not?" Indeed, at the age of twenty-one he had changed his name from Dikran Kouyoumjian to Michael Arlen.

My mother (who was American and Greek) sometimes called my father Dikran in private, and this was the only way I knew as a child that he was something other than—or in addition to—English. "It's an Armenian name," she explained to me one long-ago afternoon. For a while, I thought this referred to the kind of name—a private name. I understood that some of my far-off uncles were called Kouyoumjian—an odd and difficult word for a child to scrawl on a thank-you letter. But my father, while he was well disposed toward the uncles, evidently detached himself from the name. Reluctantly, and usually with a grimace, he would tell me again how to spell it. "It's ridiculous and unpronounceable," he once said, and I had reason to agree. For the most part, my father's Armenianness was a hazy and remote matter that rarely intruded into family conversation: a youthful stage of his life that he had apparently long since passed through—had passed through successfully, as if with a school degree—and now there was clearly no point in talking further about it.

It was at an English boarding school, when I was nine, that I first realized that I was myself in any way Armenian —or, at least, half Armenian. Before the Second World War, we lived in Europe—English expatriates in the South of France. But if in those days I thought at all about identity I thought that I was English. *We* were English. We spoke English. We traveled on English passports.

At school, I was assigned to room with a cheerful, tow-headed Scottish boy, MacGregor.

"Are you French, or what?" MacGregor asked me one day.

"Of course I'm not French," I said.

"You have to be French. You live in France."

"I'm English," I said.

"You *can't* be English!" said MacGregor.

The headmaster's wife helped set us straight. We sat at her table in the school dining room—a chill and drafty chamber where ancient uniformed waitresses clattered in with trays of dry toast and sardines, or sometimes baked beans, and on Sundays with silver platters holding pieces of bread covered with gravy. The headmaster's wife was a lady of cultured interests, who was active in the local theater group, and who often discoursed to us on the larger life that she glimpsed through avid reading of the London magazines and sometimes through abrupt, disastrous excursions to audition for historical pageants in the county seat. On this occasion, she announced that she had read somewhere that my father had recently published a new book. I never had much to say to such announcements. I knew that my father "wrote books" in his office, but writing in general, and his in particular, was another subject on which very little family conversation existed or was encouraged. She had not read any of his other novels, she continued, but she was sure they were very interesting. Wasn't *The Green Hat* the famous one? She had heard many good things about it. It must be fascinating, she said, to have a father who was a well-known writer. Did I, too, speak Armenian?

This last question took me by surprise. "No, I don't speak Armenian," I said. I think I added, "I've never heard anyone speak Armenian"—which was true.

"But I know I read somewhere that your father was

Armenian," she said, with a bright smile. "I thought all Armenians spoke Armenian."

Later, in our small room, MacGregor glanced up from the comic he was reading. *"Har-meenian?"* he said. "What kind of sports do they play there?"

"I don't know," I said. "I've never been there. Probably the same sports as here."

"Not cricket," said MacGregor.

"Yes, cricket," I said. "Anyway, I'm English."

"You can't be *English,*" said MacGregor.

At midterm, my father came alone to visit me, arriving in a chauffeur-driven car and carrying a box of chocolates. For the first time in my life, I thought him strange—almost a stranger. I remember looking at him surreptitiously, sneaking glances at his face—looking for what? I don't know. I wanted him to tell me that we were really English, but I didn't know how to ask.

Months later, home on vacation, I asked my mother instead. "Are we Armenian?" I felt that it was a daring question.

"Of course not," she replied, her tone kindly but brisk. "Your father's family have Armenian blood, but he is English and so are you." She showed me his passport.

As time went by, I went to other schools. In fact, as a result of the war, we moved to America, and I became more and more American, finally, at twenty-one, becoming an American citizen. I felt generally American, or perhaps for a while Anglo-American, but, clearly, there was also something missing. Something missing or added. I became conscious of being accompanied by a kind of shadow of "being Armenian," which other people sometimes noticed, or casually commented on, but which my father had said, in effect, did not exist. And so I, too, said that it did not exist.

I remember, as an older boy at school in New Hampshire, watching terrified from a fire escape while a gang of sixteen-year-olds taunted and pushed about one of their classmates, a sallow, spidery boy called Gordon, who was supposedly Jewish. What was I so terrified of, I've later wondered—for it is not an enhancing memory. I think probably this: I had gradually become aware that to be Jewish in certain Anglo-Saxon milieus was to be "different"—that is, to be alien and unprotected—and I knew that I, too, was "different," although I was somewhat protected by the camouflage of an accepted Anglo-American manner. But I felt that it was no more than a camouflage and might disappear any day. I know that as I looked down from that fire escape at poor Gordon, I thought: There but for *them* go *we*. Who were *we*? The truth is that for most of my growing up, and for much of my life, I didn't try very hard to find out. There seemed to be something slightly dangerous or second-rate in being Armenian; otherwise, my father would not have been so determined to move beyond it. And so I took the hint and followed him. Armenians were somebody else.

I remember also, years ago, in New York, around the time of an expected visit from my Uncle Krikor, who lived in Argentina, my father angrily brandishing some recent communication from Buenos Aires—probably a change in plans. "Why can't these Armenians ever do things simply?" he said. And "Now, isn't this just like an Armenian!" Evidently, Uncle Krikor was "just like an Armenian"; my father was something different. And, in fact, when Krikor finally arrived (a short, wiry man, with a definite nose and a face tanned by the Argentine sun) I felt him to be different from my father—darker, somehow more "Eastern"—although actually the two men were of the same size and build, had similar features (except for the Argentine suntan), and spoke impeccable English. At one point, Krikor addressed a few words to me in Armenian, which I naturally couldn't reply to. "Why, you haven't taught the boy any Armenian!" said Krikor, in genial reproof. We were having dinner in Krikor's hotel.

My father in those days had a carefully trimmed mustache and wore a flower in his jacket. "Well, it's an impossible language," he said, scowling.

Krikor smiled good-naturedly. "Ah, Dikran," he said. He was the elder brother.

In all my life, I never heard my father speak a single word of Armenian, unless one counts the occasional times we went to an Armenian restaurant and he would read, with a certain offhand professionalism, from the exotic menu, with its kebabs and dolmas, which, I later found out, were mainly Turkish. On the whole, I met few Armenians in his company, and most of these I thought of as being associated with a particular Armenian restaurant in New York, which we went to *en famille* perhaps once or twice a year. It was called the Golden Horn and was a small place in the West Fifties. Its proprietor was a large, warm-hearted man—Aram Salisian, a former wrestler, as wide as he was tall, with immense, gnarled hands and a square, rough-hewn, kind face, which invariably seemed to be smiling. When we entered, he always embraced my father; I think he was just about the only man I ever saw do so. He bowed to the rest of us. He told me that someday he would teach me how to wrestle.

I liked the Golden Horn, because it was a nice place and because as a family we were generally happy there. I also had a special, secret feeling about it—and still have to this day, although the restaurant itself has disappeared—for it was the only region or territory in which I can recall my father's being at ease with his Armenian identity, even half-way accepting it. "So-and-So was here the other day," I can remember Salisian saying, stopping by our table, rattling off an Armenian name.

"Is that so?" I can hear my father's voice reply. "Well, how is he? Say hello to him from me."

Say hello to him from me. Not what one might describe as reckless bonhomie, but in those rare and periodic moments I believe he showed more affection for his Armenian background—our Armenian background—than most other times that I can remember. Now and then, other guests in the restaurant, or at the bar, would come over to chat for a few minutes. Talk of families, of sons and daughters in school. George, the bartender, I remember, had a son studying with Rudolf Serkin at the Curtis Institute of Music, who later became the pianist Eugene Istomin.

It was a strange and friendly time—strange because the men and women there for the most part looked to me so different, as if they were from another country, and yet for a moment we were part of them, their group, whatever *they* might be. I had a sense of "Armenia" as a fragile network of restaurants inhabited by people who seemed to live elsewhere—in somebody else's country. All that seemed real to me was the affection, the mysterious bond. On the walls of the restaurant, I remember, there were photographs of various Armenians who had "made good." One of them was a picture of my father with William Saroyan, the Armenian-American writer from California, whose plays had been appearing on Broadway and winning prizes. In the photograph, the two men were seated at a table with drinks in front of them, smoking cigarettes, staring rather glassily into the flashbulb—the usual night-club snapshot. It seemed to me a romantic and heroic moment: my father together with Mr. Saroyan. My eyes always turned to it—that glimpse of an Armenian comradeship.

But then after dinner we all walked out of the Golden Horn, saying goodbye to Mr. Salisian, leaving Aram Salisian and his world behind—and were back in our own world. On a few occasions, perhaps encouraged by our moments at the restaurant, I later questioned my father about Armenia,

---

but I tried this rarely, because he so visibly wished not to be connected with the subject—in fact, brushed off such simple questions as I might have put—and because, indeed, I had no strong wish to be connected with it myself. Once, I remember, I asked him to come to the phone to take a call from a Mr. Hagopian, an Armenian professor who wished to discuss a literary project. "Tell him I'm out," my father said coldly. Afterward, I asked him why, for Hagopian and he had clearly never met. "He'll only want to talk about Armenian problems," my father said. "He'll go on for hours. They end up boring you to death." Later, more casually, he said, "They're a sweet people, but you can't let them get too close."

For the most part, I was content to leave things as they were. I was only slightly curious about my Armenian background—or so I thought, although, if I had understood how to acknowledge such matters, I might have known that I was haunted by it. Mostly, I was afraid of it. (What *were* "Armenian problems"? I supposed they must have to do with "Turkish massacres" and "starving Armenians," and such—distant and repellent events that I had vaguely heard about and that obviously had little or nothing to do with us.) What was I afraid of? It's difficult to remember now. Probably of being exposed in some way, or pulled down by the connection: that association of "difference," one's own "difference," with something deeply pejorative, with sin. I can't say that I felt sinful in any explicit sense, but I felt somehow marked—even to the extent, for much of my life, of considering myself unnaturally dark, so that a few years ago I was astonished to hear a skin doctor describe my skin as "light." And in the end (as perhaps in the beginning) I came to hate my father for my fear. It was not the only emotion I felt toward him, for I loved him, too; though he was seldom an emotionally expressive man, I knew, he was kind to me. He was my father. But also I was afraid of him. Something always lay between us—something unspoken and (it seemed) unreachable. We were strangers.

When my father died, nineteen years ago, I felt we were no closer. Even as on his deathbed he talked with me amiably and we held each other's hands. Even as, later, I wrote about him—for I myself had become a writer, although not a novelist, and tried to make a kind of contact with him, and with my mother, by writing about their life together and his career. As I remember, his funeral service was held in a Greek Orthodox church (my mother's church), rather than in an Armenian church. "All his life, he wanted to be free of the Armenians," my mother said. I missed him, although it was a relief to me in some ways that he was gone. Absent. In truth, I dreamed about him often, usually in the same scenario, or in dreams with the same feel to them: a feeling of distance between us. Sometimes he called to me and I couldn't hear what he was saying. Sometimes he merely stood apart—a solitary and somehow disapproving figure. We were still strangers.

BY THE TIME I had turned forty, my mother was dead, too. My own identity as an American seemed to me fairly definite—at least on the surface. I had an American wife and American children—a satisfactory American career and life. Then, one day, out of the blue, I was asked by an Armenian group in New York to come down and give a talk about writing. I was surprised and flattered by the invitation—for my lecture services were not in great demand—and said yes.

I can remember the evening vividly. The talk was given in an auditorium of the Armenian Cathedral, on Second Avenue—a place I had never before visited. The audience sat before me on little chairs—middle-aged Armenian men and women, for the most part, the men generally stocky, the women wearing old-fashioned flowered dresses. What I said was undistinguished, but all of a sudden I myself felt greatly moved. I remember standing at the lectern gazing into the rows of clearly Armenian faces—more Armenians than I had ever before seen together—and experiencing an extraordinary pull. My eyes told me that these people were different from me, but I knew that they were not so different. I didn't know what else I knew.

Afterward, an old gentleman with thick white hair came up to me. "An interesting talk," he said. "Although you didn't mention any Armenian writers. It's too bad we never saw your father here."

"I don't think he thought of himself as Armenian," I said. And as soon as I had said it I realized that it was untrue.

"Of course he was Armenian," said the old man. "You are Armenian. It is not such a strange thing to be Armenian. Come, have some coffee."

I think I thought something like, You can go forward here, or stay where you are. And so I went with him and had some coffee.

Such small beginnings. That evening, for the first time, I met Armenians on my own. Armenian women who laughed and asked too many questions. Thick-chested men who seemed always to have their arms around each other. Too many cups of coffee and small, sweet cakes. I was *there* —wherever *there* was. It was an uncertain beachhead, for I kept fighting off the desire to bolt. Never let them get too close! But I also knew that a corner of some missing piece had briefly become visible.

As I finally made my way toward the door, a voice called out, "You will come back!" I couldn't tell whether it was a statement or a question.

"I will," I said.

The journey had begun.

My wife said, "Did you know that Mt. Ararat was in Armenia?" She had been reading one of my new Armenian books.

I said I knew.

"Do you suppose Noah was an Armenian?"

I said I didn't think it worked that way.

Later, she said, "Tell me about the kings of Nairi."

"I don't know about them," I said.

"It says here they were your ancestors. It says, 'Many years ago, the land of Armenia was ruled over by the kings of Nairi.'"

IT IS POSSIBLE to learn nearly anything from books, except, perhaps, about the kings of Nairi. Kings, indeed! Such roughnecks as inhabited the world then! We are talking of three thousand years ago—maybe more—when the fierce and martial Assyrians clanked about Asia Minor. Five thousand years ago, when civilized life was well under way in Egypt, Babylon, and Sumer, it had also begun to appear— or, at least, leave records of itself—in certain valleys of the vast mountain plateau that stretches from the Russian

Caucasus southward between the Black and Caspian Seas and into what is now eastern Turkey. Even then, this was a land of farms and vineyards and large mineral deposits: a beautiful, remote terrain of fertile valleys and high mountain peaks, all of it, even the flat parts, elevated—much like the American West—with the average height around six thousand feet above sea level. For thousands of years, primitive peoples had lived in the valleys below the great mountains. There they had begun to tend wild vines—the vines that most likely seeded the vines of Babylon and Egypt. They had mined for tin and copper, producing bronze for the Bronze Age and metalwork for Ur of the Chaldees. They had made pottery and evolved striking geometric pottery designs, which showed up as far away as ancient Palestine and Syria. These people were a multitude of tribes, whose stock was mainly Hurrian and Hittite. Many tribes and many kings: the kings of Nairi. In fact, "Nairi" is a word that comes to us from Assyrian records, and it does not mean very much any more. It is only a word, with perhaps rather a sweet sound to it. "Twenty-three kings of the land of Nairi ordered their chariots and warriors to assemble and rose against me for war and battle," wrote a scribe of the Assyrian King Tiglath-pileser I, himself a redoubtable roughneck.

But eventually out of Nairi came the kingdom of Urartu. Now, there is a word without any sweet sound to it. Urartu . . . Ararat. Mt. Ararat, of the Genesis ark story. Later—around 600 B.C.—the Book of Jeremiah speaks of the kingdom of Ararat, as the prophet inveighs against wicked Babylon: "Set ye up a standard in the land, blow the trumpet among the nations against her, call together against her the kingdoms of Ararat, Minni, and Ashchenaz." The Urartians built towns and fortresses. They dug irrigation ditches and constructed large aqueducts. They traded with the Mediterranean communities; not only that, they bestrode one of the great natural trade routes of the world—through the mountain passes of what came to be called the Armenian plateau. The Urartians produced pottery and war chariots and armor. They borrowed cuneiform from the Assyrians, but they evolved their own speech, a descendant of the Hurrian language, which itself was unlike anything else: one of those odd languages that developed (in the remoteness of the mountains) independently of the main language systems.

The growth of Urartu threatened the Assyrians, and so the Assyrians made war on the kingdom—a difficult and essentially unrewarding occupation for the Assyrians, who year after year were compelled to march their army northward great distances into the inhospitable mountains. There is a pair of huge bronze gates now in the British Museum—carted off from an Assyrian city by some enterprising archaeologist—which depict the campaigns of King Shalmaneser III against Aramu, King of Urartu. Since this was Shalmaneser's record of the event, the Assyrians are shown to be ahead, at least to the extent of pictographs displaying burning fortresses and Urartians impaled on stakes. For the most part, the Assyrians and the Urartians fought each other, off and on, for nearly three hundred years—until both states were weakened to the point of extinction. The Assyrians probably went down first, being toppled (shortly before Jeremiah's invocation) by the Medes, and by the "Ashchenaz," who were a wave of one of the first big nomad invasions—that of the vast Asiatic tribe known to later Westerners as the Scythians, and to the Chinese as the Sai-Wang. A few years later, the kingdom of Urartu—itself beset by Medes and Scythians—started to fall apart, too, disintegrating into separate tribes, and soon ceased to exist as a nation.

Some of the tribes that had been part of Urartu remained, and in this war-torn area two new groups also made their presence felt. The smaller of these was the Armen, or Armeni, which, according to Herodotus, had migrated to the area by way of Thrace and Phrygia. The larger, and more advanced, tribe was the Hayasa, which had once been part of an ancient Hittite federation in Asia Minor. This, then, was the point at which the Armenians appeared in history—from a mingling of the Hayasa, the Armen, and the remains of the tribes of Urartu. In fact, traditionally—in their own language—the Armenians refer to themselves as Hai and to their country as Hayastan. According to ancient Armenian legend, Haik, a descendant of Japheth (one of Noah's three sons), rebelled against the Assyrian tyrant Belus some time after the destruction of the Tower of Babel and fled with his family "north to the land of Ararat." Belus went after him, "gathering a great army," and a mighty battle was fought. Haik killed Belus with a lucky arrow, and where Belus died Haik built a village, which he "caused to be named after himself." So much for legends.

The first appearance of the name Armenia is probably in an inscription set up about 520 B.C. by Darius the Great, of Achaemenid Persia, who, on a rock face about five hundred feet above the ancient road from Ecbatana to Babylon, let the world know some of the difficulties he had run into after seizing the Persian throne:

Says Darius the King: While I was at Babylon, these nations revolted against me; namely, Persia, Susa, Media, Assyria, Arminaiya, Parthia, Margiana, Sattagidia, and Sacia.

Says Darius the King: Then Dadarses by name, an Arminaiyan, one of my servants, him I sent to Arminaiya.

I said unto him: Greetings to thee. If a rebel state should not obey me, smite it. Then Dadarses marched. When he reached Arminaiya, the rebels came before him, arraying their battle. Zuzza by name, a village of Arminaiya, there they engaged. The God Ahuramazda brought help to me. My forces entirely defeated the rebel army.

There is a pictograph accompanying the cuneiform: Darius, the stern teacher, stands beside his throne; the nine rebel leaders are ranged before him with ropes around their necks. Further on in the text, there is a reference to "Aracus the Arminaiyan," who is mentioned as "usurper" of no less a place than Babylon itself. "He threw Babylon into revolt," says the Great King crossly, adding, "For which he was punished." One can imagine. Here, then, were the Armenians. Mountain people. Pupils before a stern teacher. They had fought off the Assyrians, and survived the Scythians and Medes. The Persians demanded ten thousand horses a year as tribute. Cavalry was to be the weapon of the future.

I wondered what to make of these my forebears, for it was hard not to have some kind of thought about them, usually self-serving. Were they noble or ignoble? Winners or losers? I thought, What kind of crazy notion was that: Were the kings of Nairi winners or losers? It was all so far away and out of focus. My books showed hazy photographs of excavated jars and helmets from Urartu—immense earthen jars and quaint, pointy helmets. Nairi was a word, Hayasa but a shadow. The Great King Darius (who employed his own artist) came through, somehow, more clearly: an unusually large man for his time, nearly six feet tall, with thick arms and a fiercely staring eye. But it was difficult to glimpse the Armenians: Dadarses, Aracus, and all the rest. Had they always been part of someone else's story? They seemed to swim beneath the surface, far away in eddies of time.

One afternoon, I went to have tea with the white-haired old gentleman I had met at the church. It was in his apartment, on Thirty-third Street near First Avenue—not a fashionable address at first glance. One of those silent streets, with unkempt children fighting noiselessly on the sidewalk, and the dun-colored buildings waiting patiently to be torn down. Fortunately, it was not tea but brandy. We sat in the dark sitting room and discussed the condition of the city, the matter of children, and Armenian affairs. It was a soft time of day. The old gentleman spoke about Armenian music— not the fancy kind that they played in the church but what they played in "the old country." Had I ever heard the sound of the *doudek*? It was a beautiful sound, he said. He got up and went into the next room and came back with a small case. It contained a kind of flute, or reed. "It is best when two people play," he said. "Two *doudeks*. One of them holds a single note. The other plays the song. The song always gets the applause. But to hold the single note is very hard. There is a technique for it."

We sipped at the dark brandy. There were Oriental rugs on the floor. Tinted photographs of red-lipped children on the mantelpiece. A door opened quietly (a door from the outside? from a back room?), and another man entered. He was a cousin, a frail, angular man in his late sixties. He sat beside me on the faded plum-colored couch. The sunlight grew dim outside the windows. We talked some more about music, and about my father.

"Did he enjoy Armenian music?" asked the old gentleman.

"He never listened much to music," I said.

The cousin placed a hand on my arm in a feathery grip and began to talk in an intense, low voice about his family's experiences with the Turks. He described the killing of his father and his elder brother. He described the flight of his mother and his two sisters, one of whom was captured and never heard from again. "I can imagine what happened to her," he said. "The Turks were *fiends*. They knew only how to kill. We Armenians had done nothing to them. Nothing! We were simple, God-fearing people who asked only to be left to our ways. The Turks brutalized us and raped our women." He began to weep.

The old gentleman nodded soberly from across the room. He had the *doudek* on his lap. Everything inside the room was still, and the air felt thick. There were little boxes on every table, every surface. Through the open window came the sound of distant traffic. Buses. A taxi horn. The man on the couch began to speak again, this time more softly—in a kind of croon—about his boyhood, long ago. A village somewhere, the name of it unintelligible. A Turkish village? An Armenian village? He talked of running, fleeing, as a boy, across the desert. Of hiding in a cave for days. There were dead bodies in the cave. A camel driver befriended him and hid him for three weeks—or months. The story was true, I knew—a true and moving story, and one so far beyond my own experience. But I found I wished his arm away from mine, wished away his frail hand, his tears. "My father had committed no crime—can you believe it? He had done nothing wrong." I could believe it. But I wished to be away, and out in the busy street.

Later, I thought, This cannot be Armenia, this cannot be what it is. Tears. Stories of evil times. Dark interiors and the croon of old men. "My father had committed no crime." But he was killed, wasn't he, and his brothers were killed, and his sisters were destroyed, and this old man—this boy—had been made to run and hide and to become small in his fear. What kind of son was that? What kind of father?

I sometimes wondered how I could learn anything about Armenians, or my father—or, indeed, myself—if I could not sit still with them.

Meanwhile, my wife annoyed me by making lists of "famous Armenians": Rouben Mamoulian, the movie director; Aram Khatchaturian, the composer; Garo Yepremian, the football player; Lucine Amara, the opera singer. Did I know that the television actor Mike Connors was an Armenian (né Ohanian)? Did I know that Arlene Francis (née Kazanjian) was an Armenian? Kirk Kerkorian? Charles

Aznavour (Aznourian)? Did I know that the mayor of Waukegan was named Sabonjian?

"Stop it," I said. I knew she was trying to be helpful, but it irritated me. It was like making a list of "famous graduates" of a small, out-of-the-way college. Also, it was such an *Armenian* thing to do. I was in an irritable frame of mind. This was partly because it shamed me that I had been so put off by the two old cousins—particularly by the cousin who spoke about the Turks. The sturdy old fellow with the *doudek* I had liked and felt at ease with, but the one who lamented the destruction of his family by the Turks had put a desire for flight in my bones. I knew that it was wrong of me. I knew that he, of all people, required my sympathy. But I had found it almost physically impossible to keep my arm under his hand, and myself seated beside him listening to his voice.

What had been so hard about it? At first, I thought that I had been too repelled by his tale of misery—that the details of his tragedy, as of a friend's car accident or operation, had been too rich to stomach. But as soon as I thought this I knew that it was not so. I had never been squeamish about such things, and certainly not as a result of an old man's lamentations. I realized that, instead, I was still possessed by a kind of fear. For later, walking hurriedly away from that apartment on Thirty-third Street, I had said to myself, "I know that somewhere there exists a different type of Armenian, a prosperous, vigorous, robust type of Armenian, who does not live in dark rooms and weep about the past." I had even formed the phrase "prosperous, vigorous, robust" in my mind. And afterward, when I remembered the phrase, it embarrassed me, for the feelings I seemed to express within my head were so unaccepting that I doubted whether I could ever get close to Armenians. The old cousin's words continued to stick in my mind. "My father had committed no crime . . . had done nothing wrong," he had said, and he had added, "Yet the Turks destroyed us!" As I thought about it, there seemed to be something terrible buried in that admission, although whether the negative electrical charge I felt lay in the statement or in me I couldn't tell. Only that I hated it.

Around this time, I went to a different kind of Armenian event: a concert at the Armenian Cathedral—a recital at which perhaps a half-dozen Armenian musicians performed on the piano and the violin and the cello. The musicians all seemed serious and quite youthful, and the music was good. The audience was very dressy, and I was immediately conscious of being in the presence of many prosperous and vigorous (and doubtless robust) Armenians. Indeed, some of them barely seemed Armenian—except, of course, that they were unmistakably Armenian. During the intermission, I had a drink with two brothers, both in their forties, who apparently owned a large amount of property somewhere in New Jersey and were about to erect a "total-living complex" for thousands of families. Both men had wonderful mustaches and thick, heavy faces, and unlikely, flouncy-frilly blue shirts. They spoke in a kind of duet about property values and interest rates—serious men with booming laughs, if such a thing is possible. "Were these the kings of Nairi?" I asked myself.

After the concert, a number of us went to the apartment of another man, called Bud—also Armenian. It was a fine apartment uptown in the East Seventies, with a view of Central Park. The rooms were carefully strewn with a variety of Chinese objects—vases, screens, and such. There were several drawings by Rodin and Braque and others hanging in the foyer, which had an imitation-marble floor. We sat in a row on a long leather sofa, or else stood by the large windows and looked down upon the lamplit park. Our host's wife, a handsome Armenian woman wearing mandarin pajamas, brought around liqueurs.

"How does your name happen to be Bud?" I asked the host, for I was interested in the provenance of names.

"Actually, my real name is Yeprad, which means Euphrates," he said, "but everyone calls me Bud."

We all trooped in to see the new glass table in the dining room, which had been mounted on a piece of driftwood brought back from the Bahamas.

"How is business?" I asked Bud, for it certainly seemed to be good.

"It's very good," he said. "I deal mainly in copper, and, as you know, the price of copper is up."

We shuffled along quietly on thick carpets. A large hanging carpet with a lion design had been recently brought back from Ethiopia. Several of the guests were drinking Japanese beer.

"Would you like to see a painting I have of Mt. Ararat?" asked Bud.

I said I would.

We went into a small room off the kitchen—a maid's room that had been converted into a utility room but seemed to be rarely used. A pile of women's dresses was on a narrow bed. A sewing machine stood open on a table. On the far wall, between a watercolor of some sailboats and a child's drawing of a horse, there hung an oil painting of Mt. Ararat. It was executed, on the whole, in a modernist fashion: the mountain was a deep red, the sky was a shade of yellow; in fact, it looked rather Polynesian. We stood together admiring the painting.

"The truth is I am not very active in Armenian matters," said Bud. "That is, I am not as active as I should be."

I said, "I saw in the concert program that you're on numerous Armenian boards. Also, you were at the concert."

"Yes, I know," he said. "But I am not involved the way my parents were."

It was a thoughtful moment. I did not know what else to say.

"But look here," said Bud, brightening. "I have some Armenian books." He bent down beside a small bookcase in a corner containing a variety of books, many of which were paperback or Modern Library editions and looked as if they might have been bought at college. He held up three larger volumes, two of which I recognized, for I had recently purchased them myself: a standard Armenian history text, and an account of the Turkish massacres entitled *Armenia: The Case for a Forgotten Genocide;* the third was a travel book.

"Have you read this one?" I asked, pointing to the book about the massacres. I had opened it a few days earlier and, alternately repelled and fascinated by the photographs, had soon put it down.

Bud examined the outside of the book cautiously. "No, I've read enough about the Turks," he said. "I'm not interested any more in that business with the Turks."

One of the New Jersey real-estate brothers came into the room and caught sight of the book we were examining—or, rather, not examining. "What's this?" he said sternly, but with the same booming effect. "What do you read this for? Haven't you read enough of such things?" He seemed to be laughing and scowling at the same time.

"Yes, it's all ancient history," said Bud.

"We're Americans," said the man from New Jersey. "I was in the war."

"Aram was in Korea," Bud told me. "Did you know there were Turks on our side in Korea?"

"I have no quarrel with the Turks," said the New Jersey American called Aram. "The Turks are my brothers. I embrace the Turks!" He looked at me. "Are not all men my brothers?"

"Yes, they are," I said.

He put his arm around my shoulder. "I tell you, there is no point in raking over the past."

Later, back in the living room, I asked Bud where his parents had come from.

"Fresno, California," he said. "The San Joaquin Valley. There were many Armenians there, did you know? They came from the old country." He sighed. "It's beautiful in that valley. But I have not been back there in a long time. Many years."

"Where in the old country?" I asked.

Bud looked vague, almost amused. "Oh, it was one of those small villages in the mountains," he said.

Just then, his wife, the handsome woman in the Chinese pajamas, paused on her way through the room. She glanced at her husband with a small smile—a passing look that seemed to come from somewhere else—and for a second even her chinoiserie appeared to vanish or recede. "But, Yep," she said (it must have been short for Yeprad), "you know it was Mirash, about twenty miles from Bitlis."

"That's it," said Bud briskly. "Near Bitlis. In the old country." He got to his feet—a short, energetic man in his early fifties, with only slightly graying hair and a fine suntan. He grinned. He was clearly a hospitable man. "Come on, let's feed the tropical fish," he said.

I knew I should begin to read some of the "difficult" books about the Armenians—namely, the post–First World War literature on the massacres—but I found it hard to do so. It wasn't a *simple* reaction—that of not wanting to read about dreadful things, or not wanting to read about Armenians' being mistreated. At least, I told myself it wasn't that, for I felt that by then I had surely read of enough atrocities (as had most citizens of this century), enough "case histories" of pain administered and people broken— in this fashion or in that fashion, in this country or in that country—so that there could be little reason now for me suddenly to be unable to confront what the Turks had once done to the Armenians. Still, there was something about these books—buried within these stories—that bothered me inside where I had not been bothered before: something more complicated than moral nausea, more troubling than a voyeuristic shudder.

Now and then, in the evening, my wife would peer into one of my Armenian books and call out to me across the room, "My God! You won't believe how awful it was!" Then she would show me, or leave for me to read, an account of one or another dreadful happening. I remember one such passage in particular. It was an account of an Armenian priest and two Armenian schoolteachers who had been seized in their village by the Turks in 1915. The Turkish gendarmes had handed the Armenians over to a Turkish mob. The priest had been tied to a chair, and then the hair on his head and the hair of his beard had been pulled out. Then his ears had been sliced off. Then his nose. Then his eyes had been gouged out. Nails had been driven into the schoolteachers' hands and feet, as on a crucifix, and then into their heads. The account described the "hideous anguish" and "unholy screams" of the victims. As I read, I could feel my stomach churn at the physical aspect of the atrocities. But I felt something else churning inside me as well. For there seemed to be a voice behind that terrible tale which I could abide even less than the event described. Was it the voice of "hideous anguish" and "unholy screams"? Was it a more general and pervasive voice—a voice that seemed to run as an undercurrent through much of the writing about these massacres? It was hard to tell, but it made me want to weep and also to throw the book aside, away.

I remember that my wife asked me afterward, "Wasn't it terrible, what they did?"

And I felt so angry that I could hardly speak.

She saw my mood and quickly said, "Oh, I'm so sorry. Of course, they're your people."

But inside me I knew I was not angry then at the Turks—not mainly so—or, certainly, at her. I was angry at something else. But at what? It was a mystery.

AND so I continued to read about the Armenian past —the faraway, historical past.

For example, Xenophon's *Anabasis,* which I had read thirty years before in school without noticing that much of the retreat of the Ten Thousand took place through the Armenian high country.

"They formed up together about midday and marched through Armenia [wrote Xenophon], all plain and little smooth hills. . . . This district was called Southern Armenia. The Lieutenant Governor was named Tiribazos [an Armenian, who was the King of Persia's friend] and it was his right to mount the king on horseback when he was present. . . .

"A north wind blew in their faces, parching everything and freezing the men. . . . The snow was one fathom deep, so that many animals and slaves were lost, and soldiers too, numbering about thirty. . . .

"Xenophon . . . begged them with prayer and entreaties not to fall behind . . . but they asked him to cut their throats, march they could not. . . . It was dark now and the enemy were following in confusion and quarreling over what they had. Then the rear guard [of the Hellenes] shouted as loudly as they might and banged spears against their shields."

After dodging Tiribazos and his men, the Greeks finally

descended into a warmer valley, filled with friendly Armenian villages.

"The people never let them go without offering them a feast. Everywhere on the same table there were piles of lamb, kid, pork, veal, fowl, with all manner of cakes, both wheaten and barley. . . . They found Cheirisophos and his men in their quarters, garlanded with crowns of straw and served by Armenian boys in their native costume. [Cheirisophos and Xenophon] together asked the headman, through the interpreter, who spoke Persian, which country this was. He said, The land of Armenia. They asked him for whom he was breeding the colts. He replied, They are tribute for the king. The neighboring country, he said, was the land of the Chalybeans, and pointed where the road lay."

There was something very moving in that ancient and human narrative, with its account of the dreadful march through the mountains. Tough Greek veterans, in their desert sandals, begging their commander to slit their throats in the snow! And on the rocks behind them and above them the Armenians following, a bit like Indians. Then, down in the valley, the Greeks and the Armenians had briefly come together. Sea people, inheritors of Crete, exchanging wary toasts with mountain people, inheritors of Urartu. "Cheirisophos and his men . . . garlanded with crowns of straw." Such brutal, fairy-tale times!

It seemed to me wonderful that the Armenians, *we* Armenians, should have such an ancient and textured history. Not always a glorious and victorious one, mind you. That was too much to expect of a small nation placed by God and geography on the outskirts of the world's great central empires. But clearly the Armenians had not been entirely *ignored* by large events or important empires. First, the Persians, with their ponderous palaces and their almighty god, Ahura Mazda. Compared to other nations then, Armenia was a territory of substantial size. Not only that—it was a strategic terrain, for the Armenian plateau took the shape of a kind of citadel; topographically, Armenia looked down upon the great and busy nations of the lowlands. The Persians left a local man in charge of this northern province—usually a powerful Armenian chief or landowner, whom they called satrap—and, for the most part, kept their distance, except for putting down an occasional rebellion or engaging in a religious persecution or two. And except for the horses.

In the time of Xerxes, as many as twenty-five thousand horses were sent down from Armenia to Persia every year, and in later periods the number doubled and redoubled. Twenty-five thousand horses—a considerable herd. The Armenian plateau, it turned out (in yet another parallel with the American West), was an unusually fine place to raise good horses, for the short, stubby, seemingly dry grasses were immensely rich in protein, and the high-altitude air produced a type of animal possessing exceptional speed and stamina—ideal for cavalry. Imagine a "drive" of twenty-five thousand yearlings from Armenia five hundred miles to Ecbatana!

These early Persians had such great dreams of a coherent empire. They dreamed of cavalry, the unbeatable war machine, before anyone had invented stirrups. They dreamed of a trade-and-communications network before anyone had much to trade or communicate, and so built roads westward across Asia Minor and north into Armenia. Old Darius himself always kept an eye to the north, and toward the end of his long reign—he was then an aging Persian autocrat tinkering with erratic notions of religious freedom as well as with early concepts of highway design—dispatched a military expedition into Armenia, through Armenia, through the Caucasus, and out into the Eurasian steppe, where, finding nothing, it eventually turned back. What were they looking for, these Persians standing around in the middle of the deserted Ukraine at the start of the fifth century B.C.? Darius never said.

The Persians had noticed Armenia because of its strategic position as a defense against the Scythians and because of its horses. The Greeks soon noticed it for the same reasons, and because of trade, since a natural passageway existed through the valleys and icy mountains of Armenia which connected the Eastern world with the Mediterranean and Greek world. The Urartians had sensed the possibilities of this northern route. The Persians had kept their eyes on it, though they were more interested in tribute than in commerce. Now came the enterprising Greeks. Greek trading settlements and Greek culture spread all across eastern Asia Minor and, according to Pliny, "right up to the borders of mountainous Armenia." The Seleucid governor Patrocles traveled in person to Armenia, with a corps of engineers, to see if a canal could be dug to link the Black Sea with the Caspian Sea, three hundred miles away. He decided that it couldn't.

After the Greeks came the Romans. For the most part, the Greeks, like the Persians, had let the Armenians pretty much rule themselves. Now, with the rise of Rome, as the competing powers pushed and shoved each other across Asia Minor, the Armenians declared themselves independent, grabbed off some land from the long-downtrodden Medes, and announced that their satraps were now kings. One of the first of these, King Artaxias I, determined to erect a proper capital, which he called Artaxata—"the joy of Artaxias." It was laid out on the great green plain of Ararat by no less a surprise city planner than the retired Carthaginian general Hannibal. Plutarch wrote some years afterward, "Hannibal the Carthaginian, after the defeat of Antiochus by the Romans, coming to Artaxias, King of Armenia . . . observing the great natural capacities and pleasantness of the site, then lying unoccupied and neglected, drew a model of a city for it. . . . At which the King, being pleased, and desiring him to oversee the work, erected a large and stately city." Juvenal, the Roman satirist, later spoke of "the dissident morals of Artaxata," which is an intriguing notion.

For a while, the Romans and the Armenians maintained

a distant, amicable—or, at least, standoffish—relationship, but it wasn't likely that the Romans would ignore forever the strange lights of Artaxata winking away into the darkness on the periphery of the civilized world. For one thing, by the first century B.C. the Romans had become engaged in what would be one of history's most endless and pointless rivalries—that with Parthia, an Iranian federation, which had replaced the Achaemenid empire—and were therefore continually made aware of the strategic factor of Armenia. For another, the Romans, ever businesslike, were attracted to the possibilities of East-West trade, and, what with southeastern Asia Minor generally in turmoil, they became increasingly interested in the Armenian trade route. At one point, the Roman Senate sent the great general Pompey off to Armenia to chart a better passageway to India. Pompey traveled around Armenia and the Caucasus for a while, presumably trying to imagine a Roman thoroughfare through the Hindu Kush, and then recommended much the same route that already existed—except for the addition of a road to Trebizond (where Xenophon and his men had reached the sea), which was later built by Roman engineers. Like it or not, the Armenians were getting—or finding themselves —*involved*.

THERE IS ALSO the story of Tigran II of Armenia, known to Armenians as Tigran the Great. Tigran was a descendant of King Artaxias and became king of Armenia in 95 B.C., at a time when Rome was occupied elsewhere. He succeeded his father, Artavazd I, after paying a ransom of "seventy valleys" to the powerful Parthians, who had held him hostage for several years. Then Tigran murdered a neighboring Armenian prince and took over his territory. He next made an alliance with Mithridates, a warrior king who ruled the nearby country of Pontus, and married Mithridates' daughter Cleopatra (a different Cleopatra). In the name of his father-in-law, Tigran invaded the sizable kingdom of Cappadocia. The Roman general Sulla was called in and threw him out, but Tigran nevertheless went on to invade Parthia, where he got back his seventy valleys, and overran four Parthian vassal states. Having avenged himself against his former captors, he marched his army as far as the kingdom of Cilicia, which bordered the Mediterranean. He advanced into Syria and was presented with the Seleucid crown. Finally, he invaded Cappadocia again, this time successfully. By the year 70 B.C., Tigran of Armenia was the most powerful ruler in western Asia. The "Armenian empire" extended from the Ararat Valley, in the north, to the Mediterranean, in the south, and as far as Tyre, on the formerly Phoenician coast. Tigran called himself "King of Kings" and decreed that a new and greater Armenian capital should be built near the headwaters of the river Tigris, in central Asia Minor. Ah, Tigran! What a ferocious and unlovely old roughneck he must have been! Nor were his imperial pretensions without a certain dreadful style. It was his ambition to Hellenize his rougher countrymen, by colo-

nizing the wild mountain lands of Armenia with settlements of cultivated Greeks. Alas, few cultivated Greeks
wished to move into the mountains of Armenia—not even to
Tigranocerta, the fine new city that Tigran was building on
their southern edge. Tigran marched them there anyway:
about three hundred thousand Greek prisoners from Cappadocia and Cilicia packed overland to the still building
capital. A few came willingly: Amphicrates, an Athenian
writer; also Metrodorus of Scepsis, who became a kind of
resident historian to the monarch. The Roman writer Ap-
pian described Tigranocerta as "surrounded by a wall fifty
cubits high, the base of which was full of stables," and he
noted, "In the suburbs he built a palace and laid out large
parks, hunting grounds, and lakes." A band of Greek actors
(they were also prisoners) was in residence, preparing an
entertainment for the inauguration of a new theater. Unfortunately, just before that happy event, the Romans arrived.
The Greek geographer Strabo wrote, "Lucullus, who had
waged war against Mithridates, arrived before Tigran had
completed his undertaking, and not only dismissed the
inhabitants to their several homelands but also attacked and
utterly demolished the city, which was still only half
finished, leaving a small village in its place."

Poor Tigran! But he did not give up so easily. He and
Mithridates tried to drive off the Romans. When that didn't
work, he seems to have turned on his father-in-law and erst-
while ally and attempted to have him murdered. Finally, a
unique combination of Romans and Parthians subdued

Tigran sufficiently for him to surrender to Pompey, who had taken over from Lucullus. According to Plutarch, the Roman general received Tigran graciously, and allowed him to keep what little kingdom he had left, asking only that he pay a "fine" of six thousand talents. Then the old king went back north to Armenia—the original, unexpanded, unimperial Armenia—where he ruled for ten more years as a sort of vassal of the Romans, and in 55 B.C., at the age of eighty-five and dotty, he died in his sleep in Artaxata. Doubtless the quiet sleep of ferocious old men.

Tigran, our national hero! Tigran the Great! Presumably every nation must have its own Napoleon—one of those fascinating egomaniacs, with their *gloire,* and *Blitzkrieg* empires, and dead bodies all the way back from Moscow or Cappadocia—and perhaps it is better to have one fading in the scrapbook from two thousand years ago than pinkly smiling from the turret of a tank. I think with surprise, My father's name was Tigran—for surely that is a transliteration of Dikran, his first name and a common name among Armenians. Tigran smiling from the turret of a tank! Tigran among the nightingales! Ah, but I feel there was something about that old Tigran—perhaps such *ungentleness.*

Fresno, California: *"Fresno"* is a Spanish word meaning "ash tree." There are still some ash trees here, scattered far out of town, but the Spanish influence, as they call it, is pretty well gone by now, unless you count the roadside Margarita places and Taco Pete's. The Armenian presence is a little more visible, but not much. There are two Armenian churches. An Armenian bakery. Two or three Armenian restaurants. There used to be an Armenian community—"Armenian Town"—but it has largely disappeared, torn up to make way for the new expressway and the shopping center. There is a Basque presence, also an Italian presence, and a Japanese presence, but mainly a Wasp presence, for this is a California town, a micro-city. "Fresno: Pop. 180,000," say the big green signs. What is going on here is agribusiness, which means the great earth factory of the San Joaquin Valley: untold acres of farmland, fruitland, vineland. Trees and vines and pastureland extending for miles between the invisible Pacific and the dimly visible Sierra: snowcapped blue mountains seen through a bluish haze. Over on the coast is Monterey—John Steinbeck's Cannery Row and Tortilla Flat. Here was William Saroyan's hot, flat valley filled with fruit and crops and poverty and life. "A man could walk four or five miles in any direction from the heart of our city and see our streets dwindle to land and weeds," Saroyan wrote in the nineteen-thirties. "In many places the land would be vineyard and orchard land, but in most places it would be desert land and the weeds would be the strong dry weeds of deserts. . . . Our trees were not yet tall enough to make much shade, and we had planted a number of kinds of trees we ought not to have planted because they were of weak stuff and would never live a century, but we had made a pretty good beginning. Our cemeteries were few and the graves in them were few. We had buried no great men because we hadn't had time to produce any great men, we had been too busy trying to get water into the desert." I don't know what I expected it to be like now. I know not like that, because nothing is like that any more—certainly not in California. I think I expected to see Armenian faces at the airport or on the street. I think I expected to walk off the plane and see Armenians hanging around the car-rental counters, behind the car-rental counters. Armenians—for it was our town, wasn't it?

I stood one afternoon in a field on the outskirts of the city and looked at the fruit trees, which were bare in the March wind, and looked at the grapevines, which were also bare—brown tendrils close to the brown soil, stretching out to the horizon as far as the eye could see. The man who owned the field was an Armenian named Gadalian. He had thick, graying hair and a wide, leathery face and thick hands. He was about fifty years old, but an outdoor fifty—square shoulders and a large, tough belly. He was worrying about frost. "The frost is strange here," he said. "It comes in waves across the valley. In one place there may be frost, but on the farm across the road there may be no frost. Look at this." He held up a grapevine that had been bent or broken around another vine. "Nobody knows how to work the vines any more," he said. It was a modest farm, about eighty acres. There was a comfortable small farmhouse on the edge of the property, just off the dirt road, with grapefruit trees in the front and a kennel for two or three large dogs in the back. We were standing next to a ramshackle old house or hut of dark redwood, weathered by rain and sun—a place for tools and empty boxes. "My father lived here," said Gadalian, pointing inside. "This is where we grew up. He was a good man, my father. He worked very hard."

My father committed no crime. The bare trees stretch out everywhere. Bare branches against the metallic gray sky. Plums. Peaches. Apples. Grapefruit. Grapes. Fertility. The bluish mountains swim in haze against the sky.

"Did you know the Armenians brought the melons to California?" said Gadalian. "The melon they call the Persian melon. The casaba melon, whose seeds come from Kasaba, in Turkey. Most of the melons in this valley were grown by Arakelian. They called old Arakelian the Melon King."

"Where is he?" I asked.

"He is dead, I think. Anyway, his sons have moved to Los Angeles."

"Are there many Armenians here?" I asked.

"There are some," he said. "There are not too many any more."

We stood beside stacks of empty raisin crates. Old boxes, weathered like the hut.

"Look at this one," said Gadalian, pointing to a box so old that its sides had started to split apart. "This one goes back to my father's time. Look at the way they made the corners."

"How is it your father came here?" I asked.

"I don't know," said Gadalian. Then, "I think he and my mother came from the old country around 1900, some time like that. For a while, they were in the East, around Worcester, Massachusetts. They worked in the shoe factories. There were a number of Armenians who worked in the shoe factories. Then they heard about California, where they could grow things."

"Was your father happy here?" I asked.

Gadalian seemed puzzled. "I don't know," he said. "It is hard to tell if a father is happy." Then, "He worked very hard. I remember that."

Little farms scattered around the great valley. These were some of the names on mailboxes: Pirogian, Kavanessian, Agajanian. A sign on an abandoned warehouse: "SIMOJIAN RAISINS, THE FINEST IN THE WORLD." I thought of Bud and his tropical fish in New York. I thought of my father, who had journeyed to Hollywood a number of times in his career but never to Fresno. What was here in Fresno? What had been here?

I thought of the simple warmth of a Saroyan story: "Walking along Alvin Street he felt glad to be home again. Everything was fine, common and good, the smell of earth, cooking suppers, smoke, the rich summer air of the valley full of plant growth, grapes growing, peaches ripening, and the oleander bush swooning with sweetness, the same as ever. . . . This valley, he thought, all this country between the mountains, is mine, home to me, the place I dream about, and everything is the same."

I thought, too, of what a friend of Gadalian's had said when I asked him where most of the Armenians in Fresno lived.

"Oh, now they can live anywhere," he said.

"What do you mean, anywhere?"

"There are no more restrictions," he said. "Before, it wasn't always so easy. Of course, you have to understand that a lot of the first Armenians here were country people. Farmers. Rough people." He smiled. He had enormous hands, fingers as thick as roots, palms caked with dirt. "They took away the restrictions at the end of the war," he said. And "This valley is my home. It's the place I dream about." Sometimes the dreams of people make one gasp.

AND NOW William Saroyan himself, standing in the lobby of the Fresno Hilton. William Saroyan at sixty-six. The hair thick but graying. A burly man. Stocky. A fine mustache. Also large hands. A laugh. Good eyes, a good face.

"I was out in the country," I said.

"It's beautiful, isn't it? You should come back in the summer," said Saroyan. "Of course, it is terrible in the summer. You sweat all day long. But then everybody is busy."

We drove through side streets, past the sterile glass office buildings of the new downtown, past the immense modern convention center. "Everything has changed," said Saroyan. "But of course it has changed. Look at that shopping center. Nobody comes to it. Do you see that street? I used to deliver papers up and down that street. It was a good job, too. The paper was called the Fresno *Republican,* and it was edited and published by Mr. Chester Rowell. Both are gone now, though there's a statue of the paper's founder in Courthouse Square."

We drove under a viaduct over which the new expressway was being built. The land ahead of us was mostly desolate from the bulldozers, but here and there a few small frame houses remained. "I'd show you where I grew up, but they tore that down, too," said Saroyan. "I hope for their sake more people use the new expressway than use the shopping center."

"There don't seem to be very many Armenians around," I said.

"There are still a few," said Saroyan. "Maybe ten thousand in the valley. But the town has grown, and the Armenians sold their land and moved to the cities."

"What about you?" I asked.

"I got tired of knocking around too much. One day, I decided to come back. Once you like a place, you always like it."

We drove away from the little streets and little houses, and out past the familiar landmarks of modern California: the endless strip of car lots and Mexican restaurants and bowling alleys and garden-supply stores and farm-hardware warehouses and motels with banquet and convention facilities.

I thought of a story of Saroyan's that I'd read long ago, which began, "I don't suppose you ever saw a two-hundred-and-fifty-pound Filipino." It's hard to forget a story that begins that way. I had read that story in school, when my favorite writers were Ernest Hemingway, Robert Benchley, and William Saroyan: Hemingway because he was so sexy with those sleeping bags; Benchley because he was so funny; and Saroyan because nobody could write to a person (me) the way that William Saroyan wrote.

There was another story, which I'd read on the plane to California—a story called "Five Ripe Pears." It began like this: "If old man Pollard is still alive I hope he reads this because I want him to know I am not a thief and never have been. Instead of making up a lie, which I could have done, I told the truth, and got a licking. I don't care about the licking because I got a lot of them in grammar school. . . . The licking Mr. Pollard gave me I didn't deserve, and I hope he reads this because I am going to tell him why. I couldn't tell him that day because I didn't know how to explain what I knew. . . . It was about spring pears." It was not an important story, but it was a lovely story—a story with a voice. It made one think with a kind of pleasure that J. D. Salinger must have heard that voice, and Richard Brautigan, and Jack Kerouac, and all those writers of the personal sound, the flower-writers, the writers of our modern Era of Feeling.

"I'm glad you decided to find out about Armenians," said Saroyan. "They're a crazy people, you know. Or sometimes they seem that way. But they're a very simple people."

We drove on awhile. Saroyan talked about his children—a daughter in New York, a son in San Francisco. Family talk. He asked me about my wife and children, about my sister, about my work. I felt something surprisingly paternal in his voice. It was a strange, deep feeling, as if we had known each other all along, when in fact I had met Saroyan only once before, briefly, a few years ago in New York, and had called him in Fresno only a week earlier to arrange our meeting.

We stopped to have dinner at a roadside restaurant, a roadside Armenian restaurant called Stanley's. A nice place, too, with bright lights and the ubiquitous Olde Steake House furniture and a photograph of Mt. Ararat behind the cashier's desk.

"Sometime I hope you'll meet my Uncle Aram," said Saroyan. "He's eighty-two now, and a fine man. I've written a lot of stories about Aram. People would ask me, 'Are they true stories?' I'd always reply, 'Of course not. I am a writer. I make things up. I embellish.' But it's been hard to embellish Aram."

Saroyan began to tell some stories about his Uncle Aram in a loud, resonant voice. The waiter brought some Armenian bread and a bottle of wine, then shish kebab. Saroyan laughed as he spoke. I looked at him and thought, My father was sixty when he died; he would be seventy-nine now. I thought of my father's frailness, his thin elegance; it seemed like such a different presence.

"You know, your father was a fine man," Saroyan said, as if he were reading my mind.

"Did you think of him as an Armenian?" I asked.

"Of course I did," said Saroyan. "An Armenian can never not be an Armenian. But your father went about it differently. I think he had other things on his mind."

"What kind of things?"

"I don't know," said Saroyan. "The truth is, I didn't see him often. We were different. But we were also close. I can't quite explain it. I remember the first time I met him. It was just after the war. I heard he was in New York, and I was passing through, and so I telephoned. We met at some hotel—the Hampshire House, or maybe the Pierre. I remember how we embraced; that is what I remember. Another time, this was a few years later, we had dinner at that restaurant—did you ever go?—the Golden Horn, and afterward we went back to where I was living. I had an apartment that winter on Central Park West. We talked about writing and families, I remember. Your father was about to start another book; at least, that is what he said, although I guess he never finished it. But it was a close time. I remember him standing in the corridor and looking in on our children, who were sleeping. The children were very young and they kept stirring in their sleep, and your father kept saying 'Shhh,' the way fathers do."

I thought of that photograph in the Golden Horn. The two comrades, the two Armenian writers—both of them in fact then passing the peak of their fame, my father putting on a graceful front of having "retired," Saroyan both more and less fortunate in not being able to retire but, instead, turning out a stream of novels and plays that critics were beginning to say did not compare to the early work.

A waitress came over to Saroyan with a menu she wished him to autograph. Saroyan signed it with a flourish and then asked her to sign one for him.

"I will tell you," Saroyan said to me. "If you want to know about Armenians, then you must go to Armenia, or what remains of it. You must go to Erevan—in Soviet Armenia."

"Have you been there?" I asked.

"Yes, I've been there. I went there the first time I earned any money. This was in 1935, and it wasn't much money, either. I went to New York and took one of those beautiful ships they had then. The *Berengaria*. I went to Europe and then to Soviet Armenia. They didn't have much in Armenia in those days, but it was a trip I had to make. I went back once again, in 1960."

"What did you find out when you went there?" I asked.

"I found out that there was an Armenia," said Saroyan. "Of course, it isn't what it used to be, but it *is* there; it is something."

We went back to Saroyan's house: a small tract house on one of the new streets—a modest house, on a street lined with perhaps a hundred similar houses. Inside, there was an extraordinary jumble of objects: not so much a disorder as a plenitude of things—books, and cartons, and suitcases, and boxes of this and that. In a large room off the kitchen, a tiny portable typewriter stood in the middle of a table piled with books and paper and manuscript. "I've always worked, and so I work now," said Saroyan. "Besides, I have to live."

"What are you writing?" I asked.

"I mostly write plays now. Sometimes people want to produce them, sometimes they do not. But that is what I do. Besides, my writing is better than my painting." He pointed to innumerable bright-colored abstract designs that had been pinned or Scotch-taped to the walls. Then he bent down in front of a pile of dusty magazines and pulled one out. "Did you ever see this?" he said. It was a copy of an old English-language Armenian magazine. Saroyan opened it to a picture of my father; in fact, it was a reproduction of a photograph that had appeared on a cover of *Time* in 1927—

now with a short note beside it on the "popular Anglo-Armenian novelist, formerly Dikran Kouyoumjian." Saroyan held the magazine open for a moment, and then put it down on the table. "It's a good photo of him, isn't it?" he said. "Such confidence."

"How is it that he never wrote anything serious about Armenians?" I asked.

"I think he wasn't that kind of writer," Saroyan said. "He liked to be entertaining. He made a couple of good jokes about Armenians, as I remember."

"Yes," I said. "But how is it that you wrote all the time about Armenians and he never did?"

"I don't know," said Saroyan. "Except that we all go on different journeys. Just like you. Now you come here. And soon, I think, you must go to Erevan."

We stood in the semidarkness of Saroyan's small house, surrounded by the clutter, the books, the magazines, the cartons, the jars of "treasures" that Saroyan had picked up on his travels or on the street. "I am a writer," Saroyan said. "It is something to be a writer. All my life, I have written. Also talked and drunk and gambled and everything else." He laughed. "They say that Armenians live to be very old. Did you know that? My grandmother Lucy Saroyan died at eighty-eight. My father's kid brother Mirhan died at eighty. Come on. Let's go and look at the graveyard."

It was now midnight, or a bit later. We got in the car and drove through the silent streets of Fresno. It was hard to tell in which direction we were going—out toward the country or in toward the downtown. Darkened houses flicked by in the night. "It is too bad you don't know Armenian," Saroyan said. "Although you will survive. But it is a marvelous language—marvelous sounds. Do you know their songs? I shall sing one for you."

Saroyan sang, rolling down the window of the car. Outside, it had begun to rain—one of those fine, sprinkling nighttime rains. Saroyan's voice filled the car, the countryside silent except for the sound of our tires on the wet road. "It is a song about love and injustice and about pomegranates getting ripe," said Saroyan. "In other words, about the important things in life."

The car stopped beside the road. "Come on," he said, getting out. The rain was pouring down more heavily, but the air was warm and had a kind of fragrance. "Now, over there is the Protestant graveyard," he said. "And somewhere down there are the Catholics. And right here are the Armenians." Saroyan was wearing an old hat, a kind of old newspaperman's hat—a hat from *The Time of Your Life,* maybe. Now he began to run at a trot through the graveyard. We passed dim gravestones in the darkness. "Over there is Levon!" he called. "I think one of Lucy's sisters is here!" The grass was soft and slippery underfoot. Saroyan kept up a steady jog. "I think somewhere over there is Uncle Mirhan!" He stopped, breathing heavily. "You know, everybody seems the same in a graveyard—Protestant, Catholic, and Armenian. But still there is something different. I don't know what it is." He wiped his forehead, which was damp with rain and sweat. "Come on," he said. "It's wet here. It's time to go home."

Later on, when we said goodbye, Saroyan embraced me. I could feel his rough cheek scrape against mine. His rough, robust cheek. "Fathers and sons are always different," he said. "But they are also the same. Maybe you will find out about that, too. Anyway, I was truly fond of him and now I am fond of you, and that is something, is it not?" He clasped my hand, and put the newspaperman's hat back on his head, and tugged his jacket about him more closely, for a cold wind was blowing now, and stuffed his hands in his pockets, and turned back to the car, and got in and drove away across "the valley full of plant growth, grapes growing, peaches ripening, and the oleander bush swooning with sweetness," to the house with the cartons and suitcases and the small portable typewriter.

I watched him go, still feeling the roughness of his face against mine.

And so, in due course, I journeyed to Armenia—
to Soviet Armenia, or what should be called more precisely
the Armenian Soviet Socialist Republic. Armenia *is* there,
Saroyan had said. All right, I thought, I will go see it. The
passage was not simple to arrange, nor was it extremely difficult. I was told there was a Cultural Commitee in Soviet
Armenia, which might be interested in sponsoring such an
expedition. There were letters to be written, and officials to
be seen at the United Nations. The Soviet Russians were
brusque and noncommittal. The Soviet Armenians brought
a bottle of Armenian brandy in a paper bag into the U.N.
dining room, and discussed the New York Knicks, and said
that the matter would be "no problem." Three months later,
it was arranged.

From the start, I knew that it would be a complex
journey, a journey on many levels. At the least, it would be a
voyage within an adventure, for what could a trip of six
thousand miles be—even six thousand boring sky miles—but
an adventure? A flight into the past as well as a flight into
that even more startling region of the present—although
which past I would find, and whose present, it was hard to
tell. I was excited by the prospect of the trip, and also appre-

hensive about it. With a new anxiety, I realized that although for so many years I had gone without my Armenian background—had gone without it to the point of finally feeling deprived of it—at the same time its very vagueness in my life had been a form of protection: the remote familiarity of a dream. All my life, Armenia and Armenians had been part of a dream; it and they were *out there* somewhere, hazy, nearly invisible. Now I was traveling into the dream. I would see what I would see. I would find what I would find.

FLIGHT. Flying . . . flight. One May night, I rode with my wife above the lights of the world, above the clouds—two moderns, uncomfortably seated, covered (as if in protective layers) with newspapers and magazines and books, rushing in our stale-aired Aeroflot tube through the clear black night.

My wife dozed beside me, a copy of *Time* and a book of Byzantine history on her lap. Beneath her feet was a large satchel full of books about Armenia, which I had brought with us with a view to reading about Armenians "on location." I glanced at *Time,* which showed a painting of the French Premier on its cover. I thought of my father's youthful face on that *Time* cover long ago. In truth, I never thought his face changed much with the years. It was always somehow *set*. "Your father is a very thoughtful man," my mother once said to me. I wondered what he would make of

my embarking on this trip. I thought, without quite knowing why, that he would dislike me for it.

I remembered then a dream I had had the previous night
—our last, restless night in New York. In fact, it was a
recurring dream, which I had dreamed many times in my
youth. I could not recall having dreamed it since I was
twenty-five or so, though—which, as it happened, was
around the time my father died. The dream was this: We
are in France and I am a child. My father and I drive down
a sunlit road. There are tall trees on either side. Green fields.
There is a fork in the road, and we take the turn marked
"TO THE AIRPORT." I remember the airport well, for it was a
real airport. Small, nineteen-thirties airplanes—aeroplanes.
A grass runway. A red wind sock. A large blue plane stands
in the middle of the runway, and my father walks toward it.
He climbs the steps to the doorway and then stands and
motions for me to follow. I come across the grass, running.
But as I reach the top step he goes inside. I stand on the top
step and stick my head inside. There all is darkness. *Black*. I
have never seen such empty darkness as in that dream airplane I peer into, and then, somehow, I am standing on the
grass again, the wind is blowing, and the blue plane is gone.

It had always been an unsettling dream for me, full of
sunlight and terror. I wondered why I had dreamed it again
so recently. In the stillness of our speeding jet, I gripped my
wife's hand. She stirred but stayed asleep. Inside the cabin,
there was a dim glow of light; the elbows of Russian businessmen were visible in the seats in front of me. Outside was

another blackness, the darkness of the starless night sky. For one feeble moment, I wished myself back in time, back on the ground, back even to that country road long ago—the tall trees, the fields, the green everywhere, the two of us in that car. I wondered why each time we took the turnoff to the airport. What had been on the other road?

Half asleep, I looked out into the night and saw my father's face looking in, squinting, trying to see something. I sat up. But, of course, it was my own face, my reflection in the glass, squinting, trying to see something, looking out.

Now LET ME say something of Mt. Ararat, for visibly there was a Mt. Ararat, which we glimpsed in early morning, standing far off, across the Turkish border, perhaps fifty miles away—a clear, bright early morning, with the gold sunlight glinting off the airplane's wing, and off the blue-white snow of Ararat. It was an uncommon sight. I had had no expectation that it would be the way it was. After all, how many of those wretched paintings had I seen in recent months, with their garish colors and "important" perspectives? What had I expected it to look like? It doesn't matter. Having grown up, one learns to diminish childhood legends: the oak tree in one's grandmother's garden is still there thirty years later, but it is always smaller, less substantial, *less*. How could it be otherwise (one thinks), and how could we have made up all those stories about it? But Ararat was *more*. One part of my mind, perhaps my Anglo-American mind, told me that its special presence—for truly it possessed a special presence, standing off against the horizon: enormous, by itself—was due to a trick or chance of geology. For, unlike most large mountains, it did not rise out of foothills or appear to be part of a contiguous range. Ararat was in fact two peaks: a smaller one attached to a much greater one—Ararat proper—which, as I knew, reached a height of some seventeen thousand feet. But the Ararat massif, as it was called, stood there alone: a gigantic pyramid or Mayan temple rising from the flat plain into our sky. And the other part of my mind felt a deep shiver, perhaps what an archaeologist might feel at uncovering some such towering ancient monument, some *god,* and realizing (even within his modern soul) that it was a god, and that men in distant times had surely prayed to it, had looked with joy and terror on its blank face, had lived beneath it, doubtless feeling a deeper shiver, creating legends and demigods around it. Inevitably, the Ark! Where else?

A burly Russian businessman rose and leaned across the seats behind us and pointed to the great mountain, which we were now banking away from. "Mt. Ararat," he said. "It is beautiful, no?"

We nodded. Yes.

"The Americans have radar on the back of it," he said, and he gave a short, brusque laugh and sat down.

"What did he mean?" my wife asked me.

"He meant that Turkey is part of NATO," I said.

"It seems so sad that the Armenians don't own Ararat any more," she said.

"You can't *own* a mountain like that!" I said, with a vehemence that surprised us both.

She looked at me a moment as she bent to pack the books back into the satchel. "What a curious thing to say," she said. Then, "You know, I could swear you had tears in your eyes when you saw that mountain."

"I didn't," I said angrily. And "I'm not one of those Returning Sons."

And then we landed.

Erevan: The capital of Soviet Armenia, and once the site of the northernmost Urartian fortress, Erebuni. According to the tourist brochures (simple, amateurishly printed little handbooks), it was now a city of some seven hundred thousand people, and certainly the tourist brochures appeared to be right, for on all sides of us stretched broad avenues, narrow streets, modest dwellings, offices, a few shops, and large numbers of people. It was a city within a semicircle of hills. New apartment buildings jutted up everywhere. Mostly, they were a chalky pink—pink stone blocks of buildings. Building blocks. These were neither truly graceful nor as stark and harsh as buildings I had seen in other Communist countries. The concrete blockhouses I'd once glimpsed in Moscow had seemed a kind of nightmare. There appeared to be no similar nightmare in Erevan.

May. Springtime. But it was hot. A hot haze everywhere. A haze covered the hills, which were surely leaf green but seemed a shade of olive. The sky was a faded blue. We were in the center of the town, and there was a mass of people all around us. A mass of people on the sidewalks. A mass of people filling the small parks. Suddenly I knew where we were: in a Balkan capital—a nameless Balkan capital, with dust in the air, and car exhaust fumes in the street (for there were cars everywhere), and an aura of being neither very poor nor very rich. Men in loose-fitting black suits, or else in shirtsleeves, lounged against the sides of buildings. Men played chess on benches beneath the dust-covered trees.

Men! I realized that they were all Armenian. I was in a city where virtually everybody was Armenian. For if there had been a number of square-faced, burly, blondish Russians on the airplane, they had since vanished, perhaps into some Russian *quartier,* or else into a cluster of ponderous, clearly official red brick buildings we had passed on our way in from the airport. Everywhere, now, were dark faces, dark hair, dark eyes—the faces not exactly dark in skin color but dark, rather, in some feeling or expression. Armenians!

OUR HOTEL was oddly gracious, or almost gracious: a large, old-fashioned place, also built out of the ubiquitous pink stone, and fronting on the central square. Lenin Square, although, apart from the predictable and rather modest statue of Himself—not in the middle of it, either, but off to one side—there were few signs of Soviet style either outside the hotel or within it. There was the standard Soviet watch-lady on our floor, but she had a classic Armenian face. An ample, dark-haired woman seated upon a wicker chair, looking at television.

Our room was also large and old-fashioned: the usual

bedroom and, in addition, a studio room—doubtless provided by the Cultural Committee—containing some simple wooden furniture and a piano. I sat for a moment in a chair in our room. Our room with the piano—our room in Armenia. Oh, I had mixed feelings. I knew not which.

We went out onto the street. There was a small park near the hotel. An ice-cream stand at the entrance. A bootblack with an elaborate "customer's chair," made out of leather and brass, each part of it finely polished and shining in the sun. Inside the park there were more men playing chess, and children swinging on a half-dozen swings. The children with large brown eyes. Armenian children! It was a gay scene, a summer's scene. The dust from the dirt paths rose beneath our feet. Children's laughter sounded in the leaves. I wanted to embrace them—to embrace somebody. But I could not. A voice inside me spoke: You have come this far. You must make a connection. But I could not. I knew, too, that it was a question not of my having to rush and embrace some stranger—for my temperament always stopped me short of such gestures—but only of my *feeling* something: of feeling real warmth as opposed to the pale heat of (in this case) literary sensibility. Old men and children in a park! A summer's scene! An Armenian scene! But I felt frozen.

"Now, *there's* an Armenian!" I heard my wife say.

I looked where she had been looking—toward a group of people gathered around some chess players. On the outside of the group were some young men, perhaps in their early twenties. One of them stood out from all the rest: tall, curly-haired, quite fiercely handsome. I knew which one she meant, but I said, "Who?"

My wife laughed. She was easily made shy. "Oh," she said. "You know which one." Now she was embarrassed. "The one with the blue shirt. Isn't he striking?"

I looked at him again. Yes, he was striking. He was a fine young man. But somehow I felt incapable of replying, of responding. It was quite startling. I knew that it wasn't on account of some simple jealousy—it didn't seem to have much to do with *him*. It was as if I had been found out in something—something that had to do with how *I* cared about the way Armenians looked, and that I couldn't bear to admit.

Just then, a voice behind me said, in English, "I thought I'd find you here. It is a lovely park, is it not?"

We turned to see a square-shouldered man in a brown suit—a man of medium build, of medium age, with a hard Armenian face, which seemed to be smiling.

"Permit me to introduce myself," he said. "I am Sarkis. I am not your guide. Your guide is an excellent young man who is always occupied. I am your friend." He paused, then stepped forward and shook my wife's hand in a vigorous and awkward grip, and then threw his arms around me in an embrace. "Welcome to Armenia!" he said.

How to describe this Sarkis, who had arrived apparently from nowhere, and who now walked beside us—a bustling, short-legged figure in a brown suit (an unusually warm brown suit for the season), gesticulating, talking? Our friend? In reality, the mystery of his appearance soon became less mysterious, yet it was still fascinating, for, although neither officially a guide nor precisely an interpreter, he was in private life a teacher, a teacher of English at a local high school, who maintained, as he put it, "connections" with the Cultural Committee, and who periodically offered his services to visitors—to sympathetic visitors.

"I knew right away that you would be sympathetic," he said as we walked across the street toward the central square. "Besides, you are Armenian. All Armenians are sympathetic to one another, are they not?"

I nodded. I could see my wife smiling, walking lightly. She was pleased that we had found a friend—at least, a "personal contact," not one of those mechanical guides we had dreaded. It occurred to me that she liked Armenians better than I did.

"Is your father still living?" Sarkis asked me.

I said no.

"I understand he was a writer, also," Sarkis said. "Unfortunately, I have never read his work. Did he ever travel to Soviet Armenia?"

"He never did," I said.

"What a pity," Sarkis said. "I am sure he would have liked it. He would have admired the achievements of the Armenian people."

"Yes, I'm sure he would have," I said.

Sarkis turned to my wife. "Did you know his father?"

"No, I didn't," she said. "I wish I had."

"I am sure he was a wonderful man," said Sarkis. "Armenian men make wonderful fathers. They worship their families. They would do anything for their families."

We stood now in the middle of the square, beside some fountains. I thought, Why won't this man stop about my father—about fathers, Armenian fathers? I knew it was a childish thought, and disliked myself for thinking it, and Sarkis for making me think it.

My wife apparently noticed a new expression on my face. "What's the matter?" she asked.

Sarkis overheard. In some ways, he was obviously very agile. "Is something the matter?" he said. "Probably you are tired after your long voyage. Forgive me for talking so much, but in these parts one rarely has a chance for such international conversation."

He was so singular and charming I couldn't imagine what anger, or peevishness, had possessed me. "I think it's mostly hunger," I said.

We walked over to our hotel.

"You have lunch," said Sarkis. "I have some business to attend to. Afterward, I am going to take you somewhere very special."

My wife and I found a table in the hotel restaurant—a large, high-ceilinged room crowded with customers and waiters (Armenian customers! Armenian waiters!), all of them speaking not Russian but Armenian. A beaming waiter presented an enormous menu with virtually all the items crossed out. We ordered a dried-beef dish, some kind of greenish salad, and a white wine. Four men at a nearby table were drinking brandy and singing—a soft and almost dainty melody.

Once again, everything seemed gay though somehow oppressive. My wife talked excitedly of her impressions of the new city. I felt myself silent, trying to listen, trying to listen to everything.

"What happened to you out there?" she asked.

"It was nothing," I said.

"Was it all that about your father?"

"Perhaps that was a bit of it," I said. "I don't know why."

"But Armenians always go on like that," she said. "You told me so yourself. You mustn't mind it."

"I know," I said. Then, because it was what I felt, I said, "You know, I don't think I really *like* Armenians."

"You know you don't mean that," she said. She smiled. Beside us, the singing rose into a kind of march. The waiters clapped their hands. We had more wine and finished off the greenish salad, which was mostly scallions, with a kind of bitter, pungent taste.

Sarkis reappeared outside. He was in command of an ancient Russian touring car, a definitely imposing vehicle of unnamed manufacture and of vaguely czarist inclinations: faded limousine upholstery, remains of a lap-robe cordon in the back (without the lap robe), and little, tattered curtains on the side windows, bespeaking a romantic past of modest bureaucratic trysts or kidnappings, or both.

"Naturally, it is not mine," said Sarkis, seeming very pleased. "I have borrowed it from the Committee. Naturally, it belongs to the State."

"I had hoped it was Armenian—an Armenian car," my wife said.

"I do not think so," said Sarkis. Then, "You are not joking?"

"No, I wasn't," she said.

"Armenians make many valuable things now in Armenia," said Sarkis. "In America, how do you call them—products? Armenians make electrical products. They make computers. Armenians make excellent computers. Look!" He pointed to a cloud of dark smoke on the horizon. "You call that pollution, but we are still poorer than you. We call it industry."

"Are we going to a factory now?" I asked, for I had come prepared to visit many factories.

"No," said Sarkis. "Not today. The Committee will arrange for you to visit factories. Today, on your arrival, I am taking you on a special trip—to a place that all Armenians would want to visit. I am taking you to a *hallowed* place. We call it the Monument—the Monument to the Armenian Martyrs."

We climbed into the front seat of the limousine, squeezed in beside Sarkis, who handled the old machine with a classic pedagogic mixture of vagueness and speedway fervor. "I do not drive very often," he said disarmingly, "although I had a motorcycle for many years."

It didn't seem right to inquire what had happened to the motorcycle.

We drove down one of the wide boulevards, a long, straight roadway lined with trees, which led toward the semicircle of low hills.

The olive-colored leaves were deep green as we came closer. There were flowers beside the road, and a few houses. It seemed suddenly as if we were in a different country—as if we had left the Balkans behind us in the dusty city and were now motoring through some more familiar minor bit of Europe. There were orange-tiled roofs on the poorish stone houses, red flowers in the skimpy gardens. Some goats wandered beside the road.

Then even this feeling of Europe died out. Meadows of yellow-green grass extended on all sides. The fields were flat and dry and full of stones. You could see clusters of trees against the horizon, far away, and a few scattered houses, far away—and, yet farther away, the mass of Ararat, not quite in front of us but dominating the land, its summit of snow on a level with the clouds.

"Every Armenian in the world should visit this monument," Sarkis was saying. "Every Armenian should know what it is to stand before it and feel in his bones the tragedy of Armenia." He turned to my wife. "The suffering of the

Armenian people has been enormous," he said. "Enormous. Incomprehensible. Are you acquainted with the suffering of the Armenian people?"

"I've read something about it," she said. "It seemed truly terrible."

"Ah, you've read about it," he said. "Your husband must be a good Armenian. He understands that it is necessary for us to speak out about these things." With one hand he reached out and clasped my arm. "Have you told her what happened at Van and Bitlis? Have you told her how the Turks clubbed our poor people to death? Have you told her how they tortured our men and raped our women?" He turned to my wife. "Did you know, my dear, that they burned priests on crosses and killed small infants with their bayonets? Yes, that is right. Small infants. They killed small children with their knives and bayonets. Oh, it was surely horrible, the most horrible of deeds."

I was conscious of the dry straw of the fields floating past us. Sarkis stared straight ahead. Ararat was a dream.

Sarkis said, "To be an Armenian is to have this intolerable weight of sadness on one's soul. That is what one of our Armenian poets said. Is it not true?"

In a moment, he said, "Armenians can never forget what happened to them. Armenians must never forget. It was a genocide. Do you know, it was the world's first genocide."

It seemed as if we drove for hours, but it was less than one hour. The heat was everywhere. There were no people—

only yellow fields shimmering in the sun. Sarkis stopped the car—our destination.

We climbed some stone steps. There was a stone walk. "You should take off your coat," Sarkis said. I took off my coat. I felt oddly grateful that he had said that. In front of us, about a half mile away, was an unusual structure. It had the appearance of a kind of Stonehenge—columns, metallic columns rising out of the ground, but angled inward. A Stonehenge of slanted slabs.

"How beautiful!" I could hear my wife saying. "How extraordinary!"

"Of course it is beautiful," Sarkis said. He walked just a step in front of us. For some reason, I was conscious of his stride—a stolid, heavy gait—and of his belly, which seemed not so much fat as hard, a politician's belly.

Suddenly he stooped down and plucked a little flower from the grass beside the walk. He looked at me. "For our Armenian martyrs," he said.

I was conscious of his eyes on me, my wife's eyes on me. On all sides of us I could see fields stretching away into the distance. I knew there were flowers beneath my gaze, but I could see no flowers. I kept on walking.

In the center of the slanted columns stood a large vessel—a metal bowl—with a flame burning inside it.

We stood beneath the columns looking at the bowl and the flame.

"Think of the Armenians who died," said Sarkis, almost

in a whisper. "Think of your martyred countrymen. Think what it is to be an Armenian."

Sarkis's voice was only a murmur, but it seemed to roar in my ears. I knew that I felt nothing. An image flickered through my mind of soldiers in a First World War movie advancing in slow motion across a muddy field, being mown down in slow motion by machine-gun fire, turning, falling, falling in silence. Sarkis reached out toward me and put the flower he had been holding into my hand.

"I saved this for you," he said. "For your offering."

I looked at him. "I can't," I said.

For a moment, we looked at one another. I could find no meaning in his glance or mine.

"Please . . ." my wife said.

The flower—it was a kind of buttercup, I think—was in my palm. I took a few steps forward and placed it—gently dropped it—in the flaming bowl. And turned and began to walk back slowly, away from the bowl and out from beneath the overhanging columns.

Sarkis and my wife were a step or so behind me, then beside me. They were talking about the Monument. "Each year in April," Sarkis was saying, "our people come down here from Erevan to bow their heads. Some of them even make the journey on foot."

I thought, I have come this far—so close—but I seem unable to go further, to make the connection.

Over my shoulder I glimpsed Ararat in the distance: a blue shape in a bluish haze. It seemed as silent as the dry fields, as the yellow flowers, as everything in sight. I thought quite simply, How strange to have no country. Just then, a breeze from somewhere rippled the fields. I heard my wife's laugh. The flowers swayed in the breeze from the blue mountain.

In the course of the next few days, I lived a curious interior life. That is, I stayed indoors whenever possible and read my books.

Even my wife thought it peculiar. "You've come all the way to Armenia and you won't go out and look around."

This wasn't entirely true, for we were not let off so easily, either by the official guide—a sober young bureaucrat named Vartan, who made an appearance daily, by phone if not in person, with a schedule of places (factories, schools, and churches) we should visit—or by Sarkis, who, far from being put off by my unresponsive manner at the Monument, persisted in his efforts to befriend us and to have some role in our visit.

But it was mainly true. For although I sometimes walked the dusty city and craned my neck at ancient churches, and though I sat through a performance of *Othello* (in Armenian, too) with Sarkis, I lived in those days mostly in the Armenian books I had brought, and in our rooms. I didn't even know for certain what it was I wanted to find out from these histories. I told myself, "Through the past I'll find the present"—or some such thing. At any rate, I read obsessively in the old volumes.

It continued to fascinate me that Armenia had had such a past, although the more I read, the less sure I was exactly what I meant by that—"such a past." From one point of view, Armenia existed throughout history largely as a foot-note, a cluster of footnotes. In the classic texts on Persian history, Arab history, Byzantine history, and so forth, one would scan the index for Armenia, and there it would be: "Armenia: pp. 51–57; pp. 120–124; p. 237." And so forth. But from another point of view I knew that these footnotes were the murmurs of real people, real events. My people.

I was drawn to revelations of Armenians as soldiers, as warriors. For it seemed that the martial qualities recounted by Xenophon and the horsemanship once nurtured by the Persians had propelled many Armenians into the military foreground by the time of the Byzantines. For example, in Procopius's great history of Justinian's campaign for the re-capture of Rome from the barbarians one might find the names of at least a dozen Armenian generals. There was the surreal and marvelous figure of old Narses: General Narses, also an Armenian, formerly the Grand Chamberlain (a high official in the Byzantine treasury), who at the age of seventy was appointed by Justinian to command the Impe-rial Army, which had been sent from Constantinople into the darkness of the Italian provinces to overthrow the Ostro-goth Totila. Narses had done it, too—killing Totila, and overwhelming the barbarians, who "immediately handed over themselves and the fortress," Procopius wrote. "In this way, Rome was taken for the fifth time in [Justinian's] reign, and Narses at once sent its keys to the Emperor." It seemed one of those eerie, dreamlike images that shine dimly through history—a point of light from a distant, receding star. Narses the Armenian, prefect of Italy.

What a curious people! Clearly, for hundreds of years Armenians had been among the key figures of the long-lasting Byzantine empire. They were generals. They were emperors. Consider Leo V (813–20). "As to his immediate origin, it is well known," wrote a contemporary historian, George the Monk. "He came from the country of the Armenians, whence, according to some, his obstinacy and his bad disposition." There was the dynasty started by the Emperor Basil I—originally a peasant, born in Macedonia of Armenian parents, who came to Constantinople at the age of twenty and "found favor" with the current emperor, then assisted the emperor by murdering a troublesome uncle, then murdered the emperor and took the job himself. Apparently, he made a good emperor, too—at least, the way historians like to view these things: a Byzantine "strong man," who fought off the Saracens and kept everybody in line. He increased the Army, maintained a sober interest in legal reform, and liked to wrestle after dinner.

For a while, Armenians must have been nearly everywhere in the imperial hierarchy. "The Armenian element was also prominent in the intellectual life of Byzantium, which underwent a notable revival in the ninth century," wrote D. M. Lang in *Armenia: Cradle of Civilization*.

"Prominent in this movement were such figures of part Armenian blood as John the Grammarian, Caesar Bardas, and Leo the Philosopher. . . . Also of partial Armenian descent was Patriarch Photius (820–93), whose stormy patriarchate marked the beginning of the schism between the Eastern and Western Churches."

For a while after the death of Basil I, a kind of triumvirate ruled the empire (still the most powerful political entity in the world)—two co-emperors and a general, *all* Armenian. And then, of course, there was Basil II—the last of the line. He was known at the time as Basil Bulgaroctonus, which means "slayer of Bulgars." For this reason: After a battle against the unfriendly Bulgars, whom he defeated, Basil ordered that the eyes of all fifteen thousand Bulgar prisoners should be put out save for every hundredth man, who should have only one eye put out, so that he could lead his blinded comrades home. It is said that the czar of the Bulgars, Samuel, died of a stroke at the sight of his returning army.

I COULDN'T HELP noticing how attracted I was to these terrible Armenians. First, Tigran the Great. Now the two Basils. Bulgaroctonus indeed! That was surely one of the least appealing stories I had ever read. Imagine how much time it must have taken to blind fifteen thousand men. Imagine the length of the line—imagine being the ninety-ninth man, or even the hundredth. Perhaps "attracted" is too strong a word. But certainly I was more than just aware of them.

Then, there was the interest I took in Armenian generals—the Armenian warrior spirit. I, who in my adult life had regarded myself as so devoutly anti-militarist! One afternoon, I read aloud to my wife a brief passage that I had uncovered in Procopius about John the Armenian, a commander of the Byzantine cavalry under Belisarius who by a brilliant ruse had won some North African battle against the Vandals.

Afterward, she said simply, "But what are you looking for? Of course the Armenians are brave."

"That's not the *point*," I said. I didn't know what the point was.

ANOTHER TIME, my wife said, "Sarkis wants us to go to an art exhibit with him."

I said, "Can't you see that I'm in the middle of studying?" I thought that if I called it "studying" I would add dignity to my obsession. "Besides, there aren't any first-rate Armenian artists."

"I didn't know that," she said.

"You go," I said. "If the pictures are any good, you can tell me and I'll go later."

"All right," she said.

Instead of studying, I went by myself for a walk. It was a

terribly hot day; the dust was everywhere. I walked on the shady side of the street, close to the buildings. Nothing seemed cool. Women passed by carrying large, circular loaves of bread. Men stood silently in doorways. At the end of the street, there was an ice-cream vender, selling little cups of ice cream to children. I walked along and thought, Sarkis has been trying to *define* me as an Armenian—but a certain kind of Armenian. Those damned massacres, I thought. That chauvinism, such a chauvinism of misfortune!

Across the way there was a large, shedlike building with people going in and out of it. I went inside; it was an immense farmers' market. Sawdust on the floor. Heaps of vegetables on the counters. I thought to buy some oranges for our room, because there seemed to be no fruit available at the hotel. The man behind the orange counter was young: gold teeth, a peasant's face. After I'd paid him for six oranges, he put an extra orange on the pile. "Wilcom," he said. Welcome.

I thanked him, wanted to pay him more. He declined vigorously. I gave him a ball-point pen, which seemed to please him. Wilcom, wilcom.

On all sides, there were mountains of oranges. Radishes —flowery bursts of pink and green. The old women behind the counters wore shawls about their heads, wound like a veil across the lower face, and had the skin of elephants. Armenian women from the old country. Truly, here was the old country. I had never seen such women: the skin of elephants, the eyes of bears—old bears.

Later, as I walked back to the hotel, I thought, The man behind the orange counter had seen me as American. Do I, after all, look American? And so am I American?

When my wife returned, she seemed in good spirits. "The paintings weren't very good, but they do try so hard," she said. "We ran into one of Sarkis's students—a huge, bright young boy. At least, I think he was bright. We all had a lemonade together."

I read my book. I wanted to ask her if she thought I looked American or Armenian, or what? But it seemed a stupid question.

OUTSIDE THE POST OFFICE, one morning, I had a conversation with Sarkis about literature.

"Have you read the works of Abovian?" he asked.

"No, I haven't," I said. "Unfortunately, I haven't read many Armenian writers."

"That's too bad," he said. "We have some great writers."

"I know," I said.

"In addition to Abovian, we have Toumanian, Berberian, Isahakian, Aharonian, and, of course, Raffi. You have heard of Raffi?"

"Yes. But I haven't read any of them."

"That's too bad," he said. "But you have read Saroyan?"

"Yes, I've read Saroyan," I said.

"He is a great Armenian writer," said Sarkis. "Also a

great world writer. If you like, I will lend you some books by Abovian."

"That would be nice," I said.

Sarkis and I shook hands to go our own ways for the day. He paused. "Should I have included your father?"

"I don't know," I said. "It doesn't matter."

"It doesn't matter," Sarkis repeated. "You know, I wonder was he as detached as you." He smiled and waved and walked off across the square.

Back with my books, I became absorbed in the period of the Crusades. I knew that Armenia, in 301, had been the first nation in the world to officially adopt Christianity as a state religion, but I didn't know that Armenians had later become involved in the Crusades. It seemed so unlikely. Even my ignorance interested me. Before I left New York, an Armenian priest, who told me that I could never properly appreciate the "Armenian experience" without studying the Armenian role in the Crusades, had lent me several books. One (the shortest) was by an Armenian: *Cilician Armenia and the Crusades,* by Armen Ovhanesian. The others were a French work, the *Histoire des Croisades,* by René Grousset; and two volumes from the Englishman Steven Runciman's *A History of the Crusades.*

To begin with, there seemed some variance in bias about the Armenian role in the Crusades. The Armenians, not surprisingly, generally espoused the view that had been expressed long ago by Pope Gregory XIII: "Among the other merits of the Armenian nation as regards the Church and Christendom, there is one that is outstanding and deserves particularly to be remembered; namely, that when in past times the Christian princes and armies went forth to recover the Holy Land, no nation, no people came to their aid more speedily and with more enthusiasm than the Armenians." Scholars, on the whole, were less enthusiastic than the Pope, although the French historians seemed mainly friendly toward the Armenian role. Grousset's book contained numerous references to the Armenians, especially in connection with the First Crusade. This sort of thing: "As one sees in many instances, the role of the native population was a vital factor in the success of the Crusade . . . and indeed it was the friendship between the Armenians and the Franks which set the basis for the Latin Orient." The Armenian author Ovhanesian quoted another French historian, Professor Joseph Laurent: "The Armenians guided and provisioned the Crusaders. As signs of coöperation they [the Armenians] married their daughters to them. They opened to them the cities and fortresses from Tarsus to Marash, from Samosata to Edessa. They made possible the capture of Antioch, which foretold the capture of Jerusalem and the success of the whole enterprise." The Englishman, Steven Runciman, seemed coolest toward the subject. His books acknowledged Armenian aid to the Crusaders: "As Baldwin moved toward the river Euphrates, the Armenian population rose up to greet him," and so on. But his approach was, in the modern, Lytton Strachey manner, a decidedly anti-heroic treatment of the great European adventure: a rich narrative of baronial mistrust, double-dealing, treachery, and political feuding—activities in which the Armenians appeared to have participated as eagerly and recklessly as the Crusaders.

One might well ask, What were the Armenians doing in this part of the world, on the Levant coast of Asia Minor, many hundreds of miles southwest of the Armenian plateau? The answer appeared to be that large numbers of Armenians had been driven from their homeland by increasing incursions of Seljuk Turks. Also, equally large numbers of Armenians—whole towns and counties, under individual barons or princes—had been resettled earlier by the Byzantine government to populate newly conquered territories. In addition to these displacements, until the eleventh century the defense of the Byzantine empire had been left mainly (and with relative success) to the national armies of the provincial territories, of which the Armenian was the second-largest in the empire, its borders forming the key frontier against the raiding Turks. The Byzantine government, however, in what was surely a classic example of bureaucratic wrongheadedness, decided to insure central control from Constantinople by dissolving the Armenian army, with the result that by the time of the first full-scale Seljuk invasion, in 1045, almost half the Armenians had moved off the Armenian plateau. Where had these Armenians moved to? They had migrated southwest to the next-best replica of their own mountainous terrain: to the craggy, lower, dark-green mountains of the Taurus and Amanus ranges, close by the Mediterranean coast of Cilicia, which country soon became known as Cilician Armenia.

The Arabs and the Turks were in this general area, too—at first, farther south and east. They were both Muslim. The

Armenians were militantly Christian, and since their conversion they had obdurately maintained their own branch of the Church. Then the Crusaders arrived: adventurous, belligerent, rather crude by Asia Minor standards, but also Christian. The Crusaders were short of food, of supplies, and of places to rest. The Armenians were at odds with the nearby Muslims as well as with the oppressive and distant Byzantines. Clearly, they looked to their new European friends as a counterweight to both. Such friends! In the beginning, most of the Crusaders were Frankish or Norman: Raymond of Toulouse, Godefrey of Bouillon, Baldwin of Boulogne, Robert of Normandy, Stephen of Blois—usually the younger sons of landowning families, each with a sizable private army and with distinctly secular ambitions. The Armenians, too, were a decidedly rough lot. Consider the story of Thoros and Baldwin. Thoros was an Armenian, a tough old feudal baron who at the age of sixty had driven the Turks from the city of Edessa. From far-off Constantinople, the Emperor Alexius Comnenus (doubtless short of the wherewithal for more tangible rewards) had bestowed on Thoros the title of Curopalates—Guardian of the Palace. Soon afterward, Baldwin of Boulogne arrived in the neighborhood with a private army, while around the same time a large Turkish force was threatening to move back against Edessa. Thoros suggested that he and Baldwin should make an alliance, but Baldwin demurred. Finally, Thoros offered to name Baldwin co-regent of Edessa and officially adopt him as a son. This strange adoption ceremony took place in

Thoros's palace one afternoon in 1098. According to one account, Baldwin and Thoros first stripped to the waist. Then a "doubly wide shirt" was placed over both of them, and the two men "rubbed their bare breasts against each other." Later, the same procedure under the shirt was repeated between Baldwin and Thoros's wife, "the elderly Princess Sophia." As with much of the rapport between Armenians and Crusaders, even the magic of that loony rite didn't last very long or create any very inspired friendship. The Turks were temporarily detoured from Edessa. But Thoros soon found himself on the wrong side of a palace intrigue and was "dragged from his chambers and torn to pieces by the crowd." Baldwin, who had remained tactfully neutral while the townspeople hacked up his lately acquired foster father, then proclaimed himself Count of Edessa.

Still, by the arrival, a hundred years later, of the Third Crusade—the one involving Richard Cœur de Lion and the Kurdish general Yūsuf ibn-Ayyūb, otherwise known as Salāh-al-Dīn, or Saladin—the Armenians were very much a presence in the Levant. For example, Prince Levon of Armenia was one of six noble lords in attendance at Cœur de Lion's marriage to Princess Berengaria, on Cyprus. And eight years later, when Prince Levon arranged to have himself crowned King of Armenia, it was no longer to Constantinople—his nominal source of patronage—that he looked for official approval but to the nearby, boisterous colonists from Western Europe. The coronation occurred one day in 1199, in the mountain fortress of Sis, the Armenian capital.

The Chancellor of Germany arrived from Saxony, representing the German emperor, who had just died, and brought with him a fine gold crown. The Archbishop of Mainz appeared, representing the Pope and bringing a jeweled scepter. From Constantinople, the Byzantine emperor—not to be left out—sent down another crown. Cœur de Lion himself was back in England, but he dispatched a present of a jeweled silver casket, lately stolen from a Sicilian monastery. Eight ambassadors from the Caliph of Baghdad attended, as did a retinue of eight hundred Crusader knights from Antioch, who "performed feats of jousting and brave horsemanship." Thus: King Levon of Armenia.

I thought, This was a bizarre corner of history. "Listen." I read to my wife: "At King Levon's court, Latin and French were spoken as well as Armenian," and: "He modeled his court on Frankish models, introducing many French titles for offices . . . for instance, bailiff, mareschal, seneschal, and so forth. . . . The High Court was established at the royal capital of Sis, modeled on the Assizes of Antioch. . . . There were also special courts under the jurisdiction of the Latin knightly orders such as the Hospitalers."

She laughed. "But it sounds sad," she said.

"How was it sad?" I asked. "Because the Armenians copied the French? Because it didn't last very long?"

"I don't know," she said. "Maybe because of what I hear in your voice. I mean, part of you claims to be this rational observer, and yet another part of you still seems to be trying to justify Armenians in Western terms—you know, that history we were all taught. Battles, generals, Crusades, Richard and Saladin and Robin Hood."

"That's not it at all," I said.

"All right," she said. "But why do you care so much that they seem European?"

One morning, Sarkis and we, and also Vartan, visited a refrigerator factory. It was a scheduled visit, impossible to get out of. Earlier, Vartan had announced over the telephone, "I understand you wish to see an electronics factory." What I had had in mind was computers. I had thought it would be interesting to look at an Armenian computer operation. "It has been arranged," said Vartan.

We went out to the factory. It was a large Victorian structure: bricks and steel girders and a glass roof—a bit like a nineteenth-century railroad station. Inside it were refrigerators. They dangled overhead from a conveyor cable, hundreds of white boxes swaying, moving slowly through the great room. Men in work clothes and women in scientific white coats reached up and did little things to the appliances as they passed by.

We were introduced to the plant manager, a short, fat Armenian with glasses and a harried smile. My wife asked him questions about "production volume" and "units per hour," which did not surprise him but which surprised me. Later, we were introduced to the Worker of the Month, a stout, red-faced old fellow with many gold teeth and enormous hands.

We stood in a room full of huge, silent machinery and had tea with the plant manager and the Worker of the Month. The Worker said that his son had just been accepted by the University of Erevan. He was a physics student. It was a very sweet moment. Even the plant manager seemed genuinely happy for him and clasped the old man about the shoulders. One knew that this was a model factory, but surely this could not have been a model event. I thought for a second of when I was a boy and heard the bartender at the Golden Horn announce that his son had been accepted into the Curtis Institute. Aspirations everywhere!

Afterward, outside the factory, as we were walking abreast down the sun-drenched street, Vartan said to Sarkis, "We hope to get our refrigerator next year."

Sarkis said, "We had ours last year. But we are still waiting for the telephone."

"I have the telephone," said Vartan.

"What do you think of Vartan?" my wife asked me.

"I don't know," I said. "He seems nice enough, but I can't guess what he's thinking. He seems very efficient—a young man on the way up in the Committee. I don't think he gets on too well with Sarkis."

"Sarkis is an émigré," she said.

"What do you mean?"

"Vartan was born here. Sarkis belongs to one of the

Armenian families that moved here right after the war. I think maybe that makes him more excessive."

"How did you know that?" I asked.

"He told me," she said.

"I find him hard to be with," I said.

"I know that," she said. "He feels it, too. He thinks you're finding it difficult to be here."

"That's not so," I said. It made me furious to be patronized by Sarkis.

"Well, sometimes you still act as if Armenians had nothing to do with you," she said.

ONE EVENING after dinner, we walked with Sarkis in a small park that had a pond with ducks on it and fountains splashing.

"How safe it feels here!" my wife said.

"Of course it is safe," said Sarkis. "We Armenians are a peaceful people."

We sat on benches opposite each other in the twilight. In the distance one could hear music playing—a popular tune on a loudspeaker. Some teen-aged boys walked by. They stopped at the pond, reached in their arms—shirts and all—and rubbed water over their faces, and went off laughing.

"In America, I hear, the youth are very violent," said Sarkis. "Here we have no such problem. Armenian children respect their parents."

"That must be nice for parents," my wife said.

"I know that your children are not violent," said Sarkis. "Armenian blood does not incline to violence."

For no reason, I asked, "Where were you in the war?"

"In Egypt," Sarkis said. "I was in the Armenian colony in Cairo and worked for the British. I was a clerk. They didn't treat me too badly, either, but after the war, when they had no more need of us, they went back to their old habits."

"And you came here?"

"I came here. It was the most fortunate thing I have ever done. I have returned to the Armenian homeland, and I am a citizen of the Soviet Union." He looked at me. "And you—were you in the war?"

"I was too young," I said. "I was at school."

"That was also fortunate," said Sarkis. "Armenians have no use for wars."

THAT NIGHT, I had some wretched dreams. Although the dreams (for there were several, blurring into one another) were about war and battles, in the center of each dream was a kind of dread—not so much a dread of war, or even death, as a somehow deeper dread of being *lost*. Although from whom or what was never clear. In one dream, I was alone in an unknown country. It seemed an endless dream, whose scenario was filled with ruined build-ings, vast silences, train rides in empty carriages—at one point, a wooded avenue, quite pretty, with tall trees and fallen leaves, and lined with silent, empty tanks. In another dream, I seemed more actively to be searching for some-one—my wife and children, as I imagined. There was a huge white hotel, bathed in sunshine, with orange trees in the garden and with the interior crowded with soldiers, mostly pilots. My wife and children were by a swimming pool. But my search persisted. I didn't know for what. The anxiety was quite excruciating—a feeling of being somehow kept away, or kept apart. I woke up shivering, hazily recall-ing the dream images of search: an area of rubble, wreck-age—perhaps a city—which led suddenly to a field, an endless field of tall yellow flowers.

I looked at my wife asleep beside me. I thought (the thought coming from I knew not where), Sarkis and I are both in some way lying to ourselves.

Some time went by. The days were very hot. Each morning, the sun was higher above the olive hills, and warmer—a distant, glaring white circle that hovered over the unfinished pink buildings, the trees, the statues, the jangle of the traffic.

We went to visit old churches out in the dry countryside. There was a place called Garni, on the edge of a cliff, with dark pine forests all around and the racing water of a silvery river far below. Great slabs of black stone overgrown by weeds. Broken pieces of columns lay strewn about, decorated by Armenian stonecutters of long ago with designs of pomegranates and geometric shapes. It was a ghostly place, shrouded with trees.

There was also Zvartnots. I would say the name over and over to myself: "Zvartnots. Zvartnots." It sounded somehow so Armenian: a sound not like any other. Here were the remains of a great church, now lying in ruins on the plain of Ararat. We were almost familiar with Ararat by now, accustomed to looking over our shoulder at the sky and seeing the mountain's blue mass, the rim of snow. If Garni had been dark and hidden, Zvartnots was full of sunlight and stood blithely exposed upon the plain. Wild poppies grew amid the ruins, and one could see places where the invading Arabs had once built crude, cobbled fortifications around the sculptured columns. I thought, Darkness and light, perhaps the Armenian ambivalence.

IN THE STEAMY AFTERNOONS, I continued to read Armenian history. It required persistence on my part, for many times I found it hard to understand what I was doing in Armenia, and felt discouraged, not knowing what it was I expected. My wife seemed happy, although we fought sometimes. At any rate, she liked to see new things and to observe the exotic landscape.

For example, I read about King Hetum I of Armenia, who in the thirteenth century had journeyed for seven months and four thousand miles to pay a call on the Mongol chieftain Mangu Khan, in Karakorum, the great tent city of the Mongols. Armenian historians seemed eager to note that this was the first official visit by a Western ruler to the leader of the Golden Horde. Another "first"! Apparently, Mangu —who was Genghis Khan's grandson—received King Hetum "with courtesy and high honor," and even agreed to a rather short-lived mutual defense pact against the Muslim Mamelukes of Egypt.

It was history, I knew, but it sounded dreamlike. It made one wonder: What had the Great Khan and the Armenian king talked about? Had Mangu played dumb, like Sitting Bull, puffing on his pipe while fearsome Mongols put on a casual display of flaying prisoners or shooting arrows while standing on their heads and riding backward? Had Hetum rustled about the tent city (not yet visited by Marco Polo) in royal silks, politely tasting Mongol yogurt, talking to himself alternately in French, Latin, and Armenian? Did either of them have any idea in which direction history was headed?

It was surely not headed benignly toward the Armenians. Up in the northern tier of Asia Minor, as the Byzantine empire had shrunk steadily back to Constantinople, the Armenian plateau—so-called Greater Armenia—had become literally overrun by waves of nomads from Central Asia: Turks, Mongols, and the Tatar followers of Timour Lenk, or Tamerlane.

Down by the Mediterranean, in Cilician Armenia (where Hetum ruled), the situation was not much better. Muslim warriors had recaptured for Islam most of the Crusader principalities, with the result that Christianity had virtually disappeared from the Levant, save for the islands of Rhodes and Cyprus, and for the small kingdom of Armenia. This lesser Armenia was reduced to a few mountain fortresses: a defensive Christian enclave within a sea of Islam, which now reached to the gates of Constantinople.

The Armenians, one could see, had made two crucial bets. A long time back, they had bet on Christianity. More recently, they had bet on the Crusaders and the growing power of Europe. These bets were not in themselves wrong, for the dynamics of Christianity and Europe were such that both forces would sweep over much of the world. But it seemed that the Armenians had been in the wrong part of the world to make these bets—or, at any rate, to hope to collect on them.

AN ARMENIAN CHRONICLER, who remained behind on the Armenian plateau, described the first wave of Tatar nomads as follows:

Now, however, we shall also tell what these first Tatars resembled, for the first who came to the upper country were not like men. They were terrible to look at and indescribable, with large heads like a buffalo's, narrow eyes like a fledgling's, a snub nose like a cat's, projecting snouts like a dog's, narrow loins like an ant's, short legs like a hog's, and by nature with no beards at all. . . . Their broad faces were plastered with a poisonous mixture of gum. . . . They killed without mercy men and women, priests and monks, making slaves, taking the deacons as their slaves, and plundering the churches of the Christians without fear.

THEN, there was the story of the last king of Armenia. His name was King Levon V, and, by the time he reached the throne, Greater Armenia had been totally overrun by the Turks, and Cilician Armenia was little more than the city of

Sis. Even this outpost didn't last. In 1375, within a few
months of his coronation, Levon and his subjects were besieged by an army of thirty thousand Mamelukes, half of
them mustered by the governor of Aleppo. What the governor of Aleppo wanted with Sis was never clear. Perhaps it
was "strategic." Perhaps he just knew he could take it.
Finally, King Levon surrendered Sis, and thus the Kingdom
of Armenia, and thus himself. The inhabitants were not
totally slaughtered; some were permitted to become converts
to Islam, and some escaped north to Constantinople, which
was soon to have its own troubles. The Kingdom of Armenia, however, disappeared within the Mameluke empire
—until that, in turn, was supplanted by the Ottoman Turks.

As for Levon himself, his was an odd and wistful story:
true and bittersweet and unreal in the manner of chivalric
fable, or perhaps in the manner of much of Armenian history. After the surrender of Sis, he was taken as a prisoner to
Cairo, where he remained for seven years in a royal prison,
perfecting his calligraphy and writing petitions for his release. Eventually, some European in-laws (the kings of
Aragon and Castile) provided a ransom, and Levon sailed
from Alexandria to Rhodes, and thence to Europe.

In France, ex-King Levon was received by King Charles
VI, who gave him a house and a pension and invited him
for dinner. The two men apparently became friends. The
Armenian king taught the French king to play chess, and
they often played in the evening. They also talked often
about France's endless and ruinous war with England,

which had been going on for decades, and came to be called the Hundred Years' War. Levon kept urging Charles to get out of the war—thereby, one imagines, freeing his army for one last, great Crusade to liberate Armenia from Islam. Charles invariably replied that peace with England was a fine idea, but that a cease-fire was an impractical step for him to undertake unilaterally.

In the end, Levon himself went to England, and there is a text of the speech that he delivered before King Richard II and Parliament, where *"nostre cousyne le Roi d'Armenie"* proposed an end to the Hundred Years' War—a proposal that was briefly considered and then abandoned. Levon stayed a while longer in England, perhaps peering at the dense dark woods and cold marshes and huge, coarse blond people, and then went back to Paris, where he died. King Charles provided an appropriate funeral for him, and he lies today in the basilica of St. Denis among the kings of France—in some ways as logical a resting place as any other for the last king of Armenia.

I said to Sarkis one evening at dinner, "I hadn't realized that the Armenians were so European."

"We're not European," said Sarkis. "We're Indo-European. That's not the same thing."

"I know," I said. "But there must have been a kinship between the two races—at least, at the time of the Crusades."

"Do you know something?" said Sarkis. "There should have been a kinship, but there was not. For one thing, Armenia was so far away. For another, don't you know, we were the rug merchants, the traders." As he said it, he laughed. "I remember that when I was a boy in Cairo they used to tease me about selling rugs. They did not mean it badly. It was a joke. But still I sometimes got sick of it." He looked at me. "It is something we Armenians have to get accustomed to, do we not?"

I felt a sudden rage within myself at these seemingly casual remarks, and, in fact, could hardly speak. I could see Sarkis's face staring at me, his plump hands on the table; he was wearing a gray, thickly knotted necktie. What had he said? "We were the rug merchants, the traders."

Afterward, my wife said to me, "Did anyone tease you at school about being a rug merchant?"

"No," I said. "Or I can hardly remember anything like that." But it wasn't true.

NONE OF IT was true, I realized. Not so much whether I had ever been teased for being a "rug merchant" as what I really felt about it. A great rush of memories overwhelmed me: small anecdotes from the past; trivial, unimportant remarks or jokes—many of them so petty I was ashamed to recall them. And not always from long ago: just before we embarked on this voyage, I remembered, an old friend of mine, wishing us well, said, with a laugh, "Now, don't get taken by any of those wily Armenians."

Wily Armenians! Rug merchants! Traders! What in hell did those things matter, I thought, trying to be more rational about it. But something had been let loose inside me—a shame, an anger. And I knew suddenly how it mattered. It mattered because it was supposed to matter. It mattered because I had said that it couldn't, mustn't matter. It mattered because my father had said that none of it existed.

We were walking with Sarkis through a museum, a museum of Armenian art objects: ancient pots and urns, crude wooden chariots and spears. I could hardly see any of the exhibits, let alone think about them or listen to Sarkis's incessant commentary, for I was still consumed by rage. I remember staring dumbly at an enormous orange-colored wine jar, peering at it studiously, and thinking, My secret is that I have always hated being an Armenian. I haven't ignored it or been shy about it—I have hated it. Because I was given the values of the Europeans and *they* despised the Armenians. And I have hated my father not, as I have thought all these years, for being too strong a figure or too authoritarian but because he, so to speak, stepped back and gave me to the Europeans.

What was that refrain I so recoiled from? "My father had committed no crime . . . my poor father . . . my father . . ."

And then, as if the rage had burst, I thought, Ah, fathers! How hard it is to be a father. And I thought of mine: his cool, elegant, impassive face, the face that sometimes smiled in public but rarely in private; the sad eyes; the English manner; his care that I become English, American—anything but Armenian.

We had moved on past the orange-colored urn and were standing in front of an ancient chariot. "A war chariot of the middle Urartian period," Sarkis was saying.

I said, "When did the Armenians stop being warriors?"

"What do you mean?" he asked.

"I mean, when did they stop being warriors and start being traders or rug merchants?"

Sarkis laughed. "Ah, rug merchants!" he repeated. He didn't know whether I was joking or not, and I didn't, either. "If you are serious," he said, "I think the answer is that there was no one time when they started to become traders. But the period you were just reading about, when the Armenians migrated from the mountains to Cilicia—

that was when they gave up their historic pursuits and turned to trade."

"What about the horses?" I asked.

"The Armenians were historically great horsemen," said Sarkis.

"What about the soldiers and the commanders of cavalry?"

"Yes, Armenians were great soldiers," said Sarkis.

I realized that he didn't understand me, and that in reality I was asking questions of myself, or perhaps of my own fantasies.

MY WIFE AND I sat out alone on a kind of restaurant terrace. It was early evening, the sky still light. People were lined up opposite for a movie.

I said, "All along, I've been trying to prove something, and it's not provable."

"But who said you have to prove anything?" she said.

That seemed sensible, although it was a hard idea to accept. I thought, People don't know anything about Armenians. Even Armenians don't seem to know about Armenians.

The next day, we were parading around yet another fine old Armenian church, out in one of the valleys, about an hour's drive from the city. It was a tranquil place: an ancient stone structure set against the dark trees and alpine meadows—a structure of dark-brownish stone slabs, smooth and weathered by age, which was quite small but very compact and stocky (like the Armenians), with a conical roof over the center, covered by tiles.

It was pleasant to be up near the mountains, where there were wild flowers and the grass looked less dry. Sarkis, in his ever-present brown suit, tightly buttoned, clambered over parapets and gravestones discoursing on Armenian architecture. It seemed that he especially favored the Austrian art critic and historian Joseph Strzygowski, who in 1918 had formulated the theory that key elements of both Byzantine and Western European religious architecture derived from the Armenians. "You know, Strzygowski has said that the Greeks with Saint Sophia and the Italians with Saint Peter's only elaborated on ideas that the Armenians first developed," said Sarkis. "Is that not something, my friends? Is that not a proud claim for Armenian architecture?" Sarkis bent down and picked a wild poppy from near a gravestone and handed it to my wife. I considered for a second whether Sarkis might not in some way be fancying her, but it didn't seem likely.

"What made Strzygowski think that?" I asked.

"It is very simple," said Sarkis. "It is a matter of the dome's being placed over the *square*. The Romans, as we know, placed their domes over circles, over circular structures. But the great architectural achievements of the medieval period and of the Renaissance came from the dome's being placed over the square. Strzygowski said that this form evolved first from the ancient wooden houses of Central Asia and was then perfected by Armenian architects as early as the fourth century." Sarkis sat down on a low wall, partly in the shade, and mopped his forehead with a handkerchief.

"Can we see some of those fourth-century churches?" my wife asked.

"Alas, that is a problem," said Sarkis. "They do not exist any longer."

"Did they exist in Strzygowski's time?" I asked.

"Alas, no. That was Strzygowski's problem, too. None of our early domed churches were still standing when he wrote his thesis." Sarkis got to his feet, pulling his jacket tightly about him, although the day was warm and becoming warmer. "It could have happened, you know," he said. "It is a plausible theory. But I admit that it remains controversial." He suddenly waved his arms, a stout figure in the middle of a graveyard, waving his arms at the passing clouds. "Look at the flowers!" he said. "Are they not beautiful? This lovely old church! Is it not beautiful here?"

ON OUR WAY BACK to town, we stopped to have lunch beside the road—sandwiches out of paper bags. There were some scrawny cattle in the distance. Fields on either side of us. Two trucks of laborers passed by—men of all ages, with dark eyes and mustaches, and holding long-handled hoes. I was aware of something's having happened yesterday, but I wasn't sure what it was, or how to talk about it. Before going to sleep the night before, I had been conscious of having admitted something shameful, having admitted some deep and shaming secret in simply acknowledging my revulsion (my shame) at this disparaged side of the Armenian character—the rug dealer, the wily merchant, the Levantine trader. But somehow today I didn't think I felt ashamed.

I asked Sarkis, "What was it like when you worked for the English?"

"It wasn't so bad," he said. "I had had a good schooling. I was the assistant to the head of a large warehouse. A military warehouse." He smiled. "That was when I had my motorcycle. 'Motorbike,' they called it."

"I meant, what was it really like?"

"What do you mean?" said Sarkis.

"I mean, what was it like to be an Armenian?" I said.

We were sitting on a rough stone fence. Sarkis had an

orange in his hand, which he was peeling with a penknife. He peeled it slowly, with a practiced hand—the orange-and-white skin unwinding in a steady ribbon.

"It was difficult," he said. "It was a very difficult time. It is hard to explain. You see, I had much ambition then. I was a young man. I was not bad-looking, either. I always liked the English."

"What did they think of you?" I asked.

"Oh, I was Sarkis, Sarkis the Armenian. But, you see, they were kind to me. When I was eighteen, I was chief assistant to this man, Mr. Peterson. He said he thought of me as a son."

"Where did you live?" I asked.

"I lived with my family, naturally. Where else should I live? We had a small house—part of a house, with another family. We lived in the Christian quarter. It was not far from the English."

"What went wrong?" I asked.

"What do you mean, what went wrong?" said Sarkis.

Sometimes he exasperated me. "I mean that you left Cairo, and this fine English employer, and you came to Soviet Armenia in 1948, when it couldn't have been much fun here."

"In 1947," said Sarkis. "No, it was not what you call fun." Then, "I don't know why you ask me these things."

"Because I want to know about you," I said. It was true.

"I'm not sure I can tell you," said Sarkis. "You ask me why I left Cairo. There were two reasons. The stinking poverty there had forced me toward the Communist teachings. And I was Armenian. I wished to return to my homeland."

"And what else?" I asked.

"There was nothing else," said Sarkis. The uneaten orange rested on the stones beside him. His eyes seemed to roam across the empty fields. "There was one thing," he said. "I fell in love with this girl, an English girl. She was going to the college. I would meet her after working. She was not very pretty, but I liked her very much. It is all so long ago that it is hard to remember. She had very long hair, and sometimes she used to ride behind me on the motorbike. We never really had plans to marry."

"But you were both in love?"

"Yes, but I was ambitious. Mr. Peterson had said he might take me into the business."

"Didn't he help you with the girl?"

Sarkis laughed. "No. You see, she was his daughter. He said that I had betrayed him. Oh, it was a terrible time. For a while, he wouldn't speak to me. The girl was sent away. You know, I don't remember her very well any more. Long hair and skinny legs—too skinny, I always thought. But I remember Mr. Peterson and Mrs. Peterson. One afternoon, I went to their house. I had been there before, of course, because I was his chief assistant and had taken messages, but I had not been there many times. She was very upset. Mr. Peterson kept saying, 'Don't get so upset, my dear,' but she got upset anyway. She kept calling me 'Jew' and sometimes 'Armenian' and sometimes both—'Armenian

Jew.' It's funny—I have often heard the English use that expression, although I think it is impossible. Catholic Protestant!"

"And so you left?"

"Yes, naturally. I had no choice. At first, I went to work for a rival company. I had this plan that I would rise high up in the rival company—control it, maybe—and then drive Mr. Peterson's company out of business. I had dreams that I would someday drive up to the English club in my motorcar and my girl would see me—how well I looked, how prosperous—and would know what she had missed. Oh, I had many youthful, vengeful dreams. In the end, I was ashamed of my desire for vengeance. My brothers wanted us all to move here, and so I did."

The afternoon was silent—silence everywhere. A large bird, perhaps a hawk, floated over fields far away. Sarkis slowly ate his orange. Then we walked down the dirt path to our car, which stood baking in the sun. Pausing beside the car for a moment, Sarkis said, "You know, about all I can really remember of that time is the day when Mr. Peterson said he thought of me as a son."

LATER THAT NIGHT, I thought, I am a son, and how can a son turn against his father? How dreadful it is! But then what strange creatures are fathers: these household Abrahams, with their knives raised on high—knives that take on all manner of shapes and forms, that descend in all manner of arcs. I thought, My father never raised his knife over me. I am no Isaac, and he was no Abraham.

I fell into sleep, half sleeping, thinking of how we were all together once, some long ago—a place of green fields, a picnic place. I remembered our dog had been there. My father wandered off. I could see him, a slim figure standing silhouetted beside a tree. Then, somehow, there were soldiers, and black shapes of airplanes overhead. We were in a prison above a rushing river—dark rocks below. I thought I saw Sarkis somewhere. I thought, If only Sarkis and my father can somehow meet, they will arrive at a plan—or at least an understanding. But my father was nowhere to be seen. Men with helmets roamed the hills. My wife was shaking me. "It's all right," she said. And, again, "It's all right."

After a while, I got out of bed and walked over to the chair by the window. It was quite late. The lights of Erevan were low. The square was dark. Everything seemed still. I watched a distant red dot blinking in the sky—a far-off plane—and remembered the figure standing silhouetted beside the tree, and thought, I love him anyway.

It had been agreed that around ten in the morning my wife and I should go with Sarkis to the Institute of Ancient Manuscripts: the Matenadaran. But by the appointed time, and even thirty minutes after the appointed time, Sarkis had not shown up, so for a while we milled aimlessly around the steps in front of the hotel—an area, scantily shaded by two or three frail trees, where, as always, a certain proportion of the male population appeared to spend part of its morning, leaning against the wall or standing in little conversational groups beneath the low branches.

My wife seemed irritated with me anyway. I wasn't sure exactly why. I thought, Perhaps because I woke her up with my nightmare. Then I thought, Perhaps because I embarrassed Sarkis in getting him to tell us his story. I asked her if that was it. Naturally, she said no. A bit later—we were still pacing about in front of the hotel—she said, "Well, of course. When someone like Sarkis puts his chips on the Soviet Union, on Soviet Armenia, it's the bet of his life. You can't just *talk* about it. I mean, it's not a matter of easy choices—like does one prefer Coke or Pepsi."

"I didn't think we were talking about that," I said.

"I know. You thought you were talking about Egypt.

Egypt and his English girl. But you kept raising these *questions.*"

"Is that bad?"

"I don't know," she said. "I've never been in his position. But I'm sure that's why he hasn't shown up."

"I'll go and call him," I said.

"He doesn't have a phone," she said.

We waited a little longer. There didn't seem anything else to do, and it was entertaining, in a way, to observe the drama—or, rather, the non-drama—of the shifting, leaning, standing, quietly talking groups of men. There seemed to be more tourists in the hotel, too. Two days ago, we had seen a handful of elderly French people—with a little tricolor provided by the management upon their table—seated primly in the noisy restaurant, surrounded by Armenians, but they had soon vanished as mysteriously as they had appeared. Now onto the steps emerged some German businessmen with dour faces, carrying briefcases and wearing raffish, double-knit suits. And then, unmistakably, there were some English. Evidently not businessmen but tourists. They stood there on the hot sidewalk in front of the hotel—oh, unmistakably English! First the voices. Then the *aspect* of the group, which numbered about a dozen. The men were middle-aged, save for one or two, and wore safari jackets, thick twill trousers, and sort of fly-fisherman hats. The women were of comparable age, surely wives, and were dressed in cardigans and tweed skirts. Some wore hiking boots, and there was a pile of camping gear behind them on the steps.

"Perhaps they're spies," my wife said. "Trying to blend into the surrounding countryside."

They seemed quite marvelous. Only yesterday, I realized, I had been cursing the English, sharing Sarkis's bitterness—in fact, extracting his bitterness to somehow accompany my own. And now here they were—an English touring group in Armenia. I decided to talk to one of them, and went over to an elderly fellow standing about, puffing at his pipe.

"Are you going to be here long?" I asked.

"In and out," he said. "We'll be in and out."

It turned out that they were members of a Yorkshire bird-watching club and were engaged in a spot of hiking and bird-watching around the Caucasus. "Last year, we went to some of the southern regions of America," he said. "By any chance, are you American or Canadian?"

"American," I said.

"Well, then you must know the Carolinas. Simply extraordinary shore birds. I knew we'd be in for a treat, but I had no idea of the actual *variety* of the specimens."

I asked him what he thought of Armenia.

"Oh, fascinating. A fascinating place. Yesterday, we were climbing that mountain—what is it? Not Ararat. The other one."

"Aragats," said a woman in a duck-shooting jacket, who had joined us.

"Yes, Aragats." I reminded myself that Aragats itself was more than thirteen thousand feet high. "About halfway up, some of our party—I regret I was not one of them—spotted *two* varieties of hawk that I must say none of us even knew existed in this part of the world."

"One variety," said the lady. "The other turned out to be a rough-legged hawk."

"Oh, yes. Well, it was a rough-legged hawk after all. Not so rare, but still rather unusual in my opinion."

"And how do you find the Armenians?" I asked.

"Which Armenians?" said the man. "Oh. The people?" He took a puff at his pipe. "Fascinating," he said. "Utterly fascinating."

"They're really quite charming," said the lady.

"Of course, I wouldn't *haggle* with any of them if I were you!" said the man, with a laugh.

My wife was tugging me by the arm. "Come on! Come on!" she said. "Vartan is waiting."

You bastards, I thought. "Those bastards!" I said to my wife. And "Why did you pull me away just then?"

"I don't know," she said. "I didn't think you were interested in birds. Besides, Vartan *is* waiting."

Vartan, our official guide, stood beside a car. In the last few days, he had apparently acquired a slight suntan. His hair was tousled, and he seemed hot—although he was coatless and tieless, for a change, which gave him an almost sporty look.

He said, "Sarkis is indisposed, and so he has asked me to accompany you."

We decided to go, as scheduled, to the Matenadaran. "I am not too familiar with the books," said Vartan, "but I will try to be helpful."

"I really just want to look inside it," I said.

It was a large and churchlike building set against the side of one of the hills. Within were a number of people, mostly schoolchildren on a tour—giggling young faces, the girls with great red bows in their hair, everyone being shushed by the teachers. The old manuscripts were locked away in glass cases. There were displays of tiny Bibles, no larger than a couple of thumbs, and of huge volumes in ancient, hand-worked leather.

"How meticulous and delicate the workmanship is," my wife said.

I thought, How meticulous and delicate and obsessive. I remembered those tiny carved boxes in the apartment of the old man on Thirty-third Street. His whole apartment had a kind of miniature, concentrated, hand-carved look—obsessive, and airless, too.

We looked for a while at the bright colors of the illumi-nated pages: the tiny, glowing figures in red, blue, and gold; the angular Armenian lettering of the Gospels. It was hard to know what it all meant. The manuscripts and old Bibles rested serenely under the glass. The schoolchildren giggled and poked one another. "Here," said Vartan, and he read dutifully from a display card, "This is part of the Bible from the Armenian church at Van, which was smuggled away by two sisters when they fled from the Turks. When one of the sisters died by the roadside, the other one retained the Bible and brought it here." The book in question was a considerable volume—perhaps two feet in length. There were dark stains across one of the pages. It was hard to know what any of it meant.

Vartan was clearly not in his favorite milieu, although he was trying to be polite. "Let's take a walk somewhere," I said. Outside, it was a changeable kind of day. Gray clouds were moving across the hills, and a cool wind blew.

"Perhaps you would like to see the new football stadium?" said Vartan. Clearly, Vartan wanted to see the new football stadium.

"All right," I said.

We left the car where it was, and walked for a long while down streets—streets with old buildings, streets with new buildings. Flower boxes hung from most of the windows. I said to Vartan, "Have you ever thought of yourself as a trader?"

He looked at me, smiling, uncertain. "What is that—a 'trader'?"

"A merchant," I said. "Somebody who makes deals."

"Who makes deals?" said Vartan. He laughed. "No. Why should I think that?"

We had come to the stadium. It was an enormous place, obviously very new: one of those molded-concrete structures, with a great bowl of seats rising up in a futuristic design, the oval of deep green far below.

"It is beautiful, don't you think?" said Vartan. He seemed much pleased.

"Yes, it certainly is," I said.

"I come to all the games," he said.

We wandered about the great gray concrete seats, solitary dwarf figures in an empty coliseum. Some bulldozers were still working on something down below.

"What did you mean about the 'trader'?" said Vartan. "I do not think I understand."

"I'm not sure myself," I said. "In other parts of the world, Armenians are often thought of that way—as traders. Buying, selling . . ."

"I have not heard," said Vartan. He pointed down toward the distant scoreboard, which had lettering on it in Russian as well as Armenian. "Our next game is with the Ukraine," he said. "At the present, our team is No. 2, but, of course, the Ukraine is very good."

It began to rain lightly, and we walked back in the drizzle. Gray water ran down the gutters, and the leaves on the trees looked fresh and almost glistened.

"I should have brought the car," said Vartan.

"No," I said.

We all knew it was nice this way.

Back in front of the Matenadaran, Vartan said, with a smile, "This buying and selling—I know. You mean 'businessmen.'"

"I suppose so," I said.

"Yes, we have *businessmen*," said Vartan, relieved at having cleared up the problem. "But I am not one of them."

We said goodbye at our hotel. "Did you like the football stadium?" said Vartan.

"Yes, very much," I said.

"It is a good stadium," he said. "We will win a lot."

Inside, Sarkis had left a note and a book.

The note, in thick, measured handwriting, said, "I am compelled to give a special lesson today. But I know that you will go to the Matenadaran with a guide from the Cultural Committee, and so you will not understand anything or learn anything. Therefore, you will do this for me. You will examine the book of colophons I enclose. For there are voices in this book, and you must try to hear them. Your friend and kinsman, Sarkis."

That evening, I took up the book that Sarkis had left—*Colophons of Armenian Manuscripts, 1301–1480*. It was in English, and handsomely designed, although at first glance it seemed an obdurate and unlikely thing to read. Colophons, after all, were short notes or messages "written, as a rule, by the scribes upon the conclusion of the production of a manuscript," according to their translator, Professor Avedis Sanjian. "Occasionally, they were written at the end of long sections of a text; there are also brief colophons which appear on the margins." My wife was sitting on the bed reading a book about the California Gold Rush. Outside in the square, there was the familiar sound of loudspeaker music. A casual crowd of people had gathered by the fountains—men and women idling in the warm summer's night. I began to read:

VILLAGE OF SERKWILI: At this time there occurred a massacre of innocent Christians. . . . For, instigated by Satan, Djihānshah Mīrzā, of the Scythian race, assembled many legions of troops, besieged the citadel for four months, and caused them much anguish, for many died of grief.

MONASTERY OF SEWERAK: . . . The accursed dog [from the nation of] archers, Shāhrukh Mīrzā, arrived with numerous . . . troops. He devastated Armenia, carried off many into captivity and slaughtered them, he demolished and burned, and forced many to renounce their faith.

MONASTERY OF HERMON:
> . . . *In bitter and grievous times,*
> *When many in the land were persecuted,*
> *Some dwelt among bushes,*
> *Some fell prey to the wolves,*
> *Many became victims of the famine,*
> *Fathers disavowed their children.*

VILLAGE OF SORI: . . . This holy Gospel was copied . . . in bitter and anxious times, during the khanate of Uzun Hasan, who in this year . . . shed much blood.

ALT'AMAR: . . . [This was copied] during the khanate of Iskandar Mīrzā of the nation of the archers, a Turk by race, who . . . caused ineffable and unrecountable bitterness throughout our land, and I cannot describe in writing the destruction of our country and the decimation of its population. For this is the tenth year that the tempest of God's wrath has visited our country on account of my multitudinous sins.

Page after page was filled with such notations. Brief jottings, as it were, from a bygone time: from the fourteenth and fifteenth centuries—that period, known to us in the

West as the Renaissance, when in the East the plains of Asia Minor and the Armenian plateau were at the mercy of various Turkish, Mongol, and Arab invaders.

At first, I found these colophons difficult to read, for there seemed to be no "story" to them, no order, no purpose. A list of messages from a remote time: disjointed messages, messages of woe and anger about unknown persecutors and nameless victims, about long-vanished, exotic-sounding tyrants. Djihānshah, Iskandar, Uzun Hasan, Bayandur Beg, Shāhrukh, Kara Yūsuf.

"And in this year there occurred a severe plague in our land. . . . And for two years he [Iskandar] ransacked and plundered our country. . . . We took to flight and wandered about in numerous places."

The sense of misery—for it was a litany of lamentations—appeared endless.

"It was a sight to behold the awesome moaning and lamenting over the dear ones, for the mother wept over her son, the sister over the brother, the bride over the bridegroom; and they received no consolation from any quarter, neither from God nor from man."

All the same, I kept reading, and I soon realized that I was strongly affected. Perhaps it was the mood of the evening—although, as I remember it, the only quiet was in our room, for the night's street noises continued for a long while unabated outside the open window, and at one point you could hear a dance band from the hotel's dining room playing nineteen-forties American foxtrots in a cheerful, stately measure. Perhaps, too, it was that something had changed between Sarkis and me, for he had asked me to try to *hear* something in these colophons. I believe "hear" was the key word, for what had at first seemed like dry words upon a page—a catalogue of dry words—now began to come through to me as voices.

I thought of the history I had read in the past few months, with its careful narrative of events and wavelike happenings. Battles. The death of kings. "At this time, there occurred a massacre. . . . In this year, there arrived locusts." I thought, too, of the ancient Armenia I had read about: the kings of Nairi; the sturdy mountaineers who clambered around the rocks above Xenophon's army; the horsemen and horse breeders; old Narses at the gates of Rome; even Thoros and his double-shirted ceremony. I had supposed that all that was real enough, and had clutched it as if it were some solid family tree, some solid *warrior* family tree that I might hold on to and be enhanced by. But surely *this* was real, too—these bitter and anxious times, these Hasans and dread Iskandars and poor, shame-ridden monks huddled in the cellars of their dark churches. More real, perhaps.

"This Holy Testament was begun and completed in bitter and anxious times when we were quivering at the hands of the infidels, for charity and mercy among men have disappeared."

"Sultan Mahmat . . . raised an intense storm upon the Christians and also upon his own people, by transplanting them from place to place, by imposing levies, and by causing other anguish."

Sultan Mahmat, I remembered, was the Sultan Muhammad II, who finally wrested Constantinople from the last, shadowy Byzantines; who transported eighty sea galleys overland to the Golden Horn; who employed the greatest cannon anyone had seen in the world; who was a leader of warriors, a collector of Greek books. The man who captured the One Great City, the city whose magic presence even the Turks Greekified—εἰς τήν πόλιν ("ees-teen-polin," or "to the city"), which five centuries later officially became Istanbul—and who instantly decreed its improvement, commanding the "importation of the skilled artisan populations of the Greeks and Armenians."

I thought, But what do I care about this Sultan Muhammad, with his fine cannon and his Greek books? What I care about are the people buried in the historian's sentence—the "skilled artisans," the Armenians.

By then, it was late at night. Over on the bed, my wife was long asleep. The lights in the square had gone out. The music had stopped. The summer crowd had vanished. A white moon had moved halfway across the sky.

As I read the colophons, I thought, They are like messages in bottles, messages from some long-ago sea wreck, messages written by men.

"They put the wondrous bishops to the sword; they ground the heads of the pious priests between stones; they cast the flock of Christ as food for the dogs. . . . Like the threshing-floor of flails, they thrashed the children with their horses; and, in place of grain, rivers of blood began to spring forth, and in place of straw the bones flowed forth like dust."

I thought, Perhaps strangest of all is now to be a modern man, an advanced citizen of an advanced country, and to scarcely conceive of the possibility of an unreceived message, a communication without a communicatee, a bottle that does not drift up to shore—some friendly shore somewhere.

The sky outside my window was clear, blinking with stars. But just then the darkness of the world seemed overwhelming, as did the sense of unheard voices.

A conversation with Sarkis.

I said, "I would like to know more about the Turks and the Armenians."

"The Turks are a despicable race," said Sarkis. "They massacred our people."

"Yes, I know that," I said. "But there must have been more to it."

"*More* to it!" exclaimed Sarkis. "What more can there have been? Murder is murder, is it not? Did you read the book of colophons I left for you?"

"Yes, and I was very moved by them," I said. "The Armenians seem to have suffered a great deal."

"You see, even *then* they were killing our people," said Sarkis. "For hundreds of years, we were persecuted by the Turks. What is it you want to know?"

"I want to know why."

"Because the Turks were savages," said Sarkis. "Have you not read what they did to us? To our women and children? Were these not the acts of savages?"

"But what did the Armenians do?" I asked.

Sarkis looked at me. "What do you mean—what did they do?"

"What did they do?"

"The Armenians did nothing," said Sarkis. "They were the slaughtered."

I thought, It keeps coming back to that. The Armenian refrain: "We were murdered. We were innocent. We were slaughtered. We did nothing." It was supposed to evoke compassion, I knew, and each time I willed the compassion forward, but it would not come. I felt a shame before Sarkis and myself. I also felt, There is something amiss with that refrain.

WHO were the Turks? I tried to read about them in books. For example, in *Turkey* (Geographical Handbook Series): "Chinese annals also record in A.D. 545 the rise of the Tukiu clan of the Hsiung-nu . . . who gathered other tribes and settled before 600 near the Caspian Sea, extending their rule thence to the Sea of Japan." And Professor David Bivar, in an anthology entitled *Central Asia*: "The expulsion of the Juan-juan dynasty from the Mongolian steppe was the result of the rise of the Turks, who thus make their first appearance in history. . . . The founder of the Turkish empire was the chief called in the Chinese sources Tu-men."

The Turks had been a huge association of nomad peoples, an amalgam of families and tribes, some strong, some weak, some primitive, some more advanced, most of them warrior-herdsmen shifting about on the ocean of the central Asian steppe, doubtless much like the North American Indians of long ago—sea creatures of the great land mass, drifting, grazing, hunting, fighting, propelled periodically by waves (of competition or of hunger) toward a distant shore, which in the case of the Turks was generally westward. Among the great nomad tribes were the Oghuz, the Uighur, the Kirgiz, the Pecheneg, the Kipchak, the Khazar. Even the names, at least in Anglicized form, had a somehow American Indian sound to them. The Oghuz in western Asia had been conquered by the Arabs and converted to Islam. At the beginning of the eleventh century, about the same time that the Byzantine Emperor Basil II was dismantling the native garrisons of the Armenian plateau, the Oghuz overthrew their Arab governors, and one of their more advanced and aggressive clans—that of the Seljuks—moved farther west, across the formerly Arab-dominated regions of Iran, and then north into Armenia and the Caucasus, and south to the Persian Gulf. From *Turkey:* "Though originally not very numerous, and wandering herdsmen rather than warriors, the Seljuks easily imposed their rule over the settled populations . . . while they adopted Arab and Persian cultures and combined them with Greek craftsmanship, as their fine buildings show. They left no literature; but their Ottoman successors owed much to their administrative experience."

"THE TURCOPHILES are always speaking about 'the glories of Turkish civilization,'" said Sarkis. "There has never been a 'Turkish civilization' to speak of."

"What about the Ottoman empire?" I asked.

"To begin with, the Ottomans were a minority among the Turks," said Sarkis. "By far the majority were the Turcomen—bandits and barbarians. But the Ottomans were cleverer than the majority. Do you know how they became so great? They persuaded the Turcomen to do the fighting for them. The *razzia*, they called it. The raid for plunder. The ignorant Turcomen did the fighting, and the Ottomans advanced their empire."

"Then the Ottomans were civilized?"

"They were civilized for Turks," Sarkis said.

THE TRIBE OF OSMAN, it was once called. The Arabs spoke the name as "Othman." The Byzantines transformed it again, to "Ottoman." The Ottoman Turks. By all accounts, they were one of history's great success stories. Back in the thirteenth century, Osman's tribe had been granted a small fiefdom in western Asia Minor by the dominant Seljuks. One hundred years later, the Ottomans controlled most of Asia Minor. Soon, they overran the Balkans. In 1453, Sultan Muhammad II captured Constantinople. His grandson Sultan Selim I defeated the Persians in the east, and took Syria and Egypt from the Mamelukes—in the process becoming the protector of the sacred cities of Mecca and Medina. Selim's successor, Sultan Suleiman I (the Magnificent), pushed farther into Europe, capturing Belgrade, defeating the Hungarians, and reaching the gates of Vienna.

By the end of the sixteenth century, the empire of the Ottomans was at its peak. The Ottoman Navy roamed from the Persian Gulf to Libyan Tripoli and Algiers. Ottoman beys governed territory that reached from the Armenian plateau across the extent of Asia Minor, Egypt, Libya, Greece, and the Balkans—an empire larger, even, than that of the Byzantines.

It was hard to consider this empire of the Ottomans without a certain astonishment. For it was so extensive, and powerful, and disorganized—and full of paradox.

I MADE some notes about the Turks:

From the start, the Ottoman state was autocratic, militarist, and religiously conservative. Temporal and spiritual leadership were combined in the person of the sultan, who was regarded as "the Shadow of God on Earth." Beneath him was the grand vizier, who managed the government—called "the Sublime Porte"—with the exception of the royal palace. In charge of religious matters was the sheikh-ul-Islam, who from the time of the magnificent Suleiman was head of the Ulema (Assembly of Learned Ones), and who did not manage the royal palace, either, although in some respects he was superior to the sultan, for only with the sheikh's final consent could a "holy war" be declared or the sultan himself be deposed.

The Janissaries: The name comes from the Turkish *"yeni cheri,"* which meant "new troops." As the wars in

Christian Europe ended, thus ending the supply of slaves, a policy of *devshirme* ("tribute children") was institutionalized. Young boys were taken from Christian parents, especially in the Balkans, and were farmed out to Muslim families in the provinces, converted to Islam, and then removed to Constantinople. The most physically fit were inducted into the Janissary Corps. They were trained rigorously in the arts of war, and lived apart from the regular army, in their own barracks. They were a dangerously independent elite body of troops. On initiation, they took a vow of celibacy and kept religious vigils. They prayed frequently, and doubtless furiously, and practiced "mortal combat" on one another, and in the heyday of the Ottoman empire they were the most feared—the cruelest and most efficient—body of troops in the world. By the sixteenth century, they were becoming decadent and more trouble than they were worth. Celibacy ended; free-born Muslims were admitted, many of these the sons of Janissaries; and the membership grew to an unwieldy peak of a hundred and thirty thousand. In keeping with the original savage monkishness of the order, their military titles were drawn from humble kitchen nomenclature. Thus, the senior commanders were Soup-Men. Other officers were Cook, Head Scullion, Water Carrier, and so forth. One of the traditionally dreaded moments of Ottoman political life was when the Janissaries overturned their giant soup kettles in the barracks square—symbolically indicating their displeasure with some recent action of the government's, and the likelihood of an imminent coup d'état. The corps came to an end when masses of Janissaries were cannonaded to death by a fed-up sultan in 1826—an event referred to in Turkish history books as "the Auspicious Incident."

The Harem: The word originally derived from the Arabic *"harām,"* which meant "that which is unlawful." For example, the area around Mecca and Medina was said to be *harām*—and so consequently the word came to signify "holy," "protected," "sacred," and, finally, "forbidden." The Ottomans did not invent the harem, for it had existed as far back as the empires of Assyria and Persia, but, as with many features that they borrowed from other cultures, they formalized and expanded it. The nominal head of the Ottoman harem was the sultan's mother, the *valide sultan*. Beneath this august personage stood the various mothers of the sultan's children. Beneath them were the favorite ladies, the novices, the female slaves, and also, as the enterprise grew, the royal princes, who received vague educational courses in Islamic doctrine and court protocol. The actual head of the harem was the chief eunuch, who after the sixteenth century was invariably black. He was known as the *kislar agha* and was a considerable figure in the royal harem—or, rather, in the seraglio, which was the name given to the entire palace complex of fourteen mosques, military school, ten kitchens, two bakeries, two hospitals, sports fields, arsenal, and harem. As a child, he had probably been sold into slavery by his parents somewhere in Africa; then he had been castrated en route to Constantinople at a desert stopping place along the

Nile, with everything removed by knife or sharp stone, and the patient permitted a few days to heal, buried in the sand. Now, with such traumas behind him but surely never completely out of mind—for it appeared that even total castration, if it took place after the onset of puberty, did not always remove sexual desire—the *kislar agha* was both a political and a military power in the capital. He had a small private army of his own, and three hundred horses for his personal use, and he also had his own jail and torture chamber. He maintained a steady level of income by his right of "inspecting" the funds of the imperial mosques. He alone might be the confidential messenger between the sultan and the grand vizier. He alone might approach the unapproachable sultan at any hour of the day or night.

It seems odd to think of the notions of masculinity and virility so often associated with this fussy and peculiar institution, which in fact contained the corrupt and neurotic *aghas,* the hundreds of aimless and unoccupied women, and the young princes, almost actively barred from any kind of serious education. To be sure, now and then there were some lighter moments. "It has been repeatedly affirmed," wrote N. M. Penzer in an excellent book, *The Harem,* "that when . . . favoured concubines enter the sultan's bedroom, which is not allowed until his Majesty has already retired, they approach the foot of the bed, lift up the coverlet, and raise it to their forehead and lips. They then creep in humbly at the foot of the bed, and gradually work their way upward until they are level with the sultan." Still, for both parties—the man in the bed as well as the girl crawling up it—it must have been the most confining of prisons.

The *Millets:* The Turks followed the Arabic pattern of dividing society into religious rather than national units. After the capture of Constantinople, each of the major *rayas* —or "flocks," as the non-Muslim populations were officially called by the Turks—were formed into separate religious entities known as *millets,* or "communities." Thus, all Greek Orthodox members of the empire were placed under the Greek patriarch, and all adherents of the Armenian Church were placed under the Armenian patriarch. In a sense, this office of patriarch was a considerable one, although—as with an ambassador from a foreign state—it was apart from the mainstream of official Turkish life. Even so, the Armenian patriarch, for example, ranked on a level with the higher Turkish pashas. He maintained a small police force of his own, and a private jail (although presumably not a torture chamber). Moreover, he was responsible not only for the spiritual life of his community but also for such matters as public education, civil administration, and the collection of taxes—the taxes due to his own administration as well as the "annual tribute" owed to the sultan.

This *laissez-aller* policy of the old Ottoman empire was a peculiar thing to observe. On the one hand, there was the autocratic sultan, and a rigid state belief in conservative Islam. On the other hand, there was the Armenian patriarch, with his own police force, collecting taxes. What did it mean? From *The Emergence of Modern Turkey,* by Bernard Lewis: "The Ottoman empire was tolerant of other religions, in accordance with Islamic law and tradition, and its Christian and Jewish subjects lived, on the whole, in peace and security. But they were strictly segregated from the Muslims. . . . Never were they able to mix freely in Muslim society. . . . If the convert was readily accepted and assimilated, the unconverted were extruded." One thing it seemed to mean was that the Armenians were second-class citizens.

I TRIED to discuss this matter with Sarkis—not to complain about the situation, Lord knows, although that is what I felt like doing, but because there were things about the position, or role, of the Armenians in the Ottoman empire that were not yet clear to me.

I said, "You know, in some of the books I've been reading the Armenians don't seem to have come off too well beside the Turks."

"Of course they didn't," said Sarkis impatiently. (We were sitting on a bench near the middle of Lenin Square.) "The Armenians were *conquered* by the Turks. The Turks conquered everybody in those days." He stared down at a spot between his shoes. "Savages!"

"I meant afterward. When the conquering had stopped."

Sarkis looked up. "The *conquering* never stopped. The Turks were the masters of Asia Minor, of Armenia, of the

Balkans. They had their governors everywhere; their militia—"

"Well, that's what I meant." I don't know why I wanted so to pursue the matter then, when I could see that it offended Sarkis. I think I felt that there was some clue to be found. "At least, from what I've read," I continued, "it seems to me that the Turks were very much the masters, and that the Armenians had only a very token independence."

"What did you expect?"

"I don't know," I said. "But it seems to me the Armenians were placed in a subservient position. They accepted subservience—"

"You are wrong!" said Sarkis, suddenly red in the face. "You are wrong! You have read very wrong! The Armenians were better than the Turks. The Turks knew nothing! All they cared about was making war, and soon they stopped even doing that. The Armenians were civilized. In this so-called Ottoman empire, it was the Armenians who knew about administration, who knew about business, who knew about architecture, and agriculture, and—" Sarkis paused. I had never seen him so angry or upset. He looked at me, his eyes quite hard. "You come here to Armenia and all you care about are the Turks," he said. "What is it you want?"

"Maybe you won't understand this," I said, "but I want to know everything about the Armenians, and that seems to include knowing something about the Turks."

"I know what you want," said Sarkis. "You want to tear down your father."

"It has nothing to do with my father," I said, feeling angry myself.

"Of course it has," said Sarkis. "Fatherland, father. It is the same thing."

"My father is dead," I said. It seemed an insane argument. "Besides, I love him. I've always loved him." I knew that the last was not true, but I hated Sarkis then.

"Is your father dead?" asked Sarkis sarcastically. Then, "I could tell this from the start, when I first saw you. All that Anglo-Saxon coolness and detachment. Yes, that detachment! Not like a proper son!" I looked at him. He seemed to be shaking—his thick, compact body rocking forward at the waist. I wanted to say to him, "How dare you?" or some such thing. But then he turned his head away. "Your father was an Armenian," he said, in a voice that seemed quite hoarse. "You must respect him!" And then Sarkis suddenly took my hands in his, and I looked into his face and saw that he was crying.

After Sarkis had left—for he claimed a meeting or appointment at his school late in the afternoon, and soon departed by bicycle down one of the side streets, pedaling in a slow and stately fashion, his brown-jacketed back vanishing in the traffic—I wandered off on my own across the square, past throngs of men and women on their way back from work, past small children playing tag beside the fountains, past a gathering of Armenian policemen in Russian uniforms standing solemnly around a broken green motorcycle, past newspaper kiosks selling only *Pravda* and coffee shops selling only tea, and, not wishing to walk farther or to stop anywhere along the street, I made my way almost by chance into the museum.

Inside, it was quiet and nearly empty. Two elderly guards in rumpled uniforms sat at a card table near the entrance playing dominoes and drinking soft drinks. Behind them I glimpsed the hall with the war chariot and urns which Sarkis had led us through some days earlier. Downstairs, it was a museum of brittle artifacts and of domino playing. Upstairs, the wood floor of the exhibition rooms stretched out, gleaming and lately polished, beneath my feet.

Costumes and pieces of faded peasant dress hung on the walls.

What in hell had Sarkis meant, I wondered. I knew what he had meant about my "coolness and detachment," because I had heard that many times before—indeed, had heard it for much of my life, had come to know such a quality in myself, for apparently it was part of me, a segment of my nature, a character trait that friends could spot and discuss perceptively. *You're very analytical, you know. You have this detachment.* I knew that on a deeper level I wasn't detached or cool. I was anything but cool. But I also knew that I often seemed that way. It was a kind of curse, which I tried to escape from in my writing.

I padded through the hushed museum, alone in the empty halls, the floor shining like ice and having an air of inutility about it, like the floor of some aristocrat's ballroom. I attempted to keep my mind—or, anyway, my eyes—on the exhibits, with a view to educating myself and learning more about Armenia, not wasting the moment, and so forth. There were displays of metal bowls that had been made (or so a card declared) by Armenians in Persia. Some embroidered jackets from Armenians in Poland. Some wooden boxes from China. Armenians apparently were everywhere—blown like poppy seeds, sending back obscure handicrafts instead of postcards.

You must respect your father. The phrase ran through my head. It still made me angry that I should have been told this—by a stranger, by this Sarkis, this volunteer kinsman

and friend! Did I not already respect my father? Did I not
love him? To be sure, at times I experienced the reverse of
such feelings—the child-rage of a forty-year-old son who
had once felt threatened by his sire. But wasn't this common? And even these hard emotions were surely dwarfed
by the compassion I had learned to feel for this man, who I
knew had himself suffered greatly in his life, his fortunes,
his career. If anything, I thought, I respected him too much.

By then, I had walked nearly to the end of the floor. I
was about to turn around when, down a small corridor to
the left, a solitary portrait suddenly caught my eye. Indeed, it did more than that—it gave me quite a jolt. At
first, I thought it was a trick of lighting or perception.
Then I thought it was a trick of the mind—my recent pre-
occupations having somehow jammed my optic nerve. There,
at any rate, at the end of this narrow corridor (which led, as
far as I could see, nowhere), hung a painting of a man in
period costume. The background of the painting was dark
and nondescript. The face of the man, however, was sharp
and luminous, either from the gleam of the paint or from
the museum lighting: my father's face.

As I came closer to it, my sense of normality returned,
for clearly it was a painting of someone else, someone particular. The typewritten title card, taped to the wall, described him as a merchant of Erzurum, from the eighteenth
century. But the face seemed uncannily like my father's.

I stared at the canvas closely, trying to see the markings
of the artist's brush, the placing of the pigment, as if by

observing it as an object, as paint on canvas, a man-fash-
ioned likeness, I might separate the two presences.

It was a simple portrait, really—on the whole, pleasingly
and conventionally done. The merchant wore a hat of dark-
blue velvet and a ruffled white silk shirt. A gold chain hung
from his neck. The look of the dress was *soigné* and European. The face itself was small-featured and intelligent, with
a not large but definite nose, a thin mouth, and quiet, glowing eyes. The expression of the face was composed. Over all,
the appearance of the merchant was of a man assured, elegant, in control. But how remarkable was the quiet, almost
withdrawn brightness of the eyes!

I thought of my father, and, as I so often did when
summoning him back from death, from incorporeality,
from inside my head, my dreams—whatever "memory" is—
in my mind I saw his face (was it from a photograph, an
actual scene, an imaginary moment?) looking wordlessly
back at me. Not really looking at me—just *looking,* looking
out from somewhere, from himself, the way he often did.
"Impassive": that word always came to mind. Yes, composed, elegant, coolly assured. And then I saw the eyes
again, for if there was a silence to his eyes, there was also a
glow, a heat, the most noiseless of passions. The eyes seemed
almost to burn out at me. Burning eyes in a frozen face! I
thought suddenly, It wasn't coldness or coolness that I had
felt in him. It was never coldness. It was— How might one
put it? An absence of temperature. A redirection of tempera-

ture—inward. But whose face was it I was looking at—the face in my memory or the face on the canvas? Or both?

The merchant of Erzurum stared down from the pale-green wall. Erzurum: I knew it from my readings as a moderate-sized provincial capital on the western edge of the Armenian plateau. Once, it had been the site of a Roman garrison. In Byzantine times, it had become a major caravan stop and the center of a flourishing textile and carpet industry. Since then, it had been under various Turk and Mongol administrations culminating in its capture in the sixteenth century by the Ottomans. I wondered how our composed and elegant merchant had fared with the Turks. From the dignified presence in his portrait, he had done reasonably well. Clearly, he was a man of substance, one of the top businessmen of the town—doubtless a leader of the Armenian *millet*. Did he sometimes have dinner—or, anyway, take coffee—with the Turkish bey, and discuss the new tobacco taxes and the gossip of distant Constantinople? Did he send away for shirts? Did his wife read aloud to him in French? Did he mind it that he could never have a serious place in governing his country, or that his Turkish neighbors sometimes called his son *"giaour"*—"infidel"? Or did he set his expression, freeze part of himself, his face—all save the eyes, which no man can control—and tap his finger on the coffee cup, and nod, and curl and uncurl his hand inside his well-cut pocket . . . and *manage?*

For an instant, I tried to imagine my father in the merchant's blue velvet hat. At first, I thought of it as a game, a conceit, but then my imaginings began to seem all too apt, even obvious. The obviousness of the image took my breath away. A merchant! Why not, I thought. The remote, vivid, controlled expression looked back at me from the dark canvas. I thought of Sarkis, standing on the stone wall in the graveyard, talking, gesticulating, waving hands and arms, profuse, volatile, excessive. So far removed from control and impassivity. And it came to me then and there that, all along, the two sets of mannerisms had been a variant of a single response—this cool, "un-Armenian" control and the shrill, "Armenian" excitability. They were twin symptoms, one bursting wildly outward, the other absorbed coldly inward. The merchant, my father, Sarkis—and how many others?—were the same.

I realized at that moment that to be an Armenian, to have lived as an Armenian, was to have become something crazy. Not "crazy" in the colloquial sense of quirky or charmingly eccentric ("My crazy old man!"), or even of certifiably mad. But crazy: crazed, that deep thing—deep where the deep-sea souls of human beings twist and turn.

It was near twilight. The sound of an old man coughing in a distant room sounded like falling china. I could not bear to stay in the museum any longer, and went down the stairs, past the empty card table, out into the soft and choky dusk, walking quickly across the square, as if on important business, and back to the hotel.

Up in our room, my wife had recently returned from

buying fruit and bread at the market. The hotel radio was playing Russian folk songs—the sounds of static and a bala-laika. It was a tranquil domestic scene.

"Sarkis phoned," she said. "He was concerned that he'd offended you. What's been going on?"

"Nothing much," I said. "We were talking about Turks. Turkish civilization."

"You'd think that two Armenians could talk together about that without fighting," she said. She had a pile of strawberries beside the sink and was washing them. She seemed in a happy mood, and tapped her foot to the scratchy music. "A while ago, you didn't seem to want to get involved with Turks and Armenians," she said. "'All that massacre business,' you called it."

"I never called it that."

"Oh, you did. But what do you suppose changed?"

"I don't know," I said. "Maybe it's not a very easy subject to jump into."

"I guess it isn't," she said. "But I'm curious. What bothers you most about it?"

"You know, I don't think I'm really bothered," I said.

"Is it that the Turks were such bastards? Does it remind you of the Germans and the Jews?"

"All that," I said. "And the fact that the Armenians were so helpless."

She sat at the wooden table, plucking the green sprigs off the strawberries and putting the berries in a bowl. "How do you know they were?" she said.

"Because everyone says so."

She looked at me. "Maybe," she said. "But I don't believe it." And then, "You know, I wish just once in this whole damn time you'd *admit* to being really bothered!"

I thought of the frozen man in the blue velvet hat. Perhaps I, too, was the man in the blue velvet hat. And how could I explain to anyone about that?

We went on an expedition to Byurakan. Very touristic and semi-official: five of us packed into the ancient, run-down limousine, which was driven, fortunately, not by Sarkis, who—along with Vartan—sat in the front, generally silent, with a straw hat on his head, but by a tall, elongated teacher of mathematics named Arak, a "professional colleague" from the school, who smoked cigarettes incessantly and evidently enjoyed himself rushing through the yellowing countryside.

Byurakan—it was a little village, about an hour's career from Erevan, and also the site of a great observatory. The little village possessed such charm as similar places everywhere possess—which is to say, largely in the eye of the beholder. Tiny plots of dry soil with a goat, perhaps; some frantic chickens; one or two fruit trees bearing little bulbs of orange. The houses were of stone, and many of them contained new window frames but no windowpanes.

"Look," said Arak, puffing wreaths of smoke. "They will not have windows by Christmas. In my mother's village, it required two years."

"Christmas is six months away," said Sarkis, as if imparting official information. "They have things speeded up this year."

"Ah, yes," said Arak. "I can see."

A cluster of old women—or, anyway, of women who looked old—stood near the road, some twenty or thirty feet into the field, leaning on their hoes. Arak waved a smoky hand. One of the women waved back—surely the wave of a younger sister. I thought of a passage in Osip Mandelstam's *Journey to Armenia,* written during the dreadful nineteen-thirties, when the great and persecuted Russian poet was briefly "vacationed" to Armenia. It was about a visit to Byurakan, and it went like this (as translated by Clarence Brown):

> Everywhere there were peasant women with tearful faces, shuffling movements, red eyelids, and cracked lips. They had an ugly way of walking, as if they had the dropsy or had strained a tendon. They moved like hills of weary rags, stirring up the dust with their hems.
>
> The flies eat the children, gathering in clusters at the corners of their eyes.
>
> The smile of an elderly Armenian peasant woman is inexplicably beautiful—there is so much nobility, exhausted dignity, and a sort of solemn, married charm in it.

I liked the part about the "exhausted dignity" and "solemn, married charm," and wondered if it was true—although perhaps, as with van Gogh's pictures of country life, it was enough that the artist had seen whatever he had seen.

Mandelstam had not mentioned the great observatory, and so probably it had not yet been built. Or maybe they would not show it to him, fearing that the Jewish poet might spot some altogether marvelous Jewish star out in the cosmos and publish the news abroad in literary quarterlies. Or maybe Mandelstam had been uninterested in observatories.

In midmorning, we trooped about like schoolchildren through the scientific facilities. There is this to be said about observatories in general: they are inevitably disappointing, because of their lack of frightening equipment and size, and because when photographers take pictures of giant telescopes they usually try to please by making the telescopes appear far larger than they are, and so when you finally see a giant telescope up close, you think, So what? Although, not being a child, you do not say it but instead mutter, "Ah, very interesting." There was this to be said about the observatory at Byurakan in particular: it was certainly disappointing in the traditional way, but there was also something appealing in its lack of pretension. There were no intimations either of importance or of the lack of it. Everything looked as if it needed paint, although when you examined things closely this was not always so. Here were some filing cabinets, there some telescopic equipment, also several old chairs, a table, an urn of coffee, a studious young man who disappeared, two amiable women, and on the outside there were flowers everywhere.

One of the amiable women showed us photographs of whitish spirals, some of which were very poetic and familiar. The roof was made to open by a push button, much like a garage door, and revealed a wedge of pale-blue sky. As it happened, the chief of the observatory, Distinguished Scientist Ambartsumian, was not in residence. He was in Houston, Texas, delivering a lecture. And why not?

Thus, instead of being able to interrupt the Distinguished Scientist and drive him mad with witless questions, we sat on the green grass outside amid the beautiful flowers and had lemonade in paper cups. Behind us rose a dome of the observatory. There was an air of calm, and even laziness, around us. We were in the presence of science.

I felt sad for a moment, sitting on the rough grass and thinking one of those banal travelers' thoughts: that soon we would be leaving Armenia, and—

And what? And would never tour the observatory at Byurakan again? It was not a thought that one pursued relentlessly.

"It's too bad you didn't get a chance to see Professor Ambartsumian," said Sarkis, in his hortatory manner. "He is a great Armenian scientist. There are many eminent Armenian scientists." And so forth. After a while, Sarkis wiped his brow, took off his hat, and lay back upon several flowers.

We were on the top of a hill, looking down on a valley filled with green and haze, and it seemed that one might be able to see far away, into other places and countries.

I asked Vartan, who had been silent for most of the trip, if he had ever traveled outside Armenia.

"I have been to Moscow," he said. "It was noisy, with many huge buildings."

"Have you been outside the Soviet Union?" my wife asked.

"No," he said shyly, as if harboring a secret thought. Then, "My wife wishes to go to California and see Mickey Mouse."

"Mickey Mouse!" said Sarkis.

"The amusement park," said Vartan.

"Amusement parks?" said Sarkis. "What foolishness! Listen to the dreams of these young people!" He sat up on the grass, blinking in the sun. "There is only one place to go, my friends. That is Paris."

"Ah, you and your Paris!" said Arak.

"It is truly the City of Light," said Sarkis. "Not even Leningrad can compare. Paris has everything—culture, beauty, beautiful gardens, exceptional food. I was there once, do you know?"

"He was there for two days," said Arak.

"Three days," said Sarkis. "What does it matter? I was at an educational congress—a congress of philologists. Many noted experts. We were in a tiny hotel, squeezed into rooms. They took us around in buses. But I was in heaven, every minute of it. I felt my soul purified."

"By the French women?" asked Arak.

"I was talking about my soul," said Sarkis. "The soul is the important thing."

"My wife would also like to see the Beatles," Vartan said.

"You know, I was inside the Louvre," Sarkis said. "All my life—in Egypt, here—I have heard about the Louvre. On the last day of our congress, I left our lecture—I was with Szabo, the Hungarian—and we raced to the Louvre. We looked at the Winged Victory of Samothrace. Such a beautiful thing, although it was surrounded by Japanese. I said to Szabo, 'Can you imagine that we are inside the Louvre?' He was very happy, too. Then we had to leave right away, or we would have been missed. But I am going to go back one day and see the Venus de Milo."

"You will never go back," said Arak. "One rapture is enough."

"I have already applied," said Sarkis. "There is a linguistic congress in two years."

"In Paris?" said Arak.

"In Helsinki," said Sarkis. "It's not the same thing, but it's almost the same."

A matronly woman from the observatory appeared carrying two handfuls of paper-wrapped sandwiches, which she placed gently on the ground one by one, as if they were turtles, and then she beamed and ambled away. We opened our sandwiches in the warm sun. I thought of the poor poet Mandelstam wandering about Armenia in the nineteen-thirties. Across the valley, far away from us, there stretched another range of mountains, dim and gold. I wondered if Turkey was beyond those mountains.

"What was it like here in the thirties?" I asked Arak, knowing that it was an impossible question.

Arak sat cross-legged on the grass, the sun glinting on his wide forehead. "It wasn't like this," he said. He started to eat his sandwich.

"How was it not?" I asked.

Arak looked at me as though to say, "If you have to ask the question, there is no way I can properly tell you." His face seemed very angular—chipped out of fine, hard wood and covered with pale skin. He put the sandwich in his lap and said, "There was no food." He said it flatly, almost in an amused manner, as if recalling a certain feature of the landscape. "I remember other things, of course, because I was a child. But what I remember most is that there was no food."

"In those days, there were many problems with agriculture," said Vartan, in his guide's voice.

"Yes," said Arak. "I think there were many problems with agriculture. What do you think, Sarkis?"

Sarkis was silent; shook his head. "I don't know," he said.

Arak said, "You know, we lived in Alash, a small village about forty kilometers from Nakhichevan. My father was a schoolteacher. Later, he was killed in the war somewhere in east Poland. It was a poor village—turnips, radishes, and rocks. Some time past, I think there had been cattle—or, anyway, people used to speak of it. 'We must get some cows or move,' my father would say, but, of course, we never did."

"Your mother is still in Alash?" asked Vartan.

"She was buried there," said Arak. "She was seventy-two." He stretched out his long legs. "One whole winter, she made us soup from grass. Grass soup! It was terrible. My mother didn't tell us at first. 'It is spinach soup,' she said. But, of course, there was no spinach. Then we saw her with the grass. My sister used to cry all the time, because she was hungry. Sometimes I think of that now and want to beat her with a stick, although she herself is now a grown woman with grandchildren. Imagine—a child who is always crying and you have no food to give it!"

"I have heard such stories," said Vartan, "but from earlier times."

"What do I know of stories?" said Arak. "But I will tell you about my mother's aunt. She was married to Melikian— old Melikian, they called him—and lived in the mountains. The village they lived in is no longer even there. Every springtime, we used to make the journey up into the mountains to visit them—the old people. The old man kept some bees, and he would make us presents of sticky combs of honey. Well, one winter it was very bad. It was the winter of the grass soup. Even in our valley we had almost no turnips left. And the snow was everywhere. The world was buried in snow! Nothing stirred. We tried to catch rats, you know, but even the rats had gone. My mother worried about the old people up in the mountains, because we heard reports from other villages of how bad it was. I can tell you that they did not tell the children much about it, but children always find out, do they not? And so one day—in March, I think, long before spring—we set out for the mountain village. It was right after a snowfall, I remember. We carried sacks of bread and also turnips. We could hardly find the village because of the snow, and when we got there the first person we saw was a woman huddled in shawls on a doorstep, crying in the cold. I think my father knew her, and he gave her some of the bread we had brought, and she took the bread and was eating it and crying."

"What about your mother's people?" asked Vartan.

"The old people," said Arak. "Yes. We came to their house. My father could tell right away. 'See, there is no smoke,' he said from the road. They must have been dead nearly a week—perhaps more. It was a good thing, too, that it had been so cold, for they were frozen solid. And their feet were bare. I said, 'Father, why were they not wearing shoes?'—because I had never seen the old people's feet like that, naked. And my father cuffed me with his hand, so that I nearly fell down. 'Enough of your questions!' I think he said. Have you ever eaten shoe leather, Vartan?" Arak asked.

"I never have," said Vartan.

"Me either," said Arak. "At least, I don't think so." He laughed and stood up, still holding his sandwich. He looked at it and began to eat. "Not bad," he said. "Our scientists have good mayonnaise."

It seemed to be much later than it was. There were a few white clouds in the sky. Far down in the valley, some cattle stood beside a grove of trees—black and brown shapes. Two slender birds, like swallows, turned in the cool wind.

"Let us be off," said Sarkis, hands in the pockets of his brown jacket. We trooped to the car, in single file, along the gravel path that led down from the observatory.

On our way back through Byurakan, we saw some schoolchildren standing by the side of the road throwing pebbles at a dry stream. "Do they still have many flies here?" I asked, thinking of the children in Mandelstam's journal.

"There are no flies here any more," said Arak as the yellow fields sped by.

As I thought about it later, there was something about Arak's coolness on the subject of those early hardships that took my breath away. For it wasn't necessary to have digested each word of *The Gulag Archipelago* to realize that death by starvation had been only one of the forms of horror visited upon the length and breadth of Russia during the Stalin years. (What estimate had Solzhenitsyn made—that one out of four citizens of Leningrad had been sent to prison or to a labor camp? One out of four!) Yes, one knew that death in the snowy silences of Armenia had been but one of the terrible acts that men had been required to contend with in those days, and that Arak's refusal to discuss the rest, to describe the whole of the iceberg—while somehow implying its presence—had been a stroke at once of bravery and of a frightening realism.

Beyond that, something else remained and worked in my mind as a result of Arak's story about the old people in the village. It was this: If Arak had been speaking the truth about the hunger and starvation of those times (and why should he not have been?), and if Solzhenitsyn had been writing the truth about the prisons and labor camps (and why should he not have been?), then how unbelievably terrible it must have been to exist anywhere in Russia—certainly in Soviet Armenia—during the long Stalinist nightmare of the nineteen-thirties and forties! Yet—and this was what I now noted—here was Arak, and here were how many others of his generation, and older, whom one saw every day on the street, overheard in cafés, observed standing upright on the buses returning from work, upright and proud. That was it! Not only had they survived the terrors and persecution but now they were on their feet, well on their feet: building soccer stadiums, pink stone apartment houses, statues, refrigerators, computers; fashioning fine, tall children; and talking of the past without that coloring of lamentation and self-pity which so many Armenians elsewhere seemed to employ when they talked about the Turks. For it seemed that even those who had not been personally involved, such as Sarkis, carried with them an "experience" of those earlier massacres—perhaps some racial memory of the events—like a poison.

I decided then and there to set down as directly as I could my understanding of what had actually happened between the Armenians and the Turks—in other words, to confront some of the things that I had read and thought about and kept myself detached from—and to see if some sort of meaning or coherence might not eventually emerge. Somehow, whatever had happened to the Armenians seemed to have been more than murder. But what, one wondered, could have been *more* than murder?

THE KEY to the puzzle lay, surely, in the nineteenth century, for it was toward the end of the nineteenth century that the so-called Armenian Question achieved a kind of international prominence, and that the proverbial roof started to fall in upon the Armenians in Turkey. It was strange to have studied nineteenth-century history so often in my youth but never with regard to Armenia. To be sure, Armenia did not occupy a large place in many history books. The Turks, for example, generally ignored the subject, dismissing the Armenians as one among "many Asia Minor peoples" who for obscure reasons had betrayed the Turkish trust and created trouble. The Europeans, principally the English (who, after the English custom, journeyed to remote places and turned out obtuse, carefully phrased journals), took much the same line, with a few notable exceptions, such as Arnold Toynbee, and with the added angle that any misfortune that had befallen the Armenians had doubtless been the result of their low—and, presumably, un-English—instincts for "trade." The greater part of Armenian history books were in their way no more helpful than the Turkish accounts, or non-accounts. If the Turks ignored the subject, the Armenians usually overwrote it. That is, the Turks were innately murderous; the Turks were savages.

Much of the story of the Armenians in nineteenth-century Turkey seemed to be closely connected to the person and personality of the thirty-fourth Ottoman sultan, Abdul-

Hamid II. When Abdul-Hamid succeeded to the sultanate in 1876 (as a result of his older brother Murad's having succumbed to a "nervous disorder" after three months in office), he looked out upon a still large but disorganized and declining empire of roughly thirty-five million people, of whom around thirteen million were Christian subjects of the Ottoman provinces of the Balkans, and around two million were Armenians, also Christian—some of them in Constantinople, some in Europe, a few in Syria, most of them spread out across Anatolia and the classic Armenian plateau, which had been divided into the six *vilayets* of Turkish Armenia.

For years, the Balkan Christians had been in revolt— inspired by the example of the French Revolution, incited by the liberal movements in Europe, at times assisted by the autocratic, imperial-minded czars of Russia. Lord Byron had died for "Greek freedom" at Missolonghi in 1824, five years before Greece gained its independence. (Not the least remarkable act of Byron's life was that he had spent the winter of 1816–17 in a Venetian monastery learning Armenian.) The Russian czars spoke solemnly about "protecting" the Balkan Christians. The majority of the Ottoman empire's Christians might be restive; the Armenians were not. The Turks regarded the Armenians as the *millet sadika*— the "loyal community."

In May of 1844, while on a state visit to Queen Victoria, Czar Nicholas I had observed to Lords Aberdeen and Palmerston: "Turkey is a dying man. We can try to keep him alive, but he will—and he must—die. I am afraid of no one except France. With so many tons of gunpowder close to the fire, how can we prevent the sparks from catching?" Thus, Turkey became known as the Sick Man of Europe, although its possessions were mainly outside Europe and although, as it happened, the word and concept of "Turkey" were still alien to the Turks. The French "Turquie" and the English "Turkey" derived from Medieval Latin: "Turchia" or "Turquia." However, the Turks thought of themselves as subjects of the Ottoman empire; "Turk" was a vaguely pejorative term applied to the peasantry. When, finally, in 1923, the Turks officially adopted the name, they transposed it from the European usage—"Türkiye."

By the time of Abdul-Hamid's accession to the throne— or, rather, to the sword of Osman—the "sickness" had grown worse. In part, this resulted from continued troubles in the empire's European provinces. More directly, it resulted from the magnitude of the Ottoman debt and the weakness of the Ottoman financial structure. Stated simply, European industry and capital were in the saddle. The Ottoman ruling caste, classic conservatives—still prisoners of a fading racial memory of war and plunder—had established neither; they had little to sell the world, and everything to buy. In the course of one twenty-five-year period, the rate of the Ottoman piaster relative to the pound sterling fell three hundred per cent. And when, in 1840, the government created a national bank, it fell hopelessly in debt within a few years, as it doubled and redoubled its borrowing—at the same time reducing its interest payments—so that the European central banks, which had gladly contributed to the sickness, were compelled to take a more active role in Turkish affairs in order to protect their investments.

Abdul-Hamid could do little about his European provinces' demands for independence except to try, with increasing trouble and bad publicity, to repress the demands, and, in the main, to watch with anger and impotence as the provinces broke away. He could do little about the financial mess—or, rather, *would* do little in the way of cutting down official expenses—and so was forced to accede to growing European control over the Ottoman treasury. In fact, for a while representatives of European banks administered the Ottoman debt from a special European office in Constantinople, placing liens against portions of Ottoman tax receipts in order to pay off their loans.

Impotence: an absence of potence. What little actual power Abdul-Hamid retained, he kept close to his vest and dealt out sparingly. He was an autocrat who liked surprises. For instance, soon after he became sultan the European powers and Russia held one of their conferences—in Constantinople, of all places—on what might be done about Turkey's disaffected European provinces and on the general question of Turkish reform. No Turks were invited to any of the high-level discussions. Abdul-Hamid remained quietly in his palace, playing Offenbach on the piano and watching the pennants on Lord Salisbury's yacht. One morning in the early days of the conference, while the dele-

gates were seated at table drawing up their agenda, the guns
of the Topkapi fortress commenced firing a salute. One
hundred and one rounds. When the cannonading had
stopped, the delegates were informed that the Sultan had
just announced a constitution, which would make their
presence no longer necessary. After the conference had
broken up, Abdul-Hamid consigned the constitution to the
limbo it had come from, and sent the Minister who had
drawn it up for him into exile—and then had him murdered.

In many ways, Abdul-Hamid was an unusual man.
Thirty-fourth Sultan of the House of Osman, Caliph of
Islam, Shadow of God on Earth, he was of moderate height
and slender build, with a pale, gravely handsome face, dark,
watchful eyes, and a normally quiet and withdrawn expression. He was afraid of the dark. Also, fearing assassination,
he rarely slept in the same room two nights in a row. For the
same reason, on his weekly appearances in public—riding in
a carriage to the Hamidiyeh Mosque—he kept a small child
on his knee. No decent assassin, he reasoned, would be likely
to kill a child. Indeed, Abdul-Hamid's feelings about assassination were such that he would not permit the word (or any
of its synonyms) to appear in print. "So the Turkish newspapers attributed the sudden and simultaneous deaths of the
king and queen of Serbia in 1903 to indigestion," wrote
Bernard Lewis. "In the same way, the Empress Elizabeth of
Austria died of pneumonia, President Carnot of apoplexy,
President McKinley of anthrax." Abdul-Hamid maintained

an extensive collection of pistols and other hand weapons, which he ordered continually from Europe, and one of which he kept at his side at all times. He was a good but impulsive marksman. On different occasions, several gardeners and a footman were shot by the Sultan as a result of coming upon him unawares. Also, the Sultan was fond of animals, and kept a private zoo on the grounds of Yildiz Palace. At Yildiz, too, he caused to be built two private cafés, which were modeled on ordinary Constantinople cafés and were at all times staffed with waiters, and where now and then the Sultan would stop (always the only customer), order a coffee, and express polite surprise that it should arrive so quickly.

IF ABDUL-HAMID felt impotent rage against the Europeans, who seemed to have a mortgage on his empire and were always trying to tell him what to do, his feelings toward the Armenians were more complex and, in the beginning, less visible. One of the least visible threads, perhaps, was this: Since birth, Abdul-Hamid had been dogged by the rumor that his own mother was Armenian. It was not impossible, considering that the Ottomans favored non-Turkic *shiksas* for the royal harem. Rumor had it that she was either Jewish or Armenian. Her name comes down to us as Pirimujgan, which, at any rate, doesn't sound Jewish. No official announcement of Abdul-Hamid's birth was made until harem records were checked and rechecked. Finally, after an unprecedented three-day delay, the new heir to the throne was acknowledged, but a cloud hung over the event. Piri-mujgan herself died of consumption shortly afterward, and Abdul-Hamid was said to have always thought fondly of her. But all his life his attitude toward Armenians remained markedly private and intense.

Who were the Armenians—this "loyal community"—in those days? Much has been made in novels and histories written by Europeans of the Armenian merchant and trader —the thorn in the side of the more manly and hardworking Turk. Thus, recently an English writer, Joan Haslip, noted in a biography of Abdul-Hamid, *The Sultan:* "Owing to the aversion of the average Turk to any form of commerce, most of the business of the empire was in the hands of either Greeks, Jews, or Armenians. . . . [Abdul-Hamid's] interest in every form of finance was so contrary to the tradition of the well-bred Turk as to revive the rumor of his mother's Armenian origin." Miss Haslip doesn't explicitly criticize the Armenians (or the Greeks or the Jews) for engaging in trade, but the implication seems fairly clear: The Turks were a jolly lot, perhaps not clever in certain ways, but good fellows, full of breeding—probably rode well, too. The Armenians were genetically mercenary and obviously *foreign.*

The truth of the matter seems to have been better and worse than that. In a majestically dry and scholarly book about Armenian communities in the Ottoman empire, written by the same Professor Sanjian who translated the colophons, there is this revealing passage: "In the Ottoman administrative system the high-ranking officials of the Porte and the provincial governors derived their income not from a government salary but from legal taxes and extortions levied on the population over which they had jurisdiction. Each official was dependent on a banker, usually Armenian, who furnished him with capital on interest for securing an appointment and for the surety required by the central government for the proper transmission of revenues to the imperial treasury." This implied a fascinating state of affairs. First, the Ottoman ruling caste, while expanding its bureaucracy in the modern manner, had retained its anachronistic traditional method of dealing with it—disdaining to pay its administrators salaries and instead letting them somehow make it up in the field, skimming taxes here, taking bribes there. Then, on top of that, the Ottoman state had required these officials to put up capital for their jobs, and to maintain them with additional deposits of capital (against tax receipts) throughout the year. Thus, since the warrior Turks (who had not been successfully at war for two hundred years) had neglected to develop either capital or a banking system, or even bankers, the result was that their growing civil service was virtually pushed by its own government into a debtor-creditor relationship with the Armenian merchants and bankers. What folly for the Turks to have arranged things so badly! What folly for the Armenians to have let it happen!

ONE HAS, then, a picture of a developing Armenian elite in Constantinople. The Turks needed the Armenians, who understood the new worlds of capital and commerce. Also, the Armenians, armed with a literacy taught by their church schools, often spoke several languages. They were needed as translators and interpreters—as connections with the Western world. A relationship almost of dependency existed between Turk and Armenian, but it was a unique and dangerous sort of dependency. For the creditor Armenians were in the minority and were Christian, and the needful Turks were in the majority and were Muslim.

The mutual unawareness of these Turks and Armenians seems astonishing, albeit human. Still, the Constantinople Armenians were only a minority of their own people. The majority of the Armenians lived where they had always lived—in villages and towns across Anatolia and the Armenian plateau, side by side with the Turks, with whom they had shared their homeland for over four hundred years.

In a little book called *Travels in Armenia,* by the Honourable Robert Curzon, published in London in 1860, and lent to me in New York by the writer Peter Sourian, I found the following description of the building of a "country house" in Turkish Armenia:

When a house is to be constructed, a space of ground is marked out, perhaps nearly an English acre, and then part of the whole is excavated to a depth of five feet. Eight or nine tree trunks are placed in two rows as columns, with the larger branches planted across the columns as roof-beams. The center of the house is the stable. In a richer house, there are two stables and the roof is a snow field. A fire of dung, called *tezek,* is continually smoldering. There is a divan covered with the most beautiful carpets and large wooden pegs for pistols, guns, cloaks, anything else. The chimney rises two feet or so above the ground, with a stone on top to keep lambs or children from falling in, for these habitations are constructed on the side of a gentle slope with no fences to keep people off the roof.

Toward the end of the book, Curzon tells the brief story of Artin, the *oda bashi:*

In the month of August of last year, a [Turkish] merchant named Mehmed brought his merchandise to the inn, where he slept. Two soldiers were asleep next to him. In the morning, his merchandise had vanished and he accused the two soldiers of stealing it, but they denied it and were let go.

As it happened, a woman had seen them burying the merchandise, and when these were ordered to be dug up and found incomplete, the soldiers said that the *oda bashi* —the inn-clerk—had stolen the other half. The *oda bashi* was an Armenian, Artin by name. When he denied the theft he was ordered to be tortured into the truth. A metal drinking cup was heated over a fire and placed over his head. Then a cord was tied around two pig's knuckle bones and this was tightened around his temples until his eyes nearly came out. His front teeth were extracted and pieces of cane placed under his nails.

Unfortunately, under Turkish law only two witnesses are required for a conviction, and no testimony is accepted from women, foreigners, or Christians. I heard about this poor wretch's story and took the matter to the Pasha. He said it was not true and I believed him for I had found him to be at other times a straightforward and honest man. My servant, however, had looked in through the jail window and seen Artin's pitiable condition. I said to the Pasha: "This man has been tortured because he is Armenian." The Pasha again denied it, but the next morning released Artin, who was about thirty-five years old and bore terrible scars.

A few days later I was writing at my desk, when I heard a most extraordinary shuffling and screeching, as if several cocks and hens were suffering from strangulation. Along the floor of my house advanced the most strange and incomprehensible procession of men and women, crawling on their hands and knees, each with a rooster in their hands! One woman grabbed hold of my foot and began kissing it. Being horribly alarmed, I kicked as well as I could and asked my servant to get rid of the unsightly group.

Later he informed me that they were the family of

Artin, the *oda bashi,* and although they were pained that I did not accept their poultry, they expressed gratitude to him that I had saved their kinsman. In truth, it is clear that fashions change everywhere, and that Turkey, like the United States of America, is no longer a land of laxity, where every free and independent citizen has the right to beat his own nigger, or where the Sultan could cut off fourteen heads a day!

At first, I felt furious at this Englishman's story. Had he become "horribly alarmed" that those poor wretches were trying to kiss his feet? And, as for the right of independent citizens to beat their own niggers, was he trying to say that the Armenians were the niggers of nineteenth-century Turkey? And was he right? That was a mind-stopping thought. In a rage, I read the story of the *oda bashi* to my wife. She said, "But what are 'niggers,' anyway, except people whom the ruling majority never looks at?"

I said, "But the Armenians seemed so badly off. Houses underground! Fires of dung!"

She said, "Surely their Turkish neighbors were as badly off, or worse. Look, Artin at least had an education. He could read and write. He was a clerk."

All the same, something seemed true and sad about the story—sadder, even, than the spectacle of the inn clerk being tortured. Indeed, the act of torture seemed but an outward sign of a far worse disease. For the first time, I had a profound sense of the depressed condition of the Armenians.

"Depressed condition"—the phrase went through my mind. No, I thought, it had been worse than that: *depression.* Might not a people existing too long in an untenable position, a barely tenable position, a diminishing position, experience the same symptoms of clinical depression as an individual? Might not a *people* show signs of listlessness, a glazing of the eyes, a lack of motive, an inability to get out of bed in the morning and look for better work?

My wife was looking through the Haslip book on Abdul-Hamid. "Listen to this," she said. " 'Both Abdul-Hamid and his immediate predecessors had treated the Armenians with tolerance and justice.' " She closed the book. "Obviously, everybody has different standards of tolerance and justice," she said.

As the nineteenth century wore on, Abdul-Hamid's troubles increased, and it happened that the Armenians did nothing to lessen them. For the winds of reform and European liberalism had reached even the *millet sadika,* the "loyal community." The first indication of a change in temper occurred during the Russo-Turkish War of 1877–78 —a war disastrous to the Turks—when the Russians, eager to hasten the Sick Man to his grave, invaded not only the Ottoman Balkan provinces but also, on the other side of the Black Sea, Turkish Armenia. Abdul-Hamid, furious and helpless, was compelled to ask "the English woman," as he always called Queen Victoria, to stop the Russian advance, and after a display of Her Majesty's warships in the Dardanelles the Russians halted, and grudgingly pulled back from both fronts, although they were allowed to keep the three Armenian districts of Kars, Ardahan, and Batum. Abdul-Hamid was enraged to learn that some of the Armenians had actually welcomed the Russians. It was soon after this that England, anxious to keep Russia out of eastern Turkey, where it was always threatening to "protect Christians," became interested in the so-called Armenian Question—and Abdul-Hamid's dormant paranoia toward the Armenians intensified.

Liberal England, under Gladstone, was eager to take up the new Armenian cause. Conservative England, under Disraeli, preferred to accommodate the Sultan and keep the Suez route free of hazard. On either side of the issue, the English appeared to be involved. But what was the Armenian cause? It was a fairly modest one, by European standards: equality and freedom of opportunity within the Ottoman empire. Unfortunately, the European liberals, who were far away and remained far away, never seemed to realize that the implicit basis of the Ottoman empire was inequality. The sons of Islam had to be first. Therefore, somebody must be second.

What is interesting about this whole period is the mildness, almost the naïveté, of these early reform movements, with their political and literary ties to Rousseau and Montesquieu.

Life, property, and honor are the candles
of our hearts. . . .
Your law informs the Sultan of his limits.

Thus went a Turkish political ode of the eighteen-fifties, which was considered dangerously radical. Inform the Sultan of his limits? *What* limits? Early Turkish and Armenian reform groups seem to have been very close, for many of the young Turkish and Armenian men had studied together in Paris and London, and shared a wishful admiration for European liberalism. The first Turkish group, which was established in 1865, called itself *Yeni Osmanlilar* (New Ottomans), or, alternatively, *Jeunes Turcs*. The Armenians, some years later, formed two parties, one called Hentchak (Bell) and the other called Dashnaktsutiun (Federation). Though both were founded by Russian rather than Turkish Armenians, they were actively concerned with the plight of Armenians in the Ottoman empire. The chief aim of the Turkish intellectuals in those days was to obtain a constitution and a more representative government, and better controls on the state treasury. The chief aim of the Dashnaks—the more effective (and less Marxist) of the two parties—was to obtain religious freedom and tax relief, and also the right to serve in the armed forces. Neither Turks nor Armenians then seriously entertained the thought of abolishing the sultanate. Nor did most Armenians, unlike the Balkan Christians, express any wish to break away from the Ottoman empire. The great majority of the Armenian reformers—tinged, like the Young Turks, with varying shades of constitutional Socialism—wanted mainly to work within the system.

Abdul-Hamid's response to these new winds was probably predictable. Reform groups and political parties of any description were declared illegal and de-facto "revolutionary." Intellectuals, both Turkish and Armenian, were arrested, sometimes exiled, sometimes murdered. The Sultan seemed to have a special anxiety about the "Armenian revolutionaries"—the several hundred activists, mostly students. He forbade the Armenian language to be taught or to be spoken in public, and ordered that no mention of Armenia or reference to anything Armenian be printed anywhere in the empire. Also, he created an irregular force of Kurdish tribesmen—fierce, primitive Muslims who for years had drifted across eastern Turkey in a state of feud with the settled Armenian communities, which they periodically ransacked. These detachments of newly uniformed Kurdish cavalry were called the Hamidiyeh, and were posted as garrisons near the major Armenian towns, whose Armenian inhabitants Abdul-Hamid ordered to give up any weapons they might possess. In the meantime, the Sultan's private surveillance network was expanded to around twenty thousand agents, who dutifully filed reports with their employer; these eventually filled several rooms of the palace, and were read each day on their arrival by the Shadow of God, who soon read little else.

Abdul-Hamid's massacre of the Armenians began in the summer of 1894, with the capture by a Turkish patrol of two members of Hentchak who were traversing the mountains in the Armenian district of Sassoun. Orders were immediately sent from Constantinople for Turkish troops, accompanied by a detachment of Hamidiyeh, to raid Sassoun, in order to uncover such additional "revolutionaries" as might be hiding there. As it happened, the district of Sassoun was a natural fortress—a collection of villages perched high in the rocky mountains and inhabited by hardy and independent-minded mountaineers. The year before, they had refused to pay their taxes, complaining that the Kurds had already exacted tribute from them. They had demanded that the Porte control the Kurdish chiefs. Abdul-Hamid had responded by sending in troops, who, after encountering unexpectedly heavy opposition from the Armenians, ended by killing nine hundred of them.

Now the people of Sassoun again resisted the advance of the Turkish troops, and again they resisted effectively. For two weeks, the Sultan's soldiers and the cavalry that bore his name were held at bay on the craggy mountainside beneath Sassoun—and some were killed by the Armenians. Abdul-

Hamid, keeping himself more closely than ever within Yildiz Palace, reading his spies' reports, attending to the messages from his new telegraph, evidently believed that the moment he had feared and expected was now at hand: the Armenians within the Ottoman empire were in revolt. Down the same telegraph lines that had told him of the existence of the rebellion, word was sent to the beys of the eastern provinces to suppress the Armenian uprising before it could spread.

Far away from Constantinople, then, out of sight of the ambassadors of the European powers, a loosely organized process for the killing of Armenians spread across the towns and villages of Turkish Armenia. In some instances, an "official pretext" was found for massacre. For example, in the town of Bitlis a quarrel between an Armenian and a Turk over the price of two oxen resulted in the arrest and execution by Turkish police of a hundred and fifty Armenians as "revolutionaries" and the subsequent slaughter by an aroused Turkish mob of nearly two thousand. More usually, an Armenian was discovered—or merely suspected of— keeping a firearm or sword, whereupon a hundred or so of his neighbors might be rounded up and shot, as in Marash, or decapitated, as in Diyarbakir. In some places, hanging was preferred—Moush, for example, where twelve Armenian teachers from the local school were hanged, and left hanging. As time wore on, however, and there were no signs of interference from the ambassadors of tenderhearted Europe (who, to be fair, did not have their own telegraph lines to the eastern provinces), and no change of instructions from the Sultan, the matter of "official pretexts" came to be pursued ever more casually. That is to say, the idea of putting down a rebellion or of capturing dangerous revolutionaries seemed less and less to occupy the official mind. Instead, the procedure appeared to be generally like the following, which occurred in the town of Urfa.

There, one day, into the populous Armenian section rode the soldiers of the local Hamidiyeh regiment, which had been garrisoned some four or five miles out of town. Some Armenian shops were looted by these Hamidiyeh warriors. When a shop owner protested, his shop was set on fire. At one point, two Armenians tried with their fists and linked arms (since they had no weapons) to keep a group of the Hamidiyeh troops away from some Armenian girls. The two Armenians were seized and decapitated with cavalry swords. When other Armenians began to protest, the Hamidiyeh rode away, for they had done their job. And in an hour's time (some have said less) a mob of Turks approached the Armenian section. For two and a half days, this Turkish mob, soon joined by other Turks—all of them average Turkish citizens, ordinary co-inhabitants of the picturesque town of Urfa—roamed at will through the streets of the Armenian community. Most of the Turks carried clubs—thick hardwood implements that had the look (some said) of having been specially fashioned for the event—and not a few carried the *yataghan,* a kind of machete used in vine cultivation. Armenian men were killed wherever found. When some of the younger men attempted to fashion weapons with which to defend themselves, they were seized and killed in particularly horrible and degrading ways.

By the evening of the second day, many Armenians, especially women and their children (who had not been in any sense exempt from persecution), had taken refuge in their church, a moderate-sized and ancient edifice at the intersection of two streets. The Turks nailed broad wooden beams across the doors of the crowded church, so that they could not be opened from the inside, and then set fire to it. The blaze lasted all night long and into the morning, and, when it was over, it was estimated that around two thousand had perished inside—although some said later that the exact figure was closer to seventeen hundred but had been "rounded out," as is often done in matters pertaining to crowds and attendance. At any rate, none came out. Over all, in Urfa in those three days approximately ten thousand Armenians had been killed—a figure that has doubtless also been "rounded out" to some degree but that those who have studied Ottoman census and taxation records have in the main attested to.

This general procedure—of Hamidiyeh provocation followed by Armenian protest and culminating in rampage by Turkish mobs—was pursued, or by peculiar coincidence was adhered to, in most of the towns with large Armenian populations: Van, Bitlis, Erzurum, Diyarbakir, Marash, Trebizond as well as Urfa. After the Hamidiyeh troops had galloped away from the scene of looting and sudden violence, the Turkish mobs were never long in taking to the streets. Nor were the victims of these mobs always randomly selected; in numerous cases certain individuals, notably priests and schoolteachers, had clearly been singled out beforehand for special attention, of which death by hanging was not always the unkindest form.

IN A PERIOD of two years, about three hundred thousand Armenians were thus put to death within the confines of the Ottoman empire—and in a peculiar kind of silence. There was a special quality to the silence that enfolded those "events." It was not the heavy historical silence that in times past had usually enveloped the murderer and his victim—the silence resulting from the remoteness of the deed and the ignorance of the listener, which had kept so many terrible actions hidden from the eyes and ears of the world. Think of the massacres of ancient history: tribes or armies caught in some unmapped valley far from home and slaughtered to a man, with no storybook messenger or herald to announce even the "facts" of the event. Think, for that matter, of the Armenian colophons: those despairing messages stuffed into the shipwreck bottles of history, actually buried in cellars—uncommunicated to anyone save God (who never answered), and scholars many hundreds of years later. "Like the threshing-floor of flails, they thrashed the children with their horses; and, in place of grain, rivers of blood began to spring forth, and in place of straw the bones flowed forth like dust."

What loneliness and silence surrounded these words when they were written! But consider: By the year 1894, the silence of the world had become less complete. For instance, a species of modern traveler had come into being, assisted by the railway and the steamship, tramping about the globe, busying himself here and there, observing this and that. In the fall of 1895, a group of German and Swiss schoolteachers were traveling through eastern Turkey. They passed a village where not a soul appeared to be alive. "A terrible plague," explained the guide. The schoolteachers saw blood on the walls of houses, and a village square where jackals and vultures still fed off the unburied dead. The advanced nations of the world had evolved postal services, and from this development came the "correspondent"—originally a simple letter writer in a distant place, eager to use the new system, to communicate. For instance, a Swiss schoolteacher traveling in eastern Turkey. Then, too, there was the telegraph—the "long wire"—still in its infancy. Like many infants, it was closely guarded by its parents—not its true parents, for those were the inventors, but, at any rate, its adopted parents, as perhaps one might call the proprietary governments. Consider the role of this new invention in the Turkish massacre of the Armenians. It was in many instances the telegraph that had transmitted the "information" about the Armenian unrest and "revolutionary societies." It was the telegraph that had then transmitted the "information" about the suppression of this "revolutionary activity." Finally, it was the telegraph that speedily and efficiently communicated to the world the Sultan's denials of wrongdoing. For, because of this partly broken silence of the new era of communication, some word, at least, had reached the outside world of the murderous happenings in eastern Turkey. Travelers had written letters, which were then published in European newspapers. Minor consular officials of the great powers, stationed in towns such as Erzurum and Trebizond, had communicated what they had seen or heard of the massacres—at least, as far as their embassies in Constantinople. In Europe, hundreds of miles away, spokesmen of the liberal movement (which had originally given voice to the Armenian Question) now expressed moral outrage at the reported excesses of Abdul-Hamid's Turks. In England, in 1896, former Prime Minister Gladstone, then eighty-six years old, emerged from retirement to make the last speech of his life, in Liverpool, where he inveighed for ninety minutes against the plight of the Armenians and characterized Sultan Abdul-Hamid as "the Great Assassin." In France, Georges Clemenceau proclaimed Abdul-Hamid *"le Monstre de Yildiz"* and *"le Sultan Rouge."* Even Queen Victoria wrote a letter: "Her Majesty would earnestly beg of the Sultan to enquire . . ." But the Sultan would have none of it. In a rare interview, granted to a representative of the London *Times,* he declared that the reports of Armenian massacres were "gross exaggerations." To the mild inquiries of the English and French Ambassadors, the Sultan's Ministers replied politely, or sometimes not so politely, that the situation of the Armenians was an "internal matter," and that, in any event, it had resulted from Armenian provocation. How many times in the course of the yet more murderous twentieth century would the world listen in to such verbal remonstrances and such official excuses and denials: "exaggeration," "provocation," "an internal matter." It almost seems as if with the arrival of communications it had in certain ways become easier to lie officially. Which is to say that a question-phrasing apparatus had been invented and developed, with its wires and transmitters and its appearance of communicating answers. But one man, or government, might still control the apparatus and the answers. And perhaps there was more to it than that. For previously the world had abounded in lies that no one heard. Now lies were heard all over the world, somehow dignified by their transmission through the apparatus, and even listened to with a kind of respect by the machine's new clients.

MEANWHILE, across the eastern provinces of Turkey—a Turkey whose political health was an object of such concern to European statesmen—the Turks continued killing and persecuting the Armenians. A letter from another Swiss teacher, who had been traveling in Anatolia, and whose correspondence was printed in a Zurich paper, read partly as follows:

In all the village of B—— I found not a sign of life. The houses all stood empty and the doors of the small shops were open as if waiting for customers who were never to arrive. It was as if life had vanished from that section of the world. Later, as we were on the road to K——, from behind some rocks appeared six women, although so emaciated and miserable it was hard to tell what they were.

They were Armenian women who had survived or fled the massacre of their village by the Turks. We gave them pieces of bread which they stuffed into their mouths like wolves, or perhaps camp dogs. It was a pitiful sight. They said that their menfolk had been slain or else had fled north toward Russia, as one of them hopefully prayed. They asked us if we would somehow get word to the men that they might return, or get word to someone about what had happened. We said we would do what we could, and gave them more bread, and the poor wretches fled back behind the rocks.

Get word to someone. The modern prayer. At around the same time that the schoolteacher was writing to Zurich, the French Ambassador in Constantinople, M. Paul Cambon, was communicating as follows to Paris: "The [Turkish] Government acknowledges that there has been widespread unrest in the eastern provinces between the disaffected Armenians and the Government troops, and doubtless excesses have been committed on both sides. But I am confident that the [Turkish] nation will soon return to stability and that it is not in our interest to engage more fully in the matter at the moment."

The termination of the Hamidian massacres occurred in this fashion: At one-thirty on the afternoon of Wednesday, August 26, 1896, a band of two dozen young Armenian activists armed with primitive revolvers and sticks of dynamite walked into the main office of the Ottoman Bank, in Galata, a Christian quarter of Constantinople, across the Golden Horn from the Turkish quarter of Stamboul, and seized the premises. The purpose of the seizure of so visible an institution, the Armenians declared, was to attract the attention of the European powers, who would then compel "constitutional reforms" on the part of Abdul-Hamid. But clearly the Sultan had somehow been apprised of the plan beforehand, for as soon as the Armenians appeared inside the bank, a cordon of Turkish troops arrived to keep the Armenians within the building, sealing them off from the rest of the city. Then, less than an hour after the capture of the bank, mobs of Turks, armed with the same hardwood clubs that had been seen in the country, began storming into Galata. The Turks fell upon Armenians wherever they could find them. In some cases, specific individuals—usually leaders of the professions—were sought after and, when found, were dragged into the street for instant execution. Generally, the mobs roamed through the streets and houses, breaking up shops, clubbing the inhabitants to the ground. For three days, the destruction and killing continued. M. Tissot, an attaché of the French Embassy, wrote in a letter to *Le Matin* that the soles of his shoes had been sticky with blood from his walk to the office. A young secretary at the English Embassy, Henry Graves, wrote in a journal, which he subsequently published, that he had seen a "mob of several dozen Turks, among whom were two personal aides of the Sultan, stamping upon the dead or dying bodies of an Armenian family." There were reports of disemboweling, of heads being split by stones, of the rape of small children. An American clergyman, Dr. George Hepworth, who visited Constantinople the following year, wrote about this frenzy of killing for the New York *Herald:*

> It is difficult to obtain the number of those murdered, but it is clear that there were quite enough. My informants, who are by no means all Armenian, tell me that they lay in the streets by the dozen, by the score, and in some places by the hundreds. Cold, stark bodies of men who had committed no crime. . . . I inquired how the evil work was done? "Mostly with clubs," one of my friends answered. "There was rarely any noise, no shouting, only the soft thudding of the clubs. The Armenians, who had no weapons, fell like wheat before a scythe." I have often thought of the terror of that image: the "soft thudding of the clubs."

An hour or so after the bank's capture, the Armenians who were now virtual prisoners there, and whose presence had provided an "official pretext" for what the government described as a "public protest," began to throw out some of the dynamite, with a view to attracting European notice and support. One stick exploded, and damaged a cornice on one of the bank's walls—the falling stones from which were reported to have injured the arm of a Turkish soldier. Apparently moved by the possibility of damage to the bank, its English director, Sir Edgar Vincent, requested the Sultan to give safe-conduct to the young activists. Finally, about midnight, they were permitted to leave the bank and were then convoyed to sanctuary on Sir Edgar's yacht.

For the next couple of days, Turkish mobs took to the streets of the Armenian neighborhoods, and by the end of the rioting the French and English consular attachés estimated that somewhere between five and eight thousand Armenians had been killed. On the morning of August 29, an open telegram, written in French and signed by the major European powers, was delivered to the Sultan. The message said that it was the "advice of the Signatories" that the massacres "must cease immediately." It also stated that "continuance means danger to [the Ottoman] throne and dynasty." That was certainly the right note to strike with Abdul-Hamid. The same day, the command went out from Yildiz Palace, confirmed by the sheikh-ul-Islam, that the Sultan had "forbidden to kill."

I had the illusion of finally beginning to comprehend something important about the Armenians—something that might at least partly explain the peculiarly shrill and wounded quality of the Armenian response to the trauma of the Turkish massacres. For ever since I began my "investigations" of the Armenians I had been perplexed as to why so many of them, even today, still seemed inextricably fixated on the evil times that had befallen their people in Abdul-Hamid's Turkey, and later, in 1915, at the hands of the Young Turks. In a sense, I knew that this was an inexcusably insensitive thing for me to think or write—for me, a comfortable American in the nineteen-seventies, to wonder why my people (or any people) should still respond deeply or with passion to the fact of their countrymen's having been killed in the thousands, in the hundreds of thousands. And yet it was what I wondered.

It had never occurred to me that what happened to the Armenians was *worse* than what had happened to numerous other peoples, nations, creeds in the course of man's long inhumanity to man. What could be worse than death, worse even than death by pain? And was there an appreciable difference to the victim in being hanged, decapitated, clubbed, gassed, or starved, or undergoing any of the other nearly endless methods that men have developed for administering physical pain to one another? Even so, the response of the Armenians to the bygone brutalities of the Turks seemed of a different nature from the response of other groups to massacre. It was as if a particular poison had entered the system several generations back, and had remained within it: a poison that one might up to a point live with but that caused the limbs suddenly to twitch, or the mouth—perhaps in mid-sentence—to grimace grotesquely.

After all, what invisible "virus" was it that had reduced to tears that old man I talked with a few months earlier in New York, on Thirty-third Street, and that had brought so many other Armenians of my acquaintance to the equivalent of gnashing their teeth? What was it that had caused such a marvelously tough writer as William Saroyan to manifest an unearthly sweetness? What had driven my father to write about everything except his Armenian background, and all his life to refuse to weep over anything? What of Sarkis—surely also a tough and rational man—and his wild diatribes against "the Turks"? Some writers, I knew, had ascribed the emotional or ingratiating aspects of the Armenian temperament to the Armenians' long history of being a conquered people. But the main fact to emerge from the lengthy and curious history of the Armenians seemed to be that though much of the time Armenia had been controlled by a greater power, the Armenians themselves had remained independent of mind and spirit. They had been hardy mountain people first, perhaps not very cultured or clever—people who grow up in the mountains are rarely cultured or clever—but direct, practical, and physical. And if the depressing and isolating experience of several centuries of Ottoman Turkish rule had turned the Armenians inward, had sent them down the roads that were then most practical—the roads of trade and commerce, of interpreting, of "being useful"—today one might see for oneself on the streets of Erevan the still direct, clear-eyed, at times quite fierce look of younger Armenians, who were now left (more or less) to pursue their own instincts. No, it was not so simple a matter; one could not "explain" Armenians by saying that they had suffered a great deal, or that they had always suffered a great deal.

In obvious ways, the closest parallel lay with the Jews, who had undergone, numerically, an even larger genocide in Hitler's Germany. But here, too, there seemed to be a difference. Certainly there were many Jews I knew, or knew of, who still looked back to the terrible period of the concentration camps and gas chambers as if it were an open wound, a fact of everyday consciousness. But, for one thing, the Jewish experience in Germany had been fairly recent. For another thing, it seemed to me that a majority of the Jews did not look backward in this way—in the manner of people bearing a permanently open wound. Of course, the issue might be forced: a careless or abrasive remark, sometimes only remotely anti-Semitic in intent, and even the most assimilated American Jew might respond with a flash of anger about the Six Million. Indeed, I had sometimes noticed a curiously proprietary air on the part of Jews and Armenians alike toward the misfortunes of their own peoples—proprietary and almost competitive, in the fashion of two insecure strangers trying to narrate two similar nightmares in an inattentive room. "Now, these Armenians," an intelligent Jewish friend had once said to me, with studied vagueness, "didn't they once have some *trouble* with the Turks?" Another time, I had overheard an Armenian say outright, "The way they talk, you'd think the Jews invented genocide." Doubtless this was original black comedy—perverse and deeply human. But generally it seemed to me that the Jews had handled their nightmare better than the Armenians had handled theirs: had somehow resolved it, or, at least, incorporated the trauma into everyday life—were more nearly free of it.

And what of the countless other peoples who had undergone massacre and genocide: the Ibos of Nigeria; the Communists of Indonesia; the Hindus of Bangladesh; the Incas of South America; the Indians of North America; the Ukrainian peasants of the U.S.S.R.; the black slaves of Haiti and Guadeloupe; the Protestants; the Catholics; the Muslims; the Cappadocians whom Tigran of Armenia had marched across the wilderness to his new capital; and all the rest, whose names and stories were never entered, or entered vividly enough, in history books—for the list is surely long and ancient? Had not all these suffered, and suffered very greatly? What, then, was different about the Armenian experience? Perhaps it had not been so different? Perhaps some peoples were created with more self-pity, shrillness, and vulnerability than other peoples? It seemed an unlikely proposition. I thought of something I had increasingly noticed in Armenians: an absence of a profoundly convincing "flash of anger"—at least, in this matter of their feelings against the Turks. An absence of a rage that *they* seemed to believe in. Or maybe it was not so much an absence of rage as a rerouting: a rage trapped underground. Beneath the skin.

I THOUGHT of my father often in those days, for I was conscious of many things about him: conscious, for example, that he was born in 1896, the final year of Abdul-Hamid's massacres, and had never talked about any of this in my presence; conscious that, to that degree, he had tried to free me. It seemed no small thing to have tried to free a son from one's own pain. There was also something about it of the story of the man and the fox: the man who, for fear of being caught with contraband, clutches the animal so close beneath his shirt that the animal tears at his stomach.

It was hard to imagine what this pain had been. The pain of being hated—hated unto death. For what was genocide except an expression of generalized hate, a hate so wide and encompassing that it included everyone—man, woman, child—within a certain national or racial group? If a "crime of passion" was particularizing—*you* stole *my* wife—at least it defined the victim as himself. Genocide not only killed its victims but dehumanized them, in the ultimate sense of ignoring the particulars that had made each one individual: save only the most basic and unindividual of all characteristics—the supposedly racial.

I wondered what *his* father had told him about the massacres, about Abdul-Hamid, about the Turks. A certain amount, I imagined. Probably rather more than he—an uncertain Armenian-English youth—had wished to hear. "Your grandfather," an elderly Armenian once told me, "was very active in Armenian affairs." Sometimes it was hard to believe that my father had had a father—this more distant father I had never seen.

My father was born in Bulgaria, where his family had been settled for several generations. Before that, the Kouyoumjians had been in Constantinople. Before that, they had lived in the ancient city of Ani, on the Armenian plateau. In the town of Rustchuk, in Bulgaria, the Kouyoumjians owned and ran a department store—the Kouyoumjian store. It had been described to me only a short while before by the aged grandmother of a school friend of my daughter's, who remembered it from her childhood. "A very fine place," she said to me reassuringly. "You could buy everything there."

The Kouyoumjian store. The man in the blue velvet hat. Some odd memories of my childhood came back to me. I remembered my father standing on the lawn of our house and telling me that I should learn how to box, how to defend myself. I think he used the phrase "self-defense." I was eight years old at the time and had given no thought to "self-defense"—at least, not beyond what basic skills were required to scuffle with the neighbor children. He had his hands on his hips and wore a white shirt and white trousers. Perhaps he had been playing tennis. I think he even briefly struck a boxing pose and made a show of sparring with me. I was a most reluctant partner. "You have to know how to defend yourself," he said, with surprising severity. He seemed very intense about— I never knew what. Boxing? We never talked about it afterward.

What had Miss Haslip written in her book *The Sultan*? "The Armenians . . . with a courage which belied their reputation, succeeded in beating off the [Hamidiyeh] attack."

My father was a short man, although wiry, and carried himself with a certain brittle strength. I believe I remember his saying once, "All Armenians are short." (There are no piano tuners in Japan. All Swedes are drunks.) It made me weep inside my head to think of him sometimes. That figure in the white shirt and white trousers, hands on hips. That figure whom I later saw inside his coffin, wearing some appropriate suit, the necktie well in place, everything motionless, the impassivity a final fact. I used to think that what he had wanted of me had been hard. But what he had wanted of himself turned out to have been literally unspeakable.

We were at Sarkis's house one evening, having supper and supposedly engaging in a "discussion of international literature." First, let me describe his house, for we had not been there before. His wife had been "down with the grippe," he had explained on several occasions, although I had hardly pestered him for an invitation. The main thing I think one would want to say about it is that it was rough-hewn and small (or, from another point of view, sturdy and compact), and occupied a pleasant plot of ground perhaps two miles outside Erevan, on the far side of the olive-green hills. The house was at the end of a dirt road (for the countryside seemed to start up right at the outskirts), which was lined with tall trees and dusty shrubs and was in every respect rural, except that one could glimpse two or three new, pink stone apartment buildings through the trees, barely a half mile away. All the same, there was a feeling about the area of tranquillity, and small gardens, and lazily barking dogs. "As you see, we are in the suburbs!" exclaimed Sarkis. He was clearly pleased with himself in his role as host. He showed us his garden—a tiny plot that contained mostly dirt, but where a few purple flowers and green shoots struggled through the light-brown soil. "I always tell myself that I must work in the garden on weekends," said Sarkis, "but I never do." The house was fashioned of gray stone, somewhat in the manner of a peasant house, and the outside was not especially lovely. There was a tin roof and a weather-worn wooden porch, with several very old chairs set against the wall. "You can't imagine how many rubles I had to pay for all this," said Sarkis, "and I will never tell you. But it is charming, is it not? Imagine living in an apartment building when one could live in such a house!" Inside were three small rooms, like boxes, on the ground floor and, presumably, a few more small rooms upstairs. Everything was spotless and in order, with lacelike covers on the armrests of the faded sofa, and numerous tinted family photographs in oval frames set out on the polished side tables. The whole effect was rather Victorian. Sarkis's wife appeared: a cheerful-seeming, dark-haired woman, slightly younger than her husband. She was shy as to language, but she shook hands cordially and did not appear shy about anything else. Nor did she seem to have suffered much from the grippe.

We sat around a shining dark-wood table in the small living room and consumed quantities of shashlik and green onions; also Armenian pastries, newly baked, and black, smoking coffee, and brandy out of a bottle obviously not often used, which Sarkis produced from a cupboard, set before us, beamed at, and began to pour seigneurially. In one corner of the room stood a large—or, rather, thick—wooden television set, itself quite Victorian, and beside it, against the wall, was a display chest, made of the same shining wood as the table, and containing plates and pinkish glassware.

"The crystal is from Czechoslovakia," said Sarkis. "My wife admires it, although I don't see what is wrong with our Soviet glassware."

His wife said something to him in Armenian, and he laughed.

"She says the Soviet glassware is no good," he said. "Imagine that such a statement should be made in my own house!" He laughed again and poured some more brandy.

We had many toasts: to Ararat, to Armenia, to America, to friendship between our two peoples. "I wish my son were here," said Sarkis. "He is nearby at the university, but he never comes home. That is the way with sons, is it not? He makes this joke all the time: 'I have to work hard, Papa, so that I won't have to teach English to high-school students.' But he is a brilliant boy." I tried to imagine what Sarkis's son might look like. He got up and showed us a photograph: Sarkis and a thin young man standing in sunlight beside a low hedge—perhaps on the dirt road outside. The boy (for even at nineteen or twenty he still seemed a boy) had a grave, sweet expression on his face and stood nearly a head taller than his father, who had his arm around his son's waist, as if holding on. Respect thy father! We drank a toast to Sarkis's son.

After dinner, two of Sarkis's friends (or, as he insisted, "colleagues") came by—Arshil, a youngish man with a pale face and eyeglasses, who also taught English at the high school, and Kevork, an older man, thickset, with thick hands and a coarse face, who was a member of the local Writers' Union. It had been Sarkis's notion that we should meet to discuss the literature of our two countries, but from the start it was clear that the emphasis was to be on American writers.

"Of course, it is hard to obtain translations," said Kevork, lighting up an evil-looking brown cigarette, "but it does not seem to be a high time in American literature."

"Which American writers most interest you?" I asked the two colleagues.

"I have read both Jerome Salinger and Scott Fitzgerald," said Arshil. "This year, I have read the story of Gatsby."

"I find both writers childish," said Kevork.

"Yes, Fitzgerald is undeniably childish about capitalism," said Sarkis. "But you must agree that he is an excellent writer of short novels."

"A great writer must write more than short novels," said Kevork.

Arshil said that he had also read Walt Whitman, John Steinbeck, and Edgar Poe. Sarkis and Arshil discussed Walt Whitman and Stephen Crane. It was strange to be gossiping about so many dead writers.

Kevork remarked that he preferred Dostoevsky to Edgar Poe. "Edgar Poe is a miniaturist," he said.

"Of course, Poe is not as serious as Dostoevsky," said Arshil.

I made the mistake of asking about Solzhenitsyn, partly

lulled by the warmth of the brandy, and doubtless also out of sheer hostility to Kevork, who seemed exactly the sort of person who might have made trouble for him. In what I meant to be a harmless, literary manner, I said, "How do you compare a modern writer such as Solzhenitsyn, who deals in large themes, with classical writers such as Tolstoy or Dostoevsky?"

There was the proverbial moment of silence.

"Nobody can be compared with Tolstoy," said Sarkis.

Then Kevork spoke. He looked not at me but toward the floor. "Solzhenitsyn is a special case," he said. "He is a national writer, a national writer of talent. But he is one who chose to abuse his talent with self-service." He looked around at all of us. "Besides, if a writer wishes to attack his country, then he should not expect to be honored by it."

There was another moment of silence. I thought Sarkis seemed pained, and I felt bad about having brought up the subject, or perhaps about having brought it up so trivially. Arshil got up from his chair and poured everyone some more brandy. He seemed a kind man, with many obscure feelings, and probably not very forceful—the traditional high-school English teacher. Now he said, "In America, would you say that the hippies are still a serious problem?"

"There are few hippies any more," my wife said.

"Everybody must have a job and do productive work," said Sarkis. "Is that not so?"

"In Armenia there are no hippies," said Arshil.

There was a prim, genteel quality to the conversation—

almost "un-Armenian," it occurred to me. Then I thought, Whose idea was it, anyway, that Armenians were somehow picturesque or offbeat? Surely all along they had been so palpably, doggedly, almost pathetically straight. Through one of Sarkis's small windows, the lights of a tall building blinked in the distance. It seemed all too plausible that the kings of Nairi had built those solid pink apartment houses.

We talked for a while longer about novels and novelists. There was something cheerfully indiscriminate in the other men's tastes—an absence of modishness, of topical shading. It made one think of the way a starving man might overlook the need for spices. I remember Arshil's saying at one point that in Moscow two years earlier he had bought two books by "the novelist H. Robbins," and had found them "vigorous but insensitive."

Then Kevork rose to his feet, excused himself shyly, and said that he must return home. He shook hands all around. "Someday, I should like to visit America," he said to me.

My wife asked, "Where would you most like to go?"

"I have heard of the Widener Library at Harvard," he said. "I should like to go there. Also to Niagara Falls."

After he had left, we sat together in the living room. Sarkis said, not unkindly, "You should not have asked him about Solzhenitsyn."

"I know that," I said. "I'm sorry."

"It's all right," said Sarkis.

"I thought things were more relaxed," I said.

"Yes," said Sarkis.

Arshil said, "Four months ago, the police took away his son."

I looked at Sarkis, who was staring at the carpet. His wife stood in the doorway to the kitchen drying a glass. "That is true," he said. "Yes, those things also happen." He looked up at us. "Young men do foolish things, do they not?" he said. And "Young men are crazy!" For a second, he seemed close to tears. Then he said, "Come. I will show you my library."

We all followed him up some narrow stairs into a small room, apparently adjoining an equally small bedroom. Its walls were tiers of bookshelves jammed with books. The books were mostly English and American, some French, quite a few Armenian, the majority of them ancient—or, anyway, well-thumbed—paperbacks with titles ranging from *A Farewell to Arms* to the *Sunset Barbecue Cook Book*. "You see, I take whatever I can find," said Sarkis.

"It's a wonderful library," said my wife.

Arshil held up a loose-leaf ledger, filled with names and dates. "He lends us all books," said Arshil, and suddenly he hugged Sarkis.

My thoughts were still on Kevork and his son—though I was aware not so much of this nameless, faceless boy, this "foolish young man" (had he, too, been photographed with a grave, sweet expression?), or even of his father, who had not wished to be made to express himself on Solzhenitsyn, as of all the other dark corners in the lives of these people: Sarkis, Arshil, Arak, doubtless Vartan, all the rest.

I said to Sarkis when we were back downstairs, "How is it that so many hard things have happened to Armenians everywhere, and yet it is still the Turks they hate so much?"

Sarkis looked at me evenly, his composure recovered. "Because they killed so many of our people. Your people and my people."

For a moment, I felt I might hit him, beat at him with my fists. There was something so confining in that thought. Then I felt ridiculous and embarrassed. All evening, I had wanted to embrace him.

Sarkis's wife came up and gave us a small package of her pastries to take back to our hotel. She stood in the low doorway of the little house, her hand briefly in Sarkis's. She shook our hands again. Goodbye, goodbye.

Arshil and Sarkis walked with us down the dirt road toward the bus stop. The night was clear and fragrant, with half a moon above the hills. An invisible dog barked far away. The great trees rose overhead, dark shapes against the blue-black sky. Arshil walked along beside me. Ahead I could vaguely hear Sarkis telling my wife some amusing story about the building of his house. How he had tried to fix the roof, or build the roof. His voice rose and fell in the warm night.

Arshil said quietly, "Do you know what I think was worst about the trouble with the Turks? It was that the Turks and the Armenians were brothers."

I said, "But I thought the Turks hated the Armenians."

"Don't brothers sometimes hate one another?" said

Arshil. In the dim light (from the moon? from a distant street lamp?), he seemed to be smiling, but I imagined that his face was often set that way. "Now and then, my grandmother used to speak of those times," he said. "You know, in 1915, or perhaps 1916, after my grandfather was killed in the great massacre, she fled here from Van. In wintertime, too. She was a hard old lady."

"What happened to your grandfather?" I asked.

"He was a doctor," said Arshil. "He was also in one of the resistance bands that used to attack the Turkish convoys. Of course, they caught them finally and brought them to the square where they were to be hanged. But first they were beaten—beaten terribly, I can well believe. I can still remember my grandmother's voice as she used to say, 'But the man who gave the worst beatings was Djebal, our neighbor, Aram's patient—a man whose wife he had saved from the typhus.'"

"What are you two talking about?" said Sarkis as we reached the main highway.

"History," said Arshil.

"It's too nice an evening for history," said Sarkis.

We stood together beneath the street lamp waiting for the bus to come.

"Was it not a fine evening?" Sarkis said. "I think even our English teacher is pleased." He embraced Arshil. "Do we not live well?" he said.

Soon, a bus appeared out of the dark. Sarkis stayed by the open door as we climbed aboard.

"We are friends!" he called from the street.

"We are friends," I said.

Behind us, Sarkis and Arshil stood in the pool of yellow light, arms around each other, waving. Brothers.

On the subject of brotherhood, at least this much was true of Constantinople in the summer of 1908, when the Young Turks took over control of the Ottoman government from the declining and elderly Abdul-Hamid II. In the words of the British historian Bernard Lewis: "The long night of Hamidian despotism was over; the dawn of freedom had come. The constitution had once again been proclaimed and elections ordered. Turks and Armenians embraced in the streets."

The popular Turkish poet Tevfik Fikret, whose work had often been suppressed for its anti-Hamidian views, poured out his enthusiasm as follows:

> *Now we are far from that accursed night. . . .*
> *Our eyes have opened to a radiant morning.*

Some years later, after the debacle of the First World War and the eventual collapse of the Young Turk government, an American journalist, H. G. Dwight, who had been in Turkey during that period of hope and wishful thinking, wrote in a book about Constantinople: "Although time has only partially fulfilled so many generous aspirations, or has turned them to bitterness, I refuse to believe that they were totally insincere. I shall always count it, on the contrary, among the most enlarging experiences of my life to have been in Constantinople in 1908, and to have seen a people at one of those rare moments when it really lives."

From many accounts, there was literally dancing in the streets during the midsummer weeks, and if Turks and Armenians embraced, small wonder, for the "long night of Hamidian despotism" did appear to be over. Abdul-Hamid himself was still sultan, but he was no longer an autocrat. The cause for celebration was the relatively bloodless coup d'état whereby units of the Ottoman Army controlled by the Young Turks had compelled the Sultan to restore the constitution—the same modestly liberal instrument that he had pulled out of a hat in 1876 and then abandoned. However, Turkish political life had changed since the more innocent days of 1876 and the Yeni Osmanlilar—the nineteenth-century Young Turks, with their romantic, Europe-inspired constitutional-reform movement. The men who made the revolution of 1908 belonged to a more recent and far more authoritarian Turkish political party, called the Committee of Union and Progress (Ittihad ve Terakki). Furthermore, they were mostly from the military wing of the Committee—disaffected junior officers of Ottoman Third Army units in Macedonia. For another thing, in the ten-year interval since Abdul-Hamid's massacre of the Armenians an important split had developed between Turkish and Armenian reformers, who nonetheless continued to meet together regularly until 1913, in an attempt to reconcile their diverging aims.

Essentially, the chief source of disagreement between the Turks and the Armenians was the issue of European intervention. For ever since the Hamidian massacres the Armenians (notably the members of the political party Dashnaktsutiun) had felt that the best possibilities for reform lay in the intervention of liberal Europe, whose leaders continued to profess concern and sympathy over the "Armenian Question"—needless to say, without having done much of anything about it. The Turks, on the other hand, had become more and more hostile to the notion of imposing European political ideas on ancient Turkish Islamic life. Thus, just as the Armenians (who had recently lost an eighth of their population to the paranoia and displeasure of Abdul-Hamid) were looking increasingly to Europe for guarantees of safety and political reform, the Turkish political and military activists were growing steadily anti-European (chiefly anti-English and anti-French), and turning more nationalistically Turkish and Islamic in their plans for a new nation. But even after the 1908 coup neither the Turks nor the Armenians had any very radical program for the old Ottoman empire, which both groups still conceived of in its traditional form, including the sultanate.

Such solemn and almost shy ambitions—the shyness of political children! In our starker and more violent century (a Lear among centuries), scarcely a political manifesto has

been issued that does not have the smell of murder somewhere about it. Years after the genocide of the Armenians in
Turkey during the First World War, some would say that
the Armenians had been trying to secede from Turkey—and
by the time of the genocide to some extent that was true. But
in 1908, far from wishing to break away from, or even over-
turn, this backward and bankrupt "empire," they seem to
have wanted mainly to regenerate it, and piously, in the
manner of self-absorbed children, worried that someone
might misunderstand and think they wished to do away
with the office of sultan, to take that step so final in any
family—parricide, regicide, sultanicide.

But time never stays still for anyone, perhaps least of all
for reformer-revolutionaries. In April 1909, after the dancing
in the streets of Constantinople had died down, Abdul-
Hamid (whose telegraph system had provided him with
such inferior information concerning the coup d'état) attempted a last maneuver. Still in Yildiz Palace and still sultan, knowing that the Young Turks were tinged with
liberalism (although very slightly so) and that any liberalism implied religious liberalism, even secularism—which
had traditionally been anathema to the conservative rural
Turks of the provinces—Abdul-Hamid, together with the
conservative priesthood and reactionary elements in the
Army, concocted a counter-revolution. For a short while, the
new government was in danger of falling. Muslim dissidents
gathered in Saint Sophia Square chanting, "The Holy Law
is in danger!" Several Army garrisons in Anatolia, protest-

ing that they did not wish to be governed by "college-trained officers," threatened to march on the capital. But the Young Turks still controlled the majority of the troops, and the counter-revolution was quelled.

Thus, Abdul-Hamid was finally deposed and sent into exile in Salonika, taking with him but a few retainers and only four members of his harem, the rest of which was disbanded, with the women (many of them of mature age) left to be called for by parents or relatives—who now came in from remote sections of the country—in the fashion of schoolchildren being picked up at the end of term. A new sultan was installed, but merely as a figurehead. The Young Turks were firmly in power, having perhaps learned an early lesson: never to underestimate the religious conservatism and fervor of their countrymen. If Turkey should be for the Turks, then it was worth remembering that the Turks were still predominantly and passionately Muslim.

CONSIDER SOME snapshots of the Young Turks who ruled Turkey on the eve of the First World War. They were taken by an official Ottoman photographer and reprinted in an *Illustrated London News* of 1913:

The first man has a large head, with a round, heavy face. He is forty-one years old, but he looks much older—middle-aged. There is a fringe of dark beard around his chin, and on the whole he seems to have a sober, almost bureaucratic expression, which belies his braided uniform. He is Jemal

Pasha, once a colonel in the Third Army, now Minister of Marine.

The second man is different. He is short, slender, with a decidedly Gallic look to him. He has a thin, trim mustache and dark, carefully brushed-back hair. His face is fine-boned, with intense eyes. There is something of the dandy in his appearance. He is Enver Pasha, thirty-two years old, formerly a major in the Third Army, now Minister of War.

The third man is from the same mold as the first: a round and heavy Turkish face, with ample cheeks and a bearded chin. His eyes seem more alert than Jemal's, and more concentrated than Enver's. There is something even of a professor in his gaze—but a rough-hewn, almost coarse professor. He is Talaat Pasha, forty-one years old, formerly a telegraph clerk in Edirne, now Minister of the Interior.

TURKEY for the Turks. Once the Young Turks were in charge of the country, they struggled with such noble matters as "land reform" and a reorganization of the Constantinople Fire Department. The Young Turk government also solved the long-standing problem of the roaming dog packs of Constantinople. It collected all the stray dogs of the city and shipped them to a deserted island in the Sea of Marmara, where in due course they starved to death.

Nor did the great powers now choose to sit around for very long placidly observing the new government, in the fashion of benign uncles looking upon a small child. In

1908, Austria-Hungary, with Russian approval, dived into the Turkish European provinces and extracted Bosnia and Herzegovina. In the same year, with Austria-Hungary's approval, Bulgaria declared its independence. In 1911, Italy, with the endorsement of France and England, acquired the Ottoman North African province of Tripoli. In 1912, Greece, Serbia, and Bulgaria formed a loose confederacy and pushed Turkey almost completely out of the Balkans. Indeed, on the eve of the First World War, Turkey's best friend appeared to be Germany.

For perhaps thirty years before the war, Germany had made no secret of its special fondness for Turkey—a fondness that could easily be explained as the desire of a belatedly colonial, modern state to exploit the considerable economic possibilities of the unindustrialized Ottoman empire. Twice —in 1889 and 1898—Kaiser Wilhelm himself had traveled by yacht to Constantinople, where he had stoutly shaken the hand of Abdul-Hamid, kissed him on both cheeks, and been shown at least a small degree of affection in return. German track had been laid down for the Berlin-Baghdad Railway. A German telephone system had been installed in Constantinople. In 1913, the year before the outbreak of war in Europe, the Young Turk government accepted a detachment of German "military advisers," under General Otto Liman von Sanders, who were attached to the Turkish Army with a view to instructing and training it in new techniques.

In the summer of 1914, however, as the World War crept

closer, with the swift moves of Germany and the great mobilizations of the Entente powers, Germany was not eager to have Turkey come in on its behalf. The Kaiser felt that Turkey's armed forces were too ill-equipped and disorganized to be of much use in a military alliance. Perversely, it was some of the more ambitious Young Turks, notably Enver Pasha, who pushed the matter, for evidently they wished to be allies of mighty Germany in the great adventure that was just beginning. On August 2, a secret military alliance with Germany was signed, which left Turkey with only the appearance of neutrality. England then forced the issue by impounding two Turkish warships that were under construction in English yards. In retaliation, Turkey permitted two German warships in flight across the Mediterranean to seek refuge in Turkish waters. England, France, and Russia demanded the immediate disarming of the German warships and the repatriation of their crews. At first, the Young Turks hesitated, and then they announced that they had "purchased" the warships from the Germans. On October 29, the two ships, still manned with German crews under a German commander but flying the Turkish flag, attacked Russian shipping and ports in the Black Sea, and shortly thereafter Russia declared war on Turkey. The Ottoman empire was finally in the war, on the side of Germany.

Why should the Young Turks have been so eager to bring their impoverished and backward country into the World War? It is hard to say. Economically as well as militarily, the Turks were in poor shape when they entered the war, and they were a good deal worse off when it was over. On the other hand, one might ask what rational basis any of the more advanced nations had for entering that wretched war, with its self-destructive eruption of dammed-up aggressions. Doubtless, in the dim mind of each nation there existed a kind of dream: *Drang nach Osten;* Ruling the Waves; *La Gloire;* Pan-Slavism. In the case of the Young Turks, it seems to have been a dream (albeit a vague and hazy one, like all their dreams) of a new Turkish empire, which would incorporate the Muslim population of southern Russia and also the Muslims of Iran and Egypt: a pan-Muslim empire.

In any event, with much of the civilized world resounding to such hunting calls as "On to Paris!" and "On to Berlin!" how is one to blame Enver Pasha—still a young man, full of odd bravadoes and conceits—for mounting his own cavalry charge toward "the East"? Which is to say that soon after Turkey was officially in the war Enver Pasha, Minister of War for the Ottoman empire, took passage with a small staff across the Black Sea to Trebizond; from there rode eastward into the Turkish Armenian provinces where he rounded up all the available troops of the Turkish Ninth Army; and then headed northeast into the Russian Caucasus. Precisely where he was going, nobody knows—and nobody knew then. In the manner of Darius the Great, he was possessed of some grand intuitive "northern vision." General Liman von Sanders had strongly advised against the enterprise—whatever it might be—and he was right.

Enver, at the head of a column of one hundred thousand hastily assembled Turkish soldiers, most of them still wearing summer uniforms, enjoyed a few well-acclaimed initial victories, surprising some Russian detachments and capturing several villages. But in short order the situation fell apart. The Russians reorganized and counterattacked en masse. Besides, Enver had chosen to conduct this campaign in what was now the early Russian winter, and great numbers of his troops began to succumb to frostbite and disease. By the first week in January 1915, the Turkish Ninth Army had been virtually wiped out, and Enver—unusually subdued and sullen—returned to Constantinople.

In the middle of that month, Jemal Pasha led another Turkish army, including a company of whirling dervishes, south toward Egypt. Jemal's force reached the Suez with very little difficulty, but upon encountering the British, opposite Ismailia, they were thrown back. From the start, there was little logic anywhere in the Turkish military position, with slight vitality in the ill-equipped troops and few resources at home. The dream had apparently been of short duration and now seemed to be over. Enver, in Constantinople, went to his office each morning and, sitting behind his desk, attended to paperwork. He refused to discuss the Russian campaign with anyone. Jemal had fallen back to Syria, his army now in the role of a defensive garrison. Then, late in April 1915, the English, assisted by a force of Australians and New Zealanders, landed at Gallipoli.

A student of the drama might say that at this point the

stage was set for a variety of possible dénouements. Turkey might be swiftly forced out of the war by the Allied landing. Or the Young Turk government might be overthrown, either from outside or from within—for there was increasing dissatisfaction with the adventurous but unsuccessful pashas on the part of the conservative faction in the country, especially out in the provinces, where the lot of the poor Turkish farmer had become even worse as a result of war taxation. Consider the situation for a moment: Enver and Jemal—the warriors—were on the defensive in Constantinople and Syria. The hated English were on the doorstep in the Dardanelles, where they were opposed by sixty thousand Turkish troops under General Liman von Sanders and his second-in-command, an early leader of the Young Turk movement named Mustafa Kemal. And then there was the matter of the Armenians.

For immediately after the outbreak of the war both sides had made special efforts to gain the support of the Armenians, inasmuch as the Armenian mountain plateau was considered as strategically valuable in the twentieth century as it had been in ancient times. Perhaps more so. Not only did it represent a "buffer" between Russia and Turkey but its mountainous and central position made it a key to the Black Sea, and even to the northern access to India. Furthermore, since the great oil discoveries of the eighteen-nineties Armenia's proximity to both the Russian fields at Baku, on the Caspian Sea, and the English wells in Mesopotamia had made the region an object of marked interest to most of the great powers. In the autumn of 1914, Count Vorontsov-Dashkov, viceroy of the Transcaucasian provinces, promised the Russian Armenians on behalf of the czar that if they should unreservedly support Russia in the war, then after the war Russia would grant autonomy to the six Turkish-Armenian provinces. At about the same time, in Turkish Armenia, officials from the Young Turk government appeared at a Dashnak convention in Erzurum and promised the delegates that if they should unreservedly support Turkey, then after the war the Turkish government would grant all Armenians autonomy in a "Turkish protectorate" to be made up of certain of the Russian-Armenian provinces as well as parts of the Turkish provinces of Erzurum, Van, and Bitlis.

Now, one should point out that the Ottoman law that had forbidden Armenians to serve in the Turkish armed forces (a restriction that to modern minds might seem like an exemption from death but to earlier minds often seemed more like an exclusion from manhood) had been suspended by 1912, when the Turks needed soldiers for the Balkan War. Many Armenians had then begun to serve in the Turkish Army, and a number of them had been praised for their heroism by Enver Pasha. In fact, at the time that the Young Turks at Erzurum were asking for unreserved support, full conscription was in effect throughout the Ottoman empire, and Armenian men between the ages of twenty and forty-five were already serving in the Turkish armed forces. At Erzurum, therefore, the Armenians replied that those of them who were Turkish subjects would continue to behave in uniform as Turkish subjects; as in the Balkan War, they would do as they were commanded. But the Turkish officials wished for something more. They wanted the Dashnakists to recruit a special Turkish-Armenian detachment, whose purpose would be to fight the Russians on its own and liberate Russian Armenia. This the Dashnakists said they would not do.

Into our dramatic equation, then, one must add the refusal of the Armenians—not yet twenty years after the Hamidian massacres—to put together a special brigade with which to make war against a Christian country that had traditionally expressed sympathy for their cause; and one must also add what, specifically, they were quite agreeable to doing: namely, being conscripted into the Turkish Army, putting on the coarse, dun-colored uniforms and puttees, and being shipped to various barracks in Anatolia, where many of them had already begun their training.

There was another factor that one should not ignore—the so-called Armenian Volunteers. These were a loosely organized collection of irregulars—most of them Russian Armenians recruited from the Tiflis and Erevan branches of Dashnaktsutiun—who served in the early days of the war on the Caucasian front, sometimes as scouts or advance units, more often in guerrilla squads of a dozen or so men, and who engaged in raiding forays against the Turkish troops. The active number of these Volunteers rarely exceeded one thousand (not a sizable force compared to Enver's army of one hundred thousand), but they knew the terrain, and they fought well, and—perhaps more to the point in the Turkish view—they existed. As with many guerrilla operations in our own era, a situation of paranoia and rigidity seems to have prevailed in Turkish official minds whereby merely the idea of such a group—of such an unasked-for and impertinent entity—evoked a specter of rebellious Armenian legions. The Armenians, too, recognized that these Volunteers existed; and their occasional guerrilla raids into the northern sector of Turkish Armenia were regarded by the local inhabitants, variously, as heroic or unsettling. Some photographs of these Volunteers remain, collected in a book, *The Memoirs of Rouben Der Minasian:* amateur snapshots of different bands of ten or twelve men, each group posed formally and rather quaintly, almost in the manner of an eighteen-nineties football team—the men usually with mustaches and fierce expressions, wearing lamb's-wool mountain hats, and carrying bandoliers of cartridges. Der Minasian himself was one of the early leaders of this resistance movement, as were such Armenian heroes as Kevork Chavoush, Aram of Moush, and Andranik. There is a picture of Der Minasian: a man in a wool hat, perhaps twenty or twenty-two, brandishing a grenade as he kneels at the front of a group of guerrillas. There are also numerous accounts of ambushes and escapades, of Turkish platoons and sometimes companies engaged, of nighttime rides and river cross-ings, villages defended, supply trains looted, exchanges of rifle fire. "At the outskirts of the village of S., I ordered the people to scatter, everyone for himself. I was now all alone with my company of twenty-two, and the dying Kevork. I took stock of the situation and saw that we were securely hemmed in in a tight triangle. On one side was the village of B., crawling with soldiers. On the other side were the swollen waters of the Euphrates." Much bravery, foolhardiness, and youth.

The Volunteers had originally been formed in order to catch the eye of England and France, the two Allies who would soon be so near, in the Dardanelles, and remain so far. But the strongest impression they seem to have made was on the hard-pressed and suspicious Turks. In December 1914, when Enver's ill-fated northern expedition had already begun to falter, a company-strength unit of Volunteers stationed in the snowbound Keri Pass on one occasion held off an entire Turkish division long enough to permit a trapped Russian force to escape. The story was not reported in the distant European press, which in any case was preoccupied with matters on the Western front. But after Enver had returned in defeat to Constantinople, in early 1915, the account began to be noised about in Turkish government circles—and was picked up by the German Embassy—that the chief reason for the failure of the Turkish advance had been "mass defections" of Turkish Armenians to the Russian side. Moreover, a short while later—toward the end of

April 1915—an "incident" took place in the predominantly Armenian town of Van, in eastern Turkey.

ACCORDING TO an American, Grace Knapp, who was in Van at the time, visiting the medical mission, and who later provided a lengthy eyewitness report, the trouble arose shortly after the Governor General of the province of Van, Djevdet Bey, who was a brother-in-law of Enver Pasha, returned from the ill-starred Caucasian campaign. First, on the pretext of asking for their cooperation, he arranged for the murder of four Armenian leaders. Then Turkish troops were instructed to dig entrenchments around the Armenian sector of the town. "On Tuesday, the 20th of April, at 6 A.M., some Turkish soldiers tried to seize one of a band of village women on their way to the city," wrote Miss Knapp. "She fled. Two Armenian soldiers came up and asked the Turks what they were doing. The Turkish soldiers fired on the Armenians, killing them. Thereupon the Turkish entrenchments opened fire. The siege had begun." The Turks had artillery and around four thousand soldiers. "The Armenian force consisted of 1,500 trained riflemen possessing only about 300 rifles. . . . They began to make bullets and cartridges." The Armenians of Van held off the Turks for five weeks, until advancing Russian troops diverted the Turks' attention. Meanwhile, the Turks had massacred most of the Armenians in the surrounding villages and had destroyed much of the Armenian section of Van. "There will either be nothing but Turks or nothing but Armenians left in this city," Djevdet Bey had said on one occasion. In Constantinople, where the foreign press and diplomatic corps had little knowledge of or interest in remote eastern Turkey, the German Embassy sent this dispatch to Berlin: "The Turkish Government has informed us of an attack by armed Armenian insurrectionists on Muslim inhabitants of the town of Van. Many Muslims have been slain. The Turkish Government has been forced to take steps to put down the rebellion." The dramatic equation, whatever its seemingly random or unconnected components, appeared to be in the process of resolution.

"A decree went forth that all Armenians should be disarmed. The Armenians in the [Turkish] Army were drafted out of the fighting ranks, reformed into special labor battalions, and set to work throwing up fortifications and constructing roads." So reads an excerpt from what is probably the most substantial report on the Armenian genocide, *The Treatment of Armenians in the Ottoman Empire, 1915–16,* which was published in London in 1916 under the signature of Viscount Bryce. James Bryce, then an old man, was one of those noble establishment figures—a statesman and scholar, at one time or another Regius Professor of Civil Law at Oxford, President of the Board of Trade, Chief Secretary for Ireland, Undersecretary of State for Foreign Affairs, Chancellor of the Duchy of Lancaster, and Ambassador to Washington. He had once climbed Mt. Ararat, and had been a friend of Gladstone's. The book is an immense undertaking, running to nearly six hundred pages of case histories and eyewitness accounts, and its assembly was the work not of Viscount Bryce but of a young Oxford graduate. "I had the good fortune," wrote Viscount Bryce in a prefatory note, "to secure the cooperation of a young historian of high academic distinction, Mr. Arnold J. Toynbee, late Fellow of Balliol College, Oxford. He undertook to examine and put together the pieces of evidence collected." The Bryce-Toynbee report (Professor Toynbee today is several years older than Bryce was in 1916, and is the possessor of a parallel eminence) continues: "The disarming of the civil population was left to the local authorities, and in every administrative centre a reign of terror began. The authorities demanded the production of a definite number of arms. Those who could not produce them were tortured, often in fiendish ways; those who procured them for surrender, by purchase from their Muslim neighbours or by other means, were imprisoned for conspiracy against the Government. Few of these were young men, for most of the young had been called up to serve."

From an *Address delivered in America, 13th December, 1915, by a professor from the college at X.:* "Persons suspected [of keeping arms] were arrested and taken to the Government Building, where they were subjected to the cruelest forms of torture. Usually they were bound and bastinadoed until they became unconscious. Boiling water was sometimes poured on the soles of the feet, to increase the pain of the bastinadoing. . . . At least two men of our city died under this torture. . . . They took [the blacksmith] to the Government Building. There they bound him, and four brutal men stuffed his mouth with filth, and beat him with rods all over the body until he became unconscious. As soon as he regained consciousness, they repeated the process. . . .

We learned afterward that the occasion for this man's torture was that he was seen casting a 16-lb. shot, which we had ordered him to make for our college field-day sports this year. The man who saw him reported to the police that he had been making bombs."

From a *Narrative of an Armenian lady departed from C.:* "The Turkish officials searched the Armenian churches and schools of G., H., C., AQ., AR., AS., and the surrounding villages, but without finding anything incriminating. . . . After that, they arrested from the town of C. the following persons: Professor B., Mr. H., and his brother J. . . . as well as many others old and young. . . . They took them to the house of V. Agha, stripped them one by one, and gave them 300 lashes on their backs. When they fainted, they threw them into a stable and waited until they had revived, in order to beat them again. . . . After beating T. Effendi in H. and tearing out his fingernails and the flesh of his hands and feet they put a rope under his arms, dragged him to C., and threw him into prison."

From a *Narrative of a foreign resident of German nationality:* "I was called to a house one day where I saw a sheet which originated from the prison, and which was being sent to the wash. This sheet was covered with blood, and running in long streams. I was also shown clothes which were drenched and exceedingly dirty. It was a puzzle to me what they could possibly have done to the prisoners, but I got to the bottom of the matter by the help of two very reliable persons who witnessed part of it themselves.

"The prisoner is put in a room . . . and gendarmes standing in twos at both sides . . . administer bastinadoes, each in their turn, as long as they have enough force in them. In Roman times forty strokes were administered at the very most; in this place, however, 200, 300, 500, even 800 strokes are administered. The foot swells up and then bursts open, and thus the blood spurts out. . . . On the next day, or, more exactly, during the night, as all ill-treatments are carried on at night . . . the whole bastinadoing is repeated again, in spite of the swollen feet and the wounds. . . . I was then in R., but in that prison there were . . . no less than thirty prisoners, who all had their feet in such a state that they began to burn and had to be amputated. . . . A young man was beaten to death within the space of five minutes."

These accounts from the Bryce-Toynbee report were selected more or less at random. At least, they are not notably more sensational than the hundred and fifty or so other statements in the book, the majority of which were "drawn from neutral witnesses who were living in or passing through Asiatic Turkey while these events were happening, and had opportunities of observing them."

THERE IS ALSO another voice from that period—that of Henry Morgenthau, United States Ambassador to Turkey during the early years of the World War, who published his recollections in 1918. From *Ambassador Morgenthau's*

Story: "In the early part of 1915, the Armenian soldiers in the Turkish army were reduced to a new status. Up to that time most of them had been combatants, but now they were all stripped of their arms and transformed into workmen . . . road laborers and pack animals. . . . They had to spend practically all their time in the open, sleeping on the bare ground. . . . They were given only scraps of food; if they fell sick they were left where they had dropped. . . .

"Let me relate a single episode which is contained in one of the reports of our consuls and which now forms part of the records of the American State Department. Early in July, 2,000 Armenian *amélés*—such is the Turkish word for soldiers who have been reduced to workmen—were sent from Harpoot to build roads. The Armenians in that town understood what this meant and pleaded with the Government for mercy. But this official insisted that the men were not to be harmed, and he even called upon the German missionary, Mr. Ehemann, to quiet the panic, giving that gentleman his word of honor that the ex-soldiers would be protected. . . . Yet practically every man of these 2,000 was massacred, and his body thrown into a cave. . . . A few days afterward another 2,000 soldiers were sent to Diyarbakir. The only purpose of sending these men out in the open country was that they might be massacred. In order that [they] might have no strength to resist . . . these poor creatures were systematically starved. Government agents went ahead on the road, notifying the Kurds that the caravan was approaching. . . . Not only did the Kurdish tribesmen pour down from the mountains upon this starved and weakened regiment, but the Kurdish women came with butcher's knives in order that they might gain that merit in Allah's eyes that comes from killing a Christian."

There is a photograph of Ambassador Morgenthau in the front of his book: a spare, elegant diplomat in his early sixties, with that look of nineteenth-century probity about him, and the same partly bald head and rimless eyeglasses one associates with his son, Henry Morgenthau, Jr., who was Secretary of the Treasury under President Franklin Roosevelt. The Ambassador's account continues:

"Yet these happenings did not constitute what the newspapers of the time commonly referred to as the Armenian atrocities; they were merely the preparatory steps in the destruction of the race. The Young Turks displayed greater ingenuity than their predecessor, Abdul-Hamid. . . . Instead of massacring outright the Armenian race, they now decided to deport it. In the south and southeastern section of the Ottoman empire lie the Syrian desert and Mesopotamian valley . . . a dreary, desolate waste, without cities and towns or life of any kind, populated only by a few wild and fanatical Bedouin tribes. . . . The Central Government now announced its intention of gathering the two million or more Armenians living in the several sections of the empire and transporting them to this desolate and inhospitable region."

FROM the Bryce-Toynbee report: "On the 8th April [1915] the final phase began, and the process . . . was applied to one Armenian centre after another throughout the Ottoman empire. On a certain date, in whatever town or village it might be (and the dates show a significant sequence), the public crier went through the streets announcing that every male Armenian must present himself forthwith at the Government Building. . . . The men presented themselves in their working clothes, leaving their shops and work-rooms open, their ploughs in the field, their cattle on the mountain side. When they arrived, they were thrown without explanation into prison, kept there a day or two, and then marched out of the town in batches, roped man to man, along some southerly or south-easterly road. They were starting, they were told, on a long journey—to Mosul or perhaps to Baghdad. . . . They had bidden no farewell to their families. . . . But they had not long to ponder over their plight, for they were halted and massacred at the first lonely place on the road. . . .

"After the Armenian men had been summoned away to their death, there was usually a few days' interval in whatever town it might be, and then the crier was heard again in the streets, bidding all Armenians who remained to prepare themselves for deportation, while placards to the same effect were posted on the walls. This applied, in actual fact, to the women and children, and to a poor remnant of the men who, through sickness, infirmity, or age, had escaped the fate marked out for their sex. . . .

"There was an official fiction that their banishment was only temporary, and they were therefore prohibited from selling their real property or their stock. The Government set its seal upon the vacated houses, lands, and merchandise, 'to keep them safe against their owners' return'; yet before these rightful owners started on their march they often saw these very possessions . . . made over by the authorities as a free gift to Muslim immigrants, who had been concentrated in the neighbourhood in readiness to step into the Armenians' place."

In some areas—for instance, in certain towns in the province of Bitlis—there was little pretense of deportation; most of the inhabitants were massacred instead.

From a *Statement by a German eyewitness . . . communicated by the American Committee for Armenian and Syrian Relief:* "In Harpoot and Mezré the people have had to endure terrible tortures. They have had their eyebrows plucked out, their breasts cut off, their nails torn off; their torturers hew off their feet or else hammer nails into them just as they do in shoeing horses. This is all done at night-time, and in order that the people may not hear their screams and know of their agony, soldiers are stationed round the prisons, beating drums and blowing whistles. . . . Harpoot has become the cemetery of the Armenians."

The sufferings of the deportees were of a different order. From a *Report by Fräulein M.* [a Swiss resident in Turkey], *dated 16th November, 1915:* "I have just returned from a ride on horseback through the Baghtché-Osmania plain, where thousands of exiles are lying out in the fields and on the roads, without any shelter and completely at the mercy of all manner of brigands. Last night about twelve o'clock, a little camp was suddenly attacked. There were about fifty to sixty persons in it. I found men and women badly wounded—bodies slashed open, broken skulls and terrible knife wounds. . . . In another camp we found thirty or forty thousand Armenians. I was able to distribute bread among them. Desperate and half-starved, they fell upon it. . . . I often saw them break down under their burden, but the soldiers kept on driving them forward with the butt-ends of their rifles, even sometimes with their bayonets. I have dressed bleeding wounds on the bodies of women that had been caused by these bayonet thrusts."

From a *Report by Fräulein O.* [another Swiss resident] *on a visit to the exiles' camp at Mamouret, 26th November, 1915:* "We saw thousands of tiny low tents, made of thin material. An innumerable crowd of people, of all ages . . . looking at us partly in surprise, partly with the indifference of desperation. A group of hungry, begging children and women were at our heels: '*Hanoum,* bread! *Hanoum,* I am hungry.' . . . Soon the immense procession was moving on. Some of the most miserable were left behind (others rested there already in the newly-dug graves)."

From a *Report by Fräulein M. on a visit to the exiles' camp at Islohia, 1st December, 1915:* "It had rained three days and three nights. . . . Many women had their feet frost-bitten; they were quite black and in a state for amputation. The wailing and groaning was horrible. . . . Though I had seen much distress before, the objects and the scenes I saw here defy description. A frailly-built woman was sitting by the roadside with her bedding on her back, and a young baby strapped on at the top of it, and in her arms she had a two-year-old child—its eyes were dim and it was at its last gasp. . . . The filth in and around these tents was something indescribable. On one single day the burial committee buried as many as 580 people."

The Berlin-Baghdad Railway, a joint German and Turkish enterprise, had been only partly completed, and the Anatolian portion ran from the suburbs of Constantinople southeast as far as Aleppo, on the edge of the Syrian desert. There were breaks in the line at both the Taurus and Amanus ranges. The use of the railroad to deport Armenians began in June 1915. The Armenians were packed into cattle cars and transported to the railheads, driven across the mountains on foot, and then taken by rail to Aleppo. Owing to a lack of engines and cattle cars, and the movement of troops up and down the small line, the Armenian deportees were frequently halted along the way and compelled to wait by the roadside for weeks, until new transportation could be found for them.

From a *Narrative of a journey . . . by a physician of foreign nationality, who had been resident in Turkey for ten years:* "At the first large station a sight burst upon my view which, although I knew and was prepared for it, was nevertheless a shock. There was a mob of a thousand or more people huddled about the station and environs, and long strings of cattle-trucks packed to suffocation with human beings. It was the first glimpse of the actual deportation of the Armenians. . . . There was no confusion, no wailing, no shouting, just a mob of subdued people, dejected, sad, hopeless, past tears. . . . At the station of K., as I looked across the fields to the river, I heard the Turkish commander say: 'Yes, I have 30,000 here under my charge.' Then I looked as far along the river as I could see, and it was one mass of improvised blanket tents."

From a *Letter, dated* . . . *22nd November, 1915, from an American traveller:* "We began to pass one train after another, crowded, jammed with these poor people, being carried away. . . . At every station where we stopped, we came side by side with one of these trains. It was made up of cattle-trucks, and the faces of little children were looking out from behind the tiny barred windows of each truck. [At one station] the Armenians told us that they had been in the station for three days with no food. The Turks kept them from buying food. . . . One woman gave birth to twins in one of those crowded trucks, and crossing a river she threw both her babies and then herself into the water. . . . A German officer was on the train with us, and I asked him if Germany had anything to do with this deportation, for I thought it was the most brutal thing that had ever happened. He said: 'You can't object to exiling a race; it's only the way the Turks are doing it which is bad.'"

From a *Report from Dr. D., dated* . . . *8th September,*

1915: "In P., the exiles are encamped in the open fields. . . . No protection is provided for them. . . . I have no knowledge of how many deaths have taken place. . . .

"The whip and club are in constant use by the police, and that upon women and children too. . . . A woman with a fractured thigh at the station was being helped by friends intending to bring her to the hospital. A commissary of police came along and ordered her to be dragged back into the carriage. . . . Soldiers' families are . . . said to be exempt from deportation, but in countless cases they are swept away with the rest. The men . . . are serving in the Turkish Army as loyally as any, and their families . . . are driven off in this inhuman manner."

From a *Letter from Dr. E., dated 27th October, 1915:* "Half a mile from the station I found two old women who were crawling about on hands and knees, too weak to walk; they had been carried off on a wagon, ostensibly to go to a village, but, once out of sight of the gendarmes, the driver had dropped them in a field and hurried away. . . . [They] looked forward to certain death by starvation, nor could we see any other future for them. A few miles farther on, we found a little heap of clods . . . and near it a bundle of rags full of a child's bones. The skull, with the scalp still clinging to it, was lying a yard or two away. Evidently there had been a hasty burial, and the dogs had come and torn the grave to pieces and devoured the body. That same day we found another dead body by the roadside—an old woman wrapped in a torn quilt; also a woman about forty years old sitting alone by the road, miles away from any city or village, with feet bare and swollen, almost pulseless, and evidently crazed from terror and exposure, muttering something about Turks who were coming to cut her throat, about her people who had left her behind. . . ."

WHILE the Armenians were thus being killed across Turkey in the middle months of 1915, either by massacre or by starvation, what of the great powers, notably England and France, whose attention the Armenian activists had so hoped to attract? These Allies, it seemed, had their hands full with the war. The Dardanelles campaign was at a standstill. Ambassador Morgenthau wrote: "When it at last became definitely established . . . that the traditional friends of Armenia—Great Britain, France, and Russia—could do nothing to help that suffering people, the mask began to disappear. In April I was suddenly deprived of the privilege of using the cipher for communicating with American consuls. The most rigorous censorship was applied to letters. Such measures could mean only that things were happening in Asia Minor which the authorities were determined to conceal."

In the spring and summer of 1915, at the height of the Armenian deportations, the two principal foreign presences in Constantinople were Morgenthau himself and Baron Hans von Wangenheim, the German Ambassador. Wangenheim, a career diplomat, regarded it as his main mission to keep Turkey in the war and so worked hard not to offend the Young Turk leaders. Generally, he passed on to Berlin without comment the Turkish government's prima-facie declarations that there was nothing much amiss in the Armenian provinces, that reports of massacres were exaggerations, and that such trouble as had occurred had been provoked by Armenian rebelliousness. When, in June, Talaat Pasha acknowledged to a German Embassy official that the mass deportations were not based alone on "military expediency" (as had previously been claimed), Wangenheim wrote to Berlin: "Talaat Bey has . . . openly stated that the Porte wished to take advantage of the opportunity offered by the war to make a clean sweep of their enemies at home without being troubled by foreign diplomatic intervention." On July 7, he pointed out again that the methods by which the Armenian deportations were being carried out "show that the Government is really aiming at the extermination of the Armenian race in the Ottoman empire." One of his stronger protests appears to have been a memorandum addressed to the grand vizier after the deportations had been in progress for nearly three months, in which he deplored the bad impression created abroad, and, in a kind of postscript, asked the Turks to watch out for "the manifold interests of German commerce and of the German welfare institutions in those provinces where the expulsion of Armenians is now being carried out."

Morgenthau in this period evidently felt different concerns, and conducted himself with less sense of diplomatic correctness—even with a certain largeness of spirit. "Two missionaries had just called upon me, giving the full details of the frightful happenings at Konia," he wrote. "After listening to their stories, I could not restrain myself, and went immediately to . . . Talaat. . . . I began to talk about the Armenians at Konia. I had hardly started when Talaat's attitude became . . . belligerent. His eyes lighted up, he brought his jaws together, leaned over toward me, and snapped out: 'Are *they* Americans?' In a moment Talaat said . . . 'The Armenians are not to be trusted. Besides, what we do with them does not concern the United States.'"

Morgenthau's *Story* continues: "I find in my diary on August 3d 'that Talaat is the one who desires to crush the poor Armenians.' He told me that the Union and Progress Committee had carefully considered the matter in all its details and that the policy which was being pursued was that which they had officially adopted. . . . 'Why are you so interested in the Armenians, anyway?' he said on another occasion. 'You are a Jew; these people are Christians. The Mohammedans and the Jews always get on harmoniously. We are treating the Jews here all right. What have you to complain of?'

" 'You don't seem to realize,' I replied, 'that I am not here as a Jew but as American Ambassador. . . .'

" 'We treat the Americans all right, too,' said Talaat. 'I don't see why you should complain.' "

Morgenthau had numerous meetings with the Young

Turk leaders—especially with Talaat, the Minister of the Interior, whom he regarded as having become the most powerful figure in the government: "I might as well have been talking to a stone wall. . . . 'These people,' he said, 'refused to disarm when we told them to. They opposed us at Van and at Zeitoun, and they helped the Russians. There is only one way in which we can defend ourselves against them in the future, and that is just to deport them.'

" 'Suppose a few Armenians did betray you,' I said. 'Is that a reason for destroying a whole race? Is that an excuse for making innocent women and children suffer?'

" 'Those things are inevitable,' Talaat replied. This remark to me was not quite so illuminating as one which Talaat made subsequently to a reporter of the *Berliner Tageblatt*, who asked him the same question: 'We have been reproached,' he said, according to this interviewer, 'for making no distinction between the innocent Armenians and the guilty; but that was utterly impossible, in view of the fact that those who were innocent today might be guilty tomorrow.' . . .

"I argued for a long time along these and similar lines. 'It is no use for you to argue,' Talaat answered. 'We have already disposed of three-quarters of the Armenians; there are none at all left in Bitlis, Van, and Erzurum. The hatred between the Turks and the Armenians is now so intense that we have got to finish with them. If we don't, they will plan their revenge.' . . .

"Talaat's attitude toward the Armenians was summed up

in the proud boast which he made to his friends: 'I have accomplished more toward solving the Armenian problem in three months than Abdul-Hamid accomplished in thirty years!' "

Morgenthau also attempted to put pressure on the Turks through the German Ambassador: "As soon as the early reports [of the massacres] reached Constantinople, it occurred to me that the most feasible way of stopping the outrages would be for the diplomatic representatives of all countries to make a joint appeal to the Ottoman Government.

"I approached Wangenheim on this subject in the latter part of March. His antipathy to the Armenians became immediately apparent. He began denouncing them in unmeasured terms. . . . 'The Armenians,' said Wangenheim, 'have shown themselves in this war to be enemies of the Turks. It is quite apparent that the two peoples can never live together in the same country. The Americans should move some of them to the United States, and we Germans will send some to Poland and in their place send Jewish Poles to the Armenian provinces—that is, if they will promise to drop their Zionist schemes.'

"Again, although I spoke with unusual earnestness, the Ambassador refused to help the Armenians. Still, on July 4th, Wangenheim did present a formal note of protest, but he did not talk to Talaat or Enver, the only men who had any authority, but to the grand vizier, who was merely a shadow. . . . [His protest's] only purpose was to put Germany officially on record. . . . Callous as Wangenheim showed himself to be, he was not quite so implacable toward the Armenians as the German naval attaché in Constantinople, Humann. . . .

" 'I have lived in Turkey the larger part of my life,' he told me, 'and I know the Armenians. I also know that both Armenians and Turks cannot live together in this country. One of these races has got to go. And I don't blame the Turks for what they are doing to the Armenians. I think that they are entirely justified. The weaker nation must succumb.' "

THROUGH MOST OF 1915, the deportations continued. From a multitude of eyewitness reports, it is possible to determine that the first convoys started from the Armenian mountain town of Zeitoun, in Cilicia, on April 8, 1915 (almost two weeks before the allegedly provocative "rebellion" in Van), and thereafter steady streams of deportees were driven from the various Armenian centers of the Ottoman empire south toward the desert. According to the Bryce-Toynbee report, there is no record of any interruption or cessation of this mass movement until November 6, 1915: "On that date, an order from Constantinople reached the local authorities, at any rate in the Cilician plain, directing them to refrain from further deportations; but this applied only to the remnant of the local Armenian residents, and the masses of exiles from the north and the northwest who were still painfully struggling across the barriers of Taurus and Amanus were driven on remorselessly to their journey's end." This was either along the wayside or, finally, in the dry and barren deserts of the south, where—for example, outside the desolate and malarial village of Der-el-Zor, which was virtually uninhabited—an evolving twentieth-century institution (borrowed from the Spanish practices of 1896 in Cuba as well as from the British in the Boer War) made its appearance: the concentration camp.

In the first phase of the over-all process, Armenian men had been drafted into the Turkish Army, then disarmed in the labor battalions and massacred, and the men who remained in the towns and villages had also been disarmed, sometimes imprisoned and tortured, and then either killed by the gendarmes or marched out to be massacred by the Kurds. In the second phase, the remainder of the Armenian population, which meant mostly women and children and older men, had been either packed in cattle cars on the Berlin-Baghdad Railway or driven south on foot across the mountains.

From the Bryce-Toynbee report: "From the moment they left the outskirts of the towns, they [the deportees] were never safe from outrage. The Muslim peasants mobbed and plundered them as they passed through the cultivated lands, and the gendarmes [in charge of the convoys] connived at the peasants' brutality. . . . When they arrived at a village they were exhibited like slaves in a public place . . . and every Muslim inhabitant was allowed to view them and take his choice of them. . . . The gendarmes themselves began to make free with the rest. . . .

"There were still more horrible outrages when they came to the mountains, for here they were met by bands of 'chettis' and Kurds. The 'chettis' were brigands recruited from the public prisons. . . . When these Kurds and 'chettis' waylaid the convoys, the gendarmes always fraternised with them and followed their lead. . . .

"It depended on the whim of the moment whether a Kurd cut a woman down or carried her away into the hills. . . . But while the convoy dwindled, the remnant had always to march on. The cruelty of the gendarmes towards the victims grew greater as their physical sufferings grew more intense. . . . The passage of rivers, and especially of the Euphrates, was always an occasion of wholesale murder. Women and children were driven into the water, and were shot as they struggled. . . .

"The last survivors often straggled into Aleppo naked. . . . [Others] were transported to Aleppo by rail. . . . At Bozanti, the railhead west of Taurus, and again at Osmania, Mamouret, Islohia, and Kotma . . . vast and incredibly foul concentration camps grew up, where the exiles were delayed for months, and died literally by thousands of hunger, exposure, and epidemics."

The third phase began with that remnant of the Armenians which reached Aleppo, for Aleppo was the point upon which all convoys converged, and those few who had survived the deportations that far were soon marched off again, southeast, into the Syrian desert.

From *Armenia and the Near East,* by Fridtjof Nansen, High Commissioner for Refugees under the League of Nations, published in 1928: "At Meskne on the Euphrates, east of Aleppo, where the Armenians were starved to death in one of the great concentration camps, 55,000 people, according to Turkish figures, lie buried. It is estimated that during 1915, 60,000 deportees were sent to Der-el-Zor on the Euphrates; and the majority of them disappeared. On April 15, 1916, 19,000 were sent in four batches to Mosul, three hundred kilometres across the desert; but only 2,500 arrived. . . . Some of the women and girls had been sold to Bedouins on the way; the rest had died of hunger and thirst. In July, 1916, 20,000 were deported to Der-el-Zor; eight weeks later, according to the testimony of a German officer, only a few artisans were left."

IN 1912, the Armenian patriarchate in Constantinople had estimated the Armenian population in Turkey at two million one hundred thousand. This was considered a fairly high figure, since the patriarchate traditionally inflated its membership rolls. After the war, the Turks retroactively released their own pre-deportation figures, which placed the Armenians at one million one hundred thousand—an implausibly low figure. According to the several religious and relief agencies that looked into the situation, the most likely total for the number of Armenians in Turkey before the war fell somewhere between the two statistics. Thus, the American Committee for Armenian and Syrian Relief in 1916 estimated the prewar Armenian population of Turkish Armenia at a million eight hundred thousand. Statistics from 1916 show that there were about a hundred and fifty thousand Armenians in Constantinople and Smyrna who, owing mainly to their visibility, were not subjected to deportation; approximately a hundred and eighty-five thousand Armenians, mostly from the province of Van, who accompanied an invading Russian force when it withdrew to the Russian Caucasus in 1915; approximately eight hundred thousand Armenians, the majority of them in clearly moribund condition, who were uncovered by relief agencies in the concentration camps of the desert and elsewhere across Turkey.

Thus, it is possible to say, not precisely but with a general respect for accuracy and plausibility, that in the course of the 1915–16 massacres and deportations close to one million Armenians—more than half the Armenian population of Turkey—disappeared; which is to say, were killed, outright by police or soldiers, or by roadside massacres, or by forced marches, or by starvation, or by sickness, or by conditions in the concentration camps.

On August 31, 1915, Talaat Pasha declared to his German allies, *"La question Arménienne n'existe plus."*

What was one to make of such a story? I use the word "make" in the sense of "to fashion or create"; or perhaps, in this instance, "to re-create," for there was no point in claiming either that nothing—no myth or dream—had been made of the Armenian story up to now or that what had been made had been in any way useful to the Armenians or to the world. For could one say that self-pity had been useful? Had anger been helpful or creative—this special anger of the Armenians, sometimes wild and childlike, as in the case of men such as Sarkis, for whom the Turks (turned into devils by one set of myths) had been stuck in the Armenian belly like a lump of hot coal; and sometimes an anger ingrown and self-deceiving, as I supposed was felt by men such as my father, for whom the slaying of their forebears (perhaps Christified by the same set of myths) represented such pain and mortification that they could never turn their faces to it?

On the other hand, was it in the end possible for any citizen of the twentieth century—this century of genocide, and bloodshed, and napalm-bombing, and police interrogation—to find some particular meaning in one example of political terror and mass murder as opposed to other examples of political terror and mass murder; in one instance of genocide as opposed to other (smaller? larger?) instances of genocide? Was it not perhaps, finally, more to the point, more useful, to adopt the realism of the era one lived in, and to say, with the grave modesty of someone who has discovered a major truth at no pain to himself: Such is life. Such surely are the facts of life and the human condition— of the universal context of pain and misery. Has there not always been torture and mass murder?

It was easy for the soul to cry "No" to any quick agreement with this view, for souls—certainly souls on American diets—are notoriously hopeful and idealistic, ready to identify with the optimistic affirmation of the Ascension, reluctant to fasten much attention on the process of the Crucifixion. But in this matter one's reason also answered "No." For, although there were certain exceptions, certain obscurities and dark passages in history which precluded one's making a universal law on the subject, nonetheless it seemed generally untrue that life had been precisely, or even approximately, "such," or that there had "always" been such torture and killing. At least, in this one respect it was untrue: in the scale and deliberateness of the killing.

Serious students of the epidemiology of modern violence, such as Hannah Arendt, have written amply and cogently on the increase in mass violence which has taken place in the twentieth century as the energies of technocracy and of the technocratic mind have been added to man's ancient propensity for aggression and murder. It was banality, Dr.

Arendt noted—the methodology of an advanced bureau-cracy—that made possible the extent of the slaughter of the Jews in Germany, and not necessarily some spurt in man-kind's inherent wickedness.

There is reason to believe that this harnessing of modern technology to political mass murder began with the instance of the Turks and the Armenians. Or, if it did not actually begin on such-and-such a date, at such-and-such a place (for one should be wary of asserting such "firsts"), then one can say at least that the Turkish massacres and "deportations" of the Armenians were the most notable early example of the employment of modern communications and technology in the acting out and realization of political violence.

For, clearly, the entire production—or orchestration, if one will—of the Armenian genocide was based on the im-perfectly utilized but definitely perceived capacities of the modern state for politically restructuring itself, which were made possible by the engines of technology. In due course, to be sure, Hitler's Germany was to perfect the process of rail-way deportation and to develop the gas chamber and the crematoria, and Lenin's and Stalin's Russia was to evolve further the institutions of the concentration camp and secret surveillance—as most modern nations now, in scientific con-cert, have advanced the techniques of efficiently adminis-tered torture by the use of electric current. But in virtually every modern instance of mass murder, beginning, it ap-pears, with the Armenians, the key element—not the only element but the key element, which has raised the numerical and psychic levels of the deed above the classic terms of massacre—has been the alliance of technology and communications: interior communications, such as permit concerted action on the part of a government and its agents, enabling the "net" to be widely cast and the casting of it to be part of a unified procedure; and what is by no means the lesser system of exterior communications, whereby the facts about these objects of government action (these "victims," or "rebels," or "freedom fighters," or "anarchists") are communicated to witness-populations, although they have usually been transformed to the convenience of the government that controls the system. This transformation has the effect of disconnecting the victims from the rest of the world, and even from their own people.

Was the Armenian story, then, a fable of communications, a parable of the failure of language? At this stage, one might acknowledge the obvious: that it was a story composed of a multitude of parts. It was a story of unresolved hostility (the Turks) and of a prolonged national psychic depression (the Armenians); a story of misconceived brotherhood (the Turks and the Armenians) and of bravery and pain and the reduction of personality through terror; a story, also, at least by indirection, of the moral ambitions and ambiguities of the great European Christian democracies; and, not insignificantly, a story, running as a generality—indeed, one might call it a bloody river linking the great murderous events of our century—of the intrinsic weakness, perhaps a weakness identical with that of human nature itself, of the modern system of communications, in which in recent eras virtually all nations have at some crucial point acquiesced.

Acquiescence. What if the witness-clients of the world-wide communications systems had not acquiesced in 1915 and 1916, when letters from schoolteachers and missionaries first began appearing in the Zurich and Basel papers? It is a question impossible to answer, and perhaps pointless, ignoring, as it does, the profound unseriousness of human beings everywhere, and their insistently parochial concerns. What if? Would the English and the French have returned to the Dardanelles? Would a Crusade of Zurich schoolteachers have departed for the Golden Horn? What if? Perhaps one might say that it had been a challenge to a small, unreliable element of the human spirit—a challenge that was never taken up, that was put forward again later, and again, and again, and again, and has still not been taken up. According to documents presented at the Nuremberg trials in 1945, Adolf Hitler, in a discussion with Hermann Goering about the imminent invasion of Poland, asked, "Who still talks nowadays of the extermination of the Armenians?" It was another question without an answer.

BUT IF IT WAS POSSIBLE, and perhaps necessary in a rationalistic sense, to view the Armenian genocide from a political level, even from the rather cool perspective of a student of technology and communications, maybe this was

something of a luxury for an Armenian—even a part-Arme-
nian, like me. Somehow it begged the question. For the
question was: What—beyond the journalistic facts—had
happened to the Armenians? All along, in my search for
Armenia and the Armenian ethos, I had found that Armenians—in their books or in their statements, in their cups or
sometimes matter-of-factly on the street—always came back
to this matter of the "massacres," of the "genocide." It
would have been cruel or trivial to align this refrain with the
standard simile of the broken record: the sounds of a needle
that would not, could not, lift itself out of a particular,
twisted groove. One knew that this fixation came from
something deep, as deep as trauma. One knew that the question (What had really happened?) was not answerable entirely in terms of history or politics, or even of technology or
communications, of fixing blame on this side or that side. In
the end, one guessed, it was not even answerable mainly in
terms of how many had been killed, as if the sheer numerical dimensions of the act (a million dead!) might somehow
explain the particular condition of the survivors. This last
was not an irrelevant statistic, but it referred backward more
than forward, more to the dead than to the living. One
hoped that if the question was to be answered at all, it was to
be answered for the living.

Ever since I began this journey to Armenia, my father's
presence had hovered near me, by no means always approv-
ingly. I had seen his face in dreams and in museums, and
had come to find that natural. He was my father. I felt a

presence—no, more than that, an invocation—of fathers
everywhere around me. What had Sarkis said that afternoon, almost in pain? "Your father was an Armenian. You
must respect him." It lingered in my mind. Fathers and
sons. Phrases echoed in my head: "My father had committed
no crime." And "We were innocent, we were helpless."

A picture began to form of yet other fathers and other
sons. I thought of all the Armenian fathers who had been
drafted into the Turkish Army in that year of 1914: men
who were fathers, in dun-colored uniforms, shipped away
from their towns and later killed; fathers sent to prison or
else massacred along a roadside. How many Armenian children had seen their fathers killed? Or—worse, perhaps—had
watched their mothers and sisters brutalized to death, or
close to death, in their fathers' absence? In that one trau-
matic period, how many Armenian sons had felt betrayed by
their fathers' absence—for what do children comprehend of
reasons and explanations, what does a child understand in
his soul of a father's nonappearance in a time of need?

Abraham, the father, threatened his son Isaac with a
knife stroke—an act of demonic or holy passion, a massacre.
Jesus was killed out of hate, but first He was brutalized with
the torture of crucifixion. And then the Son called to his
Father: "My God, my God, why hast thou forsaken me?"

Betrayal breeds hatred, but how does a son hate his
father? How does a son knowingly hate a father who sired
him, protected him, and only then (and for the rest of the
son's life) abandoned him as the result of his own murder?

Or knowingly hate a mother whom he has been compelled to watch being reduced to a subhuman level?

The Turks, yes. It was possible for an Armenian to hate the Turks. But here one noticed something interesting. For the Turks had never accepted this hate. Unlike the Germans after the Second World War, who had (albeit with difficulty and disclaimers) acknowledged the fact of war crimes and war guilt toward the Jews, who had even fashioned grisly shrines out of Dachau and Buchenwald and had held trials of their own, the Turks had made no official admission of guilt or criminality toward the Armenians.

Where else might the hatred go?

Toward the self: self-hatred. One hesitated to advance so simple an explanation of such a complicated subject; still, that was what it seemed to come down to. One thought of the wailing or hand-wringing quality of many Armenians—especially the older men, but also the sons—whose physical gestures seemed directed more against themselves than against the alleged object, the Turks. The diatribes against the Turks—tantrums, as it were, carried down now through three generations. Wasn't the surest way of tormenting an angry child as follows: to leave it alone, ignored in its rage?

Self-hatred. "We were innocent, we were helpless." The fact that had emerged from a study of the Armenians in Turkey at the beginning of the First World War was that they had been neither entirely innocent nor altogether helpless. Where there had been any possibility of resistance—at Van, at Zeitoun, at the small settlement of Mousa Dagh, which had been near enough to the Mediterranean coast for a French warship to intercede briefly—the Armenians had fought with skill and courage. Nor had the guerrilla operations of the Armenian Volunteers been on the level of prankish afternoon escapades of Constantinople rug merchants. The majority of the Armenians in Turkey, one realized, had been put on the defensive not so much by actual disarmament (that had been the final stroke) as by the cumulative years of mental and social depression which had led to the disarmament—disarmament at the hands of their brothers the Turks.

Did not suicide studies of various European nations in the Second World War reveal that in periods of resistance, or of the greatest danger, the suicide rate fell? In periods when resistance dwindled, when the enemy occupation became more entrenched, men again began to kill themselves —the ultimate act of self-hatred. After five hundred years of living as "*giaours*" or "*raya*" in a Muslim society, the kings of Nairi had been gradually changed into the likeness of Artin, the inn clerk. And these Artins had one day looked in their mirrors and detested what they saw.

For the first time in my life, I thought I saw my father clearly. Some little while ago, I had seen how his face, with its coolness and authority, its supposed impassivity, concealed within it the silent, helpless fury of that man in the blue velvet hat. But it had taken me this long to understand where the fury had been directed: at himself, Dikran Kouyoumjian. I thought, This proud and sensitive man—how he must have hated growing up an Armenian in England, not so much because of being condescended to by the English (although there was bound to have been that) as because of being himself marked, or feeling marked, by the collective guilt and self-hatred proceeding from a race that had been hated unto death. For that was the curse of genocide: death took the victims, but over the survivors settled a mark, a "fallout," of having been hated unto death.

I thought of the struggle, all the wriggles, he had made throughout his life to avoid being Armenian, to escape from this "collective unconscious." His detached manner. The mask of not caring about, not bothering about, his racial past. Not even writing about it—the "it," after all, being his identity, the one solid piece of wood that any writer has.

I wondered how many Armenian sons had felt abandoned by their fathers: abandoned into nothing more than their Armenianness, that racial psyche of guilt, of anger without an object and always disguised as something else— braggadocio or saturnine lament, darkness or light. Such a *waste,* it seemed. I thought, If only he could have told me about this! Then what? What would I have done? I realized I would have done nothing, except be more afraid. Besides, he hadn't known it himself.

And so one afternoon, with the sun pale and glowing in the gray-blue sky, my wife and I drove out once again with Sarkis in the borrowed limousine toward the plain of Ararat. It was our last expedition, although none of us had said so. Sarkis sat behind the wheel of the car, driving quite slowly—or so it seemed—past fields that were now yellow everywhere, fields of rock and yellow grass. Once, we stood in line for perhaps fifteen minutes behind three bullock carts, which gave Sarkis occasion to display his patience and to discourse on the necessary mechanization of rural life. Back in the hotel, our suitcases had already been lifted down from the top of the tall cherry-wood armoire and were waiting to be filled.

It had been my idea that we should drive out in this direction for a final look at Ararat. Sarkis had said that there was a little village along the way which we should examine—or perhaps it was a church within a village. My wife sat close beside me and held my hand. I knew she was genuinely sorry to leave. "I remember this road so well," she said at one point. I thought, Yes, I remember it, too, but differently—as if I had been different when I last went down it. For it was the road to the Monument, which we had visited on our first day in Erevan: the Monument on the plain of Ararat. Had Sarkis known that I wished us to go there again? Had I wished us to go there again? I thought the answer to both questions was yes.

Sarkis blinked in the glare of the sun. He seemed uncommonly vulnerable then: a creature blinking.

"Would you like my sunglasses?" I said.

Sarkis shook his head. "No, thank you. I must train my eyes."

In front of us, perhaps a mile away, some red buses were parked.

"See, we are at the Monument," said Sarkis.

"Let's stop here," I said.

"If you wish," said Sarkis.

I felt a nearly unbearable closeness to Sarkis just then, so that I wanted to touch him. No, it was more than that: an intimacy. But what is intimacy? I was intimate with my wife, but I wished to embrace Sarkis. As I looked at him, I could see the pores of his face sweating—this alien face that I wished to embrace. I could feel my wife's hand tighten its grip on mine.

Sarkis parked our car beside the red buses, and we walked up the incline and then out across the open field toward the familiar structure of angled columns, slanting together, in the mid-distance, almost like an incomplete metal tepee. Sarkis walked ahead of us. To the right of us—a moving, shifting cluster of white shirts and bare legs—a group of schoolchildren formed a circle of their own in the field. Were they standing? Listening? Their voices, like the cries of tropical birds, floated across the silence. In the far distance, Ararat (that primeval monument) rose from the open plain. Again I thought, We are in the middle of nowhere.

The snow gleamed white around the peak of Ararat. Ararat . . . Urartu. What a noble fantasy it was to have conceived of waves lapping beneath the peak of Ararat. I thought suddenly of Viscount Bryce, who, in the eighteen-seventies, at the age of thirty-eight, had climbed to the summit. Afterward, two members of his expedition reported that they had found several pieces of wood—"possibly driftwood, for which there was no logical explanation, owing to the barrenness of the summit." Bryce, however, had refrained from stating that the wood had been left over from the Ark. "A spectacular view is afforded from just below the main peak of Ararat," he wrote, "and in every respect it is a most inspiring and exhilarating climb; although if it was here that Noah rested his Ark we shall have need of further proof." A measured man, Viscount Bryce—not one to jump to hasty conclusions about driftwood on mountain peaks.

I heard Sarkis's voice in front of me, talking once more to my wife about the Monument: "Each time I come here, I marvel at the ingenuity of our Armenian architects. Look how these great slabs lie at an angle without support! See for yourself—there is nothing holding them up."

I thought, How strange to finally meet one's past: to simply meet it, the way one might finally acknowledge a person who had been in one's company a long while. So, it's you!

I was standing by myself beneath the overhanging slabs of the Monument, looking into the fire. I remember thinking that if I had had a flower in my hand I would gladly have thrown it into the fire, but that I hadn't remembered to pick one. My eyes went out to the open fields beyond the fire, the fields of yellow flowers. I thought that it didn't matter about the flower; I thought suddenly that I was home. It was the flattest, simplest, lightest of feelings. I thought, So this is what it's all about.

And then I felt my father's hand in mine. It was so strong a feeling that today I can almost (but not quite) recover that imaginary touch. But what I responded to was not merely the "touch"—I had felt that before, at many moments in my life. One of the key memories of my childhood had been a nearly tactile recollection of being pulled by the hand (were we running? walking?) by my father down an unremembered street—an unremembered time except for the pull of the hand, even his face out of sight, his expression unknown, only his arm extending from a dark overcoat.

But I knew that this time it was different, and as I stood there I knew that it would always afterward be different (as it has been). For the hand I felt was not pulling me; it was the hand of a man which I had briefly held in my own one afternoon in New York, the hand of my father dying. His hand had been so frail in mine that afternoon, so frail, and even small—smaller than mine—and I remember how the feel of this hand had been such a shock to me then (more than his fading speech, or pale features, or struggle of recognition): this hand of my father, who was releasing me, releasing himself from me, and me from him (as if either thing were possible between fathers and sons). And I had not known how to grip him back. But here his hand was again. I felt that I held it in mine. I felt that somehow I had brought him here—to this place. I didn't know what else I felt or knew, but I wept, large tears streaming down my face. I wasn't even sure for what. Nor did it feel bad. On the contrary, it felt quite natural.

"I knew that you would be overcome before you left," said Sarkis, who had come up beside me. I could see my wife looking at me, at the tears that were on my cheeks. Sarkis clasped me by the shoulder. "No Armenian can stand here," he said, "and not be moved by the suffering of the Armenian people."

I could feel Sarkis's arms around me, his warm bulk against mine. I thought, Kinsman, brother . . . so be it. I thought, We Armenians sweat a lot.

"Did you bring flowers?" I asked.

"Of course," said Sarkis.

My wife and I each took a yellow flower from his hands and tossed it into the fire, which consumed the flowers in its orange flame.

The three of us walked together, slowly, away from the Monument, along the narrow path that led across the yellow fields. The schoolchildren seemed to be playing far in the distance, arms and legs moving, their voices unheard. My wife had her arm in mine. Sarkis was talking of the last year his father had been alive, when he and his brothers carried the old man onto the plain of Ararat and the old man spent the afternoon asleep in the field.

I wondered if in early spring the whole valley was filled with flowers. I wondered if the snow at the top of Ararat ever melted. It seemed hard to comprehend that there should always be so much life and death side by side. I thought that, although I could never explain it, it was true that I had somehow brought my father here. I thought, How long and circuitous the voyage has been that brought all of us here—Armenians forever nearly sailing off the edge of the earth.

And then we left: one morning, early, with the sun slowly rising above the rim of the olive-green hills.

The hotel porters were scrubbing the well-worn floor of the lobby as if one of the archangels were shortly to arrive. Such seamen's labor! Vartan appeared to bid us goodbye. His mood was even more matter-of-fact than usual, but one guessed that he had arisen an hour or so earlier than he normally did, and was making his clarity of vision a present to us. He asked if we had heard that the Armenian soccer team had just achieved first place in the Soviet Union.

No, we hadn't—although, now that I thought of it, there had been much shouting late the previous night down the hotel corridor where the television set was kept.

"Yes," said Vartan solemnly. "Last evening, we defeated the Ukraine. Now we are No. 1." He could hardly suppress his pleasure, and I wished we might exchange cigars or all rush off to a crowded tavern and have several drinks, for in my present mood it seemed indeed a wonderful piece of news—a fortuitous piece of news. Somehow it answered well: the Ararat team was No. 1.

"Of course, they won't stay up there," said Vartan. "They play Moscow next weekend."

Of course. We shook hands with Vartan, shyly, like parents leaving a boy at school. Vartan seemed to become younger with each moment that the short ceremony extended. Finally, he clutched his briefcase, almost waved it as a talisman against the leave-taking process. "Have good luck in your journey!" he called.

"I hope you stay No. 1," I said inanely.

Vartan grinned like the Cheshire Cat and vanished.

SARKIS TOOK US out to the airport. He wore the familiar brown suit and clutched two packages: a book and a colored calendar he had bought for us—in return, perhaps, for some all too inconsequential gifts we had presented to him the day before. There was an exchange of addresses, with that formality which comes upon people who have been unexpectedly close and are now parting. I kept wanting to say, "Something important has happened to me here." But it seemed too imprecise—and also too important—to speak about on that basis. I talked instead of the "good times" we had had—the interestingness of the visit, and so on. The streets and pink stone apartment houses of Erevan sped by outside the car window. There were suddenly so many things I wanted to say to Sarkis, for I had found out in my soul that we were both Armenian, which I knew in a certain sense was neither here nor there but in another sense was nearly everything; and now he was staying here in this hard and unsafe place, and I was going home—to another home—sailing softly in my soft boat to my calm American harbor, where "starvation" and "disease" were words one read in newspapers, and "murder" was what one watched on television, and "massacre" was a synonym for what happened in athletic contests. Clearly, I was no different from my countrymen. On the other hand, I had found out that I had many different countrymen.

"Look!" said Sarkis, pointing to a somber brick office building under construction. "We are always working."

"Sarkis, it's a fine place here," I said.

"I knew you'd be proud of it," he said.

It was true. I was proud.

IN THE AIRPORT, a different reality intervened. Our Aeroflot plane was bound for Beirut, where we were to change for a flight to Istanbul, and then New York. Now, in the little Erevan airport, which decidedly had the air about it of a Balkan border crossing in wartime, well-armed soldiers in gray uniforms and Armenian passengers, mostly in peasant costumes, mingled with one another, body pressing against body in the crowded chamber, all somehow bound together in the modern police ritual of Search and Examination. Everywhere on the gray concrete floor the suitcases of these passengers had been flung open. Articles of clothing were scattered as in cartoons of department-store bargain sales. The Armenian peasants scrambled about on the floor picking things up, stuffing them back, taking more out. The soldier policemen walked about in the disorder. They, too, were Armenians.

A young man stood next to us in line—by no means a peasant, either, but wearing a proper dark-blue business suit, and clutching two suitcases, a couple of enormous and grotesque dolls, a paper bag filled with pastries, and a large gift-shop oil painting of a sunset, the sun setting over Lake Sevan. After spilling out the contents of his suitcases, the soldiers produced knives and slashed open the fabric lining at the top and bottom of each one. The young man was compelled to pry off the heads of the two dolls he was carrying; having done that, and now holding the two heads in his arms, he pushed the painting toward a soldier, who took his knife and proceeded to remove the picture from its frame, and the canvas from the cardboard backing.

When we reached the inspection point, our American passports were produced and briefly examined, and (surprising to someone who grew up with the drama and myth of the Cold War) we were let by without any search. Except for our book satchel, which weighed an unusual amount and was opened. Books on the Crusades and Abdul-Hamid and the Turkish massacres were blandly riffled through and returned. Two volumes remained on the counter: *A History of Russia,* by Sir Bernard Pares, and *Twenty Letters to a Friend,* by Stalin's daughter, which my wife had been reading, and which now stared up at us— burglar tools uncovered in the trunk of our car. A stern young Russian officer came along and picked up the books.

"We will hold these," he said. I nodded agreeably, quite icy with tension.

Behind us lay the litter of clothes upon the floor. The young Armenian with the two doll heads was trying to join his picture frame back together—a fairly hopeless task. An old woman bent over several empty suitcases, stuffing all sorts of clothing back in. It was a miserable sight, a miserable and hateful process, and there seemed to be something evil in our having been even partly exempt from it: power politics once again working their will upon common humanity. Sir Bernard Pares and Svetlana Alliluyeva had been slight hostages to fortune compared to that knocked-about sun setting over Lake Sevan.

As we walked out toward the airplane, we could see Sarkis standing in a knot of people just outside the airport building. There were gray-uniformed soldiers in front of the small crowd. Sarkis waved and called out something, which was lost in the noise of the plane engines. We waved back, and kept walking—across the runway and up the steps of the aircraft. The noise of the engines was very loud. The snow on Ararat gleamed in the distance. Sarkis still waved, his small, stocky, brown-suited figure planted beside the small stone building, waving, a hand waving. Going, gone.

Our leave-taking had seemed oddly abrupt and disjointed, but perhaps it was truer to life that way, or, at least, truer to itself.

In the plane, my wife asked me, "Are you sad to leave?"

"No," I replied.

I had embraced this stranger, Sarkis, as my kinsman, and had felt it, or had thought I felt it; and had come to comprehend things about my father that I had not known before; and had seen churches and refrigerator factories; and had heard Armenian spoken at breakfast, lunch, and dinner. And now it was time to get back.

My wife said, "How do you suppose the story ends?"

The Armenian story? Far below us now, and swiftly receding, could be seen the outline of Erevan: smoke rising from one or two factories; the buildings pressed together as if in a large village. Of course, it was more than a large village; the soccer team was No. 1. I thought, Perhaps if the Armenians have a good enough soccer team they will forget the wretched Turks.

We were flying toward Ararat now, its peak nearly level with our airplane, perhaps ten miles away. It seemed exciting that we would pass so close to Ararat. Then, suddenly, we banked—a steep bank that clattered some loose objects in the rear of the cabin. Somebody behind us said something with the word "Turkish." Of course, we were avoiding the Turkish border. Turkish air space—what an odd concept! Ararat, with its driftwood and radar.

"Where are we heading?" my wife asked.

"I think east toward Azerbaijan and then south."

OUR AIRPLANE sped high above the dark-green ridges of the Caucasus. Below, there seemed to be nothing except trees and rock outcroppings and, here and there, the slender brown line of a country road. From this perspective, the region appeared utterly wild and empty of all life. And Armenia, one realized, was so small that by then we had almost surely passed beyond it—a tiny island in the ocean of the Soviet Union. It was impossible not to think that here was a difficult place for the Armenians to have ended up— squeezed into this rock-strewn, harshly beautiful, relatively infertile northern sector of the old Urartian perimeter, as subject-citizens of yet another great autocratic empire. On the other hand, I remembered something that Sarkis had said one afternoon as we tramped around the ruins of an ancient Armenian church—the remains of walls and cornices tumbled, as usual, about the ground by unnamed invaders, or pillagers, or natural forces. "Tell me, my friends, where are the Lydians and Phrygians today?" he called cheerfully, standing on an overturned slab of basalt. "Where are the mighty Assyrians and the Cappadocians?" In some ways, doubtless, history was like a game of musical chairs, although it was hard to tell whether the Lydians, Phrygians, etc., had sat down too early or too late. But I also remembered what Sarkis had said, in a different mood, only the evening before, when, as we walked across the square, I asked him if his colleague Kevork had received any news yet about his son. Sarkis had shaken his head. Then, pointing to Lenin's statue ahead of us, which seemed suddenly obtrusive in the gray twilight, he had said simply, almost casually, "Try to understand, we have many necessary modern advantages this way. You might say it is a bargain that Armenians have made with the world—perhaps not always knowing we were making it."

Probably that was so, I thought—although when I remembered the scene at the airport it seemed a heavy dosage of reality for radish-growers, distinguished astronomers, soccer players, and even bargainers to live with. In any event, Armenians had certainly not reached their present geographical or political situation as a result of any *Armenian* grand design. Stated simply, what had happened was this. A large number of the survivors of the Young Turk massacres—roughly a hundred and eighty-five thousand of them—fled north to the protection of the Russian Caucasus. There they joined with the Russian Armenians in the Transcaucasian provinces, chiefly in Tiflis, Erevan, Elizavetpol, and Kars, to form a scattered Armenian population of around two million. For much of the previous century, the czarist government had expressed at least a public concern for the Armenians in Turkey, and at the beginning of the war it had declared a willingness to grant autonomy to the territories of the Turkish Armenians. By mid-1916, Russian troops had advanced well into the now nearly desolate provinces of Turkish Armenia, reaching a line as far west as Trebizond and as far south as Bitlis. Then, having benefited militarily from the help of the Armenian Volunteers, the czarist government dissolved them, and it became clear that Russia intended to annex rather than liberate Turkish Armenia.

But early in 1917 the Romanovs were overthrown. Under the new Provisional Russian government, the provinces of Turkish Armenia were given a civil administration, with many posts being filled by Armenians. Refugees began returning to Erzurum, Van, and Bitlis. However, in the fall, when the Bolsheviks took power, the tide turned once more. Lenin wanted to take his new government out of the war, and Russian forces everywhere began to fall back. In March 1918, Lenin signed the Treaty of Brest-Litovsk with the Central Powers and Turkey, which, among other things, permitted the Turks not only to regain the Turkish-Armenian provinces but also to reoccupy three northern Armenian districts that the Russians had taken in 1877. As the Russian troops withdrew from the Turkish front, with Russian soldiers heading homeward in thousands, a Turkish army corps marched north again, pushing well into the Caucasus, and by early April of 1918 had moved almost to the old prewar boundaries.

Centuries of powerlessness under the Turks and years of political anti-establishment activities in czarist Russia and the Ottoman empire had not produced a very sizable cadre of Armenian governing experts and administrators. Even so, in May of 1918, while the Turkish army corps continued to push northward, the Armenians concentrated themselves in the province of Erevan and announced the formation of an independent republic—as did the Georgians to the northwest, and the Muslim Azerbaijanis to the east. Starvation was widespread in the Caucasus then, because grain shipments by railroad from the Ukraine had ceased, and it was perhaps especially harsh in the less fertile areas of the new Republic of Armenia. To make matters worse, the Armenians, now virtually alone in their battle against the Turks, had also to fight the Azerbaijanis, who had formed an alliance with their fellow Muslims. Clearly, it was not a propitious time or place for the founding of small independent states. Some of the alternatives were not especially appealing, however; for instance, when a combined Turkish and Azerbaijani force captured Baku—then a Bolshevik-Armenian enclave in Azerbaijani territory—General Halil Pasha tactfully kept his Ottoman units from entering the city for twenty-four hours, while the Azerbaijani troops and the citizenry massacred the fifteen or twenty thousand Armenians who had remained behind.

Still, when the First World War ended, in the autumn of 1918, the Turks were compelled to relinquish Baku and to fall back from their recent advance. The Armenians believed that their time had finally arrived. An Allied fleet steamed into the Bosporus and anchored off Constantinople. The incumbent sultan, Muhammad VI, was in effect an Allied puppet, willing to accept Turkey's partition if he could hang on to whatever was left. When the European powers began assembling in Paris for the peace conference, the Republic of Armenia dispatched emissaries from Erevan to Paris, where, joining with a delegation of émigré Turkish Armenians, they sought to persuade the Allied delegates to create—from the expected dissolution of the Ottoman empire—an independent Armenian state that would include not only the provinces of the Armenian plateau but also Cilicia, and would receive protection from the Turks by being mandated to one of the great powers.

But even as the Armenians lobbied in Paris for their new nation—spreading out their maps before President Woodrow Wilson, who on several occasions had expressed himself in favor of an autonomous Armenia stretching from the Caucasus to the Mediterranean—the situation changed again. For the victorious Allies had overplayed their hand in parceling out defeated Turkey to the British, the French, the Italians, and the Greeks, with the result that an intense new Turkish nationalism had been aroused, personified by the "hero of Gallipoli," Mustafa Kemal. While the delegates in Paris and, later, in San Remo deliberated on their reapportionment of the Ottoman empire, Lenin, in Moscow, and Kemal, who had raised a rebel army in Anatolia and got himself elected president of a new Nationalist government, reached a private understanding of their own. The Soviets were given a free hand to overthrow the independent Transcaucasian republics. The Turks were given a free hand to regain Turkish Armenia. In addition, Kemal's Nationalist Army was provided by the Bolsheviks with much-needed weapons and funds to help in removing the European powers—especially the Greeks—from Turkey. By the fall of 1920, the Turks had moved north across the Armenian plateau to a frontier that included Ararat—the border that exists today. The Red Army then entered Erevan and, using the Turkish threat as a lever, "sovietized" the two-year-old Armenian Republic. In March of 1921, the Treaty of Moscow was signed by the Soviet Union and Turkey, formalizing the arrangement. It was a fait accompli, and was accepted by the European powers. In 1922, as a kind of coda to Europe's involvement with the "Armenian Question," Kemal's freshly armed troops pushed the Greek occupying army to the sea at Smyrna, which was set on fire, and there approximately a hundred thousand Greeks and Armenians were killed while Allied warships sat in the harbor.

I thought, In some ways, this has been the most miserable of stories. It made one weep for the hopes of the Armenians: those Armenians who for so many years had trafficked with the liberal sentiments of the West, attending like children to the "interestedness" of certain politicians and missionaries, watching the great nineteenth-century wave of nationalism confer nationhood on states and provinces whose own ethnic "unity" had long been fragmented. For Armenians what else had it been but an illusion, a political dream whose bridge to waking life was mainly this—the inconsistent support of the powerful constitutional democracies of Europe and America? On the other hand, what folly it had been to expect anything else of the world than what had happened! What a persistence of dreaming! Or perhaps in the end it had been a matter neither of folly nor of, let us say, victimization, for there was something quite grandly human in the Armenian experience, with its misfortunes, and pride, and survivorship, and hope: the hope of something better to come, periodically dashed. If the Armenians had been lately afflicted with self-hatred, they had also throughout their existence (like certain children) been afflicted with hopefulness. In some ways, this was probably an affliction like any other, not easily cured.

Far down, below the scattered clouds, there were endless green mountains and, in the distance, a lake and plumes of smoke. Then clouds obscured the ground.

THE PLANE whistled through the hazy air. I slept a long time, or so I thought. At one point, my wife said to me, "Didn't it seem wrong leaving Sarkis behind there?"

"It's his home," I said.

"I know," she said.

"They have hydroelectric stations and computer factories and oranges," I said. "Politics always change."

"I think I know that, too," she said.

ANOTHER TIME—perhaps it was only moments after the first question, or maybe it was an hour later—my wife said, "Do you know why I wished they hadn't kept those two books?"

"They cost money."

"No. In the Svetlana book there was the craziest reference to your father. I was going to show you."

The air in the cabin was warm and heavy. It all felt like part of a dream: I was half waking, half asleep.

"I didn't know they knew each other," I said. "What was it?"

"It was about your father's book *The Green Hat*. Her mother read it shortly before she committed suicide, and Stalin claimed that it had brought about her death. Had you heard that?"

No, I hadn't. I thought, How queer everything is sometimes—how unutterably *queer*. It was probably true—Stalin supposing his wife to have been corrupted by a modish, English, nineteen-twenties novel. My father's novel. A picture came into my mind of Arak trudging through the snow toward old Melikian's house. Armenia at the dawn of the Jazz Age. I thought of Sarkis standing in front of the airport building waving his hand.

"Do you think your father knew about the Stalin story?" my wife asked.

"No, I don't think so," I said.

FOR SOME REASON, I remembered the old women in the market shed, and the piles of radishes. I thought of a certain phrase in Mandelstam's *Journey to Armenia*—a reference to the Armenians' "inexplicable aversion to anything metaphysical." The full quotation runs: "The Armenians' fullness with life, their rude tenderness, their noble inclination for hard work, their inexplicable aversion to anything metaphysical, and their splendid intimacy with the world of real things—all of this said to me, You're awake, don't be afraid of your own time, don't be sly."

Down below, the clouds parted. There was sea—the bright blue of the Mediterranean. We were coming in to land.

We stayed a few days in Istanbul—new Constantinople. Each morning, the sun came up glowing across the Bosporus, which lay a half mile or so below our window: a river of black water filled with little craft, and dozens of ferryboats that crossed incessantly from bank to bank, and sometimes the massive, quiet shape of a Russian tanker returning empty to the Black Sea.

Across the Bosporus stretched the shore of Asia, house-crowded and tree-lined. About two miles upriver, a great new bridge now connected the two sides; it was a graceful green construction, with two tall towers and curving suspension cables. There was talk in the hotel of traffic problems during the rush hour. A little way downriver, right at the edge of the water, stood the gray stone expanse of the Dolmabagdshe Palace, that ponderous, frilly, nineteenth-century strudel of a royal edifice which had been built for the Ottoman sultans by the Armenian architect Balian. "The Armenian architect Balian." It said so right in our Turkish guidebook. And if that was not exactly the only reference to Armenia or Armenians visible in standard Turkish touristic publications, it was nearly so. With the exception of an occasional inclusion in a list of the "polyglot mixture of ancient races" that had once inhabited "pre-

Turkic Asia Minor," the name, the presence, the idea of Armenians appeared to no longer exist in modern Istanbul. It was not so much that there was no sense of an Armenia here (in this nation that contained the classic home of the Armenians), for in political terms that was comprehensible; it reflected a political fact. What seemed less comprehensible and much harder to accept was the extent to which the Armenian connection had been erased. The slate had been wiped bare, as though by an act of will—or, if not absolutely bare, then as close to absolutely bare as was possible.

The first afternoon, I remember, we drove past an old church, so unmistakably Armenian, with its conical roof, that we asked our Turkish guide if we might stop. "It's a Greek church," he said. "I know it very well. It is of no interest."

My wife said, "It looks Armenian."

"There is nothing Armenian around here," the guide said. "It is Greek." And he drove on.

Later, we went back on our own. On the ancient stone above the church entrance, part of the Armenian lettering had been literally erased—rubbed off. But not all of it. The church itself was closed, and a new apartment house had been built in such a way as to wall off the side entrance and the stained-glass windows. Two men in rough clothes were playing cards at a table in the alley. One of them looked at us quizzically.

"Armenian church?" my wife asked.

One of the men shook his head and said something in Turkish. The other man scowled and got to his feet. We left the alley.

"I didn't like that," my wife said as we walked down a more crowded street.

"He didn't understand us," I said.

I don't think that either of us thought he hadn't understood us.

Once, I knew, Istanbul had been filled with Armenian churches and with Armenians. Armenians had formed a key element in the life of the great city—especially, perhaps, as artisans and craftsmen. I had read how in the late Byzantine period, when the western arch of Justinian's Saint Sophia collapsed, an Armenian architect had been called in to study the problems of stress and geometry, and undertake the restoration. Later, when Muhammad the Conqueror captured Constantinople, the people he summoned to build up his new capital were the Armenians and the Greeks, and also the Arabs.

For centuries (regardless of their political position), Armenian artisans had been masters of tilework, of stone-cutting, masters at working with things—perhaps that anti-metaphysical instinct that Mandelstam had spoken of. How strange, then, to be in Istanbul and learn that it had never happened. "Observe this unusual tilework," another guide remarked, pointing to some beautiful orange and blue tiles that adorned a sixteenth-century mosque.

"Who made the tiles?" a fellow tourist asked.

"Turkish craftsmen," said the guide. "There were some Arab tilemakers, too."

On the outside of the mosque stood several twenty-foot columns of basalt, each elaborately, even obsessively, adorned with stone-cut designs that were the familiar geometric figures we had observed on so many old Armenian churches—even the smooth, eroded shapes of grapes and pomegranates I remembered from the fallen cornices at Garni and Zvartnots.

"Who did the stonework?" I asked.

The Turkish guide was middle-aged and accommodating. He gazed upward, examining the designs, which he had surely looked upon each day. "Turkish stonecutters from Anatolia," he replied.

In a sense, all this felt unreal, and almost comical. I realized that I had traveled a long distance from my previous disdain of most things Armenian to my present barely suppressed chauvinism in Istanbul. Perhaps too far. (Had I really become offended by that remark about Anatolian stonecutters?) On the other hand, I felt something faintly evil in the air. Or perhaps it was this: As an Armenian, for the first time I had a sniff, a scent, of what it was like to be hated for being Armenian. Because what was it except hatred to say that a people did not exist?

ONE MORNING, we went to visit another Armenian church. There were a few Armenian churches listed in the phone book. We picked one out, wrote down the address, and asked a driver to take us there. He seemed surprised and then amused that we should want to go to such a place. "Much better Greek church near the hotel," he said. He was a young man with a friendly manner and explained that he wished to save us trouble.

We went anyway, and on our arrival I could appreciate the driver's preference for the Greek church. We were in a shabby part of town, a place of narrow, dirt-strewn streets and few people. The Armenian church seemed run-down and derelict: cracked walls, no paint, few ornaments of any kind. Although it was evidently still in use, it seemed like an abandoned shell; there was something of the look of a cave about it. Next door, however, there was an Armenian school, its courtyard swarming with children. I had grown accustomed in Erevan to seeing large numbers of Armenians, and these Armenian faces in Istanbul seemed surprisingly familiar. Indeed, these children were like children everywhere—energetic, shy, curious. In broken French and English, they asked about the Beatles and Bob Dylan. We replied in kind. Then an Armenian priest appeared. I told him we were Armenians from America. He seemed vague and unresponsive, and led us away from the children into a tiny office, where he sat down behind a small, bare desk and, from its lower drawer, produced an electric hot plate and a jar of instant coffee and a saucepan, which he proceeded in silence to assemble into three cups of coffee.

The coffee made and sipped, I tried to ask him routine

questions about the school. The priest's English was not bad, but his desire for conversation seemed slight. Talking with him was like interviewing a government official on a sensitive subject. I wondered what the sensitive subject was. On his desk was a small plastic Turkish flag, and behind the flag were two photographs—one of Mustafa Kemal, the other of the present Turkish president. What I had wanted to ask him, or somebody, was: What was it like to be an Armenian in Turkey now? Was it hard? Was it easy? Was it routine? My wife pointed to the flag on his desk and asked him if he felt more Turkish or more Armenian. The priest had been talking in a slow monotone about the school curriculum, and changed neither the rhythm nor the subject of his discourse. When he finished, he sipped his coffee.

I finally asked him, "Well, how is it being an Armenian in Turkey today?"

The priest looked pained, or else confused. He gave a sort of smile, and a sort of shrug. He replied something in such a low voice that I couldn't hear it and asked him again.

He looked across at me. "I am sorry, but I have the answers only to other questions," he said.

After leaving the Armenian priest, with his Turkish *drapeau de la patrie* and his photograph of Kemal, I felt depressed, although I knew that this was a foolish response. After all, I lived in America and was American. He lived in Turkey and was Turkish. All the same, there were some differences. Earlier, I had wondered how even in Abdul-Hamid's time Armenians could have chosen to continue living in Turkey. And what in hell's name was any Armenian doing here now? I thought of Erevan, with its inelegance and dust, its rocks and factory smoke and pink stone apartment buildings, its Stalinist graves, its airport police, its decided lack of anything as lovely as the Bosporus at sunset, and thought, Well, at least you were on some kind of solid ground there—you were somebody there.

BACK IN OUR HOTEL, we had arranged to have drinks with some American acquaintances: friends of a New York friend—two professors of English who had taught for many years at the American college up the Bosporus. It was a pleasant, even romantic time in the late afternoon, the garden smelling sweetly in the still air, the coolness of the shade settling around us. It was easy to imagine at such a moment why Constantine had chosen to place his new Rome here, why the failing Byzantines had stayed on and on and on, why Sultan Muhammad had taken care not to destroy too much on his arrival.

We chatted of this and that. The expatriate professors seemed politely interested in our travels but obviously perplexed as to why even an Armenian should wish to sojourn in Soviet Armenia. It was a bit like trying to explain living in Chicago to a Bostonian. "Of course, the Armenians were once a sizable population in Istanbul," said one of the professors, a man in his fifties—thin, sparely elegant, tweedy, perhaps himself a Bostonian.

"There doesn't seem to be much sign of them here any more," I said.

"Yes, it's a pity," he said. "But you must understand the Turkish point of view. The Armenians were a great nuisance to the Turks, and, after all, the country belonged to them. Those things are probably brutal, but they're life."

"They were a nuisance? How?" my wife asked sharply.

The professor smiled. "Well, I'd have imagined you'd know that by now. It's surely in books. I mean that the truth which seems to emerge from those dreadful massacres is that the Armenians basically provoked them, you know—more than anyone would admit to at the time."

"That's true," said the other professor—a younger man, with glasses and a seersucker jacket. "I have several Armenian friends here, and they all readily agree to that. They say, 'On account of the crimes of selfish revolutionaries, we were nearly wiped out.' Actually, you know, even the massacres weren't quite as terrible as they were made out to be."

We all had a fight—one of those dispirited, civilized fights in which the other side is terribly cool and conversational and doesn't care very much. "My dear fellow, as I'm sure you know," the older professor kept intoning, ever calmer and more controlled. Our side verged on shrillness and disarray. I heatedly quoted statistics, doubtless with the air of someone making them up on the spot. "Yes, that's very interesting," said the other professor, gazing out toward the water. Finally, my wife said, "I think you're both fools for sitting here on your damned Bosporus and not knowing what really happened." It was one of those scenes that cause people at other tables to begin to turn their heads and the waiters to become unusually attentive. The two American professors (our new friends) became ever more cultivated and ironic. "Damned Bosporus?" said the older man slowly and quizzically, as if the point at issue were now an attack on an innocent body of water. "My dear, I'm not sure I really care to argue on that level." Well, no. In the end, nothing of further interest was said; no views were exchanged. We somehow patched the "disagreement" together on the surface, and ordered the additional, unwanted drinks in order to show that we were all chums, and gulped them down, and said goodbye. "Be certain to say hello to Henry back in New York!" the tweedy professor called, disappearing into the twilight. Yes, we'll be certain to, we said. Civilization triumphs.

Upstairs in our room, my wife said, "No wonder so many Armenians sound so shrill."

"You mean, because 'nothing happened'?"

"Because the Turks don't admit to anything. And nobody else still gives a damn. There's no release."

It never seemed more true than there in Istanbul. The Armenians were once a great nuisance. The sounds of a dance band floated up to us from the hotel gardens. The lights along the Asia Minor coast began to glow—yellow reflections in the dark Bosporus, where two large cruise ships had lately moored, their masts lit up like Christmas trees. The sky above and around us was a dark blue, growing darker: still and deep and almost transparent. The bell of a ferryboat clanged far away. I thought of what I had seen and read about, trying to hold on to at least the texture of what it was. Actually, you know, even the massacres weren't quite as terrible as they were made out to be.

Yellow flowers burning in a metal bowl. The music of a South American song throbbed lightly against the window-panes—a girl's voice and guitars.

THE NEXT DAY, I couldn't stand the thought of touring any more Turkish mosques. The younger of the two professors had telephoned in the morning with a suggestion that we might wish to be introduced to a friend of his—a Mr. Dermejian, an elderly Armenian, although brought up by Turkish foster parents, educated at Oxford, a gentleman of many cultural interests, most charming, a connoisseur of Iranian art. Somehow, I could not abide, either, the thought of meeting Mr. Dermejian, for all his cultural interests and charm. I imagined that he, too, wore English tweeds, or else a Magdalen College boating blazer. I could see his pale, soft hands resting on an old Iranian chessboard. My dear fellow, you must understand, the affair was blown quite out of proportion.

Instead, without having any conscious plan in mind, I walked over to the Istanbul phone directory and began flipping through the pages to the letter "K." Kouyoumjian: my father's family name. Indeed, there were four or five Kouyoumjians listed, and that didn't surprise me, for it was a common Armenian name and it was evident that there were still a fair number of Armenians living in Istanbul. There was even a Dikran Kouyoumjian—my father's exact name. On impulse, I picked up the phone and asked the operator for the number.

Against my ear I could hear the other phone ringing, ringing. Then a click. A man's voice answering in Turkish.

"Hello," I said, wondering if I should hang up, wondering what would happen next.

The man's voice changed. "Hello," he said with an educated but imperfect English inflection.

I explained that I was an Armenian from America. That my father's name had been Dikran Kouyoumjian. That although we surely weren't related in any way, I had seen his name in the phone directory and had called to say hello.

"But you must come over," he said.

We talked briefly of the Kouyoumjian family. "There was a distant branch in Bulgaria, then England," he said. "Perhaps your father was connected to that one."

I said, "Yes."

"You and your wife must come for tea," he said.

In the hot midafternoon, we drove down one of the main boulevards, crowded with traffic, then through a network of narrow side streets, also crowded, into another shabby section of town. Our driver—the same sweet young Turk who had taken us to the Armenian church and elsewhere—let us off on a narrow, unkempt street lined for the most part with small, dark shops; it had scattered newspapers and orange peelings on the pavement, and all manner of filth in the gutters. At the end of the street there was a modest four-story apartment house of crumbling brown stucco. Some urchins played inside the lobby, or what had once been a lobby. Kouyoumjian was on the fourth floor.

He opened the door—a pleasant, quiet, slightly smiling man of perhaps fifty. His hair was thinning to the point of baldness, but otherwise he seemed in good trim. In fact, he had the appearance of a fairly successful professional man, or else a small-shop owner. He was an engineer, he said—an electrical engineer. His apartment, sheltered from the grubbiness of the street, seemed composed and well furnished. There were chests and tables, rather massive but highly polished. A bowl of cut flowers stood on a mantelpiece. There were some pinkish crystal glasses in a glass case which made me think for a second of Sarkis's house outside Erevan, with its Czech glassware and well-polished furniture.

On the table in the main room there was an array of English books: *Lord Jim, The Mayor of Casterbridge, Pride and Prejudice,* a thick Oxford dictionary.

I said, "Are you studying literature?"

"I am trying to learn English in order to emigrate to Australia," Kouyoumjian said. "I have been studying for three years." He looked at us shyly, as if we might not understand, or approve.

I thought, Everything becomes clearer. An Armenian

still in Turkey—my father's namesake, even. Dikran Kouyoumjian, of Istanbul, with the orange-leavings and mosques and recorded-prayer minarets of this finally Muslim city outside his windows, and, inside, the domestic talismans of the Armenians: the clean, polished furniture, the cut flowers, the careful displays of glassware. And now, at last, the escape route: Joseph Conrad, Thomas Hardy, and Jane Austen. Australia.

"Are you sorry to be leaving?" I asked.

"It is no good here any more," Kouyoumjian said. "I think it has probably not been good here for Armenians for a long while, but it is difficult to know these things when it is your home." Then, "But I love Istanbul." It seemed such a heartfelt statement, almost as if he were saying it to himself. "My father always loved Istanbul," he went on. "It was he who brought us back here, after the war. I think that was a mistake, for we had been living in Paris, but he said he loved this city. He loved to drive down toward the coast in the spring and see the orchards and flowers." Then, "I think he thought it would get better here after the war."

Kouyoumjian smiled. He seemed not to be a tough man. One imagined that the tough Armenians in Turkey had been killed long ago, or else had extricated themselves. No, he was a modest man, but in a difficult position; he was trying for something difficult. "Sometimes I become afraid when I think of leaving. You see, I am fifty-one years old and have a nice business here. Also, the Turks will let me take no money with me. It is a fact that they want all the

Armenians to leave Turkey. They want no trace of Armenians in Turkey any more—and most of the Armenians have already gone. I think there are only about fifteen thousand remaining. But they will not let us take anything with us. They will not even let us take what we can get for selling our possessions. In Australia, I must start again with nothing."

"What finally made you want to leave?" I asked.

"Because it finally made my heart sick," he said. "You know, under the old sultans they called us *'giaour'* and kept us down. Today, they still do the same thing. 'Father, what is *"giaour"?'* my daughter said when she first went off to school. 'Are we *"giaour"?'* It is true—for a while I thought things became better. But I was deluding myself. Lately, there has been a growth of Muslim feeling here—especially in the countryside, which is where it usually starts. A while ago, do you remember, there was an incident in America: a crazy old Armenian in California shot two Turks in a hotel. There was a trial about it over there. But here Turkish mobs took to the streets. You could see that they had been officially encouraged. In Erzurum, they hanged two Armenians as reprisal, and beat many others. In Istanbul, they were prepared to hang perhaps a dozen, but they thought it might be noticed, and so instead they beat them savagely, and one of the Armenians can no longer see. I think I finally despaired of life getting better here for our children."

Kouyoumjian's wife entered the room, carrying a tray of tea and little European cakes. She was a quite tall and hand-

some woman, fair-haired, with her hair piled up—seemingly
European. In fact, she was French, and spoke English halt-
ingly. "I worry, too, how we will do in Australia," she said.
"But I hear they are kind there. I am glad that Dikran reads
all these books. He says, 'I may not speak much English, but
I speak fine English.'"

"How has it been, living all these years side by side with
the Turks?" I asked.

"There has been no trouble," said Kouyoumjian.

"We have many Turkish friends," said his wife, as if it
would be disloyal to suggest otherwise.

"The Turks are nice people, gentle people," said Kouyoumjian. "But sometimes they have a craziness. A crazy
feeling comes over them."

"Is it only crazy?" I asked. "It isn't that they hate
Armenians?"

Kouyoumjian looked into his teacup, then over at his
wife. "I suppose there is some truth in that," he said.

In some ways, it was a charming and hospitable moment—the four of us seated in that small, carefully tended
apartment, sipping tea and eating cakes, while Dikran
Kouyoumjian discoursed on the good and bad points of life
for an Armenian among the Turks. But it was also a bit
eerie, as if something were being left out—not so much un-
said as unthought, beyond thought. One knew that a curse
had been placed on the Armenians in Turkey, and here we
were—in Turkey, smelling the curse. It hovered over
Kouyoumjian's cut flowers and plate of little cakes. It waited

on the outskirts of our conversation. But no one would name it. Perhaps it was unnamable.

My wife asked if they had other children. It turned out that they had a son about twenty-two years old, who had already gone to Australia. One could see that Kouyoumjian was very proud of his son. "He trained here as an engineer also," he said. "He did very well in the national examinations here, and on the strength of his final score he was given a good job in an important company. But then the man looked at his name—clearly an Armenian name. The man said that he was sorry but he had made a mistake—the position was already taken. This happened once again—in fact, I think more than once—and then my son decided to go to Australia. He has a job in an engineering firm in Sydney."

So that was it, I thought. The young were at last going to extricate the Armenians. I looked at our host and his shy French wife—Dikran Kouyoumjian, with his pleasant face and polite, uncertain manner, his engineer's skill, his volumes of Conrad and Jane Austen on the tabletop, his pink crystal glasses, and bald head, and many friends among the Turks—and thought, How could you have come back from France when they didn't want you here, when they so didn't want you? And then I thought, I bet that your son is tall and impatient, and that you can't tell him anything.

I had one more question, which I wanted to phrase courteously, with due respect. In the end, I simply said, "But why did it take you so long to leave?"

Kouyoumjian looked at me as if he were uncertain what I meant. Then he reached over and touched my arm in the Armenian manner, and leaned back in his chair. "I could give many reasons for why I stayed so long—my business here, our children in school, perhaps the hopes we had right after the war. I have thought about such things often since my son left, for now I have to follow him. A middle-aged man following his son. I think the reason I stayed so long was this—that it was home."

Kouyoumjian's wife stood up and moved behind her husband, her hands on his shoulders. "I've never known any people to care so much about their *homes* as the Armenians," she said, as if neither approving it nor disapproving it. A fact of life.

"But soon we are going away," said Kouyoumjian. And just then he seemed not at all uncertain, not regretful, or even modest: a decent man, a decent middle-aged man following his impatient son; perhaps even shortly to be released from something—an unnamable curse.

At the door, Kouyoumjian extended his hand and shook mine with sudden firmness. "Someday, I hope I will travel to America," he said. "I hear Armenians are happy there."

"As happy as anyone else," I said.

Then he said, "If you have a chance, you should drive down toward our coast. Not on the coast but before the coast there are such flowers, such fruit! Truly, there is a sweetness there. We try to make a motor trip each spring." He waved goodbye.

And so we left. Kouyoumjian in his shirtsleeves, hand outstretched. Kouyoumjian sailing close to the edge of the earth. Behind him, the teacups and half-eaten cakes and *Pride and Prejudice* on the table. We left crowded, shambly, half-elegant Istanbul—the One Great City—with its Bosporus, and curving mosques, and jostle of shipping; the blue-black Bosporus, with its banks of trees, and great green bridge, and tankers gliding by in the twilight.

We never went south toward the flowers and fruit.

Back in New York, some time later, my wife said one evening, "Then does the Armenian story end with Kouyoumjian going to Australia? With Sarkis in Erevan, waving behind the police? Here in America?"

It seemed to me that probably the only point to the "Armenian story" was that it continued. As with other aspects of nature—a waterfall, a rock—there was no way to gauge the merit or demerit of its existence, but the persistence was worth noting. Ultimately, there was bound to be a kind of nobility in this persistence.

Back in America. An Armenian American traveler returned from a voyage among the Armenians—in some ways like the proverbial Indian who has been brought up by white men and who years later makes and returns from a visit to his old tribe. *Where do you stand now, sir? Are you with us or with them?* Alas, by then the alternatives are mostly rhetorical.

The texture of my life is American. My kin are the Armenians. Sometimes like brothers, other times like cousins—even distant cousins. At times, I wish we were closer, but it is not always a sincere wish. We are as close as we will be.

I often wonder what it really is to be *Armenian* in our world—what message it is that we Armenians carry down from our own journey through the centuries. One hears of "Armenian culture"—at least, from Armenians—but it is surely not that. Or the smoky gravity of the Armenian Church. Or even mercantilism—the "trading instinct." For Armenians have turned out to have no greater racial bent for commerce than most other educated peoples—certainly not since the Western nations discarded the pretense of dressing up their shopkeepers as hearty yeomen (nature's noblemen) and joined the group.

Armenians were a—one cannot quite call them a "nation," but at any rate they were a presence long before the world conceived of nations and nationhood in the modern fashion. They are a presence even now—scattered about the globe, or gathered once again, as in tiny Soviet Armenia, in the province of yet another ambitious empire. Armenians, or some of them, at times profess a passion for this nationhood—this organism like the ones from whose madness and pride the Armenians have suffered as much as any people. But perhaps in the end the message of the Armenians is more particular than mere persistence. Perhaps, if there exists a deeper possibility in the psyche of this ancient, sturdy, and minor race, it is this: the capacity of a people for proceeding *beyond* nationhood. For to be a nation—a member of a modern nation—is to inherit territory, and pride in property, and to be connected to collective dreams of quite impossible grandeur and savagery, fertility and hatred. To be an Armenian has meant that one has been compelled by circumstance to rise above or fall below—or, anyway, to skirt—these so-called imperatives of nationhood and property, and thus has been free to attempt the struggle of an ordinary life, and to dream more modest dreams, and to try to deal with one's dreams as best one could. Oh, it is true that for some years Armenian dreams were in a most dreadful tangle. The kings of Nairi enmeshed in liberal political adventures. The kings of Nairi dreaming dreams of grandeur, adrift in foreign courts. Mountain kings with crowns of branches and palaces of rock. Such unmetaphysical kings! But this much seems to be also true: there is a good chance now that the clearheaded, impatient young will begin to set their fathers free.

I HAVE THOUGHT OFTEN about my father since our journey, although I no longer dream about him as much. Once, I remembered a dream of his that he had told me long ago—I think the only dream I ever heard him describe. And then it was with rather gruff perplexity, for it was during the last year of his life, when he slept unevenly—frequently sleeptalking, or waking in starts. It had been about *his* father. "You know, he was just as I remembered him as a boy," my father said that morning. "Except his hair was white—but very thick. He wore a frock coat and steel-rimmed spectacles. He stood at the end of our road speaking to me, calling. But he was speaking in Armenian, and I couldn't understand a word."

Sometimes I think it is as if a circle, once broken, had been completed or recompleted. What circle? We were kin to begin with.